Praise for

My Summer Darlings

"A potent cocktail of desire and deceit. Spicy enough to make you sweat—until the suspense chills you to your core."

—Riley Sager, *New York Times* bestselling author of
The House Across the Lake

"*My Summer Darlings* sizzles with small-town secrets, backstabbing besties, and the year's darkest take on 'summer romance.' This sultry, soapy thriller just might be the perfect poolside read."

—Andrea Bartz, *New York Times* bestselling author of
We Were Never Here (Reese's Book Club Pick)

"*My Summer Darlings* is addicting, twisted, and a whole lot of fun. It's a steamy thriller that goes down with a bite, like a cold margarita on a hot day. A perfect summer read."

—Simone St. James, *New York Times* bestselling author of
The Sun Down Motel

"Full of big houses, teenage attitudes, and snarky housewives, and would be the perfect companion to a beach vacation."

—*San Francisco Book Review*

"Nobody writes deliciously wicked and devious housewives quite like May Cobb. *My Summer Darlings* will tease, shock, delight, and enrage you. But most of all, it will leave you pleading for the next Cobb thriller!"

—Jesse Q. Sutanto, national bestselling author of *Dial A for Aunties*

"Bold, sultry, and unapologetic, *My Summer Darlings* is destined to become your next obsession. May Cobb is the queen of complicated female characters, and the ladies of Eden Place won't be ones you'll soon forget. A simmering, sexy read best accompanied by a strong cocktail."

—Laurie Elizabeth Flynn, author of *The Girls Are All So Nice Here*

"With friends like these, you won't need enemies. . . . This dark, devious, sexy tale of duplicity and one-up(wo)manship sizzles so much it'll practically burn your fingers as you turn the pages. *My Summer Darlings* is sure to be another unputdownable hit!"

—Hannah Mary McKinnon, author of *You Will Remember Me*

"May Cobb has done it again! *My Summer Darlings* is a sexy, sassy, scary page-turner. I couldn't put it down."

—Robyn Harding, international bestselling author of *The Perfect Family*

"[*My Summer Darlings* is] an intensely suspenseful and deliciously entertaining novel. May Cobb writes as though she's been hanging around your neighborhood, listening to all the conversations, and taking notes with a pen as sharp as a fish hook. This book should be required poolside summer reading."

—David Bell, *USA Today* bestselling author of *Kill All Your Darlings*

"[A] smart, fun thriller about obsession and friendship."

—CrimeReads

"A searing suspense that gets under your skin and raises the heat level, *My Summer Darlings* by May Cobb sizzles with fiery intensity. The magnificently drawn characters; dark, delectable plot; and a neighborhood bubbling with sex, secrets, and lies make this sensational novel perfect for anyone who loves Jackie Collins and Liane Moriarty. An absolutely electrifying read."

—Samantha M. Bailey, *USA Today* bestselling author of *Woman on the Edge*

"Sexy, addictive. . . . In Cobb's signature stylish prose, small-town East Texas is lush and vicious, teeming with that most dangerous and all too relatable temptation: to fulfill unspoken desires, to become someone new, to leave it all behind—no matter who gets hurt. As seductive and irresistible as the mysterious man at its center, *My Summer Darlings* exposes the messy pulsing heart of female desire and friendship—likeability be damned. This thriller is set to become your new obsession."

—Katie Gutierrez, national bestselling author of *More Than You'll Ever Know*

"Sexy, fresh, and fun, *My Summer Darlings* tells the story of three friends who go after what they want—even when what they want is the same man. Cobb's sophomore novel is unputdownable and devious, a twisty thriller that threw me for loop after loop."

—Stephanie Wrobel, *USA Today* bestselling author of *Darling Rose Gold*

"May Cobb delivers another firecracker of a novel complete with her signature scandalous leading ladies and steamy suspense—this is not your mother's thriller!"

—Chandler Baker, *New York Times* bestselling author of *The Husbands* (*Good Morning America* Book Club Pick)

"Fabulous, sexy, thrilling, and hot, *My Summer Darlings* is the perfect escape. May Cobb is a gorgeous writer and kept me guessing until the final pages. I loved this book!"

—Amanda Eyre Ward, *New York Times* bestselling author of *The Jetsetters* (Reese's Book Club Pick)

"Compelling and compulsively readable. If you haven't read May Cobb yet, now is the moment."

—Liv Constantine, international bestselling author of
The Last Mrs. Parrish

"My Summer Darlings is sexy and suspenseful and I could not put this fast-paced romp down. Three friends are all attracted to the new, handsome stranger in town—what could go wrong? Everything of course! Twisty and fun, you need this on your summer reading list!

—Catherine McKenzie, *USA Today* bestselling author of
I'll Never Tell and *Please Join Us*

"[A] dark tale of psychological suspense that will keep readers involved until it ends with a final twist."

—*Booklist*

"My Summer Darlings is an excellent, character-driven illustration of how each woman puts on a different face to the public, keeping angst to themselves."

—Shelf Awareness

"May Cobb's follow-up to her acclaimed 2021 thriller *The Hunting Wives*, solidifies her identity as an East Texas Jackie Collins with better prose and a gift for high-octane twists."

—*TexasMonthly*

My Summer Darlings

MAY COBB

Berkley
New York

BERKLEY
An imprint of Penguin Random House LLC
penguinrandomhouse.com

Copyright © 2022 by May Cobb
Readers Guide copyright © 2022 by May Cobb
Excerpt from *A Likeable Woman* copyright © 2023 by May Cobb
Penguin Random House supports copyright. Copyright fuels creativity, encourages diverse voices,
promotes free speech, and creates a vibrant culture. Thank you for buying an authorized edition of
this book and for complying with copyright laws by not reproducing, scanning, or distributing any
part of it in any form without permission. You are supporting writers and allowing
Penguin Random House to continue to publish books for every reader.

BERKLEY and the BERKLEY & B colophon are registered trademarks of
Penguin Random House LLC.

ISBN: 9780593101179

The Library of Congress has catalogued the Berkley hardcover edition of this book as follows:

Names: Cobb, May K., 1973– author.
Title: My summer darlings / May Cobb.
Description: New York : Berkley, [2022]
Identifiers: LCCN 2021034434 (print) | LCCN 2021034435 (ebook) |
ISBN 9780593101162 (hardcover) | ISBN 9780593101186 (ebook)
Subjects: LCGFT: Novels.
Classification: LCC PS3603.O225554 M9 2022 (print) |
LCC PS3603.O225554 (ebook) | DDC 813/.6--dc23
LC record available at https://lccn.loc.gov/2021034434
LC ebook record available at https://lccn.loc.gov/2021034435

Berkley hardcover edition / May 2022
Berkley trade paperback edition / April 2023

Printed in the United States of America
1st Printing

Book design by Alison Cnockaert

To the wonderful men in my life: my dad, Charles, and husband, Chuck, who, thank God, are nothing at all like Will Harding.

My

Summer

Darlings

Present

MY JAWBONE THROBS with scorching pain—whoosh whoosh whoosh—keeping time with my heartbeat.

I can't move my head; my neck won't budge an inch. But that's not the worst of it; the worst of it is that I know he's coming back for me.

I'm lying on my back on the silty floor of the forest, and even though it's a boggy summer night, my teeth clatter with chill—I can't feel my toes or fingertips. My mouth is bitter with the rust taste of blood and my head rests in a sticky pool of it.

Inky pines sway above me, their trunks groaning in the breeze. It's not the first time I've been out here, not by a long shot, but it's the first time I've been in this position where all I can see is the sky above me. The moon is like a silver hook caught in the treetops, and as I gaze up at it, I want to yell for help, I want to shriek, but I can't form the sounds, so the scream stays trapped in my throat.

1.

I HEARD HIM before I saw him. He arrived in the middle of a hot, balmy morning, a week ago today, the low rumble of his 1967 Chevy pickup snaking around the block as I was bent over, twisting the rusty nozzle on the garden hose. Tepid water sputtered out of the warm rubber and oozed around my flip-flop-clad feet as he slowed his truck and rounded the bend in front of my house. Did he wink at me? I'm still not sure, but a small grin crept across his face and he gave me the quickest of nods.

Even in this brief exchange, I could feel the fever of attraction. My neck flushed and my hand shot up of its own accord, waving maniacally at him.

I could tell he was dead handsome through the windshield, the glaring morning sunlight catching blond streaks in his short sandy hair. His toned lean arm slung across the blue steering wheel. His honey-kissed skin and that perfect mouth I could already imagine pressing my lips to.

After the truck coasted up the hill and out of sight, I doused the row of tropical plants I'd recently planted—pumpkin-colored cannas, a stand of banana trees, and a bed of waxy elephant's ears—my pulse thrumming from this brush with him.

This had been the first task I'd thrown myself into upon moving back to Cedartown eight months ago: ripping out the generic, predictably cheesy flower beds tended to by the landscapers—geraniums and petunias—in an effort to make the yard as lush and verdant as possible.

And as opposite as possible from the yard of my failed marriage: the arid xeriscaped rock lawn with jagged succulents that rimmed our modern two-story farmhouse just south of downtown in Austin. Fucking Felix with his fucking minimalism.

I've likewise tried to eradicate all signs of Felix from inside the house. Or as much as my son, Kasey, can bear. I left behind all of Felix's hard-edged furniture but kept his Danish sideboard and matching table made of teak. Because those were two pieces of his I genuinely liked, and also, because I knew he adored those more than anything else. And after what he had done to me, I had to jab back at his heart a little. Make him bleed a bit.

In the house, on the mantel, there's a lone picture of Felix holding two-year-old Kasey. Snapped thirteen years ago. Long before the string of affairs. At least that's what I tell myself—I don't know what to really believe anymore—and long before Felix's descent into his full-blown midlife crisis. In the photo, a rough beard frames his strong jaw and he's flashing a bright smile. A father beaming at his dumpling-faced toddler. Kasey is bundled in a red parka, his golden locks springing from beneath a hand-knitted toboggan.

When I unpacked the photo from the tissue paper, my intention was to put it on Kasey's dresser, but it's always been on our mantel and Kasey lifted it from me and parked it there. I wasn't in a position to argue with him—he's been snippy with me ever since the divorce, as if his father's philandering was somehow my fault—so I have to pass by Felix every time I walk through the living room. But I've already managed to autoblock him each time I glimpse it, focusing instead on Kasey's crimped face, captured midgiggle.

At least my bedroom is one hundred percent Felix-free. No more stacks of serious, severe books of music criticism and design magazines, arranged to disguise poorly hidden issues of *Playboy*.

Now my weathered wooden nightstand holds my ever-growing collection of self-help books: Pema Chödrön's *When Things Fall Apart*; Melody Beattie's *Codependent No More*; a few of Brené Brown's books, which I have yet to crack; and various yoga/meditation books.

I've recently taken to reading a book of mantras just before I doze off at night:

I am already complete, whole, and loved.

The universe provides.

I attract abundance.

Love surrounds us in each moment of every day.

My thoughts become my reality; think positive ones.

And so forth. I feel slightly ridiculous chanting these out loud to myself while I'm out in the yard gardening; I realize that most people would cringe if they heard me, but I swear they're already starting to help just a tiny bit.

The yard work is helping, too. And not just with my sanity. Now that my parents don't have to pay for the landscaping service, they apply the savings to the monthly stipend they give me to keep me and Kasey afloat. Between that and living in their rental (my childhood home) rent-free, we just about manage to scrape by each month. Of course, there's alimony and child support, but Felix's lawyer friend managed to ensure the settlement was as favorable to Felix as possible. And seeing how I haven't worked since Kasey was born, it's not as though I have any income of my own to contribute to things, which is something I need to figure out.

So each morning, I work for an hour or so in the yard, tearing out weeds, plunging my hands into the ruddy clay earth, and sizing up the jade-colored carpet of Saint Augustine grass to see where I might lay more beds for tropicals and possibly even some herbs.

It's a nice-sized lot shaded by a stand of stately pines that thud their cones to the ground in winter. And it's calming for me to be out there in the early hours, listening to the backdrop sounds of my childhood: the sizzling hiss of cicadas, the drilling of woodpeckers, the gurgling of the neighborhood creek that winds along the back side of our property.

Our small town in northeast Texas may not have the hipness and glossiness of Austin, but it's serene and it's home.

Home. I'm home again. That's another mantra (but one that I made up) that keeps running through my mind while I'm out there tending to the property, as if to solidify the fact that this *is* my new home and as if to make that fact less surreal.

THE MORNING THAT Blond Man drove past, however, I cut my work short. As soon as I finished watering the plants, I turned off the faucet and dropped the hose to the ground without even bothering to coil it back around its stand, the tip of it chinking against the concrete drive.

I padded inside and pulled my sweaty hair into a quick ponytail before grabbing my keys and hopping into my white Honda Accord.

I set off in the same direction as Blond Man, taking the long way around my street, Azalea Circle. I live on the far end, near the edge of the forest, and normally I turn left out of the drive and head straight out of the neighborhood. There's never a reason to turn right and circle around the back, past the row of houses that grows more opulent as the street climbs the gentle-sloping hill.

I used to bike this route as a kid and all the homes and families who lived there are imprinted on my mind like photos in an album: the Carters' colonial mansion with its chalk-white columns; the Dickensons' sprawling 1970s ranch with its endless wings; the Wards' elegant contemporary—all glass and blond wood, as if it were built out of the earth itself.

I eased up the incline and I saw his vintage blue truck parked at the curb in front of Dr. Ellingsworth's old estate, the grandest home in all of Eden Place, the pseudoparadisiacal-sounding name of our neighborhood. A shock of adrenaline jolted my chest and I yanked down my sunglasses to help shield my face as I neared the house.

When I was just a little girl, Dr. Ellingsworth was already a widower living in his storybook mansion all alone, his children all grown and living in far-flung cities along the East Coast.

The kids in the neighborhood used to call the Ellingsworth mansion the fairy house, and I for sure imagined little elves and fairies, just out of plain sight, running through the halls and skipping around the rolling backyard. Once, when I went knocking door to door through the neighborhood, selling spices for our elementary school fundraiser, I got to glance inside Dr. Ellingsworth's house as I waited in the foyer for him to fetch his checkbook. The floor was paved with milk-white stone and amber light filtered through the diamond-shaped windows, filling the foyer with a honeyed hue. The house smelled like a church—beeswax and mustiness—and standing on my tiptoes, I peered around a corner and glimpsed a room that looked to be the doctor's library. Floor-to-ceiling shelves crammed with leather-bound books, the room laid out with dark wooden furniture. I wanted to take stock of the rest of the place, which was so different from any other house I'd ever stepped foot in. But soon Dr. Ellingsworth appeared with a freshly written check, handing it over to me with a warm smile.

The outside of the mansion is just as enchanting as the inside: pitched rooflines, thatched siding, arched doorways, a quilt of glittering windows in all sorts of odd shapes, and an ivy-covered wooden gate that leads to a pocket side yard.

A S   I   N E A R E D the house, my pulse whooshed in my ears when I caught sight of a long white moving truck parked in the long drive. Blond Man was standing in the plush grass, gesturing to the crew of movers before disappearing through the giant mouth of the front door. I pressed on the brake and took stock of the pile of boxes being shuttled inside the house.

My shoulders sagged.

It was obvious he was moving in, but clearly—from the looks of the conveyor belt of furniture streaming from the back of the moving truck—he was most likely soon to be joined by a wife and four kids.

T H I S   W A S   S E V E N days ago and I haven't caught sight of him since. His truck has been parked in the same spot, and whenever I drive or stroll past and do a quick nonchalant sweep of the windows with my sunglass-clad eyes, the rooms inside look still and uninhabited. Like a stage set awaiting its actors.

I don't know anything about him, really. All I know is that I can't quit thinking about him. I don't even know his name. But I'm hoping to find out more tonight at wine with Kittie and Cynthia.

2.

Cynthia Nichols's Diary

THIS IS MY first official entry. Well, my second, actually, but it's the first in this black leather Moleskine journal.

I started the first one on my laptop, but then got paranoid that Gerald might see it. It's not like he's a snooper or anything, but my laptop is so clutter-free and devoid of files that a new one would jump right out at him if he happened to plop down in front of it to read the *Washington Post* or check the *Wall Street Journal*, which he routinely does.

The Moleskine I can stash in my lingerie drawer. God knows he'd never go looking in there.

It's evening, just after eleven o'clock, and he's asleep. I don't know whether or not Tyson is; I've been banned from his room at nighttime ever since he turned fifteen two springs ago. But on nights when I do edge down the hall toward his room—even if it's way past midnight—

blue-white light flickers beneath the door, which means he's either watching TV or playing *Minecraft* or whatever the hell teens are obsessed with these days.

So tonight I'm tucked into the study, my little sanctuary, on the creamy white chaise, a chenille blanket pooling around me. The sky outside is bruised black and a ragged cloud the color of slate scrapes across the moon.

What am I supposed to be writing about? Surely not this mundane stuff, but Dr. Whitaker—Sally Whitaker, my newfound confidante and shrink—told me not to filter my thoughts, just to write everything down. All of it.

This was at our second meeting, last Thursday. Thursdays have become my therapy days, I guess, even though it's just for an hour. But it's something I already look desperately forward to. I found her online and instantly trusted her for some reason. Maybe it's her smart silver bob or her kind eyes, or the fact that she raked up the most positive reviews online, but I phoned her the next morning to make an appointment.

I have never in my life gone to therapy. My parents—if they were still living—would be horrified. You didn't go picking apart your emotions in the White household. Virginia and Frank believed, instead, in bettering yourself with more expensive private lessons. English horseback riding, ballet, etiquette class. All activities that would mold me into a well-rounded housewife instead of the overly sensitive, overly analytical little girl I once was.

And as secretly excited as I am about it, I do feel a prick of shame about going to therapy. Not that Gerald would judge me—easygoing Gerald; it's just that I don't have some giant issue or trauma to recover from. I don't, in fact, know *what's* wrong with me or if anything actually is. Maybe it's the prospect of turning forty this September, but I'm tired of waking up in the middle of the night with my thoughts racing, my heart rate speeding, and then descending into a sinkhole of depression where I fester until Tyson or Gerald comes home and I'm forced to put on my cheery face.

And I cannot talk to Kittie about it. She's like my parents, never self-reflective or wanting to appear weak. She's all take-charge. She'll listen to my bedroom problems and every shard of gossip I have to share, but she's got no appetite for my navel-gazing.

I'm sure Jen would lend a more helpful ear, but her life is such a shit basket right now that I can't bear to burden her with my own.

I mean, I have a happy marriage. Or at least a stable one. And I *do* love Gerald; I really do, and I can't imagine being with anyone else. It's just sometimes when I catch sight of him lounging in a chair in his bathrobe, with his perfectly coiffed brown hair that's beginning to gray and immaculately manicured hands, I sigh. At this stage, we're more like roommates or old friends than lovers.

Not that we don't have sex. We do, and quite often, only it's the same routine every single time. His eyes fill with desire. He leads me by the hand to the bedroom, kisses me while caressing my hair. Lays me down on the bed with him on top. Every time. Nibbles on my ear and, afterward, holds me and tells me about his day or how he's feeling. Asks how I'm feeling. During our courtship, I loved this about him. Loved his strong hands stroking my forehead while we bonded. Loved this intimacy, which I could've never imagined having with a male. But now, eighteen years into it, it's making me batty. Making me cringe. Making me want to scream and rip my hair out. It's crushing my soul.

And all my attempts to shake things up go unnoticed. Like the new pair of lacy black panties I recently selected from the lingerie department at Dillard's. He didn't even give them so much as a second glance as I paraded in front of him with them on.

Of course, I've read *Cosmo* and all the women's sites that urge you to speak your fantasies out loud to your partner. And I know I should tell him exactly what I want, what turns me on, but to do so would seem to break the illusion that things are wonderful between us, that we're one of the lucky ones. Plus, I'm afraid of what he might think of me if I told him all the dirty thoughts running through my mind.

It feels weird to even be writing this stuff down in the privacy of my own diary. I've already said too much tonight. I'd better stop now and turn in.

3.

Kittie

I'M STALLING; I know I should get my ass out of this patio chair and start my day for real.

But instead, I allow myself to sink farther into the deep cushions and tear a fresh sheet off my pad of monogrammed to-do lists. I've already made one list today, but now it sits crumpled next to my lukewarm cup of coffee.

I jotted down far too many things on it, and that makes me crazy—not being able to cross everything off by the end of the day and start fresh the next.

This morning, I don't feel so fresh. It's ten o'clock and I'm still in my pj's—a cotton cami and matching shorts—my eyes fixated on the rippling aquamarine surface of the pool. I'm in a hungover trance, lulled by the sound of pool water bubbling into the filter and the sticky breeze that makes my whole body feel damp.

The coffee has yet to chisel its way through my foggy head, so I slam the rest and turn my focus back to the list.

Chloe's cheerleading uniform to cleaners

Leave Gloria a check

Hank's insulin

Gather donations for League drive

Book facial for next Fri.

Harley's for case of wine tonight

Store: cheese, crackers, olives, salmon spread, gluten-free crackers for Cynthia (sigh), almonds, prosciutto, figs, cheesecake, ice for wine

I gnaw on the tip of the pen and scrutinize the list.

This will have to do. Given how I feel—headachy and dry mouthed—that's more than enough to accomplish today.

But I'm leaving something off, which has been eating at me for weeks now. It's been on my mental to-do list every day this summer and it's the one thing I can't bear to write down, to eventually cross off:

Driving school for Chloe

She turns sixteen in August, so she should already have her learner's permit, but I cannot handle even the thought of it—the thought of her having a traveling domain of pure freedom on wheels unchaperoned by adults. I well remember myself at her age, which is precisely why I can't let her completely out of my clutches just yet.

I've always given her space and I've never wanted to be controlling, but I'm an overbearing mom on the inside, even if I won't allow anyone else, including Chloe, to see it.

I've somehow managed to grant her the illusion of freedom, while always knowing exactly what she's up to. The pool, for instance, was my idea for this very reason. I knew (and was right) that her friends would practically move in over the summers if we had the biggest, splashiest pool in town. And even though I stayed out of their way and left them to it and earned the reputation as the "cool mom," I always kept tabs on who was coming and going, who was fighting, and who was making out with whom. I managed to do it all undetected. It's one of my superpowers.

But now I sense that Chloe is pulling away from me. Where she used to trail me and look up to me—asking my advice on what to wear, confiding in me about her friends and even boys—I'm now sometimes met with slammed doors and rolled eyes. Not all the time, of course, only when she's in one of her moods. Usually, she's the same old sunny Chloe, which makes her outbursts even more jarring.

And it's not just her moodiness that gets to me. It's the fact that she's becoming increasingly secretive. When I enter the room while she's on the phone, for instance, her voice drops and she twists her head away from me, cupping her cell with her brightly manicured hand. Or even worse, she dissolves into giggles and I can tell she's talking to a boy, but I have no idea which one.

So the thought of her in a car alone with one makes my stomach clench. I know I should be letting her practice behind the wheel, especially since it's summer and she's home all the time—and Lord knows she hounds me enough—but I always find a convenient excuse not to. To delay it a little more.

Hank lets her drive the old truck out at the farm. It's not a farm, really, just a hundred-acre piece of land that he uses as a hunting lease. The three of us used to go out there on Saturday mornings to hike and picnic, and it was nice; it was the most outdoorsy thing I've ever done other than drinking by the pool. We haven't been out there like that in years, but recently, Chloe's been begging Hank to take her to the lease to practice driving. And of course, Hank lets her do anything she wants.

THE SUN IS splitting through the pines and the mosquitoes are already grazing on my legs, so I plant my hands on the glass table and finally push myself out of the chair. I'm thinking too much and I hate it when I get like this, so I go inside and head for the shower.

I peel my pajamas off and drop them to the floor. And stare at myself in the mirror, sighing. I don't look bad, of course, but I wish I could shed that stubborn weight around my belly. But worse than that today is my face. I passed out before I washed off last night's makeup, so my eyes are smudged with the remains of charcoal eyeliner and mascara, my skin still sealed under a layer of base.

It was just a Junior League happy hour and I hadn't intended to get so bombed, but I lost control after the first two martinis. I even allowed myself to come home and have drunk sex with Hank, flashes of which are coming back to me now in waves, making my neck burn as I remember how much I enjoyed it. Or how much I enjoyed turning him on, after all these years. Me riding him, hearing him moan my name, his blue eyes glinting in the dark.

4.

Jen

IT'S MORNING. JUST before seven. It's been a while since I've watched the sun rise but I've been up since five, heart racing from all the wine I drank last night.

I'm out on the back patio, unrolling my yoga mat to do a few poses once I fully wake up. But first, I sink down onto the springy foam and sit cross-legged, watching the sun finish its ascent over the stand of rain-spattered trees. It poured last night after I got home and the creek is gushing over its red-clay banks, rippling around weed-strangled bends.

Kittie kept pouring, and we kept drinking. I think we finished four bottles between the three of us. But even with all the imbibing, it was the first time at Wine Night that I didn't go on and on about Felix.

Mainly, it's because I found out about Will.

Will Harding. That's his name.

Kittie was already lit by the time I arrived, apple cheeks blazing from the rosé she had been guzzling, her jade eyes burning with the fever of gossip she was so obviously anxious to share with me.

She shepherded me through the great hall, her strappy sandals slapping the marble floors, and led me out to the pool area, where Cynthia was already seated, all olive-toned legs and yoga-sculpted arms escaping her crisp white sundress.

I could hate Kittie for her backyard—a fern-lined oasis complete with a country-club-sized pool tended to by a staff of caretakers—but it's so glorious out there, I'm just grateful I get to hang out in it at all. And the food. I'd be embarrassed if Kittie and Cynthia suspected me of this, but I purposely skip dinner on Wine Night to save money and instead gorge on the spread that Kittie's housekeeper, Gloria, sets out for us.

My mouth watered at the sight of meats and dips, and I stabbed a shard of cracker into a fluffy mound of goat cheese and was cramming it into my mouth when Kittie started in about Will.

"Girl," she said, her red-glossed lips curling into a smile, "found out some stuff about your boy."

"And?"

"Well, don't kill me, but I got pretty bombed at League happy hour last night and nearly forgot to ask, but then I remembered. And first off, he's on Brandi Stephens's radar, too."

A zap of jealousy coursed through me. Brandi went to high school with us and had soap-opera-star looks even then. Dark wavy hair, her porcelain face always overly made up, her figure trim and leggy and with cleavage for days. She had a reputation for being promiscuous, but we were *all* promiscuous, so I never really understood why certain girls got tossed into that category.

"But isn't she married?" Cynthia asked, her bunny-slope nose crinkled in judgment.

"Like that's ever fucking stopped her before." Kittie emptied the rest of her wine down her throat and poured herself another glass.

"But anyway, turns out it's a good thing he's pricked her interest because no one else knows a goddamn thing about him. He's like . . . Mr. Secretive, evidently."

I shifted in my seat, tipped my wineglass back, and took a long, burning sip. "So, what'd she find out?"

"Well, of course, I didn't talk to *her*; I mean, *as if*. But she told Margaret Anne what she knew. I guess he bought the old Ellingsworth mansion, like you were saying, but since it was listed by Sotheby's and not by a local Realtor like Brandi, details were hard to come by. But apparently, he paid 3.75 million dollars for it. Full asking price. Cash."

"Wowza," Cynthia chirped.

"Does he have a wife? A last name?" I asked.

"That's the thing, and it's driving Brandi nuts; she hasn't dug that up yet. I mean, she found out his name. It's Will Harding. How prep school is *that*?" Kittie hooted. "Anyway, crazy bitch says she saw him coming out of Frosty's." Kittie paused over the word "saw" and put rabbit ears around it. "And as soon as he pulled out of the parking lot, she ran inside and asked Miss Sheila who he was."

Frosty's is the local dry cleaner; I made a mental list to dredge up a few things to drop off, even though I have only two or three articles of clothing that actually require that service.

"So, yeah, that's all of Brandi's intel. Not much, I know, but it's something, right? How fucking hot *is* he, by the way?"

"Seriously? He must really be something," Cynthia said, smoothing down a sheet of her glossy chestnut-brown hair. But even as she said this, I could detect an air of preoccupation about her, as if she'd already grown bored and exited the conversation.

"He's delish, but I mean, I just saw him for a sec the other day. And he's probably married."

"Hope not. That would be the best fuck-you to Felix ever if you guys got together!" Kittie placed her bronzed hand on mine. "And don't you worry. I'll make sure Brandi keeps her slutty mitts off him."

Heat spread across my chest and I allowed myself to linger on the thought of a single Will Harding.

Kittie quickly moved on and launched into her previous night's escapades, descending into League gossip—names that brought up echoes of faces from high school, but I could remember only a handful of the women she was dishing about—her thunderous laugh clapping off the surface of the pool. Her rendition seemed to snap Cynthia out of her daze and soon their voices were buzzing in my ear like a pack of mosquitoes, but I wasn't interested in whose lives they were dissecting. I could think only about Will.

THE BIRDS ARE beginning to chirp and I know their chorus will likely wake Kasey, so I begin my yoga flow; nothing more awkward than doing downward-facing dog in front of your son. My head booms when I angle it toward the patio, but I push through until a sheen of sweat blooms across my skin and my lungs are filled with pine-scented air.

I leave my yoga mat unrolled so that it can air-dry, and pull my sneakers on. I always jog at least a mile every morning—and sometimes I meet up with Kittie and Cynthia so we can jog the neighborhood together—but last night, as we stood swaying in the doorway saying slurry goodbyes, we all swore off exercise this morning.

And I would've blown it off, given how much we drank, but my body is live-wiring with this crazy crush.

I CAN'T BELIEVE I'm boy crazy over someone I don't even know. And more than that, I can't believe I'm boy crazy period. I promised Annie, my therapist back in Austin, that I wouldn't date for at least a year after Felix and I split.

It's been only nine months.

Annie and I were sitting in her small bungalow home office—which smelled faintly of the hibiscus mint tea she was always brewing and offering—when she said, "I really want you to use this time to work on yourself. To really find yourself."

She threaded a lock of curly brown hair around her index finger, a habit she had when broaching delicate topics, and continued speaking in her signature diplomatic tone. "We know you have this tendency to get lost in the other, to dissolve into your partner. But in order to become whole and to eventually participate in a more whole relationship, you need to sit with yourself for a while."

And she's right. I've had a steady boyfriend since my senior year in high school. Cody, with his jet-black hair and dreamy eyes. Followed by Ben, my first boyfriend in college, with his long brown hair cinched in a bandanna and a guitar perpetually slung around his neck. Followed by a string of others. All versions of Felix: narcissistic types parading as sensitive, artsy types. All model handsome, too.

I'm no bombshell, like Kittie and Cynthia; I'm rather plain-looking, so it surprised me each and every time I landed one of these lookers.

Felix once told me that I resembled an out-of-focus Sienna Miller. Less blond, obviously, and I guess with less defined features? I could never really figure out if that was a compliment or not. It probably wasn't. But I theorized that what each of these guys saw in me was that I was an unthreatening asset: attractive enough to hang off their arms, but not at risk of being bedded down by one of their friends.

I PUSH MYSELF to jog up the hill, toward Kittie's and Cynthia's homes, and farther away from Will's. As much as I want to run past in the hopes of seeing him, I don't want to be *that* person.

My street is a circle, rimmed by an undeveloped lush forest. At the entrance to my block, one road leads out to the east and connects with the main thoroughfare through town. The other feeds into the more sprawling, posher section of Eden Place, where Cynthia and Kittie have always lived. That part of the neighborhood looks like a horseshoe, with little coves attached to the edges like spurs.

They now live in neighboring coves to each other, but when we were kids, Kittie and Cynthia both lived in Lilac Cove, and as I crest the hill, I turn the corner and slow to a walk so I can stroll past their old mansions.

The cove is the size of a large pond and a cluster of gnarled oaks lines the sidewalk, their tops forming a knitted canopy, splintering the sunlight. It's still early, but heat rises from the pavement, so I pull my hair into a loose bun.

To my left is Kittie's childhood home, known as the Southerland Mansion after her parents Margie and Trip. The Southerlands still live here and their house is still as jaw-dropping as ever. It's the largest lot in all of Eden Place—a sea of jewel-green grass marked off by a wrought iron gate. Margie, originally from Louisiana, commissioned a storied architect from New Orleans to design the place to look like a Garden District mansion. And it does, with its row of picket-white columns, two-story wraparound balcony, and endless windows framed by floor-to-ceiling ebony shutters.

Back when they were younger, their estate was the scene of all the high-end society parties of Cedartown. Not that my parents, Don and Lisa Miller, were ever invited. Sure, my dad made a decent living as a bookkeeper before he retired, but we were definitely middle-class compared to the dizzying wealth of the Southerlands and Cynthia's parents, the Whites. Everything about me, in fact, has always been more muted when compared to Kittie and Cynthia. My straight sandy blond hair versus Kittie's near-platinum locks, which are permanently immune to humidity. My girl-next-door looks versus Cynthia's fine-boned refined beauty. And obviously, my modest childhood home—an early 1980s ranch—compared with their tantalizing spreads. And even when I was growing up, my parents, God love them, were more boring than the gregarious Southerlands or the oil-rich Whites.

According to Annie—as she further picked apart my psychology—that's one of the things that drew me to Kittie and Cynthia as a little girl: excitement. That and the fact that we are all only children. So our bond can sometimes be sisterly, in that urgent, primal way. And even though I'm in a different social caste from Kittie and Cynthia, none of that mattered to them growing up. If I were in need of a cute outfit to wear to a party in high school, Kittie would dress me in her walk-in closet; Cynthia would loan me an expensive handbag for the night. They never made me feel "less than" for not being as outrageously wealthy as they were, and it's one of the things I appreciate about them now that I'm approaching midlife and in danger of being way more destitute than I ever was growing up.

When I left Cedartown for college in Austin, I did drift away from Kittie and Cynthia. They went to Southern Methodist University in Dallas, promptly returning home after their four years in college, but I stayed in Austin, stepping into a whole new existence, especially after I fell for Felix.

Sure, Kittie and I would drunk-dial each other and it would be as if no time had passed, but Cynthia's and my friendship dissolved into a handful of texts a year. That wasn't all that unusual for us—our friendship had always hinged on Kittie. Kittie's needs, Kittie's wants, Kittie's impulses. Cynthia and I have always been just trying to stay afloat in Kittie's wake.

I'M ROUNDING THE cove now and walking past the Whites'. Their mansion is smaller in size than the Southerlands', but no less grand: a bloodred brick behemoth set far off the street and reached by a slender drive that winds up a rolling hill. Cynthia's parents, Frank and Virginia, when they were still living, sold their house to a young doctor and his wife years ago before moving back to Dallas, where they were originally from.

Walking by their house now, I can still remember how it felt inside: distant and chilly. Mrs. White never remembered my name—if she ever even knew it—referring to me as "dear" as she flitted about the rooms like some agitated bird.

Cynthia wasn't neglected by any means; everything she ever wanted was laid out at her feet, but I do suspect she was emotionally neglected by her frosty parents, who were nearly a generation older than most.

I CAN'T BELIEVE I'm back here, strolling these streets. On the one hand, the familiarity is comforting, but on the other, I feel sucked back into a past I never thought I'd return to, like I'm living in some parallel reality to the life I should still be living down in Austin with Felix and our circle of friends.

But the night I read that text—Mmmm . . . can't wait for more of you . . . —from Kiera, his latest assistant, it wasn't my Austin friends, Evie or Samantha, I called. It was Kittie.

"You have *got* to be fucking kidding me," she said. Kittie had warned me about Felix on the eve of our wedding, hissing in my ear that something was off about him. In my backless silk wedding gown, with my hair swept up and the pop of lights from the photographer spotlighting me, I thought at the time she was just jealous that I was the center of attention for once.

"Let me guess, the little bitch is in her twenties."

"Yes," I said with tears strangling my throat.

"Want me to come down there and slit her tires? Roll her house? Or her fucking *condo*, because I'm positive she doesn't even have a house!"

She wasn't kidding, and that's why I love her.

And when I *did* reach out to my Austin friends and broke the news, they were aghast. First, with sympathy, but then they slowly retreated from me as if I'd caught a virus that they'd soon catch, too. The cheated-on, betrayed-by-her-perfect-husband virus.

No, I don't need those faux earth mamas in my life right now, now that my life is tilted on its side. I need my roots, my old friends.

And Annie is likely right: a man is probably exactly what I *don't* need right now.

5.

Cynthia Nichols's Diary

IT'S FRIDAY AFTERNOON, just after lunchtime. I'm sitting in the breakfast nook at the table. Sunlight shimmers off the pool and rose-colored buds from our monstrous crape myrtle trees bob in the water.

I haven't written in this thing in a few days, which Dr. Whitaker gently prodded me to keep up with more regularly during our therapy session yesterday.

I can't believe how much I look forward to being in her office, with its clean lines and off-white color scheme, her calm, steady voice like a purr in my ear. I feel like I'm shedding my skin in there, like I'm edging closer to becoming myself. Whoever that is. She draws things out of me that I didn't even know were there, and I feel a course of electricity zing through me when we talk.

So here I am, writing my third official entry.

My walnut dining table is littered with wallpaper samples and color chips from the paint store, spread out before me like confetti.

We've been in this house for nearly twenty years, and at least once every five, I get the itch to remodel. I'm in one of those phases right now. Gerald is the CFO of Longstreet & Gem, Cedartown's most prestigious architectural-design firm; we had them design this house when we were newlyweds, fresh out of college.

Of course I had a big hand in it—interior design has always fascinated me; it was my major in college (architectural design was my minor). I guess I inherited that from my mother, and I wanted a huge Frank Lloyd Wright–inspired home.

The outside of the house is stacked limestone, trimmed in forest green, with a bank of floor-to-ceiling windows lining the front and back. I love lounging in the sun-drenched rooms, gazing out over the green slope of the front lawn and the terraced gardens in the back that border the pool. It makes me feel sometimes like we live in an atrium, like we're encased in nature.

It helps that I have a staff to handle the upkeep, to make sure the windows are always crystal clear, the wood floors polished like a new penny, the yard trimmed and shorn, the pool skimmed.

I mean, I'm no slob; I never let a single dish rest in the sink, but I prefer instead to tinker with furniture placement, pick out new textiles, etc., rather than the rigors of housekeeping, such as scouring the floors.

I comb through the pile of color chips on the table and try to imagine the walls awash in those hues. Right now the interior of our home is all grays. I was in on that fad early—ahead of the times, I like to think. Now not only is everyone's home drenched in gray, but public spaces are as well—restaurants, stores, hair salons. And now I feel like I'm living in a mortuary; the cold, steely drabness feels prisonlike.

I'm longing for color, and I'm thinking, or predicting, rather, that global colors—fuchsias, tangerines, and teals—will be the next trend. And also, wallpapers, I think, will swing back in vogue.

I finger the edges of two fuchsia chips. Should I pick Forward Fuchsia? Or Dynamo? I'm thinking I'll have the bedroom done in this shade. Maybe if I pick Dynamo, our sex life will follow suit and heat up?

DR. WHITAKER'S OTHER assignment for me, besides keeping this journal, is to make a list of all my interests. The problem is, I don't know what those might be. Is remodeling an interest? An obsession? A distraction?

For the past seventeen years, I've poured my focus into Tyson. Tyson's toddler issues with acid reflux, Tyson's hypersensitive behavior in preschool. Tyson's now-earned status of "gifted." Tyson's tennis lessons (now abandoned) and Tyson's flute lessons (currently obsessed with) and Tyson's band practice.

But now that he's a full-on teenager with his own car, he has less time for me; he's always gone in that Nissan Sentra. And he has less patience with me, too. Yes, he's a nerd and a good boy, and he still sits down with us to eat dinner every night and stays at home after school and on the weekends for the most part. That is my fault: I've always overindulged and encouraged his geeky side.

When he was little, I allowed him to spend endless weekends inside playing with Legos. I even used to play alongside him, the two of us creating elaborate structures together, building cities and fortresses. I guess my nerdy side enjoyed it, too, but in hindsight, I fear it socially stunted him. I should have shoved him out of the house, encouraged him to play with the other children in the neighborhood.

So you'd think I'd be thrilled that he has a new best friend, Carter, but I feel a prick of jealousy when he leaves to go to Carter's house. When he speaks about *Carter* with such reverence.

But what I'm really uneasy about, I think (or, at least, Dr. Whitaker thinks), is that before I know it, I'm going to be an empty nester. And the void I'm already feeling will threaten to swallow me whole.

I confessed to Dr. Whitaker that even though it embarrasses me, I don't *know* what interests me, what fills me with passion.

"Well," she said, shifting her reading glasses to the bridge of her nose, "start at the beginning. Of your life, I mean. What fascinated you as a child? What were you drawn to back then?"

Ah, my childhood. A cordoned-off area of my mind I rarely look back toward. Not because my childhood was tragic, but because it was lonely. My parents, Frank and Virginia White, *the* Frank and Virginia White originally of Dallas, oil money leaking out of every one of their pores, had me when they were in their early forties and raised me in a distant yet strangely smothering kind of way.

Like Kittie and Jen, I'm an only child, and my parents were too old to even pretend to be my playmates. My mother, cloaked forever in her long dresses and fussy nightgowns, her bony hands adorned with knots of golden-nugget rings, always seemed too dressed up to want to cuddle or get messy playing in the dirt outside. And when my father wasn't in his dark-paneled home office sorting royalty checks from oil wells, he was perpetually crashed in his crackled leather La-Z-Boy, the newspaper pasted across his chest.

I usually retreated to my second-story bedroom and sat in the crook of the arched window seat, sketching with charcoals in a tablet or working through math problems. In elementary school, *that*'s what I was most interested in: math, and also science and art. I was Mensa smart, and my fourth-grade math teacher, Mrs. Henry, with her ropy braids, always encouraged me to enter the annual University Inter-scholastic League mathematics competition, but Mother had other ideas for me.

She pushed me into ballet classes, English-horse-riding lessons, etiquette class, things she felt would mold me into a proper young lady and, one day, a fine housewife. So I broke from the brainy, artsy kid I was long ago in the name of refinement.

I would have majored in art in college if I'd had the guts. But Virginia and Frank wouldn't have gone for that. That was something that single women did, bohemians. Not debutantes. And I wasn't bold enough to go against the grain.

So I chose interior design instead (which I do truly love), as it was more of a clear path to decorating my future house as a future house-wife. I did manage to take an elective painting class while I was there. It was in a crumbling brick building, the studio flooded with natural light, and I can remember feeling a jolt of excitement as I stood in front of my easel, a feather-soft smock on over my dress, paintbrush in hand. We worked with acrylics, and I loved the sensory input of squeezing the paint from the tubes onto the palette, moving the brush across the canvas. The intoxicating feeling of creating something of my own.

I painted one landscape that I was particularly proud of: a beach with the ocean done in a cerulean blue. I remember carting it home in my satchel to the sorority room I shared with Kittie. It was a Friday afternoon and she was sitting cross-legged in the middle of her bed on top of her floral comforter, chunky hot rollers in her hair, giving her-self a French manicure, readying herself for our evening out at a frat party.

I slid it out to show her.

"Look what I made in art! Can you believe it?"

She flicked her eyes up for a second. "Awww, that's so cute, honey!" She dropped her gaze back to her nail job. "Can you top me off?" she asked, gesturing with a fanned-out hand to her half-full wineglass.

A pang of disappointment washed over me. I was going to hang the painting on our wall near the door so it would be prominently displayed, but instead, I placed it on a high shelf in my closet. Art wasn't something girls like us focused on, and I felt silly for even al-lowing myself the fantasy of indulging in it.

Now when I think of what I'd like to do, of what might spark my imagination, I see a vision of myself in a walled city somewhere in

Europe, my heels clicking along a cobblestone path, the breeze from the Mediterranean Sea combing my hair, lifting the hem of my skirt. A tanned hand on my wrist leading me somewhere clandestine. After we graduated college, I'd begged Gerald to go backpacking through Europe for a month.

"What? Like hippies?" he scoffed.

I dropped it then and stifled it. But now, since I've started seeing Dr. Whitaker, the vision of me strolling through a narrow, sun-soaked alleyway keeps springing to mind. I've even done some furtive late-night searches for flights to Italy and Spain, fantasizing over different villas and B and Bs.

But the trouble with these visions? Gerald is not with me.

6.

Kittie

MY THIGH MUSCLES are searing and my lungs are singed from sucking in huge gulps of air, but I keep pushing.

The neighborhood's annual Fourth of July picnic—for which I serve on the committee, of course—is less than a week away, and I'll be damned if I can't squeeze into these new white shorts I picked up at Neiman's in Dallas last week.

I try to exercise every day and meet up with my personal trainer, Erica, on Tuesdays and Thursdays. Mondays are for Pilates, Wednesday is spin class, and if I'm not too worn-out from my rotation with Erica, I'll pop into kickboxing on Thursdays after our session.

I don't do yoga; it's way too Zen for me—all that ohming and group deep breathing make my skin crawl—but I do enjoy meditative strolls. It's as close to a Zen state as I can get. That and guzzling wine. Plus, I love meeting up with Jen and Cynthia to walk the neighborhood we all grew up in together.

But right now I'm pounding the treadmill in my home gym, having shut myself in here to try and put even more space between me and Chloe and her friends.

We just had another fight. It's strange sparring with her now, now that she's taller than me. I'm a petite five two, and this year she's shot up, gaining two inches on me. She stands over me when we argue, my mirror in every way except her height, which she got from Hank's side. She really does look like my clone: same heart-shaped mouth with naturally berry-red lips, same prism-green eyes, same high cheekbones, same sun-kissed skin. The only other feature that sets us apart is Chloe's blond hair, which is a shade darker than mine, making it the color of butterscotch, her nose and cheeks sprinkled with butterscotch freckles to match. And where my hair is silky straight, Chloe's is curly; coiled ringlets dipped in gold frame her face and fall past her shoulders.

We fought because when I stepped outside a few moments ago to water the rosemary (okay, I was snooping), I smelled a pungent whiff of cigarette smoke.

Chloe, Megan, and her new friend, Shelley—the bad one in the bunch—were all giggling, lounging around the pool in their strikingly sparse bikinis. I mean, thong bottoms on teenagers? I did *not* want Chloe buying that but she erupted on me one day at the mall, so I caved, yanked it off the rack, and let her purchase it on the condition she wear it only at home and never in front of Hank, because, well, just *no*.

"Chloe," I said, my face burning with anger, "a word, please?"

She huffed and rolled her eyes to her friends before trailing me inside.

"What?" she asked, her green irises spearing me, her hands parked on hips.

"I smelled cigarette smoke when I went out back a few minutes ago. Is it Shelley? Does she—?"

"God no, Mom." Her eyes skittered away from mine; her neck turned crimson.

"Don't bullshit me, Chloe. And don't cover for Shelley." My own face was scorching with anger.

"Sshhhh, lower your voice; she might hear you," she whined.

"I don't *care* if she *does!*" I pitched my voice even louder.

"Why," Chloe shrieked, throwing her hands up around the word "why," "are you acting like such a bitch?"

She spun around before I could answer, her thong bottom all but vanishing between her ass cheeks as she sashayed out the patio door.

And though I longed to reach out, grab her by the shoulder, and screech back, I decided not to give her the satisfaction.

So now I'm taking it out on the treadmill, shins splintering with pain as I pound the rubber tongue of the machine, breaking out of my jog and into a run. But even with my heavy breathing and feet slapping against the treadmill, I can hear laughter piercing the air from Chloe and those wicked girls.

I jam my earbuds in, scroll to find my Missy Elliott playlist, and jab the "incline" button until it reaches seven, the highest level I've ever run on before. I keep this up for several minutes (six, to be exact, a record for me) before planting my feet on either side of the treadmill so I can bend over and heave in some air.

My heart thunders against my rib cage and my body is drenched with sweat, but even this intense workout burst hasn't quelled how pissed off I am at Chloe for gaslighting and back-talking to me.

Slipping a finger through the slats of the mini blinds, I peer out at them. Shelley is in the pool now on a yellow float, a slender hand shading her face, the other tracing circles in the aquamarine water. Megan and Chloe are sprawled on their stomachs on chaise longues, flipping through glossy magazines.

Chloe's hair is crunchy with chlorine, but still looks print-model perfect as it trails down her bare back. Increasingly, I study Chloe—

her taut flesh, her sculpted legs—thinking of the body I once had and will never have again, and it fills me with envy.

I pause at the window for a moment longer, lean my ear closer to the glass. Their voices are somewhat muffled, but I can make out Shelley barking something out to Chloe. Chloe lowers her magazine, sits up, her loud teenage voice shooting through the window like a laser.

"Oh, don't worry about her," she says, flinging a hand toward the house. "She's in there torturing herself on the treadmill, trying not to look as fat and old as she is. *As if.*"

Shelley snorts and their trio of wicked laughter fills my ears once again.

7.

Jen

IT'S NEARLY MIDNIGHT and I'm still awake, staring up at the popcorn ceiling in my bedroom, my eyes tracing the puckered texture as if it were a constellation of stars—a leftover habit from my childhood.

Back then, I was across the hall in what is now Kasey's room, but now I'm in the master, my parents' old bedroom, which feels both comforting and somewhat pathetic to me.

I love this house and the warm memories of childhood it holds, and over the years, my parents have done some updating—retiling the bathrooms, installing wood flooring throughout—but there're still some remnants from the 1980s I'd love to shed: the popcorn ceiling being one, and the brass doorknobs and fixtures being the other.

Tonight, I miss my airy modern farmhouse in the Bouldin Creek neighborhood of Austin. Our lot was on a hilltop, and from our rooftop deck, we could glimpse the tops of skyscrapers jutting up from downtown. Our home was all natural light and blond wood, very much ahead of the whole "hygge" aesthetic from Norway that's now all the rage. Felix—Nordic fucker—was onto something there. Or self-proclaimed Nordic. He is from Minnesota but his ancestral roots are Norwegian, and he never misses a chance to drop that in a conversation.

I don't miss the sanitized minimalism of our house, but I do miss the buttery-soft light of Austin spilling through our windows, turning our crisp white walls violet at sundown. I miss sipping Pinot Noir by the fireplace while gazing out over the jagged hills and the way the Hill Country breezes in the summertime would lift the scent of lavender from our bushes outside, coating the entire house with the perfume-clean smell.

But mostly, I miss being held. I miss the feeling of resting my head on Felix's rock-hard abs while he strokes my hair. I miss him cradling my feet, absentmindedly giving me a foot rub while he tells me about his day. I miss our sex, his hands clasping my face, my legs wrapped around his jutting hips.

THE NEIGHBORHOOD FOURTH of July picnic was this evening and it made everything I've recently lost come into sharp relief. I arrived around six thirty, dragging a reluctant Kasey with me and a cooler full of watermelon slices and oven-roasted corn—the cheapest items to grab from the store. Kittie is on the planning committee, so of course I had to volunteer to bring something.

It's held each year on the third, so as not to compete with the town's fireworks display out at the lake on the official holiday. The neighbors gather at a grassy sloping park on the banks of the swollen creek that winds through our neighborhood. The banks are ruddy red from the red-dirt clay of the area, and after this most recent rain, the water is the color of dried blood.

The picnic drew out all the usual families—everyone in neat nuclear units, appropriately paired off.

The dating pool here is dismal, and the only single male I could spot at the picnic was Tony Peters, a good friend of Hank's who Kittie tried to hook me up with when I first moved back. I think she did it more so she and Hank could have someone to double-date with, and less because she thought we might make a good match. Tony is nice enough, and cute, I suppose, but in a baby-faced way that is rarely appealing to me. We spent the evening at the local Italian bistro, my cheeks sore from the fake smile plastered on my face while my insides churned at the sadness of it all.

"You're not into him, are you?" Kittie asked, midway through dinner, while reglossing her lips and patting down her spun-silk hair in the dimly lit ladies' room.

"Is it that obvious?" I gave my head a quick shake to try and stifle the tears that were threatening to strangle my throat.

"Pretty much. But only to me, don't worry." Kittie snapped her candy-bar-sized clutch shut and turned to me, reaching out and smoothing down my hair in the same way she had just done with hers. "Sorry, sister. I thought y'all might make a good match, or at the very least, I thought he'd be useful for a night, take your mind off Felix."

Her red lips curled into a half smile, a smile of concern, and then I couldn't help it, hot tears flooded my eyes, which then gave way to my chest heaving with sobs. She held me close and let me ugly cry all over her for a good long while until I was wrung out.

"Let's get you out of here," she said.

And minutes later she was behind the wheel of my car, driving me home, having steered me out of the restaurant with just a passing wave to Hank and Tony. Once we were safely nestled into my car, she banged out a hasty text to Hank, making something up about "female problems." After that, to my relief, she gave up on playing matchmaker altogether.

So when I spotted Tony at the picnic earlier, chatting with a group of men in a circle of lawn chairs, I purposely decided to avoid contact with him if at all possible.

When we arrived, I rolled the cooler across the spongy lawn, the blades of grass needling the sides of my sandaled feet. I went over to the picnic table where Kittie was stationed, ladling syrupy booze out of a spiked watermelon and passing it out in plastic cups. She was dressed in a white halter top with a plunging neckline that revealed her generous cleavage, a pair of matching crisp white shorts hugging her sumptuous curves. Her bronzed legs glistened with oil and her freshly pedicured feet were slipped into red-and-white-striped espa-drilles. She looked radiant and I glanced down at what I was wearing—last season's flowy linen pants and my freshest-looking T-shirt—and inwardly cringed.

"Jen!" Kittie cried out. "You guys made it!" She slipped an arm around Kasey's back and pulled him in for a peck on the cheek before lacing her other arm around me, giving me a tight squeeze. Her breath reeked of fruit and alcohol and her eyes were already dilated.

"Here, taste," she said, palming me a plastic cup with the pale pink liquid.

I took a sip and the hit of vodka burned the back of my throat but the cocktail tasted like an icy watermelon Jolly Rancher, so I downed it and reached for another.

A dozen or so picnic tables lined the lawn, each with different of-ferings: gourmet Jell-O shots made with real fruit chunks, wooden barrels of homemade vanilla ice cream flecked with peaches, a burger bar with a selection of fancy cheeses and toppings, and bowls full of various forms of Fourth of July–themed staples—fruit salad, chicken salad, and potato salad.

Hank was tending to the giant barbecue pit, which sizzled with sausages, burgers, and blackened chicken wings. I've liked Hank since the first time I met him in Dallas, soon after he and Kittie started dating in college. He is broad shouldered and now has a healthy-sized beer paunch, but he's still roguishly handsome: jet-black hair and blue eyes with a rugged jawline. And more than that, he's witty and welcoming. He flirts with me in an innocent way that always makes me feel good about myself and, in situations like these, less like a pariah. He beamed at me from across the park, raised his beer in a toast.

Gerald, Cynthia's husband, was at Hank's elbow as usual, chomping on a cigar, and he greeted me with a friendly dip of the head. I've always liked him, too, and find him well suited for Cynthia. Both are refined and mild mannered. Gerald's pomade-perfect dark brown hair is always slicked back in place and his taste in clothing is impeccable; his whole demeanor is endearingly effeminate. He has a pleasing Southern drawl, delicately selecting his words, putting one at ease.

I spied Cynthia one table over from Kittie's, dressed in a red sundress, her lustrous inky hair flowing between her chiseled shoulder blades. She was doling out plastic bowls of ice cream with her son, Tyson.

"Go say hi to Tyson," I whispered in Kasey's ear.

Ever since we moved back, I've tried to forge a friendship between the two boys, but it's never stuck.

"No, he's such a fucking dork," Kasey said.

"Sssshh," I hissed, jabbing him in the side with my elbow.

I then eyed Chloe on the banks of the creek with a group of teenage girls surrounding her. She was standing while the others sat crosslegged at her feet. Seeing her like this reminded me of Kittie in high school, how Kittie always commanded the attention of the group.

I remember our first cheerleading slumber party, freshman year of high school. Kittie hosted it at her mansion while her parents were out for the night on the town. Mrs. Southerland had hired a chaperone, of course, to oversee the party, but Kittie bribed her with a twenty to leave us alone.

None of us girls had ever taken a sip of alcohol before, and as the sun began to set, washing the forest behind Kittie's house in golden hues, Kittie led us outside to their sprawling patio paved with red bricks, which hugged the back of the house in a semicircle.

One of Kittie's admirers, a senior named Drew with a fake ID, had procured a fifth of Jose Cuervo tequila for her earlier that afternoon. Kittie stood before us, wielding the bottle, casually but effortlessly beautiful in a baggy SMU sweatshirt, her blond hair pulled high in a loose scrunchie.

"Everyone is doing at least one shot," she said, swinging the bottle in front of her.

Because I was standing closest to her, I took the first shot and the tequila was so strong, it made the inside of my nose burn, but I finished it, eager to go along with whatever it was she commanded of us. The rest of the squad followed suit, passing the open bottle around, a domino effect of Kittie's peer pressure.

Chloe is every bit as dazzling as Kittie, but with a bit more edginess to her. At the picnic, she wore a red string bikini top with frayed blue jeans cutoffs and combat boots. Her face was pink with the sun and her hair glowed golden as if lit from behind as sunlight shimmered off the water beside her. Her slender fingers were adorned with stacked silver rings, her hands gesticulating as the gaggle of girls beamed up at her.

Even from where I stood, I could sense a current running through the group, a restless tension that felt like they were on the edge of doing something naughty. They all clutched red Solo cups and I'm positive there was alcohol in them.

I didn't encourage Kasey to go speak to Chloe, but I didn't have to. He's been secretly smitten with her since we moved to town. He would never admit it to me, but I see the way he watches her, the way his neck blushes when he's around her, and I know he's got a crush. Maybe because they've known each other since they were little, Chloe's always playfully treated Kasey like a younger brother. She's only several months older than him, but the gulf in maturity seems a lot vaster.

When we moved back, though, Kasey had grown nearly a foot since they'd last seen each other, his body already straining toward puberty. I saw Chloe register him in a different light that day: his deeper voice, his broader shoulders, his skater haircut—all of it aged him up from the little blond boy she used to tease. She twisted a strand of her honey-colored hair around the tip of a finger and studied him for a moment before socking him in the shoulder. I think she might have a crush on him, too, but we're in a different social class from the Spearses and I can't imagine she'd ever pursue anything with Kasey. Plus, most girls only want to date guys their own age or older.

I glanced at Kasey and sure enough, beneath his blond bangs, his eyes were locked onto Chloe and her gang. But with no other boys around the girls, there was no way he'd approach them. Instead, he sauntered over to the burger bar, piling a paper plate high with toppings.

I SCANNED THE rest of the crowd for Will but saw no sign of him. I figured he might still be out of town, and my shoulders slumped with disappointment. I slunk through the boggy air back to Kittie's table for a refill.

"That's my girl," Kittie said, sloshing more booze into my cup. She wiped her hands with a napkin, circled around the side of the table to stand in the shade of a willow tree with me. Cynthia joined us.

"Well, well, look who just arrived."

Kittie motioned over to a sleek black Suburban pulling to the curb. A tall, dark-haired guy slid from the driver's side and opened the passenger door. Brandi Stephens spilled out, in all her glory. Obviously aware that all male eyes were pulled her way, she gave her head a dramatic flip, swinging her long brunette hair over one shoulder as she bent over at the waist to adjust the strap on her sandal, her breasts practically surging out of the canary-yellow tank she was wearing.

The man—her husband, I presumed—took her by the elbow and the pair coasted across the lawn, both of their faces stamped with gleaming white soap opera smiles.

"Kittie!" Brandi approached our table with an overeager smile.

"Jesus," Kittie said under her breath as Brandi walked up.

"Well, don't you just look—" Kittie paused, searching for the right words, her head involuntarily wagging as she took in Brandi's attire.

"Thank you!" Brandi threw herself onto Kittie for a hug before Kittie even had the chance to finish her thought.

As if aware of the brittle-thin social ice Brandi was skating on, the man tugged her by the wrist, guiding her away from us.

My eyes (and I'm certain everyone else's) trailed Brandi's backside— her perfectly shaped ass was squeezed into a pair of ultrahigh-cut denim shorts that exposed the lower part of her butt cheeks.

Cynthia's doll-perfect mouth hung open for a second as she gaped before taking another pull off her cocktail. The heavy, damp heat and the alcohol were making me light-headed, but I allowed Kittie to refill my cup again.

"God, the nerve on that woman," Kittie shout-whispered to me and Cynthia, "literally showing her ass at a family picnic. She knows I can't stand her but she's always gotta try."

"Is that her husband?" I asked.

"Yep. Blake Stephens. Easy to look at but also *so* bleh plastic-looking. Just like *her*," Kittie growled. "I mean, Blake and Brandi? Is that even for real?"

The strands of the willow tree hung limp around us in the lifeless air, and I grabbed a paper dessert plate from the table to fan my face with. Blake and Brandi headed to the far side of the park, where they were absorbed by a subset of Junior Leaguers, a clique of nouveau riche women whom I know Kittie all but sticks her nose up at. Kittie is part of the old guard, the old money set, the gilded lineage of ancestral debutantes coursing through her DNA.

The sun was finally beginning to drop beneath the forested horizon but sweat still glazed over my hairline and neck. I twisted my head to watch the coral smear of the sunset when I saw him walking along the paved trail toward the picnic.

Will.

He was tall, taller than I could've imagined. At least six foot three. He wore a faded denim shirt, cuffed above his sculpted forearms, the top buttons undone to show a bit of his chest. Even in the heat, his shirt was tucked into a pair of charcoal-gray pants, like he'd just stepped off a runway. I felt my mouth go dry and I must have gasped because Kittie and Cynthia both turned to me and followed my gaze.

"Is that him?" Kittie asked.

"Yes."

"He *is* hot," Cynthia said.

"Hmmmm-mmmm." Kittie inched closer to me. "And look, no wifey!"

"Should I go talk to him?" My pulse pounded in my throat.

"Yasss, bitch, yasss." Kittie put her hand on my lower back, gave me a gentle shove.

I wanted to but my tongue grew thick in my mouth and my stomach clenched with nerves.

"Okay, I will. But lemme finish this hunch punch of yours first. I need it."

"Heard that," Kittie said.

The sun was now completely set and the sky was darkening with shades of deep blue. I nursed the rest of my drink while studying Will. He moved gracefully through the park, turning heads as he did, until he reached the base of a gnarled oak tree, which he leaned against, surveying the crowd. The sea of voices from the picnic buzzed a pitch louder as if everyone else was talking about him as well.

"Fireworks are going off soon. You'd better go," Kittie said.

I set my empty cup down and adjusted my outfit.

"Wait, more lipstick," Kittie said, digging in her purse, which she had stashed underneath the table. "Here." She passed me a berry-colored tube and I uncapped it before running it across my lips.

I started picking my way across the park to Will, trying to take deep breaths as my therapist suggested to calm my nervous system down, but it wasn't working. I stared down at my feet and tried counting my paces instead. When I got halfway across the lawn, I glanced up at the tree to find Brandi planted right in front of Will, her head tilted to the side, her back arched so that her chest was thrust out.

A grin was spread across Will's face and he cupped a hand behind his head as he stared down at her, talking to her. Anger singed through me. Brandi already *had* a goddamn husband, so why did she need to talk to him? I spun on my heels and headed back to Kittie and Cynthia.

"Oh, for fuck's sake," Kittie spat. "Will you look at her? But seriously, Jen, there's no way he's into her. He's classy. I can tell that much already. He's just being polite. Go, go back over and talk to him. Interrupt them."

Overhead, the first round of fireworks popped against the now-black night.

"Ooooh, pretty!" Cynthia said, clasping her hands together. She was obviously drunk, speaking in the little-girl voice she adopts when she imbibes too much.

Kittie's elbow dug into my rib cage. "Go."

"Well, now I might as well wait until the fireworks are over. I don't want to be shouting at him," I said, nearly shouting at Kittie so my voice could be heard over the thundering fireworks.

I gazed back over at Will, and Brandi was still preening over him, her legs now spread farther apart, her hands running through her shiny hair as she nodded up at him.

Kittie leaned into me and squeezed my hand. We watched bursts of color explode against the cloudless sky, like fluorescent jellyfish expanding and contracting, as thick layers of smoke filtered down around the picnic. When I could feel the display cresting with the most spectacular fireworks, I squeezed Kittie's hand as a signal that I was heading back over to Will.

But when I looked in his direction, I saw Brandi striding across the field toward her husband, and Will was nowhere in sight.

Present

MY LIMBS ARE aching with the chill; I'm still pinned in place on the cold forest floor, where my body will most likely be found.

By habit, my hand travels down to my shorts pocket, searching for my cell, again, even though it's not on me. *He* has it.

I lost it in our first struggle, just after those few words left my lips and he struck me with the back of his hand, then grabbed me by the wrists. I wrenched my body away from his and that's when the cell inched out of my shallow pocket like a freshly caught fish wriggling to escape a fisherman's coarse hands.

It landed screen down on a mat of pine needles. He toed it hard— a hockey puck gliding across glass—and it was out of reach, out of sight.

I'm not even sure who I would call first for help if I still had it on me. Everyone is going to be mad at me, so I tell myself that I wouldn't call anyone I know. I guess I'd simply dial 911 and wait for the police, sort the rest of it out later.

No one in this town is ever going to talk to me again, will never look at me the same again, which fills my stomach with dread. I don't want to die, but the shame I will feel when I face everyone almost makes death seem like an easier option.

8.

Jen

I'M STANDING IN front of my bathroom mirror, fidgeting. I want to look good, but don't want it to seem as if I've put forth too much effort. My skin looks dewy and fresh (but only after repeatedly pinching my cheeks) and my lips are coated in a soft pink lipstick that I hope looks natural, appealing.

I pick up my cell, start to tap out a text to Kittie and Cynthia, but erase the message and set my cell back down. Adrenaline is already needling through my veins and I don't want to make this more anxiety inducing or a bigger deal than it already is.

"It's *not* a big deal," I actually say to my reflection, palms planted on the edge of the countertop.

But of course, it is. I'm going over to Will's.

Amber-colored afternoon light leaks through the blinds, tinging the room with a warm glow, picking up the ghosts of highlights in my hair. It's been so long since I've been to the salon, but I can't afford it, so I'm making do right now by teasing the roots with my fingers, trying for a beachy look.

Will's house. The thought of it sends my heart knocking against my chest. I glance at my cell, feeling another tug to alert Kittie and Cynthia, but stifle it again; I don't want to break this dreamlike spell that I'm under.

So much has happened in the past twelve hours.

This morning, I was parked at the kitchen table with my laptop open, sipping a scorching-hot latte and scanning again for jobs. My head throbbed from all the cheap booze I'd consumed at the picnic, and staring into the screen only sharpened the pain in my temples.

I actually don't do the job-search thing as often as I should. It's too depressing. There aren't a lot of opportunities here in Cedartown, and the few places I've reached out to—a wellness spa (womanning the front desk) and an interior design firm (handling the books)—I never heard back from. Who wants a thirty-nine-year-old with only stay-at-home-mom experience and an ancient bachelor's degree in English with a minor in music history?

Also, I don't want a straight-and-narrow job. I'm trying to raise Kasey all by myself and I don't need the mind-numbing pressure of having to answer to anyone else. So lately, I've been trying to visualize what line of work I'd like to explore and the thing I keep coming back to is: private yoga instructor. That or Realtor. But I'm not sure I have the extroverted personality required for that. So yoga instructor it is, but I'm lacking the motivation to even figure out the steps to make that happen.

I will soon; I have to. Every month we come up short, even with the stipend from my parents. Somehow sensing this, my dad stops by and digs a few hundreds out of his wallet, hands them over to me, eyes lowered. I don't know what Kasey and I would be doing if my parents hadn't given their renters the boot and agreed to let us live here for free. Probably, we'd be shacking with them, which is why they most likely decided on this generous arrangement.

I worked odd jobs through college—sales clerk at a party-goods store, runner for a downtown law firm—but my only other position was at the record label just after I graduated. I was interning and my paychecks were scant, but I loved the work: booking bands, overseeing promo art, scheduling travel. And that's how I met Felix. Felix Hansen, locally famed guitarist for a midlevel rock band. I was instantly drawn to his lean, chiseled body, his shaggy dark hair, his aloof, cavalier demeanor.

Before I knew it, I was in a satin gown coasting down the aisle with him, and soon after, I became pregnant with Kasey.

At the first sonogram after the doctor spread warm gel over my stomach and guided the wand across my abdomen, confirming Kasey's heartbeat, Felix squeezed my hand. And when the doctor stepped from the room to let me get dressed, Felix announced that he was going to get a real job, one with benefits. At the time we were renting a tiny duplex with a warped porch, and excitement sizzled through me at the prospect of having more.

Within a week, well-connected Felix had landed an IT position at a start-up company downtown. And I was all too happy to ditch my internship and prepare for Kasey's arrival. I always assumed I would have some sort of career, but Felix shot to the top of the start-up after a few years and was making more money than we ever needed. He urged me to stay home, and I listened to him. I never dreamed I'd be back in Cedartown, scrounging for income, with no retirement plan or assets, let alone savings.

After I closed out the job search, I logged on to my bank account, just to punish myself even further. As usual, the savings account was a flat line and I shuddered at the three-digit amount in checking, which would soon be one digit after the bills were paid.

I pressed the pads of my fingertips to my temples and rubbed in small soothing circles until my reverie was broken by the sound of Kasey flipping the guest bathroom toilet seat up and pissing noisily with the door open.

He lumbered down the hall, hair cowlicked from sleep, T-shirt tucked loosely into the waistband of his flannel pajama bottoms. My stomach clenched as I took him in—my little boy in a teenager's body with a teen's stormy vibe—and I felt a prick of guilt. Both of us are exiled in this place, but at least I have Kittie and Jen as my consolation prize. He has nobody, other than me and my mom and dad.

My parents, Don and Lisa Miller, are so dependable, so rock-solid, so the opposite of how Felix turned out to be. I even want to shed my married name and take back theirs, but I don't want to piss Kasey off even further.

My parents were one of the bargaining chips I used to lure Kasey back to Cedartown. That and the notion of more freedom and also the promise of a car.

"You'll be able to ride your bike around the neighborhood like normal kids are supposed to," I said to him one evening as I was folding towels in the laundry room.

He stood against the door, arm slung on the frame, his face darkened by my announcement that we were moving. "But I won't have any friends there."

"You'll *make* friends. I promise. And you can go out to Grandma and Grandpa's land anytime to fish. *And* you'll be able to roam the neighborhood, walk through the woods along the creek. Without me worrying about you getting stolen or smashed in traffic." My voice kept rising in pitch as if I were on midday television selling timeshares.

"I *do* like the land," he said finally, crossing his arms in front of his chest. "And you swear you'll get me my own car?" His sky-blue eyes locked onto mine.

My chest tightened with anxiety because I couldn't sort out how I was going to pay for it, but I managed to say, "I promise. For your sixteenth." I stood on my tiptoes and kissed the top of his head before scooting around him with the laundry basket bouncing on my hip.

And of course, my parents have come to the rescue on the car front as well. Dad combed through listings on Craigslist for weeks before settling on the one he thought might be best: a Toyota Land Cruiser, early nineties model. He wanted something cool for Kasey, but not a dangerous sports car, and he didn't want to plunk down a ton of cash for it.

The Land Cruiser is forest green with a tan cracked-leather interior. The shell and inside are in mint condition, but it needs some minor mechanical work. We've managed to keep it a secret from Kasey for the past few months—Mom and Dad want to surprise him with it for his sixteenth birthday next March, so it's resting under a heavy tarp next to one of Dad's old tractors.

My parents' land is a few miles north of town—fifty forested acres that they've owned since I was a little girl. When my dad retired five years ago and closed up his bookkeeping firm, my parents set out to build their dream house—a modern log cabin—which is perched on a sloping hillside and looks out over the pint-sized pond Dad keeps stocked with catfish. A few times a week, they come to pick Kasey up for the day and he always returns satiated and ruddy faced, smelling of pine needles and mosquito repellent.

I WISH HIS edges would soften like that around me. But this morning, I could feel his jagged energy without him even uttering a word. He strode past me to the cabinet, dragged down a cereal bowl, clanking it against the countertop. I felt my breathing grow shallower as I peered into my laptop, feigning focus.

He let out a sharp exhale and I looked up as he shook the dregs of the near-empty jug of milk he had pulled from the fridge.

"Sorry. I'm making a grocery run later," I said.

Before I turned my eyes away from him, I saw him shake his head in obvious disapproval.

I snapped my laptop shut, turned back to him. "Sleep well?"

He snorted, face growing red, and just shook his head again as if I were the dumbest person alive.

"Want me to get anything special from the store?" I asked, trying to break through to him.

He stirred the bran around his cereal bowl, took a mouthful, and kept his head down, ignoring me.

"Kasey, I asked you a question," I said, anger pinching my voice.

"Sorry. Yes, apples," he finally said, looking up at me, his face softening. "I'd like some apples." His voice was gentler then and had a trace of innocence that pierced my heart.

Apples. Such a simple request. He's not intentionally mean, and he's certainly not a nightmare, no more than any other hormone-surging teen would be if they were ripped away from their hometown. And he'll still, on occasion, let his adolescent guard down with me, and in those moments, he's eight years old all over again.

I'm the one who's not holding up my end of the bargain all that well. He's bored to tears being at home with me this summer while all of his friends in Austin are no doubt splashing around in Barton Springs Pool, ogling the topless women. I can't afford to send him off to summer camp, can't really force him to make friends or force other people in this tight-knit town to become his friends, so, yes, he's rightfully miserable.

And he misses his dad. We've always gotten along, always been close, but he worships Felix. And I don't want to be the one to shatter the image of perfect Felix for him, though I'm tempted to at times.

Felix has been up to visit Kasey only a few times since we moved back. He whisks Kasey away to Dallas for the weekend, taking him to NASCAR events and fancy steak houses and shopping sprees at the

Galleria. I can't compete with that, but for Kasey's sake, I wish I could.

But while I was sitting at the table earlier, just feet away from Kasey, an idea bubbled up inside and I rose and slipped out the back door to the patio. A warm breeze gushed over me, carrying the ripe, earthy smell of the creek with it, and I took in a deep breath before calling my dad.

I asked if they'd go ahead and bring Kasey's car over. This morning. I explained that Kasey needed something to tinker with over the summer, that maybe he could watch some YouTube videos on tuning up cars. And if nothing else, he could at least have something to brag about on godforsaken social media.

An hour later, my parents were at the door. Dad in his T-shirt and wrinkled cargo shorts, Mom in her customary button-down with crisp capris, every hair in place, a sweet cloud of perfume greeting me as we hugged (I'll never understand how she always looks so pulled together), me still languishing in my pajamas.

They'd pulled the Land Cruiser through the car wash and it gleamed shiny like a wet tortoise shell in the driveway, bathed in morning sunlight. My heart melted at the sight of them; I am so lucky they are always there for us.

"Let me go get him." I smiled at my parents.

I found him in his room, cell clutched in hand, playing *Candy Crush.*

"Grandma and Grandpa are here. They want to show you something."

He trailed me down the dark hall out into the drive, where Mom and Dad stood with nervous excitement plastered on their faces.

Kasey looked at the car, dropped his jaw, then ran over and hugged them both.

"Thank your mother, too!" Dad said. "She was in on this as well."

He spun around and looped his arms around me, squeezing me.

"Happy early sixteenth!" I said.

Kasey beamed at the three of us before lifting the keys from Mom's palm and climbing into the driver's side.

AFTER MOM AND Dad left, I lingered in the driveway, watching Kasey explore every inch of his new car. The interior smelled of leather polish and the faintest hint of rich tobacco smoke.

"You like?"

"I love."

The sun was now glowering overhead and sweat was making my cami stick to my chest. But I didn't care; I wanted to stretch this moment out for as long as possible.

Kasey pulled a lever under the console, popping the hood open with the sound of a muffled cap gun. He climbed out and raised it the rest of the way, propping it up with the attached metal stick. His eyes swept across the innards of the car and he leaned in closer to the engine as if examining the contents of a treasure chest.

Felix always had muscle cars and knew some fundamentals, like how to change the oil and replace a timing belt, so Kasey is already aware of the basics.

"How's she look?"

He mopped his brow with the back of his hand and a slow smile crept across his face. "Like a beaut."

From the top of the hill I heard a rumbling sound. Will's truck. I circled to the side of the Land Cruiser nearest the house, so at least my pajama bottoms would be shielded by the car. Kasey glanced up at the sound and the truck slowed as it got closer to us. My eyes locked with Will's and he stopped right in front of the drive, lowering his window.

Sweat stung my armpits and all my muscles felt frozen in place.

"I dig those wheels," Will said to Kasey, flashing him a smile.

"Thanks," Kasey said, his face reddening with shyness. "I just got it today. Early birthday gift."

Will nodded, put his truck in park, and stepped out, walking toward us. The tops of pines whirred behind him in the breeze and it took all of my focus to tamp down the eager grin cracking my face in half.

He was dressed in dark designer jeans and a white T-shirt that hugged his chiseled chest. I wrapped my arms around me, hoping to disguise the fact that I still wasn't dressed for the day.

"I thought we should have a proper introduction," he said, extending his hand for me to shake.

He towered over me, and I looked up at him. He was even more dazzling up close. James Dean eyebrows knitted over aquamarine eyes. High cheekbones. Petal-pink lips. Strong jaw.

"I'm Will. Will Harding."

I almost said, "I know," before catching myself.

"Jen. Jen Hansen. And this is Kasey, my son."

He smiled down at me, grinning more with his eyes—which crinkled at the edges—than with his mouth. "Mmmm," he muttered, staring at me, his eyes dropping for a sec to the top of my cami.

"Sorry I'm still in my pj's," I said, my neck burning with shame.

"Ha, no worries, I'm in my work clothes. And also, we're neighbors." His velvet voice had a trace of a slight accent that I couldn't place.

"Oh?"

"Yeah, I'm just around the corner. Top of the hill, ten houses from the bottom. On the right. Eight-oh-two. You guys should come up sometime."

My insides twisted and I felt like I couldn't breathe.

"I know a lot about old cars," Will said, motioning with his head to his vintage truck. "So if you ever need a hand with anything, I'm your guy. Seriously, don't hesitate."

Kasey seemed as starstruck as me, his face still blotchy with embarrassment. "That'd be cool," he said, his voice breaking.

"And you should come by as well, Jen." Will pivoted his gaze back to me. "As early as this afternoon if you like." His eyes were grinning at me again.

"Really?" My voice came out squeaky and high.

"Sure, why not? I'm in the midst of unpacking and could use a hand."

As if reading the confusion on my face, he snorted out a quick laugh. "I didn't mean you'd be lifting things and digging me out of boxes." His eyes were level with mine. "But I bet you could tell me where to put things."

My entire body felt like it was on fire, and before I could think of a reply, Will gave me a quick wink, shook Kasey's hand, and clapped his shoulder before striding back to his truck.

After he drove off, Kasey and I stood wordlessly around the Land Cruiser as if all the air around us had been vacuumed away. After a moment, Kasey was the first to speak.

"He seems nice. And what a cool truck."

I didn't want to seem all that interested in Will in front of Kasey—I'm not sure how he'd take to the idea of me dating again—so I gave a brisk nod. "Yep, nice guy. And you should take him up on his offer sometime."

THAT WAS FOUR hours ago. It's nearly two thirty now and all I've done since is rehash the scene with Will over and over in my mind, dissecting it, examining what I said versus what I should have said, and working myself up into a tizzy.

And I've been in this bathroom for the past half hour, endlessly primping, trying to calm my skittish nerves by reciting mantras to myself, especially this one by Pema Chödrön: "To be fully alive, fully human, and completely awake is to be continually thrown out of the nest."

I'm not sure if I should be going over to Will's this soon after his invitation. Does it make me seem too needy? But he very pointedly asked me to, and I don't want to overthink it.

And Kasey's gone for now—he's out walking along the creek and promised to be home by dinner—so it's now or never. I want to bolt before I talk myself out of this.

I gaze into the mirror again and check my reflection—making sure there're no lipstick stains on my teeth, making sure my shirt hangs just right.

I give my hair one final tousle before killing the lights and heading out the front door.

9.

Kittie

THE SUN IS a blowtorch on the back of my neck. It's afternoon, and I'm out jogging the neighborhood. My hair is pulled high into a ponytail, and if I stay out much longer, my skin will be singed.

But God, this feels good, letting my body tunnel out of the crushing hangover I've been at the mercy of all morning.

The picnic was a success, I guess, judging by said hangover, and also the ticker tape of texts streaming in from all the neighbors, thanking me for my part in making it happen once again.

Even Chloe seemed to genuinely enjoy herself, lapping up the attention of her crew. She walked home with me and Hank at the end of the night, instead of begging to linger at the picnic with Shelley, who was still there sipping from a cup on the banks of the creek.

The three of us zigzagged together through the darkened streets, Chloe with her arm looped through Hank's, her hair wild with sweat and sun, reminding me of picnics past when things were so much simpler.

Staggering up the drive toward our house, I could smell a trace of alcohol on Chloe's breath, but it didn't bother me, her taking nips when everyone else's kids were doing the same. At least she wasn't out riding around with her friends while drinking. And at least she wasn't outwardly defying me, like she did with the cigarette smoking, at our own house, right under my nose. That had felt like such a personal insult, such a dig—a nasty middle finger in my face.

I can see how ludicrous this logic sounds, even to my own ears, but damn it, I can't help it. I *am* irrational at times, and ragey. It's like my nerves are glass, set to shatter.

During my last checkup with my gynecologist, she explained that I was going through perimenopause and how that "transition," as she had so gently put it, is very much like experiencing a second puberty. But unlike puberty, this horseshit can last up to ten years.

Great.

One of the things that can help balance everything out, she advised, is exercise. So in addition to trying to trim up, there's the added bonus that working out can stabilize my moods.

I've already been at it for a half hour, already raced through the tangled streets on the north end of Eden Place—the section where I live—and I'm cruising past my house now.

I could call it quits for the day, but I keep pushing, jogging toward the older addition of the neighborhood, where Jen lives.

She also texted me first thing this morning to tell me what a good time she had last night. I was relieved. I felt bad for her when she showed up in her slouchy T with Kasey pouting at her elbow, so I tried to ply her with enough booze to get her good and buzzed.

And of course, I felt terrible that Jen didn't get the chance to talk to Will. But how could she with Brandi commandeering him the whole time? Fucking tramp. I felt bad, because hot damn, he is a scorcher. I tried to play down his interaction with Brandi to Jen, but he did give Brandi his full attention.

I'm turning onto Jen's circle now, the tip of my ponytail slick with sweat, whipping against my neck.

I should head over to Jen's, pop in, and chat, but instead of continuing straight and heading down the hill to her place, I feel myself being pulled to go left, to the other side of the circle. To head, in fact, in the direction of Will's house.

It does piss me off on Jen's behalf that she missed her shot to chat with Will, so I'm going to do something about it. A plan is hatching in my brain as I slow my pace to a walk, steady my breath.

I'll knock on the door, introduce myself under the guise of welcoming him to the neighborhood. I'll invite him over to our place for cocktails soon so that Jen can meet him properly.

I'd love to pull her out of her post-Felix slump, and this seems like the best way to do it.

I round the bend and spot the Ellingsworth mansion midway down the street on the left, just before the road crests down the hill, its pitched rooflines like a toy castle against the backdrop of the deep forest.

I pause in front of a towering magnolia tree, its dusky form shielding me from the sun. Blotting the sweat from my face with my tank, I suck in a deep breath. But even though I've come to a stop, my pulse is still racing and my stomach is spinning. I'm nervous, I realize.

And it's because—if I'm being honest with myself—I'm interested in Will, too. Way more than I should be.

10.

Cynthia Nichols's Diary

THIS IS MY fourth entry. Not too bad, but I've got to do better. It's afternoon and I'm in my study for a second, stretched out in a patch of sunlight on the chaise while Tyson is in the backyard and Gerald is taking a shower.

Today is Thursday, normally a therapy day for me, but Dr. Whitaker's office is closed for the holiday. When did the whole goddamn world start shutting down for the Fourth? I mean, I understand places like banks being closed, but counseling? Isn't that considered a medical service?

So I'm journaling in lieu of therapy. I guess I'm kind of out of sorts because I was really looking forward to being in her office this week, to getting things off my chest, to sitting across from her and hearing her sandy voice drifting over to me, probing me with questions, observations.

Nothing major has happened; nothing's happened at all, in fact. I'm just feeling wound up as usual.

The picnic last night was fun, but it was also unsettling. Mainly it was Jen who made me feel unsettled. It was tough, as her friend, watching her pine after Will when she doesn't even know if he's available. I mean, I hope he is for her sake—and judging by the open way he was talking to Brandi, he probably is—but the whole thing struck me as sad.

I mean, Will *is* gorgeous—I nearly gasped when I saw him. But is anything *really* going to happen with them? Nothing against Jen. She's beautiful, too, with her yoga-sculpted figure, her springy breasts, her dirty-blond hair that always looks perfectly mussed. But what if he's not single? What if he's not interested? I'm not saying he won't be, but what if he's not? She just seems to have so much pinned on what could turn out to be a nothing situation.

So watching her watch Will made a fist form in my stomach. And it made me feel grateful that I have Gerald. I know things aren't perfect between us, but I can't imagine being out there on the hunt again.

11.

Kittie

I'M STANDING AT the edge of Will's lawn, working up the courage to go through with this.

I'm never like this; I'm always take-charge, so why won't the lump in my throat dissolve? Damn these nerves. I roll my shoulders, take in a steady breath, and remind myself that even though I'm scoping him for selfish reasons, I'm also really here to help Jen.

I've got this.

I head up the sidewalk, which is pocked and weed choked. Even when Dr. Ellingsworth lived here, the place always had an aura of sweet decay about it. I'm in the shadows of the roofline now, almost to the door, and I have the creeping sensation that all eyes in the neighborhood are pricked in my direction, even though rationally, I know they're not.

The front door looks to be made from hand-carved wood, and I rap my knuckles against it quickly before I lose the nerve.

From inside, I can hear the sounds of classical music—stringed instruments chiseling through the air.

Will must be home, but he's not answering the door. I press my finger to the doorbell, ringing it. My chest tightens as I hear feet padding in the entryway and the click of the lock unlatching.

Will swings the door open, greeting me with a surprised look. He's wearing a white shirt stained with sweat, and his hair is flopped down over his eyes.

"Heeeey," I say in my best cheery voice. "I'm Kittie. Kittie Spears."

His lips curl into a small grin but his eyes stay flat and focused on mine as if he expects me to keep talking. Which I do, to my horror.

"I know you're new to the neighborhood, and I just wanted to stop by and welcome you."

"I'm sorry," he says, seemingly snapping out of his classless behavior. "I'm Will. Will Harding. How did you know—"

"This is Cedartown. Everybody knows everything," I say, jutting my hip out to one side. By now most men would have dropped their eyes to my chest, taken in my curves, and made a pass at me, but Will's gaze stays parked above my neck.

"I'm kidding," I say. "The moving truck, I saw it recently—"

"Oh, right." He flashes me another grin.

His lips are full and soft and his eyes are a glittering blue-green. My stomach clenches as they bore into me. I'm waiting for him to invite me in, but he doesn't; he just leaves me stranded on the sidewalk, panting in the heat.

"I'd ask you to come in but my place is a bit of a wreck at the moment," he says as if reading my thoughts, a hint of a European accent to his voice. "Unpacking and all."

"No worries. I can't stay anyway." My tongue feels heavy in my mouth and I'm struggling with what else to say. Flirting is my bag, but he's making this difficult; it seems as though his guard is up. "I just wanted to pop by and invite you over for cocktails sometime."

He cocks an eyebrow, shifts from one foot to the next. Impatient.

"To our house," I continue, putting a special emphasis on the word "our" to let him know that I'm spoken for and definitely not coming on to him. "We have the neighbors over for drinks around the pool every so often." I feel my face flushing and I just want this whole exchange to be over with; I want to vanish.

"Sounds nice, sure," he says. "And thanks."

He smiles at me again, a polite smile that simultaneously seems dismissive. This is clearly my cue to leave. But instead, I slide my cell from my pocket, tap the screen to wake it up. "What's your number? I'll text you next time we're doing it."

He pauses, squints his eyes, and scratches the back of his neck. Heat floods my body as I watch him; he's even hotter up close.

"I don't have a cell phone, actually."

"Ooookay. How about email?"

"I've got one of those. But mainly just for work. So best to call the landline. The number's 903-555-1904. If I don't answer, just leave a message."

"I'll try to remember to do that, Grandpa."

He barks out a laugh.

I make a point to bend at the waist a little and lean forward, offering him a view of my cleavage as I type in his number. When I'm done, I look up, expecting to find his eyes trained there, but he's looking elsewhere, out into his sea-green yard, bored of me already.

"Well, good to meet you," I say.

Will dips his head. "Thanks for stopping by." That quick smile again that flashes, then dissolves, his face tightening with what looks like restlessness.

I turn to go. I'm never one to overstay my welcome.

I'M GRATEFUL WHEN I round the bend and can take shelter once again under the magnolia tree and collect myself. My temples pound with a sharp headache, my hangover coming back full force.

What the fuck was that? I had to drag everything out of him, and he barely gave me a passing glance.

What did he see in Brandi of all godforsaken people? I saw the way he was beaming at her, the way she held his attention. Must've been her slutty getup. I glance down at my outfit—khaki shorts and a tank—and realize I *do* look a little pedestrian. A little suburban housewife-ish.

He's clearly sized me up, written me off.

Will—with his accent and soft Italian loafers and classical music— thinks he already knows everything there is to know about me. Snotty prick.

He's got me pigeonholed in his mind. We'll see about that.

12.

Jen

I'M PACING ALONG the length of my back patio, my feet pounding the sun-faded cedar planks. I'm so flustered, I can't even think straight.

The creek swirls beneath me, and I walk over to the iron gate, peering down to see if I can spot Kasey. I can't. He must be hiking through the woods—which is great. I still need another moment to process what just happened.

I set out to Will's half an hour ago. My whole body hummed with anticipation as I rounded the curve and began climbing the hill toward his house. The street was empty and quiet, with most everyone out at the lake for the Fourth, so I focused on the drone of cicadas, the shifting of treetops in the wind, the muffled sound of my sandaled feet padding against the brick-oven sidewalk.

Halfway up the hill, the dark silhouette of Will's mansion rose before me. As I got closer, I spotted someone standing on the walkway at the front door, a female form. I slowed to a crawl. When I was just three houses down, the woman came into crisp focus and I sucked in a sharp breath of air.

Kittie.

What in the actual hell? I thought.

I slid over to a thick pine, shielding my body behind it so I could spy on her.

What was she doing there? Was she coming or going?

Will stood in the doorway, not a foot away from her, looking down at petite Kittie.

She was dressed in short shorts, her hip cocked to one side, her head tilted so that her ponytail dangled over her svelte shoulder.

Fury rippled over me. I'd seen that stance a thousand times before.

Kittie flirting.

My mind spun back to an old wound that had long since scabbed over but was now being picked open wide again.

Sophomore year. In these very woods behind Will's house. Kittie and I were at a keg party in the middle of the forest in a clearing. A Friday night after a football game and Craig, the quarterback and my longtime crush, had finally noticed me. He ambled over, serving Kittie and me foamy beers in plastic cups, and when he introduced himself, he winked at me.

Cut to Kittie doing a keg stand moments later in her denim mini-skirt, spraying beer from her mouth as her laughter slashed through the din of the party, Craig hoisting her up by her ankles. I kept waiting for her to snap to, to cease being the center of attention and guide Craig back over to me, but after her keg-stand display, he draped his hunter green letter jacket over her shoulders and guided her into the woods.

They stumbled out a half hour later, Kittie's hair a tangled mess, her fingers interlaced with Craig's. Later that night as I stewed next to her in her canopied bed, she dismissed me.

"You need to get over it, Jen. It's not like you guys are a couple," she said, her voice slurry with beer. "And he only fingered me. I wouldn't let him go all the way. He's not even that good of a kisser." She hiccuped and slid her arms around my waist, holding me.

I had wanted then to kick her shins until they splintered, but I let myself be cradled as hot tears stung my cheeks.

I was pissed at Kittie for a while after that weekend, but I eventually let it slide, like I do a lot of shit with her. I decided that he was the real asshole, especially as rumors flittered around that he slept with a new girl every weekend, later tossing them aside.

BUT STANDING BEHIND the tree near Will's moments ago, fingernails digging into the soft bark, that old hurt crept over me and I wanted to scream out at her.

What the hell did she think she was doing?

I watched as she fiddled with her cell before turning to leave. She sauntered off in the opposite direction from me—thank God—golden ponytail swishing behind her, hips catwalking as if she were certain his eyes were still trained on her. When I saw her disappear around the corner, I slunk out from behind the tree and headed home.

By the time I reached the bottom of the hill, I was out of breath from stomping down the street so fast and my shirt was soaked with sweat. I fished my cell from my back pocket and called her.

"Hey!" She was out of breath as well. "What's up?" she asked.

"Ummm, I just saw you," I said, groping for words. "In front of Will's house?" My voice tilted up on the word "house," making my statement sound like a question.

Kittie exhaled across the line. "Girl, I was gonna call you as soon as I got home to tell you all about it."

Which seemed weird; why didn't she just "tell me all about it" when she answered?

I didn't say anything.

"Don't be mad, but I couldn't stop being pissed that you didn't get to talk to him last night." She was huffing even harder as she spoke. Her house is a good mile and a half from Will's. "So I went over there to welcome him to the neighborhood and to see if he'd be interested in coming over for drinks by the pool sometime. So you could properly meet him!"

"But I *have* met him," I said. "This morning. He stopped by."

"Wait. *What?*" she asked, her voice rattled. "Woman, why the hell didn't you call and tell me? I would've never gone over there if I had known. That's so exciting!" She sounded genuinely giddy.

I felt myself stumbling, felt the wall of anger begin to dissolve. "I didn't want to make a bigger deal than it already was. I mean, it's *not* a big deal. He was driving past and saw Kasey's new car—that's another story—so he stopped by and introduced himself."

"And? Tell me everything."

And I did. About how gorgeous he looked, how he offered to help Kasey with the Land Cruiser, how he had invited me over.

"Well, get your ass over there right now! And then call me back!" I could hear her grinning.

And even though I could tell she had definitely been flirting with him, she does that with *all* men, so I felt sure it was harmless.

"Kittie," I said, my stomach beginning to ache with guilt, "sorry I was all wound up when I first called."

There was a long pause before she responded, and when she did, her voice was pillowy soft. "S'okay. I understand. I know you've been through hell and back."

"Love you," I said. "I'll call ya after."

NOW I'M SOPPING with sweat and my nerves are shot. I feel sick about attacking her, about jumping to conclusions. She was clearly just trying to help me, but I had to go off and infer that she had done something sordid. I've got to get a grip. I know how sensitive she can be—even with her steely armor—how quickly her ego can bruise.

I'm sure I've hurt her feelings.

I also need to calm the F down about Will; this has already spun out of control and I don't like feeling this way.

I take a deep breath and clasp my hands together in prayer position—my favorite yoga pose for centering myself—and hold it for a few moments, closing my eyes. The bright sun beams down on me, making my muscles go slack, and I visualize all the tension streaming away.

Opening my eyes, I release the pose. I'm calmer.

And Kittie is absolutely right. I should head back to his house right now. Especially while Kasey is still out prowling through the woods.

13.

Jen

IT'S NEARLY FOUR o'clock and the sun is still planted above the tree line, toasting my shoulders as I walk to Will's.

Just before I left, I freshened up, changing from my sopping T into a lightweight sundress. Kittie probably did me a favor in delaying my trip to Will's: it's closer to cocktail hour, for one. And also, I have a built-in deadline—I'll need to leave soon to get home to Kasey, so I won't be in danger of lingering too long. *I* can be the one to shut things down.

As I cross in front of his sculpted lawn, I glimpse him through the library's window. His body is twisted down and he's lifting something from a box. I scurry up the path and rap on the ornate door.

He peers out the window, eyes narrowed at first, but when he clocks that it's me, his face breaks into a wide grin. My breath is caught in my throat and I can't keep my fingers from fiddling self-consciously with my hair.

"You made it," he says, swinging the door open, gesturing with a sweep of his arm for me to enter the foyer.

The first thing I notice is how he smells. Clean and salty at the same time. Hints of citrus and sandalwood. Intoxicating. Also, he has a different standard for personal space—instead of moving to one side and putting air between us, he steps closer to me. Leans down and pecks both of my cheeks—like the French do—and slides his hand down my back, steering me into the library.

"So glad you stopped by," he says, releasing his hand.

My cheeks flame, so I twist my neck around to make a show of admiring the space.

"This room needs the most work, as you can tell." He jams his hands under his armpits; his forearms are carved lean muscle.

The library looks to be very much the same as when Dr. Ellingsworth lived here. On the wall opposite us, the same floor-to-ceiling bookshelves—stained in a dark walnut shade—span the space, already half-filled with books. The giant picture window, rimmed in the same dark shade as the shelving, looks out over the front lawn, flooding the room with light. And the same milk-white pavers line the floor. It even still holds the same honey-beeswax chapel smell that I remember.

"Here, have a seat," he says, nodding toward an armchair in the corner of the room next to the window and bookshelves.

I move toward the chair, sink down, crossing one leg in front of the other. I feel his eyes prick over my legs and my mouth goes dry.

A heavy wooden desk is parked opposite the window, a pencil-slim laptop resting on its surface, alongside a handful of what look like antiques: a glass reading lamp, a small, wood-carved statue, a miniature slate-green globe.

Will stands at the corner of the desk facing me, his hand resting on its edge.

A neat stack of paintings leans against the far wall next to a mountain of boxes, some with their lids slashed open, exposing even more books.

"Books are my weakness, I'm afraid. This room is actually the reason I bought the place."

"It's lovely," I stammer. I'm tongue-tied, and for some reason, I decide against telling him I've been in this very room before. "I like books, too," I say stupidly.

"Oh, yeah?" He crosses the room and plops down into the matching armchair opposite mine.

"English major here," I say, raising my hand. Ugh, what am I doing? I drop my hand back in my lap.

On a side table next to him, I eye a glass of half-melted ice floating in bronze-colored booze.

Trailing my eyes, Will springs to his feet. "I'm afraid all of this unpacking has made me forget my manners. Would you like a drink? I've got sparkling water or bourbon if you want something more stiff." He motions toward his glass.

"Bourbon sounds great." It's actually one of my favorite drinks. "I'll take it neat, please."

He flicks an eyebrow up at this, a smile tugging at the corner of his face. "Sounds like you know exactly what you want. Do you mind if I put a drop of water in it? It helps to release the flavor."

"Of course. Never heard that before. Um, I can only stay for one drink; I have to—" I'm blubbering but Will has already drifted out of the room, leaving me to burn in shame.

He returns a moment later with my drink, his hand grazing mine as he passes it to me.

He settles back in his chair, leaning back with his legs slightly spread. I bring my glass to my lips, breathe in the oaky odor of the bourbon.

"Wait." He lifts his tumbler into the air. "First a toast. Shall we?"

I oblige, holding mine at eye level.

"I'd like to toast to this afternoon, and to many more like this." His voice is deep and rich, his words shaped by the lilt of an accent I still can't place.

"To this," I say, then take a tentative sip. He sips in unison but his eyes remain steady on me as he drinks.

The bourbon tastes buttery and the scorch on my throat is pleasant.

"Mmmmm, delicious."

"Glad you like it. It's vintage small batch." He leans even farther back and scans the bookshelves behind me. "So, we were talking books. You studied literature? What was your era?"

"The Victorians."

"Ahhh, yes. Right now I'm on a poetry jag—I find I can't digest novels at the moment, probably the move and all—but some of my favorite novelists are Victorian. Dickens, of course, and Thomas Hardy."

He traces the rim of his glass with his finger, circling it over and over as I imagine how his fingers would feel tracing along my skin.

"Who's your favorite?" he asks, snapping me out of my fantasy.

"Well, I did my senior term paper on the trope of the veiled lady— how women were objectified in Victorian novels," I say, surprising myself. I had forgotten all about this stuff, but it feels good to remember, to recall that I once had a brain before Felix, before motherhood. I feel my shoulders relax, feel myself opening up to him.

I take another swallow of bourbon and I can practically feel it thinning my bloodstream. My face grows warm and the edges of the room soften.

"Sounds like heavy stuff, Jen," he says, his Adriatic Sea eyes crinkling into a smile.

A laugh escapes through my nose, making me snort.

"Guess so. I can't pick a favorite, too many, but my *very* serious paper started out with Robert Browning's 'My Last Duchess.' Do you know that one, the poem about the creepy husband who presumably has his wife murdered for stepping out on him?"

He barks out a sharp laugh. "Do I know it?"

He crosses the room, scans the meticulously labeled boxes. Digs through an already-open one and pries out a red leather-bound book, holding it up as if it's a trophy.

"Special edition. Gold-leaf pages. Found it in a bookshop in London years ago."

He walks over, cracking it open and thumbing the pages. He leans against the bookshelf, standing over me; I'm aware he can see down the top of my dress. I don't budge an inch.

"'That's my last Duchess painted on the wall,'" he says, reading from the slender book, "'looking as if she were alive. I call that piece a wonder, now; Fra Pandolf's hands worked busily a day, and there she stands.'" His voice is succulent, floating down to me. "'Will't please you sit and look at her?'"

I crane my neck and glance up. But his eyes are lost in the pages. He sweeps his gold-tipped bangs back and drags a finger down the page before striding back over to his chair.

"And this is my favorite line of all." His eyes flare with delight, and it's as if he's reading it as much to himself as he is to me. "'So, not the first are you to turn and ask thus. Sir, 'twas not her husband's presence only, called that spot of joy into the Duchess' cheek.'"

He folds the book shut. "Just brilliantly dark stuff. I love it."

Setting the book down on the side table, he slings a leg over the arm of the chair and levels his gaze at me. "And where, if I may ask, is *your* husband, Jen?"

I feel my insides melt; my hands churn in my lap. My neck is on fire and I'm positive he's enjoying putting me on the spot.

I suck in a quick breath. "We're divorced, actually." I try and focus just beyond his face but I can see the hint of a grin as his leg swings back and forth. I down another gulp of bourbon and blurt out everything: Felix's philandering. My filing for divorce. Moving back into my childhood home with Kasey.

The sun has now slipped behind the fence of pines, streaming cracked orange light between us.

I return my gaze to his and find his eyes are still locked onto mine.

"I'm very sorry to hear that." He scratches his chin with his hand. "You know, I've never understood how a man—after witnessing the birth of his child—could leave the woman who went through all of that."

I can't keep the question down any longer, so I part my lips and force myself to ask, "Are you married, Will?"

His face darkens and he stares out the window for a moment before answering.

"I'm— I guess you could say I'm not ready to talk about that just yet." His eyes smile at me but his face remains closed, thoughtful. It feels as though a shade has been drawn between us.

I feel clumsy and stupid. "I totally understand," I say, hearing the jangled awkwardness of my words. "I'm sorry. I—"

Will waves this away. "Don't be. It's just, well, it's just something for another day." He cocks his head to one side and winks at me, his lips parting into a grin.

Wicks of sunlight flame against the paste-white walls, turning them copper. Kasey will be home for dinner soon, if he's not home already; I should get going. But Will's eyes are lasered onto me, skewering the outline of my body, resting on the hem of my dress.

My whole body feels drenched with heat and I follow his gaze, dropping my eyes to my lap. When I look up, he's staring straight into my eyes, chin cradled in his hand, thumb brushing his lip.

I could cross the room right now and kiss him and sink down into his lap—that's the vibe he's giving off—but I'm immobilized by his gaze. And I want—no, I need—*him* to make the first move. I'm still too vulnerable.

I shift in my seat, unsure of what to do with myself, and this movement breaks the spell between us.

Will reaches for his drink, drains the rest of it, then wipes his mouth with the back of his hand.

"Refill?"

Leave now. Quit while you're ahead. "Sure. But maybe just a short one. Kasey will be looking for me. Dinnertime and all," I say, trying to sound light.

"You got it." He vanishes through the darkened archway.

AFTER RUMMAGING IN my bag for my cell, I type out a quick text to Kasey.

> There's pizza in the freezer if you beat me home. Still
> at a friend's. Xo

I *want* to stay longer. I'm dying to see if anything will happen between us, but I'm also mortified. I'm so out of practice with all of this. What if I'm misreading his signs altogether? What if he just views me as a potential friend? Someone in the neighborhood? I can't imagine the dreadfulness of making a pass at Will and finding out that's not where his mind is at all. And that's what I'm on the verge of doing, especially with the threat of more bourbon in me.

I really need to go. Not just for Kasey's sake, but for my own.

My inner monologue is driving me batty, so I stand and walk toward the kitchen, toward the sound of ice chinking in a glass.

Like the foyer, the kitchen is still half-unpacked with boxes lining the walls; wads of tissue paper like clenched fists litter the floor. It's stunning, though, all Mediterranean tiles and golden yellow colors.

Will's back is to me; he's filling the glasses with bourbon, so I clear my throat.

He twists around, eyes the purse on my shoulder.

"Leaving already?"

"I really need to."

I lean back against the countertop catty-corner to him.

"Well, at least finish this first." He steps over, palms me the bourbon. As with when I first arrived, he stays unnervingly close to me.

The shallow serving slides right down my throat.

"As you can see, this room is a disaster, too."

He inches even closer, taking me by the wrist so lightly that his hand feels like a whisper against my skin.

"So come back soon, eh?" Electricity sizzles up my arm. "I wasn't joking when I said I need help deciding where to put things. And I'll pay you in cocktails." That succulent voice again, fizzing in my ear.

I want to lean forward, to kiss his neck, but I simply smile instead.

"Deal. This was"—I pluck my brain for the right thing to say—"nice. Thanks for having me."

Still holding me by the wrist, he leads me to the front door, opening it. Tepid night air seeps inside the foyer, coating us with dank warmth. His lips graze both of my cheeks just before he drops my hand, and my body feels unmoored, like it's filled with helium and could float to the sky.

14.

Kittie

I CAN'T BELIEVE Jen busted me at Will's. I mean, it's not like I *did* anything wrong. And even if I was checking him out, I was also genuinely trying to help her. But damn, I can't believe she caught me at his front door.

That's why I've called Emergency Wine Night tonight. I want to make sure everything is smoothed out between me and Jen, and of course, I also want to hear every single detail of her time spent at Will's.

She called last night and gave me the broad strokes—no kissing (except on the cheek), no touching, but he *was* flirty with her—and now I'm on pins and needles waiting to hear the rest.

Since he didn't have the decency to invite me in, I have to pick apart what took place between them.

It's late in the afternoon and I'm bustling around the kitchen, preparing for tonight. I've slid a pork roast in the oven—covering it with diced garlic and charred green chiles—for the taco bar. A pot of queso the golden color of corn bread bubbles on the stove, and I briskly stir it, making sure it doesn't scald.

I grab three peaches from the windowsill, their fuzzy skins warm from resting in the sun, and chop them for a syrup I'm making to glaze the tres leches cake with. I picked it up earlier at the bakery; not that I need the extra calories, but I know Jen loves it. I also have her favorite Pinot Grigio chilling in the wine fridge—six bottles, just in case—and I've already uncorked one to sip as I cook.

Hank is going over to Gerald and Cynthia's for poker night, and Chloe, predictably, is headed out with friends.

It's like Chloe and I are in a death match at the moment to see who can make the most noise. Me clanging pots and pans in the kitchen and Chloe thudding her curling iron against the bathroom counter, slamming doors behind her as she endlessly circulates from her closet back to the bathroom with a new outfit on each time.

My nerves are frazzled from her twitchy energy, and thoughts prowl through my mind about what she'll be up to tonight. She's going to the movies allegedly with Megan and Shelley in Shelley's new car, some kind of tricked-out SUV.

Eyeing the sweating bottle of wine, I realize it's nearly half finished. Maybe I'm actually gulping and not sipping. So be it; I can live with that. I'm sure things are truly fine between me and Jen, but between thinking about that and fretting over Chloe's real plans, I need the alcohol to chill me out.

I drag a tortilla chip through the gooey queso to taste it; it's not spicy enough, so I shake a thin layer of red chile flakes over the surface. I'm stirring the pot when I hear a horn blaring outside, followed by Chloe's voice.

"Ride's here! Bye!"

I round the sharp corner, a headache forming at the corners of my eyes.

"Who honks for people in this neighborhood?"

She's already at the front door but spins around to face me. She's in those damn denim cutoffs again, holes that look like gaping mouths frayed in the fabric. She's wearing a hot-pink T-shirt that exposes her midriff, her eyes rimmed with so much black eyeliner that the green of her irises almost looks fluorescent. Striking-looking but also when did her style become so Goth? She used to be more preppy. My stomach tightens just looking at her.

"It's not like Shelley *needs* to ring the front doorbell and hand me flowers, right?"

Little bitch.

Both her *and* Shelley. I claw back the drape in the front window and peer out. Shelley's got her jet-black-tinted window cracked and I hear music spilling out, thumping. Shelley's head bobs side to side and her fingers drum the steering wheel.

I narrow my eyes at Chloe. "Home by ten or your ass is grass."

Her body heaves with a huge sigh. "But, Mom, you said you'd push my curfew back to eleven when I turn sixteen. And I know that's not for another month, but Shelley and Megan are already—"

Even though her tone is haughty, there's a pleading to her voice as she says the word "Mom" that pinches my chest a little, makes me crumble.

"Fine. But eleven at the latest."

She squeals and closes the gap between us, hugging me to her bony frame. I feel at once giddy from her approval and dismayed by how gleeful she is, about what this final free hour will hold for her.

She peels herself off of me and wrenches open the door, waving to Shelley and Megan before bounding down the steps.

I can't help myself; I call out to her. "Be safe!"

But other than a quick, tight slump of her shoulders upon hearing this assault, she doesn't turn around; she doesn't acknowledge I've spoken at all. She takes the concrete steps down the sloping lawn two at a time until she reaches Shelley's pearl-white SUV and disappears inside. She can't get away from me fast enough.

15.

Jen

THE SKY THIS morning is cloudless, and even though it's not yet ten o'clock, the sun is already broiling the backyard.

I drag the hose over to my newly planted herb garden and toss water on the rows of basil and thyme, which are already wilting from the heat.

But it feels good to be out here, plunging my hands into the loamy soil, beads of sweat glazing my skin.

I dropped Kasey off early this morning at my parents', where he's spending the night. I might be seeing Will later, and I want to have worry-free time in case something develops between us.

After driving away from my parents' house, I headed to the local nursery and loaded up on more drought-resistant herbs to add to the bed: lavender, rosemary, oregano, and sage, all of which I'm anxious to get into the ground today. I also sprang for a pair of crape myrtle trees with buds the color of bubble gum, feeling a tinge of guilt at checkout when I had to throw it all on a credit card, racking up more debt.

But I'm intent on continuing my mission to transform the lot into a veritable paradise. A place that nurtures both me and Kasey.

I plan to stay out here all day—it's one sure way to clear my head—and also, my body is craving this kind of work: yanking out weeds, deadheading the manic rosebush, which is obscuring the view from the breakfast nook, and digging deep holes for the new trees.

I tip my straw hat back so that it shields my neck, grasp my trowel, and begin breaking up the soil for the remaining herbs. The fragrance of the lavender is so sweet that I roll the silver-green leaves in my fingers until they are gummy with the smell. This relaxes me, helps to lift the remnants of the hangover from Wine Night at Kittie's last night.

I left Kasey at home alone with a platter of grilled-cheese sandwiches (his favorite) and the remote. I think he prefers my being gone sometimes; he gets to watch whatever he wants on Netflix. And even though he's tech savvy, he doesn't think to clear his history, so I'm always a bit shocked when I happen upon his viewings: *Eyes Wide Shut*, *The L Word*, *Californication* (used to be a favorite of Felix's; go figure). But I don't want to shame Kasey by calling him out, and I never snoop in his browser history on his laptop. Maybe I should, just to be on the safe side, but that feels too invasive.

I C L I M B E D I N T O my Honda Accord and drove the short distance to Kittie's. It's close but far enough away where I wouldn't feel safe walking home alone at night with the trees shuddering all around me, the unsettling sounds of night birds and nocturnal creatures calling out to me from the shadows.

I pulled into her drive—a curving strip of bone-white concrete flanked by gray potters—and killed the engine. In the early-evening sun, Kittie's house positively glowed with cheeriness and opulence. Crystal clear windows flooded with warm light, every surface inside gleaming, the front yard shorn and trimmed—I could practically smell the Windex from where I sat inside my car.

Kittie must have heard me in the drive because she threw open the front door and waved me in. As we passed through the kitchen, my heart seized at the sight of my favorite cake oozing with peach glaze, and I felt lame all over again for even questioning her about Will.

"So, do tell," Kittie asked, eyebrows arched.

I took a swig of the chilled glass of white she thrust upon me as soon as I stepped out by the pool.

"Yes, dying to hear!" Cynthia sat poised on the edge of her seat, her slender elbows parked on the glass-top table.

I told them everything, sparing no detail. About the inside of Will's house; about how he stared at me; about him reading me poetry; about him asking about Felix. About him pecking me on the cheeks, holding my wrist.

As I spoke, Kittie's arms were crossed in front of her chest, her right hand seeming to absentmindedly swish the wine around in her glass.

"Sounds like a good start to me," Cynthia said, her face brightening.

"It does, for sure." Kittie tipped her glass back, downing the rest of her wine. "But I don't know. It also sounds . . . kinda weird? I mean, there's obviously chemistry between y'all, so I can't believe he didn't just jump your bones. You must've been dying to tear his clothes off."

I felt a pang of shame at Kittie's words. Obviously, I'd already had the same thought. But I had told myself it was because Will was a gentleman and wanted to get to know me first.

She must have noticed the crestfallen look on my face because she yanked me into a tight hug. "But I mean, squeeeee! I'm just anxious for you to get it on. It's what you need, and I promise that afterward you won't even remember Felix's name. So, what's your next play? Sounds like he wants you to come back over soon?"

My mouth spread into a grin. I love Kittie's fierceness about me getting over Felix.

"That's what I wanted to ask you guys about. How long should I wait?"

Cynthia clicked her nails on the side of her wineglass, then shrugged. "I'm *so* not good at this kind of stuff, but I would think you'd want to wait at least a week?"

"Hard disagree," Kittie said. "You get your ass gussied up and you go right back over there. Tomorrow night. Don't let any time lapse. Especially with that hussy Brandi on the loose."

S O   T H A T ' S   W H A T   I'm planning to do. Though I'm not going to wait until evening; I'm heading over there later this afternoon. Popping in at night feels too presumptuous—like a proposition, or a date. And I want to be as casual about this as possible.

It's now noon, so I take a break from the yard and slip inside to escape the scalding heat. I mix myself a glass of iced tea with lemon, slap together a chicken salad sandwich, and plop behind my laptop at the kitchen table.

Of course I've Googled Will before. But I've yet to find anything. No trace of this particular Will Harding exists online, at least not through my unsavvy search methods. Sure, there are a dozen Will Harding profiles on Facebook and Instagram, and even more on LinkedIn, but none so far match the mystery man.

Taking a swig of tea, I get instant brain freeze. I type "Will Harding" into Google once more, this time clicking on images. After sifting through several pages and trying to match faces to my Will, I give up. Maybe he's one of the wealthy elite who've had themselves scrubbed from the Internet for security's sake.

Gazing out the breakfast window, I survey the yard, which looks, at the moment, like a surgery patient waiting to be sewn back up. I eye a corner of the lot where I'd like to plant a vegetable garden for fall: radishes, carrots, an array of lettuces. I let my mind wander, fantasizing about carrying a basket of freshly picked produce up to Will's, the two of us standing hip to hip in his kitchen, tearing leaves together for a salad.

I snap the lid to my laptop shut and slide it across the table. My imagination is getting too far ahead of me. I hear the voice of my old therapist, Annie, gently in my ear. *You have this tendency to get lost in the other, to dissolve into your partner.*

Will isn't even close to being my partner yet and I'm already getting swept away. I don't even really know him. I don't know where he's from or anything else about him, to be honest.

But I'm determined to find out. Starting with this afternoon.

Present

I HEAR FOOTFALLS nearby. The crush of leaves, legs brushing against the tangled nets of poison ivy that strangle the tree trunks.

I knew I was right; I knew he would come back for me. Bile scorches the back of my throat as I see the outline of his tall form silhouetted above me and I shut my eyes, brace for another blow.

But he just scoffs, yanks me by the wrists, and drags me across the ground.

"Shit," he hisses.

He must have stumbled on something because his hands release my arms for a second. I've always heard that if you think your neck is broken, you're not supposed to try and move but I can't help it. I try and turn my face ever so slightly to get a better look at him.

When he first left me here, I couldn't move my neck at all but now it budges a centimeter before the pain becomes too much to bear and

I freeze, seized by the pain and the fact that I don't want him to catch me moving. A tiny flicker of hope flames within me: I can move my neck!

"Fucking bitch," he says, and I can't tell if he's talking about me or the tree root he just stubbed his toe on. But before I can even think another thought, he wraps his hands around my wrists and continues pulling me across the soil until my head thumps against the base of skinny tree, a sapling.

I shut my eyes again, wait for the sting of his rock-solid knuckles to strike my cheek. He pants above me, his breath almost like a whistle, before tugging on my wrists even harder, tying them with a strip of cloth to the tree.

Fuck.

He fastens the knot so tight that pain surges up my arms. I part my lips to speak, to plead with him, to scream, but stop myself. He'll finish me off if I dare say anything else.

16.

Jen

I'M JUST HOME from Will's, fumbling my way through the entryway to the kitchen. It's dark inside the house, the rooms lit only by dregs of early-evening sunlight that seeps through the blinds.

I click the range light on above the stove, filling the room with just enough light to make myself a cup of tea. While the water boils, I lean against the counter, hugging myself.

I'm not sure what just happened. I'm tipsy, yes, but also baffled. My nerves are jittery and my hands are shaky, slick with sweat. What the fuck just happened with Will?

I'm *so* glad Kasey's not here, so I can try and process these last few hours.

Just before five o'clock, I headed over to his house, dressed in red shorts and a crisp silk blouse, hoping to look casual. As I walked up the hill, calves burning, I spotted his blue truck, trimmed in creamy white, in the drive; my heart thumped at the sight of it. The lawn glistened with diamond-shaped droplets of water, fresh from being sprayed by the sprinklers, the clean smell of wet grass hitting my nose as I strolled up the walkway.

I rapped on the door; he didn't answer. I knocked louder, craned my neck, and peered into the library window. The lamp on his desk was on, and I could see light spilling into the library from the hallway, but no sign or sound of Will.

I pressed the doorbell.

I was debating leaving when Will answered the door, an air of distraction hanging over his face. He raised his eyebrows at me as if expectantly, but didn't step aside for me to come in.

"Umm, hey." My voice squeaked out of me. I wondered for a second if he remembered who I was, recalled that he had invited me over. "You wanted me to come back by, help you with some decorating?"

He smiled at me with his eyes, then pulled the door open. "Of course. Forgive me; I was in the middle of digging through more boxes and am kind of spaced out from it. Perfect time to take a break."

Moments later, I was settled into an armchair in the library, a tumbler of bourbon at my side.

Will stood leaning against the desk, rattling bourbon-soaked ice cubes around his glass. A hammer and a box of nails rested on the desk, and half of the wall was now covered with artwork.

He bent down toward the remaining paintings, slid one out, and held it up. "I was just thinking about where to hang this one. What do you think?"

It was a seemingly nude portrait of a striking female with jet-black hair and the same liquid teal eyes as Will's. Her body was almost completely shielded by a giant orange wildflower with petals the color of fire, her eyes peering over the top with a boldly coquettish gaze. The pale pink contours of her naked form were visible on the edges of the petals, curvy and petite.

"That's stunning," I said, crossing the room to further examine it. I traced my finger along the raised brushstroke of a petal and stared into the woman's eyes. "And she's beautiful."

"That's my mom."

"Oh?" I said, a bit shocked that he would have such a bold, nearly naked painting of his mother. But then again, Europeans are so less hung up on nudity than we are.

"This was a self-portrait, from the sixties." He crunched his ice, tossed the last sip of his drink back. "She passed away a decade ago."

"I'm so sorry."

"Don't be. She had a vivid life. She was a painter obviously and a model and had some fame in her native Georgia."

"In Atlanta?"

He snorted out a laugh. "No, like Georgia, the country."

I blushed.

"Don't worry. No one else has heard of it, either."

"Where is it?"

"Come here, I'll show you."

He led me by the wrist to the other side of his desk; his hold was delicate, his fingers sparking heat up my arm. I honestly wasn't sure how I felt about him guiding me like that. I mean, the contact felt dreamy, but like the other night, there was something unsettlingly old-fashioned, archaic about it. With all his refinement, it's as if he never got the memo about touching and personal space. I decided I was being judgy; maybe it was an old-world thing.

Will opened a slender drawer, then removed a crinkly map on parchment-style paper. I followed his finger as it veered toward near Russia.

"Georgia was part of the former Soviet Union, separated from Russia by the Caucasus Mountains."

"What's it like there? Is it warm?" I asked, clueless, eyeing the country's proximity to Turkey, which, for some reason, I think of as Mediterranean.

"No, not really. It's the same latitude as San Francisco, so pretty chilly most of the time."

We stood close enough that I could take in his salty, citrusy smell. He stood nearly a foot taller than me, and I could feel his stare, feel him looking down the top of my blouse, eyes resting on my cleavage. My breath grew shallow; my mouth turned dry as paper. Kittie was right—definite chemistry between us—and I wanted to turn to him just then, meet his gaze, lean into him.

But instead, I asked, "Are you from Georgia?"

"Why, my accent?" He grinned. "No, but I've spent a lot of time there, grandparents and all. My parents met in Paris while my mom was there modeling. My father was a banker, Danish. So I was born in Copenhagen."

"Ah, I *do* know where that is."

Will laughed at this.

"So, where do you think she belongs?" he asked, motioning toward the painting.

I eyed the span of bare wall behind the desk. "There. I think she should stand alone."

All his other artwork hung from the adjacent wall—landscapes and still lifes, classical stuff but with moody overtones.

He reached for the hammer, his forearms tanned and rippling with muscle, and my insides lurched.

"And I think you should hang her at eye level, just above the desk chair."

"Sounds like you know what you're talking about."

He hammered a long nail into the white stucco, releasing chalky powder from the wall. He placed the painting on the nail and stood back.

"Perfect. It feels like she's watching over me," he said softly.

I noticed then the tiny dark slash marks at the bottom-right corner of the canvas. Must have been her signature.

"That's a good thing, right?"

"Ha, yes. I was very close to my mom. My dad, not so much."

"Do you keep in touch with him?"

"He passed, too. Cancer. Five years ago."

"Sorry."

Will clicked his tongue. "It was difficult, watching him shrink with the disease, grow weak. But he had great care. Money can buy that."

I felt my neck grow warm; I didn't want to dig too much into the dark corners of his past. "So your mom," I said, trying to tread into lighter fare. "What was it like growing up in Denmark? Especially with such a beautiful and sounds like wonderful lady? Must've been fabulous."

Will ran a hand along the back side of his neck, scrunched up his face. "I'm . . . gonna need a refill if we're going to go there."

Those smiling eyes trained on me again, his blue-green irises glittering in the light.

"Top me off, too, if you don't mind."

He winked at me before turning to go and my pulse jittered through my veins, making my body quake. I crossed back over the room to the safety of my armchair.

Will returned with our drinks and a plate of grapes, cheese wedges, and bread balanced on top of the tumblers.

"I need to put something in my stomach or I'll get trashed, maybe do things I might later be ashamed of."

Heat rose to my face; he was definitely flirting with me, no doubt about it.

"Same," I managed to stammer out.

I chased the bites of food with bourbon, and my vision grew softer around the edges, my mind at once becoming both muddier and sharper from the booze.

He rolled a grape around with his fingers before popping it between his luscious lips. Leaning back in the chair, he stretched his long limbs out so far that his bare feet nearly touched my bare ankles.

"So, you want to know about my childhood, eh?" He thrummed his lips with an index finger, eyes boring into me.

I lifted the tumbler to my mouth, took a long, scorching sip. The bourbon tasted delicious, like liquid caramel. "I don't wanna pry, but yeah, a small-town Texas girl like me thinks growing up in Denmark sounds pretty damn dreamy."

I found it easy to flirt with him, mainly because he was so suggestive and good at it; the alcohol lacing my bloodstream also definitely helped.

"We lived in Copenhagen for the first six years of my life. The happiest years, if I must say. My parents were still young then and very much in love. I have a half brother who is ten years older than me, a product of my father's first wife, but he never lived with us. I saw him only on the holidays, so it was as if I were an only child. And as an only child, I absorbed my parents' moods. On the weekends, we'd stroll through the Tivoli Gardens or through the city's cobblestoned streets, buying loaves of bread, my parents sipping cappuccino."

"Um, yeah, there was none of that happening here in Texas during my childhood."

"Yeah, but I'm sure you had horses, a ranch, right, cowgirl?" He flashed me a teasing grin.

"My parents *do* have land, but it's more to just roam around on. My childhood was pretty suburban. Malls, soccer games, Burger King, you name it. Glamorous." I plucked a cheese wedge off the plate, nibbled at it.

"But I like it here," he said, gesturing out the bare window to his storybook grounds.

"How in the world did you ever find Cedartown?"

"Business trip to Dallas. I have my own small investment firm and some dealings with oil and gas. Anyway, I wanted to see some real Texas—something more Southern—so my associate drove me east and I was mesmerized by the thick forest here. And this town, which feels like a village, a little community. Reminded me of my youth in the countryside just north of Copenhagen. Before we moved to Manhattan." Will tugged at his jawline, his face lost in thought.

"That had to be a culture shock."

"It was. My dad's career exploded. We went from living a simple life in Denmark to a penthouse lifestyle on the Upper West Side. And the money came with all the trappings. My mom trying to chase after my philandering father." He paused, a dark gleam dimming his eyes. "And me left to a nanny most of the time."

My chest ached at hearing this, seeing the solemn look dashed across his face. "Sounds lonely."

Will slammed the rest of his drink, set the glass down with a thud, and stood. "Yep." He jammed his hands into the pockets of his jeans, paced in front of his now-stuffed bookshelf. "And that's how I got lost into books. How I fell in love with them. They were my best friends, my closest companions growing up."

He ran a finger along the top shelf, as if searching for something.

"I know a thing or two about being an only child as well," I offered. My face was flushed from the drink and my voice sounded slurry to my ears.

He turned and looked at me. "You, too, huh?"

"Yep. That's why I was so close to my girlfriends growing up—all only children, not a sibling between us."

"And are you still? Close with them?" Even though he was asking me this, his eyes were averted as he continued scanning the shelf.

"Very. It's one of the reasons I moved back here. To this neighborhood, in fact. To live near them."

I spilled this out without indicating to him that I knew he'd already met Kittie. I didn't want it to seem as though we'd discussed him, which was foolish; he must have known that we had.

"Ah, here it is!"

He held up a hardback with a glossy dust jacket, his eyes sparking with excitement. I'm not even sure he heard my answer to his question, and I decided it didn't matter.

"I've been on a real Mary Oliver kick lately. This poem in particular. It's called 'Wild Geese.'" He thumbed through the pages until finding it. Glanced up at me before he began reading. "Do you know her work?"

"I'm ashamed to say I only know *of* her; I've never read her."

This seemed to make him even more excited, as if he were about to share a juicy secret with me. "Well, behold Miss Oliver."

The sun was sinking, searing the treetops, turning the walls the same terra-cotta color as it had the other evening. Will stood before me, a foot propped on the bottom shelf, his designer jeans hanging low on his hips, the rays of warm light picking up the blond strands in his lush hair.

He read to me the poem with lines about the call of wild geese, about loneliness, about finding your place in the world. I wondered for a second if he'd been a professor in his previous life; obviously he was at home standing before an audience, carrying on. But before I could ask him about his profession, he snapped the book shut, tucked it back in its place on the shelf.

"That's how I feel about moving here. Like I've found my place. Sounds to me like you have as well." He sank back into the armchair, raised his glass. "To Cedartown."

"To Cedartown."

I clinked my glass to his before taking another stinging swig. My eyes roamed the room and I stared through the archway leading into a hallway. Through an open door, I glimpsed Will's bedroom. A four-poster wooden bed made up with a soft white down comforter so fluffy, it looked like a serving of whip cream. Beyond his bed, another picture window, bare of any window covering, just like in the library. It looked out over his rolling backyard, and beyond the wooden fence line, to the woods.

The creek and the foot trails of the forest run behind my house, but in this section of the woods, a maze of dirt lanes wide enough for cars to drive on snakes through the pines. Growing up, we used to ride four-wheelers through this part of the forest and, later, our own cars. The same spot as where we held keggers, like the one when Kittie snatched my crush away from me.

As I gazed out at the thick fence of looming pines, a flood of other memories rushed over me. Cynthia, Kittie, and me in the eighth grade racing along the dirt path with high school boys, all of us running from the cops who'd been on our trail for pelting front doors in the neighborhood with eggs.

Me at sixteen in the passenger seat of Darren Wilke's black Ford Mustang, being felt up for the first time in my life, his fingers tracing my torso until he had reached my bra, undoing its front-opening clasp.

A laugh bubbled out of me as I remembered all of this.

"What? What is it?"

"Nothing, just memories. Lots of teenage firsts happened in those woods back there."

Will chuckled. "Mmmm, sounds racy. Pleased to live in such a previously infamous spot for you and your friends." His eyes danced over me and I shifted in my seat, suddenly aware of my screaming bladder.

"Could you point me to the ladies' room?"

"Of course, come with me."

I followed him through the archway into the hall. A row of diamond-shaped windows lined the end of the hallway, casting amber light into the space, like in a cathedral. A red Persian rug lined the length of the floor, and I studied its ornate design as I trailed behind Will.

"Here you are." He cracked open the door to the bathroom, flipped on the light.

I took a few steps toward him, and my foot tripped on something, sending me stumbling. He caught my arm.

"Sorry about that. These stone pavers are exquisite, but evidently, they're old and chip easily. That's why this rug is down. Covering it up until the floor men can come and repair them."

Once inside the bathroom, I sat down on the cold porcelain toilet and waited to hear the sound of Will's footfalls retreating. I didn't. So I unleashed my bursting bladder, aware of his ear pricked just outside the door.

After washing my hands with the fig-scented pump soap, I stepped back into the hall. Straw-colored light trickled through the diamond-cut windows and Will was leaning with his back against the wall as if waiting to escort me.

His cheeks were pink in the sunlight, his eyes locked onto mine, and I couldn't help it: it was as if there were an invisible string pulling me toward him, as if he were magnetic, and before I knew it, I walked straight at him and placed my mouth on his.

His lips were firm and closed, but I grazed mine across them, closing my eyes, my pulse throbbing through my neck. I didn't know what the hell I was doing—but I figured if he didn't move me away, he wanted me to continue.

He parted his lips slightly, as if he were unsure, but then cupped his hands against my cheeks, pulling me closer. He kissed me full on then, his tongue probing but also teasing.

A shudder rippled through me. He was the best kisser, even better than Felix, and soon we were pressed up against each other, hands exploring, hips swaying. My fingers trailed along the top of his jeans and I wrestled with the button.

Will slid his hands down to my wrists, guided them away. "I'm not ready just yet," he whispered, his breath hot against my ear.

But his hips—still brushing slowly against mine, the friction down there driving me crazy—told another story. Soon we were kissing again, lips locked, and I wanted to tear his clothes off, have him strip mine off as well. I moved my body back and forth across his, the tug in my groin almost painful, and I could feel him firm against me, could already imagine him inside of me, thrusting.

He placed his hands on my shoulders, pulled back from the kiss. "I just want to take this slow." He dragged his thumb across my mouth, kissed me on the cheek. "Hope you understand."

He slid against the wall away from me, leaving me feeling raw and exposed. And also ashamed. My cheeks stung with embarrassment and I dropped my head, following him into the library.

Inhaling a slow breath, I tried to gather myself. "I should be going." I yanked my bag from the floor and headed into the foyer.

I could feel Will behind me, so I twisted the knob, throwing open the front door so I could escape.

He put a hand on my shoulder. "You don't have to rush out—"

"I do, actually." I stepped away from him. "And I'm sorry about all that," I said, waving my hand at my side. "I guess I just got carried away."

Will stared at the lawn but a grin played on his lips.

"There's no reason to be sorry, Jen. I really like you; you're different from the others here, I can tell. It's just . . . I've been through something. And also, I'd like to get to know you a little more first."

I let out a long breath. This made me feel a tiny bit better. That and the fact that he was now staring at me again, his eyes roving over my body.

"Come again soon?"

I opened my mouth but closed it before something stupid came out. I chewed on my bottom lip, nodded, and turned to head back home.

I DRIFTED DOWN the street, my silk blouse clamped against my skin like a wet shower curtain, my heart hammering in my chest.

I fumbled in my bag for my cell; I wanted to call Kittie, but I dropped the phone back down, needing to examine every detail before sharing it with someone else.

I'M SITTING AT the kitchen table, waiting for my cup of chamomile to cool. It's dark out now, and even with the windows closed, I can hear the groaning of bullfrogs near the creek, starting up their evening chants.

Will. Will. Will. I can still smell him on my skin, can still feel his lips on mine. His granite-solid body holding me. I shiver in my seat. I'm giddy, giddy as a teenager, but more than that, I'm confused. Mortified. My stomach is sick with shame.

I promised myself I wouldn't make the first move, but there I was, flinging myself at him. I wanted to hold on to that power so I wouldn't sit here and torture myself like I'm doing now, but I couldn't help it. I *had* to be with him.

And then he turned me down. I mean, I know he kissed me back, and I'm pretty confident he was into me, but it *was* a rejection. I wanted to take things further with him, much further, and he all but peeled me off of him.

Jesus fucking Christ, what a loser I am! His words keep replaying through my head as if on repeat: *I'm not ready just yet. I've been through something. . . . I just want to take this slow. I'd like to get to know you a little more first.*

He must think I'm so needy, so desperate. But on the other hand, I don't know many men who would've turned a woman down in this instance, so screw that. Maybe he *has* been hurt before. Maybe that's all it was about.

I take a sip of the tea, try and calm my monkey mind.

I should just be happy, I decide—happy with what happened, happy that we did what we did. And I *am*, but my head's still a mess, spinning scenarios. About what I should have done. Or what I shouldn't have done.

He wants me to come back, though; that much is clear. So maybe he does really like me. *You're different from the others.*

But I'm nervous about what will happen next time. I'm definitely *not* making any more moves.

I'd ring my old therapist, Annie, right now if I could, but I'm pretty sure she doesn't work pro bono. And also, I can't handle her judgment right now.

It's Kittie who I really need to download this to.

I angle my cell toward me and press her name.

17.

Kittie

I'M HAVING DATE night with Hank. Which means he's grilling steaks, I'm pouring Pinot Noir, and we might binge-watch something later. Or maybe just sit by the pool and talk and get drunk. Unlike most married couples, we actually still like each other.

Chloe, predictably, is out with Megan and Shelley, and tonight, that's just fine by me. My nerves are on edge and I'd rather not have the extra dose of stress from having her around at the moment.

An hour ago, while Hank was layering the charcoal into his customary dome shape, getting ready to light it, I was inside slathering giant russets in butter and minced garlic when I saw him motion for me.

I stepped out onto the patio.

"Phone's blowing up."

It gyrated on the glass table, Jen's name streaking across the screen.

Of course. I'd been waiting on her call, waiting for her to tell me whether she'd grown a pair and gone back over to Will's, and I knew this meant she had.

I quickly sent a text: Call you in a few! Just tossing the last of dinner in the oven!

The screen bubbled up with an instant reply: Yes call me ASAP! Am freaking the eff out! We kissed!

A lump formed in my throat, but I managed to text back: GIRL. FRIEND!

I STEPPED BACK inside the kitchen, uncorked the wine, and topped myself off. Before I called Jen, I gulped down half a glass.

"Jesus, Kittie, took you long enough." Jen's voice sounded jittery and manic.

"Sorry, woman. I had my hands full; we're grilling. But oh, my God, forget all that—tell me, tell me!"

I forced myself to sound as cheery as possible. And I *was* happy for her, genuinely so, but envy simmered around the edges of my mind.

She went into a twenty-minute play-by-play of their every move. Will's Euro background. The painting of his mom (intriguing), him reading her more poetry (gag), them getting it on (whoa), and finally, Will pushing her away (humiliating).

She was an absolute hot-mess express, doubting her every move, and I did my best to listen, squealing in all the right places and propping up her self-esteem at every turn.

"Do you think he's into me? I mean, he said he liked me. But fuck, what man shuts it down like that? Is it me?"

While she was talking, I kept thinking about his hands on her, them dry-humping, growing more jealous by the second. But Jen's agonized voice also made me feel protective over her.

What the hell is she getting herself into?

He wants to take it slow? He really likes her but wants to get to know her better first? Uh, right; sure, he does. What a gentleman.

I call bullshit on that. He's fucking with her. Period.

"Of course he's into you; who wouldn't be?" I offered, dumping the rest of my glass down my throat.

"So what's my next play here? He told me to come over again, but—"

Hank popped his head in just then—pillars of smoke from the barbecue rising behind him—but I lifted an index finger, shooed him back outside. A plan was hatching in my head and I needed to get it out.

"Jen, just listen to me. You may not be into it, but just hear me out."

"'K, I'm all ears."

She sounded open and game, just like she used to in high school. I could pretty much get her to follow along with anything. Cynthia, too. Whether it was toilet-papering the house of a girl I hated or hitching along on a double date—me with the catchier guy, Jen with the lesser one—she would put up with whatever I had cooked up.

"It's *so* great what happened between you guys, and I think you handled yourself perfectly. I mean, you left when you needed to. You didn't pine after him. You're in a very good position; I mean it. But I'd like the rest of us to size him up."

"Kittie, I—"

"Instead of Wine Night Tuesday," I soldiered on, "I'll have a cocktail party by the pool. Invite some of the neighbors. I'll invite Will; I have his number—"

"You *do*?" Jen's voice sounded wiry.

"I mean, yeah, he gave it to me when I stopped by. 'Member I told you I wanted to have him over sometime for drinks so y'all could meet?"

"Of course," she said, softening.

"I just don't want you to get hurt. And if he's for real, then there's nothing to worry about."

"I don't want to feed him to the wolves—"

I sighed. "It won't be like that, I swear. And that's *if* he even shows. It'll just be a few couples. But seriously, after Felix, don't you want to be careful? Get our take on him?"

She sighed, too, her breath sounding like a balloon deflating. "I guess so. And actually, it *could* be good because it'll take the pressure off of me having to go and see him next."

"Exactly."

AFTER WE FINISH our steaks, we sit on the lip of the pool, dipping our feet ankle-deep into the cool water. I tell Hank about my plan for having the gathering Tuesday so we can check out Will for Jen.

"Can't *wait*," he hoots, "to check out the weirdo."

"He's not a weirdo, so please don't fuck this up for her. She clearly needs—"

"A good pokin'." Hank barks out a laugh. "I get it."

I jab him in the side with my elbow. "Seriously, you boys need to be on your Sunday best. And yes, sister totally needs to get laid."

He stretches out, clasping his hands behind his head, leaning back on the concrete. "She's not the only one." He places a hand on my thigh.

I turn and grab a second bottle, slide the cork out. "I promise we will soon, honey. I'm just drained tonight." A lie.

We have sex often, and I definitely enjoy it. I'm still attracted to Hank. His square jaw, his ruggedly handsome lines. But as good-looking as he is, he's no Will. And Will's all that's on my mind tonight.

I hope he comes over; I have to see him again. And I have to see, with my own eyes, how he is around Jen.

18.

Cynthia Nichols's Diary

IT'S MIDNIGHT. I can't believe I'm still up, but after twisting in the sheets next to Gerald (who's in an alcohol-induced coma), I wrenched myself from bed and stepped outside.

I love it when I have the backyard to myself. I'm sitting on the edge of the pool, writing in this journal, dragging my ankles through the topaz-blue water.

It's my oasis out here: our yard is one of the more private ones in all of Eden Place. Terraced gardens bank to the top of the fence line walling us in, their beds studded with rows of succulents and tropicals. And I love my pool—a slender rectangular wedge of water so different from Kittie's grandiose one. Mine is something simple I can swim laps in, which I do every day, weather permitting.

I love the feel of plunging into the cool after baking in the heat, the sensation of my muscles going slack from slicing through the water, the way I'm cocooned against thought and sound.

Tonight the cicadas are sawing in the background, their song always sounding to me like the sonic version of the chills. The moon is nearly full; its watery reflection floats back at me from the surface of the pool.

So much happened tonight and I'm still trying to process it all, my journal balanced on one knee, my mind emptying every thought onto these pages.

Kittie had her neighborhood get-together so we could collectively judge Will. I wasn't exactly on board with this plan, but I bit my tongue as I always do with Kittie because she's going to do whatever the hell she wants anyways.

After she filled me in on every detail of Jen's recent rendezvous with Will, I *was* curious to scope him out for Jen's sake—to see how he behaved around her. I mean, she really is in a fragile place right now.

But I also thought Kittie was taking this whole thing and overblowing it, putting too much pressure on Jen and Will when they've only just started out. I honestly couldn't believe Jen agreed to it; it's as if she'd forgotten how Kittie can be after one too many drinks. Brash. Obnoxious. Downright embarrassing.

Kittie kept herself in check, though, for most of the evening.

It's Will who's got my head spinning.

Gerald and I arrived at six thirty, just before the other guests were due at seven, and Jen was already there, churning around the perimeter of the pool in a cute sundress with wedge sandals. Kasey sat off to the side alone, pasted against a lounge chair with a plate of hors d'oeuvres in his lap, looking pissed off as usual.

My heart goes out to him, poor thing. He's a good kid in a tough situation. Chloe and her gang of friends were grouped at the far edge of the pool, all loose limbed and teen-girl attitude, their eyes shielded with matching Ray-Ban sunglasses. I was glad then that I'd caved into Tyson's request to stay at home. He would've been even more pissed off than Kasey to be there, especially because he would've been the oldest teen at the party with no one his age to hang out with.

Jen came over to me, passing me a glass of prosecco.

"I'm so nervous," she said, twisting the stem of her wineglass around with her fingers.

"Don't be. You look *amazing*."

"You sure? I couldn't figure out what the hell to wear."

I know her wardrobe is slim pickings these days, but she really did look stunning. "Total knockout, I promise."

Kittie floated over to us, the picture of glamour. Blond hair pressed into waves, green eyes sparkling. Stark white halter dress. Skin smelling of coconut.

"Ladies!" She leaned in to hug me. "Well?"

"Well, what?" Jen asked.

"How you feelin'?"

"Nervous as fuck," Jen said, her voice teetering.

"You'll be fine, I swear. I just hope he shows," Kittie said, her eyes flicking toward the patio door. "He *still* hasn't RSVP'd from the message I left."

"Who knows?" Jen threw her hands up and I felt an ache in my stomach for her.

Gerald and Hank stood guard at the buffet, beers clasped in their hands, and I picked my way over there, sandaled heels stabbing the grass, so I could grab a plate.

Kittie flitted about, tuning the stereo to an eighties playlist, fussing over the cocktail table, which was lined with jewel-colored bottles of tequila, wines, mixers, and beer. I saw her pour a shot and knock it back.

All the neighbors seemingly arrived at once, spilling in from the kitchen to the lawn (her housekeeper, Gloria, greeted guests at the front door), and soon the yard vibrated with the sound of glasses clinking and boozy voices. The evening was swampy and hot, and I was grateful I'd chosen to wear a strapless summer dress, even if the sweat streaming down my neck would be more visible.

I grazed on chicken salad finger sandwiches and grapes before having Kittie mix me a margarita on the rocks.

"Whoa, I'll take about half that amount of tequila," I said.

Kittie rolled her eyes and splashed even more in the bottom of the glass. "Drink up, sister. We're just getting started." She clicked her glass against mine and I took a sip, the lime mix making my mouth pucker.

As if in concert, we both looked up through the glass patio door and saw Will standing there. He was still inside, staring out, as if deciding whether to join the party. When he caught us looking, he stepped outside.

Nearly all the other men from the neighborhood—Gerald included—were dressed in Tommy Bahama shirts and shorts with loafers. But Will looked like he'd just wrapped up a photo shoot for *Vanity Fair.*

He wore a long-sleeved gray shirt with the top buttons undone, the kind of shirt that looks like it cost a thousand dollars but is also casually rumpled, with a pair of khakis that had the same wealthy-chic flair. His hair was mussed with light product, and he wore weathered-looking leather sandals.

A silver linked bracelet hung from his wrist, and he was even more glaringly handsome up close than he'd been when I'd glimpsed him at the Fourth of July picnic. No wonder Jen was losing her shit over him.

"Ahhh, look who's here," Kittie said, stepping in front of me. "Surprised you made it, Grandpa." Her voice was bright and oozing with charm. And I had no idea what she meant by the pet name she'd given him.

"Thanks for having me." Will leaned in and pecked both of her cheeks. I felt the tug of the men's stares from across the lawn and noticed Will cut his eyes in their direction, too, as if to taunt them with his forwardness to Kittie.

Jen zoomed across the lawn and was at his side in no time. He slid an arm around her waist and kissed her on the cheek. Her face flushed crimson in response, and her mouth spread into a wide grin.

I felt Will's eyes move over me, and I froze in place, unsure of what to do with myself.

"I'm Cynthia," I said, offering him my hand to shake. He took it in his, and his grasp was strong and warm.

"Oh, sorry! Yes, Will, this is my other best friend, Cynthia. And, Cynthia, this is Will!" Jen chirped. "You already know Kittie—"

Jen was starting to stammer and Will blissfully came to the rescue.

"Pleasure to meet, at long last, all the members of the famed trio." His voice was silken soft, his accent appealing.

"I've told him all about our escapades in the woods in high school." Jen was still bumbling with her words, her neck clotted with red blotches.

It pained me to see her so geared up, so already openly head over heels, so I did my best to get a read on him. His arm was still laced around her waist and he'd pulled her in even closer. When she finished the last of her prosecco, he reached over to the bar with his free hand and topped her off. All good signs, I decided.

"I should go say hi to Kasey," Will announced.

Jen gazed up at him as if to ask if she should join him, but he'd already unlatched from her and was striding over to the pool.

Kasey was kicked back in his chair near the middle of the poolside, while Chloe and her friends were still huddled at the far end. There was an empty chaise longue next to Kasey, and Will sank down into it. Kasey straightened in his chair, his face lighting up under Will's attention.

Kittie slid between me and Jen. "Will you *look* at them together?"

"I know! I can't believe it." Jen's eyes were dancing, her whole body humming with energy. "Should I go over there?"

"God, no," Kittie said. "Let them bond. This is good shit, woman!"

Kittie went behind the bar and mixed us a batch of fresh margaritas.

"Do you think I should introduce him to the guys?" Jen licked a crystal of salt off the rim of her glass before taking a sip.

Kittie's eyes narrowed toward the cluster of men. "Nah, it's not like we need their input anyway."

I could already tell that there was no way Will would be accepted into their fold. He was far too worldly, far too different from the Southern preppy clique of our husbands.

"I'd better go check on Chloe," Kittie said. "See if she and any of her little bitch friends want something to eat since they're obviously too cool to come near us adults."

She picked her way around the other side of the pool from Will and Kasey, the hem of her white dress swishing against her tanned and toned thighs. I noticed Will glance in her direction as she walked past, but he quickly dropped his eyes, turned his attention back to Kasey.

"I'm *so* screwed," Jen said, her breath tangy with lime juice.

"You totally are. But I have a positive feeling about this, Jen. I really do."

"You think so? You think he's into me?"

"Well, he's *definitely* into Kasey," I joked. "Yeah, this bodes well," I added, gesturing to where they were sitting.

I heard Chloe's voice then, cruel and loud, echoing off the surface of the pool. "You didn't have to come over here and ask us that." A cascade of laughter erupted from her friends.

A taunting sneer was pressed on her face, and all eyes were now on Kittie. I inwardly cringed for her, but other than a slight twitch of her head, Kittie just smoothed her hair to one side, turned on her heels, and drifted back to the party with a tight smile crimped across her lips.

She disappeared into the cluster of men, grabbing a glass of wine along the way.

"That was brutal," Jen said. "Fucking teens. Speaking of which, think I'll go check on mine."

Jen made her way over to Will and Kasey, leaving me stranded alone by the bar. I took another pull of my margarita, rocked back and forth to Madonna's "Into the Groove," which had just started playing.

I studied Chloe and her friends. So much confidence, so much like Kittie in high school, it was uncanny. That same magnetism that made her the center of gravity, same infectious throaty laugh that made you wish you were in on whatever joke she was telling.

Will rose from his chair then, with his and Jen's empty glasses in hand, and headed toward me. My stomach clenched at the sight of him approaching. I wanted to turn and leave but didn't want to seem rude, so I stood there, frozen in place.

"Just grabbing some refills." His eyes twinkled in the early-evening sunlight.

He lifted an eyebrow and I realized I was standing in front of the bar, blocking his way.

"Sorry." I stepped to the side.

"I'd ask if you need anything, but it looks like you're good."

He was talking about my drink, but something about the way he said it sounded suggestive, making me squirm inside. I glanced over to Jen, but she was zeroed in on Kasey.

He tilted the bottle of prosecco, filling their glasses, but left them resting on the table. He slid his hands in his pockets, looked at the ground, but then traced my body with his eyes from the ankles up.

Sweat stung my armpits and I felt like he had just trespassed all over me.

Cocking his head to one side, he locked his eyes onto mine, probing and intense.

"Cynthia," he said, letting the word dangle in the air, "do you have a last name?"

"Of course." The haughtiness came out of me before I could stop it. "Nichols. Cynthia Nichols."

"You live in Eden Place, too?"

His stark blue-green eyes jetted over me; I couldn't believe he was coming on to me mere steps away from Jen. I found myself recoiling from and attracted to him at the same time.

"I live just over there, actually," I said, flinging my hand in the general direction of our street. "On Honeysuckle."

I didn't know why I was giving him my street name.

"Well, we're neighbors, then." He lifted his glass from the table, tipped it toward mine in a toast. "Cheers to getting to know each other better."

I clinked glasses with him, took in a mouthful of margarita, so much of it that I nearly choked on it.

I could feel Gerald's gaze on me from across the lawn, so I looked up and gave him a tiny wave. He was gnawing on a cigar, arms crossed in front of his chest. I knew I needed to go over to him. With a fresh beer in hand.

"Going to go deliver my husband a beer," I said, emphasizing the word "husband."

Will looked in his direction, raised his glass. Gerald lifted his beer bottle, gave Will a quick dip of the head.

"See you soon, Mrs. Nichols."

Without responding, I pivoted away from Will and walked across the shamrock-green lawn toward the group of familiar nonthreatening males.

Will slipped out about a half hour later, and after he was gone, we left soon, too. My head was swimming and I wanted to get home to process everything in the privacy of my own mind.

Kittie pleaded with me to stay, pouting when I left. Normally, I give in to all of her requests, but not tonight.

She called me over an hour ago, soused, her words slurring together like cascading waves.

She always phones after an event to pick every detail apart with me. Not necessarily to get my take, just my reassurance, which she's sought ever since we were little. Even though she's outwardly fierce and confident, inwardly, she's vulnerable. When we were twelve, she had a nasty fight with Stacey Cleaves, another girl in the neighborhood and Kittie's rival. Stacey had called Kittie a slut in front of some of our friends for flirting with her boyfriend, Dan, and the other girls had snickered when she said it.

Kittie ran all the way to my house, feet pounding the stairs as she made her way up to my bedroom.

"You'll always be my best friend, right?" she asked, her eyes bloodshot from crying as she yanked me into a damp hug, her T-shirt soaked with tears.

"Of course," I said. "I promise."

She is tight with Jen, too, of course, but Kittie has always needed me in a way she's never needed Jen. And I've always needed Kittie, too. As pathetic as it sounds, especially when I was younger (but honestly still to this day), I simply followed her lead. Let her think *for* me. She's always been so take-charge and I've always been more docile, eager to please. It's always been easier—and also more fun—to simply trail in her wake.

I answered her call tonight on the first ring.

"Hey!" I said.

"Just wanted to check in and say that Chloe and I had it *out*." She let out a long sigh.

"Yeah, I kind of saw her being snitty."

"No, not that. After you left," she said with an edge to her words as if she were clearly still pissed I'd split early. "Look, I shoved her."

I inwardly flinched but I would want to shove Chloe, too.

"There were a few other guests still left and I don't know if they saw me but . . . should I care? Should I be embarrassed?" Her voice flared and I already knew what my lines should be.

"Hell no. Chloe can be such a piece of work and everyone knows that. Believe me, if anyone did see you, they're not judging you; they're applauding you."

I was telling her what she wanted to hear to put her mind at ease, but also, so I could get off the phone and get back to my own rehashing of the night.

IT'S NOW NEARLY one o'clock in the morning. I pull my feet out of the water, let them air-dry in the still-lukewarm heat before heading inside. The pages of this journal are crunchy with chlorine; I take my dry hand, smooth one down.

I feel dirty from my exchange with Will. Gerald never said a word about it, thank God, and neither has Jen—at least not yet. But the thing that disturbs me most are my own feelings, which I can't even really identify.

Repulsion? Yes.

I mean, who hits on their girlfriend's friend? Maybe it's a European thing and I'm old-fashioned, but it felt invasive. Like he crossed a line. And yet my stomach has butterflies thinking about him. Thinking about the way he said my name, the way his accent shaped it so that it sounded like something sensual. About the way he stared at me, eyes peeling off my dress—so startlingly direct, so intimate. A shiver courses over me.

Thinking about him turns me on, but also, I'm disgusted with myself for feeling this way, for even allowing thoughts about Jen's guy to dance through my brain. He *did* seem to be into her, holding her close, making an effort with Kasey, so maybe my imagination is running loose with all this. Maybe nothing happened between us at all. But the pinprick of heat I feel in my stomach tells me otherwise.

19.

FUCKING CHLOE. I'M in the laundry room, digging through her pockets, looking for evidence. I don't know what I expect to find, but after she passed out tonight, I peeled her wadded-up clothes off the floor and dragged them in here.

There's nothing in the pockets, but when I lift her shorts to my face, I inhale the ashy smell of cigarette smoke.

Shortly after her shitty remark to me by the pool—*You didn't have to come over here and ask us that*—loud enough for Will (and hell, the whole party) to hear, she sent me a text:

> We're going for a walk around the block. Be back in
> a few.

I knew that was code for going to smoke, but what the fuck ever.

What steamed me the most, aside from her nasty mouth, was how long they stayed gone.

The party was nearly over, the sun fading behind the treetops when they returned, glassy-eyed and staggering through the back gate. Only a handful of people remained—Will was long gone, Jen and Kasey had left shortly after he did, and Cynthia and Gerald were gone as well. Worry had started to build behind my eyes—a sharp throbbing pain—and when I saw them, finally, the worry was replaced by rage.

And yes, I'd had way too much to drink, but I couldn't help what happened next. Chloe didn't even speak to me when she and her witchy trio hit the buffet, raiding it for food before taking up residence again at the far end of the pool. Clearly, they had the munchies; they were either soused or had been smoking weed in addition to the cigarettes, but something about the sight of Chloe sitting there in her tiny cutoffs and tank, snickering about me and the rest of the adults, lit a fuse. Not to mention the taunting looks she kept flicking my way.

Red-hot anger blistered inside of me and I stormed around the pool, my voice steaming out of me before I could stop it.

"You all think you're *so* fucking cool—"

I heard Shelley gasp before a hand flew to her mouth. "Oh, my God," she said, sucking in her breath before laughing. "Chloe, what is she doing?" she snickered-whispered.

"You know what? Out! Get out of here. Time to leave; shoo! And you," I said to Chloe, "inside the house. Now!"

Plates of chips and dips, pigs in a blanket were balanced on their knees.

"Ignore her," Chloe said before sliding her ankles out of the water and rising to meet me.

"Mother." Her breath was sharp and tangy, her eyes dilated and bloodshot, making their green color even more vivid. "*What* are you doing?" she hissed only loud enough for me to hear.

The lights Hank had strung from the plump arms of our oak trees twinkled behind her nest of hair, making her look almost angelic then. But I was done with her bullshit.

I grabbed her by the shoulders, spun her around, and shoved her (lightly, but yes, I shoved her) toward the patio door. "You, young lady, are going inside. Right now!" I yelled.

Shelley and Megan scrambled to their feet and slithered out the back gate.

Chloe stood there frozen, her back slightly hunched over as if I'd dealt her a sharp blow.

Hank lumbered over to us, throwing an arm around her shoulder, consoling her. He shot me a skewering look before leading Chloe inside the house, abandoning me in front of the last of the guests.

"Don't you think you took it a little too far, Kit?" he asked me later in our bedroom after the party was over. His voice was thick with drink, his eyes sparking with confusion and anger.

"Maybe, but don't you give a shit that your daughter is smoking weed and drinking?" The slate-gray walls of the room blurred around Hank's profile.

"Would you drop the church act please?"

I sank down on the edge of the bed, crossed my arms. "Okay, whatever. It's not just that; it's how she *treats* me. She has no respect for me and she humiliated me tonight."

"Humiliated *you*? How do you think she felt? You lashing out at her in front of her friends. You know how sensitive kids are at that age—"

"Kids? You need to sober up. She's not a fucking kid anymore, and that's the problem. And you *always* take her side."

He slid his leather belt from his shorts, flung it onto the armchair, where it rested like a dying snake. He undid the button, stepped out of his shorts, and plopped down next to me on the bed in his boxers. His hands found my shoulders and he started kneading them. It felt good, but I flinched.

"I'm too mad."

His shoulders slumped and he whistled out a sigh.

"Sorry." I placed a hand on his knee, leaned into his bulky frame.

"Just cut her some slack, Kit. That's all I'm saying. And don't get mad, but I think we should go ahead and get her the Pilot."

"But her birthday's still a month away."

"Exactly. It's *just* a month away and you haven't even signed her up for driving lessons yet."

My throat constricted with tears. I hated it when Hank called me out on my shit. "You haven't, either," I said.

"I know, I know; calm down. We'll talk about it in the morning. But it could be a nice early birthday surprise. And this way, she and I can go out to the land to practice driving if you're not ready to do the formal lessons yet."

He was doing what he always does, trying to smooth things out, trying to keep the peace, trying to placate Chloe—this time with a new car—but I was sick of him always siding with her.

"Whatever you think. I'm going outside for a drink. Alone."

I launched myself from the edge of the mattress and stormed from the room, slamming the door shut behind me.

I SPENT THE next hour downing the remnants of various wine bottles, trying to smooth away the pricks of anger nettling my chest. It didn't work.

Now I'm under the fluorescents in the laundry room like a manic freak, rooting through my child's dirty clothing. I twist the knob to turn the machine on and slam the metal top down, half hoping to wake the rest of the house up.

Tears build behind my eyes; I hate that I'm so steamed. Hate, and embarrassed, that I shoved Chloe tonight in front of everyone. What the fuck has come over me? It seems like just yesterday she was twelve, sitting before me in her vanity chair, begging me to French-braid her hair. I'd take the soft-bristle brush that used to be mine as a girl and start by combing through her unruly mane, smoothing it out with the brush and with my hands. She'd inevitably lean her small bony back against my stomach as I twined her sun-kissed hair through my fingers, her mouth going slack as she watched me braid in the reflection, an innocent look of admiration in her eyes.

Now she cringes at the sight of me and it's gotten to where I cringe at the sight of her, too.

I didn't go through this bullshit with my mom. I was smarter than Chloe, had my mother wrapped around my finger, manipulated her into doing anything for me.

I head to the kitchen, rake some tortilla chips out of a bag, and scatter cheese along the top to make nachos. Fuck the calories. As the nachos sear in the toaster oven, the gooey white cheese bubbling and charring like the crust on a toasted marshmallow, I finally face what's also gnawing at me, making my insides twist.

Will. The sexy bastard. I almost fainted when he showed; I was so excited—my stomach fluttering like a teenager's. And when he pecked me on both cheeks, the brush of his lips scorched my skin.

I tried to look hot tonight—I wore my most flattering halter dress, my cleavage on display, my skin nice and tanned, and I felt his eyes roving over me more than once.

But as he stood there with Jen on his arm, I felt the same smug vibe radiating off of him as I had that day I'd jogged over to his house—the vibe that says he has me all summed up. And he didn't even make an effort to go and talk to the husbands. Which, in hindsight, I'm relieved about because as he was talking to Kasey, I heard one of the men utter the term "Eurotrash" before the rest of them chuckled in response.

I *wish* I could've talked to him more; I was really planning on it, but he spent so much time with Kasey and how the hell could I interrupt that? Before I knew it, he was gone. He didn't even say goodbye. I thought he went inside to pee, but Jen explained, all red-faced and schoolgirly, that he needed to get home—some bullshit excuse about his business.

The good part of me was happy to see Will with Jen, happy to see his arm cinched around her slender waist as if marking off his territory. Happy to see him chatting up poor Kasey.

But the other part? The other part still wonders why the hell he's into Jen and so dismissive of me.

Is it because she's single? Because she's lived in a big city like him? Because she's more cultural than me? I mean, I *want* him to be into her—I really do—but of course, the other part of me wants Will to be into me, too. It's driving me nuts; I've never *not* been able to hook a man's interest, even if I don't *really* want him. Even if I just want him to want me. But I do want Will; I can't even lie to myself about it anymore.

And he put on a good show with Jen, but there's something off about the whole situation.

I'll be damned if I don't find out what it is.

20.

Jen

I'M OUT IN the backyard, buzzing with energy. It's nine thirty in the morning, but I've been up since dawn, my body humming with the glow of last night's party.

The local nursery opened at seven, and I was already in the parking lot, waiting in my car with my windows down, letting the one cool part of the day wash over my skin.

I went hog wild with my purchases, deciding this morning to go ahead with the vegetable garden. Why was I waiting until fall? I weaved between the rows of selections, filling my cart with a variety of tomato seedlings: ruby-red heirlooms, a dozen or so Romas, and a huge mess of grape tomatoes that promises to be the yellow-orange color of candy corn when it's time to harvest.

The owner recommended planting watermelon and summer squash by seed, so I nabbed a few packets of those while filling the rest of the cart with pepper plants: serranos, jalapeños, and habaneros.

While Kasey still dozes, I'm bent over on my knees in the damp grass, tugging out the weeds in the corner of the lot so I can till the soil.

You're never alone in the forest, and this morning my company is a woodpecker, drilling his blade-shaped beak into a nearby tree. The staccato sound is comforting—oddly similar yet different from the near-constant sounds of construction in our old neighborhood in Austin. Felix and I bought our place just as the reverse gold rush was taking place—Californians newly discovering Austin as the jewel that it is, razing older homes to build McMansions that blotted out the skyline of gnarled oak trees.

Today, for a change, I don't miss any of it: Austin, my former home there, or my marriage. And I know it's because of what happened last night.

Will showed!

Just before I saw him stepping through the patio door, my faith that he'd come by started to falter. But then he appeared, dripping in sexuality, like a mirage by the pool. As I crossed the lawn to greet him, my pulse throbbed in my neck, my wineglass almost slipping from my hand because my palms were glazed with sweat.

He was being charming to Kittie and Cynthia, chatting them up, which put me at ease, and then he immediately pulled me into him, clasping my waist with his ropy strong arm.

I felt like the belle of the ball, pinned to his side for all to see. After months of being the single one, the *divorced* one, I felt a sense of triumph, a flicker of pride sizzling through me. To anyone looking on, Will and I looked like a proper couple. And it made it clear to me, even after our last interaction, how he feels about me.

The best part of all, though, wasn't the attention he heaped upon me; it was his laser focus on Kasey. We left shortly after Will did (he made some excuse about needing to attend to some pressing work, but I didn't believe him. The party just wasn't his scene, and honestly, I don't care; he's in a different class from the other men), and on our walk home, I grilled Kasey.

"So, what were you and Will talking about for all that time?"

I was tipsy and the everglades heat of the evening made the night feel all the more heady. Kasey was in a rosy mood, too, and at one point during our walk, he actually laced his arm through mine.

"Nothing, just guy stuff," Kasey said as if the pair of them were too cool for me. I didn't care; I was lapping it all up.

"Tell me."

Kasey sighed. "Well, we talked about cars. Will said he's going to show me how to install new spark plugs sometime."

His neck blushed and I got the sense he was feeling territorial over Will, like I was intruding on their guy time. It made my heart melt.

"And what else?"

Kasey exhaled, blowing his floppy bangs to the sky. "He asked me if I had a girlfriend."

Will had probably picked up on Kasey's crush on Chloe. I *loved* that Will asked him this, and I stayed quiet nearly the rest of the way home, daydreaming about Kasey having an involved male figure in his life for a change. Not that *I* need that, but most of the time I feel like he's pissed off by my very existence, and since he doesn't have any close friends in town yet, he could use a guy friend.

When we got back home, stepping inside our frostbitten house, I had the urge to call Will and thank him for paying special attention to Kasey. But thank God he hasn't given me his landline yet, or I would have, the prosecco in my veins blurring my better judgment.

I did call Kittie, of course. She sounded numbed out from the alcohol, slurry and bone-tired.

"So great he came," she said.

"Well . . . what's the verdict? About him and me?"

There was a pause on the other line and I could hear her taking a drink. Most likely of wine.

"Mmmm . . . I wish he would've stayed longer; I barely got a read on him."

A sting of annoyance pricked my chest. But then she backpedaled.

"I mean, yes, honey, he obviously has the hots for you, no doubt about it. And I was thrilled"—she stretched the word "thrilled" out so that it was three syllables long—"watching the way he was with Kasey."

My frustration with her dissipated and my heart began to flutter again.

"Right?! I can't tell you how incredible that felt."

"It's all good, sister. I coulda used some more face time, that's all, but let's call tonight what it was, a success."

I knew I had to give her props then or risk pissing her off. "Thank you *so* much, Kittie, for doing it, talking me into it. I owe you big-time!"

"You sure fucking do," she cackled. "I'm already holding you accountable for tomorrow's hangover."

T H E   P I L E   O F weeds next to me is waist-high. With the back of my gloved hand, I wipe a line of sweat from my hairline. The coolness of the morning has evaporated, the sun a torch now on my skin. I take a breather, downing half the glass of iced tea I made fresh this morning.

The woodpecker continues his rhythmic drilling, and I clasp the metal handle of the hoe and return to the newly bare patch of soil. With all my strength, I raise the hoe and stab into the earth, busting up the sod. The top layer gives way pretty easily, but the next layer is when I reach the red clay, so densely packed and moist, it feels like mud glue.

I sink down to my knees and grab the trowel instead, carving jagged rows into the clay. I see something shift out of the corner of my

eye and look over the vine-choked chain link to see Will moving toward the yard.

He's at the gate before I can even rise to my feet, unlatching it and
letting himself in.

"How very Mary Oliver of you," he says, grinning down at me.

Of course, after I left his house last time, I looked her up and read
more about her, discovering that a lot of her poems are set in the
garden, but I don't lead onto that now—I don't want him to think I'm
so besotted—so I just grin back at him.

"Hope you don't mind me dropping by."

"Of course not. I actually wanted to thank *you* for being so atten-
tive to Kasey last night; it meant a lot."

"Happy to do it. You've got a special son on your hands."

I stand, peel off my mud-crusted gloves. "I'm a mess. Sorry."

"Not to me you're not."

A bolt of desire clenches my stomach.

"And it looks like you know what you're doing."

"I'm just trying to get these plants in the ground." I motion toward
the seedlings still nestled in their black plastic cubes. "But it's getting
hot and I need to take a break anyway. Want a glass of iced tea?"

"I'd love one," Will says, making his way over to a metal chair in
the shade of the covered patio.

Inside, I race to the bathroom, splashing cool water on my face
and swiping my armpits with deodorant before pouring him a glass.

"Ah, this is so refreshing. I can see why it's a thing in the South."
He drains his whole glass, setting it on the white iron table. "I'm glad
you're okay with me stopping by. I'm definitely okay with you coming
over anytime."

Goose bumps prick my arms; I open my mouth to respond but
Will keeps talking.

"I think so much is lost with today's technology. That's why I re-
fuse to have a cell phone. As Sartre once said, 'Hell is texting.'"

"I believe he actually said, 'Hell is other people.'" I laugh.

"That, too."

"It's so nice here." His eyes sweep over the lawn, taking in the array of tropicals, flowering vines, and herbs I've planted since landing back at home.

I feel a rush of pride at my handiwork.

"Could you help me with mine sometime? I want to plant some fruit trees and other things. Do peaches grow here?"

"They do in Central Texas, but you're better off if you could do figs."

"Ah, fig trees. What a perfect thing to grow in Eden Place." He clasps his hands together, slides them to the base of his neck, and smiles.

"I actually stopped by to see if you wanted to accompany me on a walk this morning. I haven't yet explored the neighborhood by foot and I thought you'd be the perfect person to show me around."

My heart fluttered in my chest. "I'd love that. Let me just slip inside and leave Kasey a note. He's still asleep. Teenagers."

WE STROLL UP the hill on the west side of the block—Will's side—making sure to stay in the shadow of pines, his shoulder gently knocking into mine every so often. When we arrive at the entrance to our circle, I guide us north toward the older pockets of grand homes, including Kittie's and Cynthia's childhood mansions.

"These are rather stunning," Will says, standing on the buckled sidewalk in front of Kittie's old home. "Are you up for continuing? I'd love to see the rest of the neighborhood."

"Of course."

We walk for a while in silence, which feels oddly intimate, and as he breaks a sweat, his salty-citrus smell perfumes the air around him, making me want to lace my fingers through his, tug him into a kiss.

I lead us down the sharp hill that connects with the new division of Eden Place, the only sound around us the rustling of doves in the waxy green holly bushes. Will stops when we reach a vacant lot, its property marked off with a low wooden fence that's strangled by honeysuckle.

He bends down, smells the lemon-yellow bud. "My God, what is this nectar-of-the-gods plant?"

"Honeysuckle. Isn't it divine?"

"I must have some of this in my backyard."

It never occurred to me before, but the next street up is Honeysuckle Cove, Cynthia's street, and I'm wondering if it was named for this near acre of honeysuckle threaded on the fence.

"Let's turn here," Will says.

We veer left, onto Cynthia's street, and start walking down the bleached white sidewalk.

"So, tell me more about your firm," I manage to stammer out, eager to know more about him.

Will stares at the ground as he answers, looking at his feet as if he's counting steps. "Like I said, it's finance. Investment banking. Sounds boring, I know, but since it's my own, it's small and not too taxing. Just a handful of clients, and it affords me this lifestyle. I can do most of my work from home, except when I need to travel."

The thought of him traveling anywhere makes my heart cinch. I never want him leaving Eden Place.

"Doesn't sound boring to me," I say. "Most people would kill to be able to have that kind of setup."

"Well, it's certainly not the bohemian lifestyle I always fancied myself having, but I'm good at it and it honestly doesn't require that much of my time."

He digs his hands in his pockets, nicks his shoulder with mine again. Heat courses down my arm.

He doesn't ask what *I* do for work, and I'm grateful. He probably

knows I'm a stay-at-home mom and doesn't want to seem disrespect-
ful by asking. But then, he never really seems to ask much about me.
I'm trying to figure out how that makes me feel, if that clouds things
between us or not. I don't know. I mean, on the one hand, he did sit
there with Kasey at the party, and he does know that I'm into gardening, wants me to help him with his. Everything else is just superficial,
I tell myself for now.

Still, I'm longing to get to know him better and for him to get to
know me better, too. But then I remember his words—*I just want to take
this slow*—and that reassures me. If he wants to take things slow, I'm
game.

We round the cul-de-sac so that we're now heading up the sidewalk that runs in front of Cynthia's house. I look up and see her standing at the top of her drive, conferring with her gardener. Her lot is
sprawling, and she looks like a small stick figure from where I'm
standing.

The whole landscaping crew is there, their truck with its long
trailer and jumble of yard tools clogging up half of her drive.

"This is Cynthia's house," I say to Will.

I've actually been here only a handful of times since moving
back—we always congregate at Kittie's—but I love coming here. Sitting in her glassed-in living room while her lap pool shimmers behind
us, surrounded by a mountain of green plants. It's a very architectural
house, with horizontal lines and stacked limestone. Something out of
a magazine spread.

"Interesting," Will says as if he isn't interested at all.

I don't want to interrupt Cynthia with the landscapers, so I wave
and she flashes a grin and waves back. Will steps around me to wave at
her, too, and Cynthia raises her hand to shield her eyes from the sun, a
scowl on her delicate face as if she's trying to make out who he is. Surely
she knows it must be Will? As if she can read my mind, she finally lifts
her other hand and gives him a quick curt wave.

Maybe she's surprised to see us together so soon. Either way, she's clearly preoccupied, so I steer us up the sidewalk and out of her cove.

WHEN WE TURN on Azalea, we take the loop around the circle toward Will's house.

"Well, I'd better get some more boxes unpacked," he says at the foot of his walkway. "But that was lovely, thank you."

He leans in, lifts my hair from my shoulder, and kisses my cheek. I want to turn my face and kiss him open and softly on the mouth, but I stifle the urge, wanting to have the upper hand. I turn and step away from him.

"Jen," he calls after me, "I'll be back over soon with a surprise for Kasey."

My cheeks ache from the grin that's spreading over my face. I look over my shoulder at him. "See you then. And thanks in advance!" I keep heading down the hill before I mess up this perfect goodbye.

21.

Cynthia Nichols's Diary

JEN *JUST* WALKED by the house with Will. At first, I saw only her, but then he poked his head around hers, waved at me with a half grin on his face, and I froze.

Why were they walking by here? At the party, I remember him asking me which street I lived on, so surely their passing by so soon after isn't a coincidence? Jen jogs the neighborhood frequently, but she rarely runs down my cove. If we're meeting up to jog, we usually congregate at the halfway point between the older division of Eden Place and the newer side, where Kittie and I live.

No, it wasn't a coincidence. He's sending me a message. I'm sure of it.

22.

Kittie

I'M IN THE corner of my bedroom, sitting on the floor, knees pulled into my chest.

I'm shaking. I can't believe what just happened, can't believe what I just did: things that I've never in my life done before.

With Will.

A shiver of pleasure zings over me as I remember how he felt against me. Followed by a shudder of disgust.

Hank, thank God, is still at work, and Chloe just shouted through the door that she was heading out for a walk to meet Megan. She's been doing that more and more lately; I'm pretty sure she's a pack-a-day smoker already, but I just don't care right now.

A few hours ago, after pounding the treadmill for thirty minutes, I found myself in the shower, sudsing up, shaving my legs. Stepping out and toweling off. Tugging on my shortest shorts with a gingham top that knots at the waist. I've been killing it with my sit-ups lately at the gym, while Erica, my personal trainer, cheers me on, so earlier today I felt like going for it. Felt like showing my tighter new abs off.

I slipped into a pair of espadrilles—even though I was going walking—and got in full makeup as well. I spritzed on some perfume just before leaving, and left Chloe a note (she was in her room with the music blaring) telling her I was heading to Cynthia's for a bit.

IT WAS CLOSE to two o'clock when I left. My feet instantly ached from walking in the high wedges. But that turned out to be a good thing. I could focus on the pinch of pain in my arches instead of thinking about what in the hell I was doing.

When I rounded the corner to Will's, I could see that he was out in his front yard, on his knees, with trimmers in his hands. I paused, adrenaline coursing through every blood vessel. But standing there, watching him, I got pissed off all over again at his arrogance, his dismissal of me.

I situated my bra and undid another button on the top of my blouse. Smoothed my hair over one shoulder and marched toward Will.

He was still crouched down, shearing the tops off the boxwoods next to the front door, when I walked up his pathway.

"Hey, Grandpa," I said, going for flirty.

But he didn't respond back that way. He just twisted around, shielded his eyes with a broad hand, and looked at me like "What did I need?"

And I exploded on him.

"You're such a fucking prick—you know it? You think you're better than the rest of us. I can't believe Jen can't see it."

The corner of his lips lifted into a smug grin, but goddamn it, when he rose to standing, his shirt soaked with sweat clinging to his rock-hard chest, I got distracted by how insanely hot he is.

"I *don't* think that way," he said, stabbing the tips of the trimmers into the soil.

"Oh, really? Well, you certainly think that way of me. I can tell."

The smug grin was still smeared on his face, but his eyes turned cold, his voice chilly. "No, Kittie, that's not it."

"Then what the hell *is* it? Why don't you like me?" I couldn't stand the teenage whine that had crept into my voice.

"Because, Kittie, you're not a good person."

My temples throbbed. "What? What did you say?"

"Why are you here? Why are you at the house of a man who is dating your best friend? That makes you *not* a good person."

Fucking prick. "Dating? Is that what you call it?"

Will snorted out a sharp laugh. "Yeah. And more importantly, I think that's what Jen would call it."

My vision blurred with anger and my limbs started to shake. I couldn't stand there any longer, letting him get the best of me. But before I turned to leave, I said in my lowest seething voice, "You know what? Fuck you. You couldn't handle me anyway."

After the words left my mouth and I spun on my heel away from him, everything that happened next seemed to happen in slow motion—a short pause and then Will grabbing me by the wrist, dragging me inside his house.

I had dared him and he'd accepted the dare.

He slammed the door shut behind us, suddenly pitching us into darkness in his creepy-ass old-school entryway. Will pinning me to the wall. His neck craned down so his face was level with mine. Our teeth bared at each other. Neither one of us searching for a kiss: we hate each other.

"What are you gonna do about it, Grandpa?" I spat out at him.

He then parted my thighs with his knee, sliding it between my legs and slowly rubbing it against me. I didn't want it to feel good, but it did. I didn't want to want him, but I did. And he could tell.

After a few moments of this, he led me by the hand to his bedroom. An airy, light-filled space with a bare picture window that looks over his chartreuse grassy lawn.

Will leaned against a wooden column of his four-poster bed, and we started to kiss. Frantically. Me rubbing my chest against his, tearing at his shirt. Gasping when I saw his rippled olive-toned chest.

Will tugging at the tie of my shirt, loosening it, and letting it fall. Unclasping my bra.

He pulled back from me then, his eyes taking in my boobs, a pained look on his face as if he didn't want to be attracted to me but was.

He grabbed me by the hips and lifted me on top of his bed, which was made up with a fluffy white down comforter. In a strip of sunlight, with me half-naked facing toward the window, Will licked his fingertips, rubbing circles on my nipples until they grew hard. I moaned, the pinch between my legs becoming almost too much to bear, and he unbuttoned my shorts, then yanked them down.

Then he was on me, turning me over onto my stomach, the jangly sounds of him undoing his belt, unzipping his jeans, making me moan again.

"Oh, I can handle you all right." His voice was tight, strained.

He roped an arm around my belly, guiding us on our knees to the center of the bed, near the headboard. I thought he would enter me then and I was ready, my hips rocking against him, but then I felt the heat of his chest dissipate as he moved away from me.

Out of the corner of my eye, I watched as he slid open a drawer on an antique-looking nightstand and removed two white cotton strips. He took each one and tied my wrists to the corners of his four-poster bed.

I've never been tied up in my whole life. Don't really go in for kink; Hank and I are definitely tame in that category. And I had lots of sex with many men before Hank, but I've never done this. To my surprise, it turned me on, and soon Will was on me again, panting in my ear. Lips brushing my back, then placing a scorching finger between my legs.

I spread them farther apart, inviting him to continue. Hank has never touched me like this—he's usually all thumbs down there, but great in other departments—but Will traced his finger expertly over me so that I was moving back and forth, my body saturated with heat, my vision clouding. And all I could think was that I had to have him.

But I couldn't, wouldn't tell him that. I just continued to grind my hips back and forth, groaning.

Then he pulled away, leaving me high and dry, with my hands tethered, so that I couldn't even touch myself. It was agony.

After a few minutes, he started back up again, this time sliding a finger inside of me. I nearly shrieked in pleasure.

"Say it. I want you to say it," he grunted in my ear.

"No, no."

"Fucking say it."

I couldn't help it. I wanted him so badly; my body was so desperate for him to finish what he had started, it was torturous.

"I want you."

"Yeah?"

"Yes," I hissed. "Fuck me."

"That's more like it."

And he started to. Slowly at first, moving in and out of me. It felt so good, I couldn't believe it. His hands skimming over me in all the right places, his mouth on my ears, nibbling with his teeth. And then thrusting faster so that we were both in a frenzy, me bucking against him, shouting his name.

Afterward, he untied my wrists and we collapsed into a loosely knitted spoon position.

I turned to face him; he was grinning.

"See, you really *are* a bad girl."

I don't normally go in for that kind of shit, but here it was applicable. I was indeed bad. A bad friend, a bad wife. What the fuck had I just done? To Jen? And to Hank, whom I've never cheated on before. The thought of Hank made my stomach churn, so I pushed him from my mind, focused instead on Will's sea-green eyes.

He traced a finger along my hairline, giving me goose bumps.

"I can't imagine you're going to tell Jen, are you?"

I recoiled. It sounded like a threat. His grin turned into a smug sneer, and I batted his hand away. I didn't know yet if I was or if I wasn't. A good friend maybe would, to warn Jen about him—that he wasn't who he said he was. But I knew I would risk losing my friendship with her and I was going to have to think long and hard about that.

I wadded up the sheets around me and moved away from him, scanning the floor for my clothes. Will stayed moored in place, his elbow propped on the mattress, his head resting in his palm, the sneer still playing on his lips as if he'd just won some chess match.

Bastard. What evil trap had I just fallen into?

Sunlight strained through the windows, catching the blond tips in his hair. And even though I was furious with him for fucking with me, my body still ached to connect with his again, to crawl across the mattress and climb on top of him.

I fought the urge, though, and slipped back into my panties and shorts, tying my shirt back into a knot.

Will pulled the sheets over his lower half, rolled on his back, and clasped his hands behind his head. I wanted to slap him, wanted to fuck him all over again.

My skin was searing with shame and I made my way for the hall.

"See you around, Kittie," he said, and I could hear the smirk in his voice.

NOW I'M IN the corner of my room, still balled up, unable to move. Hank will be home soon and I need to get up, get into the shower, wash the smell of Will off of me. But at the same time, I want to keep his scent imprinted on my skin, and I shiver as I replay all of our torrid moments together.

I'm beyond worrying about Jen's feelings at the moment. Right now I'm worried about my own.

23.

Jen

IT'S HALF PAST eleven and I'm out in the garden. Despite the blistering heat, I'm determined to get the last of my new plants in the ground today.

I saved the toughest for last—the watermelon and summer squash, which require molding mounds of dirt for each plant, their shapes reminding me of tiny freshly made graves.

Felix drove up early this morning to take Kasey to Dallas for the weekend for a NASCAR event. We barely spoke, and for the first time, our estrangement didn't bother me. And that's all because of Will. I'm half hoping that Kasey will mention Mommy's new friend to Felix.

Prick.

Pulling up in his dolphin-slick new BMW, dressed in expensive-looking jeans and a button-down. I'm fully hoping Kasey charges the room service bill through the roof.

I'm grateful for the time alone: a whole weekend to myself—and hopefully, a whole night alone with Will. Maybe I'll walk over to his house tomorrow night.

I drag the garden hose over and douse water over the soil to moisten it, making it easier to shape the mounds. My face feels flushed, my whole body is drenched with sweat, my cami soaked through, and I might just douse myself with the hose when I'm finished.

"Morning, Jen." It's Will's voice floating to me over the fence.

I freeze, embarrassed by what a wreck I look like. He unlatches the gate, letting himself in like he did the other day. He's carrying something in his hand the size of a pack of cigarettes.

Will holds the package up. "New spark plugs. For Kasey."

My heart melts inside my chest.

"I'm so sorry, but you just missed him. His dad picked him up earlier for a weekend in Dallas," I say as if it's my fault Kasey's not here. "And sorry I'm so, well, gardeny at the moment."

He sets the spark plugs on the patio table and strides over to me. He smells clean and woodsy; I'm certain that I do not.

"Please, carry on," he says, stepping even closer so that he's a foot away from me. "I love watching you work."

Bent over the plants like I am, my breasts are practically spilling from my cami. I feel Will's eyes darting over them and look up at him. He's standing directly in front of the sun, pitching me into his shadow.

"Actually, it's good Kasey's not here."

"Oh?"

"Yeah, I've been thinking about you since I saw you out here day before yesterday."

He leans down, strokes my cheek with the side of his hand. A million pinpricks tingle over my skin.

He runs a finger along my lips. I grab it, nibble on it.

He closes his eyes and groans. I want to do so much more to him; I want to shred his clothes off of him, but also want to follow his lead in taking things slow. I start licking his finger and he groans again.

He sweeps his other hand down my neck. When he reaches the straps to my cami, he unrolls them so they fall against my arms. There's enough shrubbery in my yard that I'm certain the neighbors can't see us—especially with me crouched down—but still, I feel a little dirty when I wriggle my top down and expose my breasts.

Will is staring down at me now—all of me—his lips parted, his breath rapid. "Oh, Jen."

He looks as if he wants to take me right here and now, so I reach for the waistband on his jeans, pull his hips toward me. I press my face against him, fiddle with his button.

"Mmmmm, not just yet," he says, but runs his hand down my shoulder until he reaches my breast, which he grazes with the back of his hand, cupping it and lightly rubbing my nipple between two fingers.

Blasts of heat rise from the baking soil, and I'm so turned on, I continue undoing his jeans until the fly is open.

"I wanted to wait just a little while longer. Make it special." He's breathless and almost stuttering. He looks down at me, piercing me with his eyes, and I ignore him, taking him in my mouth.

He tilts his head back, exhales a long sigh, and starts to gently thrust his hips. After a few moments, his hands begin massaging my breasts. I have to have him, so I rise, press my body against his.

Will reaches behind my neck and brushes his lips against my cheek, but when I begin to fumble with the buttons on my shorts, he pulls back, then quickly zips his pants up.

"I'm so sorry," he whispers in my ear. "I didn't want to take things this far today, but I couldn't help it. You are just *so* good, Jen."

Taken aback, I loop my arms back through the straps of my cami so that I'm fully clothed again.

I don't know what to say to Will. Part of me is so frustrated. I want to tell him that it's time, that I'm tired of this state of sexual anguish, but my head is also swimming with the very fact that we've made it this far. That what just happened between us *really* happened. He wasn't faking that.

And I want this to work between us. I want things to keep progressing.

"You're so good, too," I say, flashing him a smile.

To take the pressure off, I move to the covered patio and sink into a chair, gesturing for him to do the same.

"Kasey's back Sunday afternoon. Want to stop by then? Show him what to do with these?" I say, motioning toward the shiny package of spark plugs. "I could grill."

"Absolutely. I'd love that."

"Perfect. Me, too."

"What time?"

"Three should work."

Will stands and jams his hands in his pockets with an almost-bashful look on his face. "See you then, Jen. And this," he says with a small sweep of his hand, "is to be continued, I hope."

No more guesswork as to whether he's into me or not. It felt so natural being with him, so electric, that I can barely catch my breath, thinking about what's yet to come.

24.

Kittie

I'M A JANGLE of nerves. I'm never like this and I can't stand it.

I just got off the phone with Jen and she gave me a blow-by-blow (literally) about her little rendezvous with Will in her garden. Of course, I was sick with jealousy, listening to her describe every sordid detail, but I did my best to sound cheerful and excited even.

It sounds like Will came on to *her*, and then she started blowing him. But when she tried to take it further, he resisted. Told her that same malarkey about wanting to wait, wanting it to be special.

My stomach is a rock.

What exactly is he doing? Is he truly treating Jen extra special as if he has intentions of having a real relationship with her? Was I just one and done?

But if that were the case—if he really *is* into Jen—why did he do what he did with me?

A bolt of lust is zipping through me as I think about our afternoon together and the fact that, even though he can obviously (and repeatedly) resist Jen, he couldn't resist me.

It still bothers me, though, that he doesn't like me, that he doesn't think I'm worth getting to know the way he thinks Jen is. And I'm not sure how I'll be able to handle having a ringside seat to their budding affair if that's even what's really going on.

No doubt, he's a bastard, but I can't quit thinking about him. The way we kissed with such urgency once he led me into his bedroom. The way he looked at me when he took my top off, his eyes drinking me in. Me on my knees, my wrists lashed to his bedpost while he was having me, the scorching feel of his skin on my back. His stuttered breath in my ear. It was combustible and felt inevitable even.

And I want him again; my body craves his, even though I know it's so wrong.

Present

M Y   W R I S T S   A R E   bleeding and it's all my fault. Seized by a restless panic a little while ago, I started writhing, trying to free my arms from the cloth tie. Which only made the knot tighter and the pressure greater, and now I've really fucked myself.

My muscles have gone slack from all the adrenaline; I'm limp, hopeless. Light-headed and dizzy, and beyond desperate for a cool drink of water. But the more I think about it, the stickier my mouth gets. My anxiety starts to buzz in my chest again, so I try to glaze over, think about what led me here.

Out of everyone in town, I couldn't believe that he had singled me out to be the one.

Telling me I was different from all the others. The most beautiful thing he'd ever seen. Exquisite.

How could I have been stupid enough to fall for that?

Even at this moment, I can feel his lips against mine, his fingers tracing my curves. But instead of the anticipation I used to feel, all I feel now is dread, disgust. Dread of Will and what he's planning to do with me, disgust with myself for how foolish I've been. How I've allowed myself to lose everything.

25.

Jen

I'M OUTSIDE ON the back patio, savoring the last of the prosecco I served earlier this evening with dinner. The sun is just starting its descent, turning the sky behind the tree line the color of Tang.

Will left about an hour ago, and Kasey is inside, splayed out on the couch, watching TV. And for the first time in a long time, my heart is full.

The three of us just spent the past few hours together—me grilling us red snapper and summer veggies—while Will and Kasey tinkered with the Land Cruiser.

Will had arrived promptly at three, a wispy bouquet of wildflowers in his hand, cinched with twine. My stomach fluttered at the sight of him through the window, standing in our entryway, clutching the flowers, hair mussed with product.

A text from Kasey had just brightened the screen on my phone, letting me know that he and Felix were still ten minutes away, so after I led Will inside and told him Kasey would arrive soon, he set the flowers on the countertop and pulled me into him.

"They're gorgeous; thank you," I said.

He tucked a strand of hair behind my ear, his voice sizzling against my cheek. "Glad you like them. I picked them earlier in my backyard. I guess you could say you've gotten under my skin with the gardening thing."

I was wearing a floral miniskirt and Will placed his hand on the side of my thigh, sending a jolt of heat up my leg. He moved his lips to mine, kissing me while his hand crept up my leg.

"You look so hot right now," he said, sliding his fingers toward the elastic on my panties. He stopped just shy of going farther, his fingers a pulsing tease against my skin.

We continued making out—tender, delectable kisses—until Will broke away. "Guess we should get these in some water," he said, gathering up the bouquet and moving toward the sink. "And we should probably collect ourselves before Kasey arrives."

My shoulders sagged in disappointment. I was frustrated; I didn't want to stop kissing him. But I knew he was right—we needed to stop before we got too carried away.

I opened a cabinet and dug around until I found a vase behind a stack of metal mixing bowls. Will took it from me, filled it with water, and arranged the flowers, setting the vase on the bar.

I heard Felix's tires in the drive, followed by the sound of two car doors clapping shut. Through the front window, I could see Felix heaving Kasey's duffel bag out of the trunk. I opened the front door, and to my surprise, Will trailed behind me.

At the sight of Will, a small grin crept across Kasey's face, but Felix did a double take, his stride stuttering to a halt.

Will stepped toward Felix, extending his hand.

"Will Harding," he said as the two shook. "I'm a friend of Jen's."

Felix pushed his black-rimmed glasses up the bridge of his nose. "Felix Hansen. I'm Kasey's dad. I mean, obviously." He was squirming under Will's poise and the beam of pride bursting through me almost made me giggle.

"Great son you've got. Very mature. I've gotten to know him a bit here lately."

"Oh?" Felix's eyes darted to Kasey, who'd obviously not mentioned a word about Will to his father.

Stripes of red painted Kasey's neck and he muttered, "Yeah, Dad, we've hung out some." Kasey seemed suddenly embarrassed by Felix, as if he were ready for him to vanish.

I forced my face to become blank in order to suppress my glee.

"Thanks for taking him," I said to Felix as I lifted the duffel bag from his hands.

"Of course," Felix said as if it hadn't been three goddamned months since he'd last seen his child.

He gave Kasey a bear hug, nodded at Will, then slid back into his Beamer and pulled away.

ONCE INSIDE, WILL showed Kasey the package of spark plugs while I got dinner ready, slathering the corn and squash in olive oil and diced herbs, squeezing lemon over the fish, tossing the spinach-and-avocado salad in a large wooden bowl.

Will uncorked the bottle of prosecco and filled our glasses, coasting around the kitchen as if he were completely at home here. At one point, he snaked his arm around my waist in front of Kasey. Kasey's neck grew red again, and I saw him stifle a smile.

After dinner—which we ate out on the patio while the cicadas trilled and the overhead fan swatted at the heat—Kasey followed Will back out to the driveway.

Will was intent on finishing the spark plug lesson—how to properly clean them and how to replace them when necessary—and I left them to it so I could tidy up.

After scrubbing charred bits of fish and veggies off the grill with the wire brush, I cleared the table, bringing the dishes inside. As I rinsed the dishes in the sink, I watched Will with Kasey through the kitchen window. Will's forearm was slung over the open hood while Kasey leaned over the engine, brows furrowed, his mop of bangs nearly covering his eyes. I inched the window open so I could hear them.

They were talking shop; listening to the way Will carefully and gently explained things to Kasey made my heart burst.

"Another trick of the trade I'll let you in on is this. If you ever see your battery cables getting corroded"—Will tapped on the battery with a wrench—"grab a can of soda and dump it on the cables. The acid in the soda eats it right off."

"Cool," Kasey said, nodding his head in approval.

I was starting to hand-wash the wooden salad bowl when I smelled a whiff of cigarette smoke. I peered back out at Kasey and Will and spotted Chloe and her two friends strolling in front of the house.

"Shit," I heard Chloe say as she ground out her cigarette with her combat boot. Her two friends giggled, then stubbed their smokes out as well.

"Heeeey," she said in a lazy drawl to Kasey, stopping in front of the drive.

"Hi, Chloe," Kasey said.

She scanned the yard. "Please tell your mom not to rat us out for smoking."

"Sure thing."

"I, like, forgot you even lived down here."

Kasey's face bloomed red and Chloe and her friends laughed.

"I mean, not in a bad way, but just in a spacey way."

Her eyes were bloodshot, and to me, she looked stoned. There was no way I was planning on mentioning her smoking to Kittie. Chloe can be a pain, but I also think Kittie is a bit harsh with her.

"Is that yours?" she said, gesturing to the Land Cruiser.

"Yep. Early birthday present. And this is my mom's friend Will. He's showing me how to work on it."

Will gave Chloe a quick dip of acknowledgment with his head but turned his attention back to the engine. He seemed impatient for the girls to scatter.

"It's awesome. And would look superhot on Insta," Chloe said, twisting a lock of hair around a finger.

"C'mon, Chloe." The taller brunette rolled her eyes, tugged on Chloe's T for them to leave.

"Thanks! So glad you like it!" Kasey chirped at Chloe before she trotted off with her friends.

DIPPING HIS HEAD farther inside the hood, Will fiddled with another section of the engine until Chloe and her troop rounded the corner and vanished from sight.

"You interested in her?" Will asked Kasey nonchalantly without making eye contact.

Kasey fidgeted, shifting his weight from one foot to the next. He combed his bangs back with his hands and blew out an exhale before answering.

"Yeah. I mean, I guess. She's an old family friend. Known her since I was little. But, like, I don't think she's into *me* or anything, so it's not like I'm seriously considering something with her."

"Can I give you some advice?"

The suds from the sink tickled my arms, but I held my breath, anxious to hear what Will was going to say next.

"Sure."

"Next time you're around her, act like you don't even notice her.

Like when she's talking to you, barely look up. They like that. Trust me."

Kasey nodded. "Cool."

Will clapped him on the back.

I winced. It was such a dick piece of advice and I didn't want Kasey turning out to be the type of guy who plays games with girls; I hate that! But truthfully, though, Chloe can be such a royal shit, I can actually see Will's advice working.

And watching the two of them bonding over guy stuff, huddled over the vehicle together as if it were a campfire—their shoulders nearly touching—made my eyes prick with hot tears.

26.

Cynthia Nichols's Diary

MY HANDS ARE shaking as I'm writing this; I can't believe what happened today. It's night now, nearly midnight, and I'm curled up on my chaise in the study while Gerald's in bed sawing logs.

A mug of lavender tea rests on the tiny side table, waiting to cool, and I draw in a deep breath, taking in its floral scent. Trying to keep my head from spinning.

Earlier today—just after three—I was lying out by the pool in my black bikini, flipping through *Southern Living* for recipes for Wine Night, and also earmarking pages in the summer issue of *Veranda* for ideas for a dream pool house.

Tyson was at band camp, due home just after five, and Gerald was still at work, of course, also expected around that same time. I was just about to cool off in the water when I heard a knock at the gate.

I figured it was Mario, my gardener, popping back by to drop off bags of compost, but he has his own key and doesn't usually knock.

My cover-up was inside, so I went to the gate, opened it a crack, and looked out.

It wasn't Mario.

It was Will.

"Hello, Cynthia," he said, smiling.

I couldn't believe I hadn't at least grabbed my towel to pull around me. My heart thumped at the sight of him dressed in a crisp long-sleeved white button-down with linen pants that were cuffed at the ankles.

"Hi," I managed to say, still peering from behind the wooden gate.

"Mind if I come in?" He crinkled his features into an amused expression as if I were ridiculous for not having invited him in already.

"Um, sure," I said, creaking open the gate all the way.

Will stepped forward, closing the gate behind him. He scanned the backyard, the pool, the house. "Wow, quite a stunning spread you have here."

"Thank you," I lamely said, wrapping my arms around my body in order to try and shield myself.

After he finished scoping my property, he turned to me, raking his eyes over my body with that same probing gaze he'd had at Kittie's party. I felt naked in my swimsuit, so I walked over to my lounge chair and motioned for him to have a seat on the one next to mine.

He moved, instead, to the corner of the pool and sat on the edge, angling his body toward mine. Had he brought his suit? Have one on under his clothes? I was about to stupidly ask when he started cuffing the bottom of his pants until they reached the backs of his knees. He dunked his legs in the pool, dragging his feet through the azure water.

"Would you like something to drink?" I asked, desperate to get inside and find my cover-up.

"Sure. Anything with alcohol sounds nice."

"I've got wine, some beer, although it's gluten-free. I—" I bumbled.

"Wine sounds amazing," Will said, cutting me off.

I rose and headed toward the sliding glass door, feeling Will's eyes needling my backside the entire way. Once inside the house, the chill of the AC stung my skin and I strode to my closet to fetch a cover-up. I realized that they were all sheer—not that much covering up going on at all—but I selected a black one that at least had a silk tie I could cinch around my waist.

In the kitchen, I dragged two glasses down from the cabinet and selected a sparkling rosé, something to take the edge off the blistering heat. I gazed out the window at Will, who was leaning back with his arms arrowed out behind him, his ankle still lazily circling the water.

What the hell was I doing, offering him a drink? Encouraging any of this? But as I studied him—his full lips, his tanned chest peeking through the V where his top buttons were undone—my stomach did somersaults. Before I could think about what was happening, I grabbed the stems of the glasses and headed back outside.

The sky was partly cloudy, which somehow made the sun even more blinding, and sunspots clouded my eyes for a few moments, making Will and the pool look splintered, fractured.

As I bent over to pass him the wine, his eyes traced over my cover-up and I felt a sting of embarrassment for having put it on. For not being comfortable enough to simply flounce around in my bikini.

"Cheers," Will said, raising his glass to mine.

"Cheers." I tapped my glass to his and took a swig, rolling the wine around in my mouth.

"Mmmm. This is quite good," he said.

"Glad you like it; it's one of my favorites," I said, moving back to the safety of my lounge chair.

"Thanks for letting me in." His lips were parted as he studied my torso.

My heart raced, but instinctively, I cinched the cover-up on even tighter, shielding myself from his probing view.

"I just wanted to stop by, wanted to get to know you better. I know Jen, and I know Kittie—well, I've been to her house at least—but I don't know you. And we're neighbors." He made a circle eight in the water with his shin, flicked his eyes back onto mine.

My pulse throbbed in my neck and my mouth grew dry, so I took another long sip, buying a few seconds until I could figure out how to respond. The wine was already hitting me—I've always been a bad day drinker—and I knew I needed to take small sips from there on out or else I'd be soused.

"Well, what do you want to know?" I said dumbly.

He let out a sharp laugh. "I don't exactly have a list of questions prepared, Cynthia. But you just seem"—he paused, eyes skittering over the surface of the pool as if he were selecting just the right words—"elusive. Why is that?"

Because I have a husband. Because Jen is one of my best friends.

"I don't know what you mean." My voice was strained.

He just smiled at me, locked his eyes onto mine, holding my gaze for a long moment. "I think you have a lot more going on under the surface than meets the eye."

I felt my cheeks redden, felt exposed. This conversation was like a roller-coaster ride veering dangerously close to the edge of the tracks.

"Not much to see here," I said in protest, but inwardly, I wanted him to keep digging.

"Let's start with simple stuff. Like where are you from, Cynthia?" There was my name again in his mouth, being delicately chiseled by his accent.

"Ummm, here? This very neighborhood, actually."

"Mmmm. I can see you being shy growing up. Were you shy as a little girl?"

"I was very shy and bookish. More so than Kittie, that's for sure."

I wasn't sure why I was confiding this to him, only that I felt like he was seeing through the normal facade of things. There was a part of me that was responding to his openness.

"Yeah, I can tell you have a lot going on up there," he said, pointing a well-manicured index finger to his temple. "But you keep it hidden."

I took another nip of wine, shifted in my seat. He was reading me even better than Dr. Whitaker—like he could sense my unhappiness, my unease—and I needed to take back control of the conversation.

"And you? Where are you from?"

"Denmark. Copenhagen, to be exact."

"Wow, I've always wanted to go to Europe," I said, immediately chastising myself for sounding like such a hick.

"Maybe we will someday."

I looked right at Will to see if I'd misunderstood what he had just said, but his nose was in his wineglass.

"What?"

"Nothing. I said maybe you'll go someday."

But that's *not* what he had said; I was certain of it. The wine was making me light-headed and woozy; my peripheral vision was starting to get fuzzy, but I knew I had heard him correctly.

"You really do have a beautiful place. I dig it; it's very Frank Lloyd Wright."

Warmth pooled in my stomach; he was talking about things that actually matter to me. Not that Gerald doesn't, but Will was lasering in on them in with lightning speed.

"Yes, exactly. That's exactly what I was going for. I minored in architecture at school."

"And what was your major?" He cocked an eyebrow, took another drink of wine.

"Interior design."

"I can tell," he said, gesturing with an open palm around the yard.

"Thank you; design is a passion of mine, actually."

"Mmmm, that's a good passion." He locked his agave eyes onto mine; I felt my stomach drop.

"Oh, the places I could show you in Copenhagen. Every civic building is a monument to Danish design. And even the most modest flats have unbelievable architectural details."

"Sounds incredible." My head spun at the thought of Will showing me around Denmark.

"Tell me about your husband." He drained the rest of his wine.

A shard of guilt stabbed me and I suddenly felt oddly protective over Gerald.

"Tell me about your wife," I shot back, surprising myself with my boldness. Of course I already knew what Jen had told me—that something had happened, but she didn't know what, only that Will had obviously been wounded by it.

He stared off, scratched the back of his neck. "Let's just say I've been through something."

"So, why don't you tell me about it?" I had no idea where my forthrightness was coming from—I'm never this direct with anybody—but with Will it felt natural, refreshing.

"Let's leave it at this: she broke my heart."

He dropped his gaze to the pool; I felt bad for pushing it.

"Sorry. I—"

"Not a worry. I'm a firm believer in the past staying in the past. Rebirth and all that." He looked up, winked at me.

I studied his strong jaw, the curve of his lips. Imagined what it would feel like to kiss them. Fire sparked across my solar plexus just thinking about it.

He pulled his ankles from the water, pushed himself to standing. Shook the water off his legs and took a few steps into the grass so that he was underneath the shade of an oak.

His wineglass was empty, so I hopped up to retrieve it from the ledge of the pool.

"Let me get you a refill."

He moved out from under the shade, came over to me. Took the glass from my hand and set it back down on the ground.

"Forget the wine." He stepped nearer to me, closing the gap between us so that his chest was nearly touching mine.

Over Will's head, the sun throbbed behind a cloud, making the light around him pulse, making his skin look like warm velvet.

Leaning down so that his mouth was just on my ear, he said, "I like you. You don't just talk like most people. I like your company."

My pulse raced from his breath on my neck, his lips close to my skin. It was as if there were an electrical current running between us, and I wanted to grab the back of his head, pull him into a kiss.

I closed my eyes and he shifted his face so that his lips were on mine, barely touching them. My insides clenched and I started to kiss him, my tongue darting between his lips. He kissed me back in a teasing way that made me nearly swoon. But when I felt his hands on my hips, I pulled back, remembered I was married.

"I—I can't. I can't cheat on my husband." The words left my mouth but I still leaned in for another kiss.

Will placed his hands on my shoulders, steadying me. "That's okay. We'll take this slow. But I'd like you to do something for me."

Before I could ask what, he led me by the hand over to the lounge chairs. He motioned for me to sit where I had been lounging before, and I sank down as he walked a few paces and plopped onto the nearest one, about five feet away. He sat on the edge of the chair so that he was facing me, his forearms resting on his knees, a lock of his bangs dangling between his brows.

"Will you take your cover-up off?"

My heart banged against my chest. I had no idea what he was

after. But I shimmied out of it, releasing it into a black pool on the hot concrete between us.

His eyes widened. "You"—he sucked in a long stream of air—"are beautiful."

I squirmed in my seat, unsure of what to do with myself.

"I wanna watch you touch yourself. And this way, it wouldn't be cheating."

Heat spread all over me and I was having a hard time breathing.

As if sensing this, Will said, "Just a little. Just touch yourself."

I couldn't believe he was asking me to do this, but after Gerald, who never tells me what to do, never asks me what *I* would like to do, the request felt so bold, it turned me on even more.

He nodded. "Do it. Please."

Leaning all the way back in the chair, I slid my hand down the top of my bikini bottoms and started rubbing small, tight circles. I glanced around the yard, scanning the fence line to make sure no one could see us. Even though I know it's totally walled in and private, I felt exposed out in the open like that. Gerald and I had never even had sex out by the pool. The sun was bouncing off the glass walls to the house, turning them into mirrors, so that I couldn't see inside, making things feel even riskier. What if Gerald or Tyson came home early?

But then I heard Will's voice, husky and low. "I want to see you; take them off."

I slid my bottoms to one side.

Will moaned. "God."

I kept touching myself while his agave-green eyes raked over me, my hand moving faster, having a mind of its own, my other hand straining against the elastic of my bikini.

I wanted him to come over then, to take me. I wanted it so much, I could've screamed it. But instead I continued to grind against my hand while he watched.

"My God, you are exquisite."

My hand became frantic then, the terraced gardens blurring into a sea of green until I finished.

AFTERWARD, MY WHOLE body relaxed against the heat-baked lounge chair. I couldn't believe what I had just done. In front of Will. I knew all about Jen going down on him in her garden—and the thought of the two of them together made me feel queasy and jealous—but it sounded like he was the one to pull away from her. So unlike what had just happened between us.

I stared up at the sky, shielding the sun with my hands, and heard the scrape of Will's chair.

I rolled on my side to find him inches away from me.

"You're beautiful, Cynthia," he said, tracing a finger down my leg. "I've never seen anything so beautiful in my life."

I thought he was going to lean over and kiss me just then, but instead, he stood. "Like I said, we'll take this slow. But I'll see you soon."

And before I could respond, he was heading over to the gate, unlatching it, and letting himself out.

MY TEA HAS turned cold as I've been writing this, but I cup it in my hands and sip it anyway. My body feels as though it has a fever—at once sick with chills over what I did, betraying Gerald, betraying Jen—but also on fire, electrified.

It's not just his looks or my molten attraction to Will that has me feeling this way. It's our connection. Immediate, intimate, and yes, physical, primal, but it's also something deeper than that. The way he talks to me and what we talk about. He was able to peer inside of me so quickly when so many others can't, and he gets me.

I feel more alive than I have in a long time—or possibly ever—and it scares me.

27.

Kittie

IT'S MORNING. EARLY. The sun just rose and I'm already out jogging the neighborhood while it's still cool outside. Dew from my lawn clings to my sneakers, and I'm enjoying the crisp breezes that lift my hair.

I had Jen and Cynthia over for Wine Night last night and woke up with a tension in my chest that I needed to loosen. I'm rounding the corner, heading for the park where we held the Fourth of July party. This town is filled with parks. It's one of the nice things about Cedartown and our little neighborhood spot is one of my favorites, one of the places where I can clear my head—banked on a wide swath of the creek, rimmed by willow trees.

I jog down the rest of the sidewalk until I reach the boulevard that runs to the park. There, I break into a sprint, trying to outrun the shifting thoughts in my brain.

Last night was exhausting, listening to Jen—all doe-eyed and brimming with excitement—go on and on about Will. Even more exhausting was having to act like I was happy for her.

"That's *so* great that Felix met him. Are you fucking kidding me? I'd give my house to have seen the look on that SOB's face," I said as I slurped more wine.

I actually *was* delighted that Felix had been confronted with the smoldering storm of Will. He deserves every pang of regret and awkwardness that I'm sure racked him when he saw them together.

But it was tough putting on a cheery face for Jen, and Cynthia wasn't much help. She seemed glazed over all night; at one point, I elbowed her to jolt her back to the conversation.

"Sorry. It must be the paint fumes. The painters were over all day, taping and priming the bedroom, and I'm foggy headed."

"Have some more wine, darling," I said, emptying the bottle of Pinot Noir into her glass and clapping her on the back.

Jen could barely sit still, she was so buzzy with Will this and Will that. It sounds like he came on to her in the kitchen before Kasey arrived, and once Kasey got there, he played the role of doting stepfather to be.

I felt sick to my stomach, thinking about Will kissing her, but even more sick pondering Jen's naivete. She's *always* been like this. Always jumping into bed with the first handsome guy whose head she turned. I *knew* Felix was a snake in the grass, and I tried to warn her, but she wouldn't listen.

But how can I possibly warn her now about Will? I can't be the one to break it to her. What would I say? Hey, Jen, your new guy is scum. How do I know this? He's already fucked me when, at the same time, he's telling you he's not ready to go all the way yet.

No, I have to bide my time instead, see what develops between them. And in the meantime, sooner rather than later, I'm going to have to pay Will another visit.

28.

Cynthia Nichols's Diary

MIDDAY SUNLIGHT POURS through the window, making the walls of my bedroom glow.

The painters finished in here yesterday, transforming the mortuary gray into a vibrant fuchsia that makes me feel as though I'm nestled inside the center of a bougainvillea petal.

Dynamo. That's the shade I settled on and I'm so happy I did; the sensory ping of color matches the inward zest I'm feeling.

"Jesus, it looks like a bordello in here," Gerald joked when he arrived home from work yesterday. "But if you like it, what do I care?"

He sat on the edge of the bed, peeling off his thin dress socks.

I wanted to tell him that's precisely the vibe I was going for, but he wouldn't get it. That doesn't matter, though. Dynamo is already working its magic.

With Will.

This morning at therapy, even Dr. Whitaker could sense the change in me.

Once inside the calming womb of her office, she cocked her head to one side, studying me with a grin dancing across her lips.

"Cynthia! You're positively glowing!" Warmth radiated from her cognac-brown eyes. "What do you think the reason for the change is?"

I felt my cheeks flush pink and I folded my hands in my lap. There was no way I was going to tell her the truth. Tell her about Will.

"Well, I did as you suggested," I said, the half lie tumbling out, "and tried to focus on what interests me. And well, remodeling really does. We just had the bedroom done up in an incredible shade of fuchsia and it's really brightened my mood."

She nodded, her silver bob swinging at her shoulders. "I'm *so* happy to hear it. Sometimes, it's the smallest changes that can lead to the biggest shifts. And are you still keeping up with your journal?"

"Yes, nearly every day." Except now it's a sex diary.

I felt a prick of guilt for keeping my secret from Dr. Whitaker, who was so earnestly happy for me—I mean, wasn't I supposed to be able to tell my shrink everything?

But I held my revelation about Will close to my chest like a tight spring bud waiting to unfurl.

I SAW HIM again yesterday. I get dizzy just thinking about it; it's all I can focus on. After he stopped by on Monday, I lay out by the pool Tuesday afternoon, hoping he'd come over again, but he didn't. I felt dismayed, like I'd imagined the whole episode between us or, worse, that he'd changed his mind about me, but on Wednesday afternoon, as the painters were splashing color on the walls and I was outside roasting in the sun, I heard his knock again at my gate.

I had selected a red string bikini to wear—the skimpiest one I own—and when he unlatched the gate and saw me, his mouth hung open.

"Good Lord," he said.

He got down on one knee, ran a finger along my abdomen. "You have the most gorgeous torso."

Goose bumps spread across my skin, but I pulled on his hand until he came to standing.

"The painters are inside, so we can't stay here."

"Oooh, clandestine. I like it. So, my place?"

I nodded. He knew he didn't have to tell me where he lived.

"I'll walk over in a bit. See you soon."

I slipped inside to change, stepping into the black lace panties I'd recently bought and a white eyelet dress. On the walk over, adrenaline shot through me and my eyes kept darting over the neighborhood as if someone might notice where I was heading.

I couldn't believe I was going through with this, actually heading over to Will's house, where God knew what might happen, but it was as if an invisible string were tied around my waist, tugging me along.

He opened his hulking front door the minute I reached his walkway, like he'd been watching for me through the large window on the front of the house. I had never been inside the old Ellingsworth mansion before, but it was just as Jen had described it: breathtaking, refined, and slightly Gothic.

"Will, this is incredible. I must see every room."

He shut the door behind us and laced his tanned fingers through mine. "Every room wants to see you, and I mean all of you."

We kissed in the hall—a hot, tangled mess of hands groping—until we broke apart and he led me through his house.

First stop, his sun-filled kitchen, done in a Tuscan style with a gleaming stainless steel range and stove. Will retrieved a bottle of Pinot Noir from the wine fridge and poured us each a glass.

Next, he led me to the dining room, an intimate cloistered space with a battered wooden table that overlooked the sculpted back lawn. We toasted and sipped before moving down the hall, which was paved with milk-white tiles that were almost iridescent, glowing in the sun-light like moonstones.

We reached his bedroom, and when I stepped inside, my stomach quaked with longing. The room smelled like Will—clean, salty—and his bed was made of gorgeous hand-carved wood.

I walked around it toward the bare window and tapped my fingers along the wooden window seat stained in a dark oak color. Beyond his fence line lay the forest where we came of age as teens in middle school. First smokes, first kisses. And where we partied throughout high school. Bonfires, keg parties, make-out sessions—so many sordid memories in those woods and in the trails snaking through them.

He came up behind me, clasped his arms around my waist. Pull-ing my hair to one side, he nibbled on my ear. "I lied; the rest of the house will have to wait."

His hands trailed down to the hem of my dress, and he slowly started rolling it, inching up the fabric until my panties were exposed.

"I also lied about taking things slow." His breath was rapid against my ear and my own breath was shallow, ragged.

He bent to his knees as if inspecting me, hands moving over my ass, lips kissing a hip.

"You look absolutely stunning in these," he said, tugging on the waistband of my panties.

A thrill shuddered through me; I began to unzip my dress and felt Will's fingers fold over mine, guiding the zipper the rest of the way down until the dress fell to the floor. He pressed his searing chest against my back, tucked his chin over my shoulder, and peered down the top of my bra, which was black lace to match the panties.

Guiding us back to the edge of the bed, he said, "I can't wait to ravish your body."

I wanted to turn to him, kiss him full on again, wrestle his jeans off, but he roped an arm underneath my breasts and moved his other hand down the top of my underwear.

What we did next happened in a fever, and every hair stands up on my arms as I remember it.

Will flinging off my bra, hands roving all over me, caressing me, his tensile arms arching over me like a cellist playing a cello. His lips on my ear while his fingers touched me until I couldn't take it anymore. Both of us glazed in sweat. Me turning to face him, pushing him on his back, yanking his jeans down.

A strained look on his face as he grasped my hips. "Are you sure about this, Cynthia?"

His question did give me a moment's pause; Gerald sprung to mind. His toothpaste-white flesh against his rust-colored bathrobe. The monotony of our lovemaking. I shoved him from my thoughts. No, I deserved this. It was through no fault of mine that Gerald and I were dead in bed. Sure, he'd be devastated if he ever found out, but what was happening between me and Will in that moment—by my logic—had nothing to do with him.

Next: me climbing on top of Will, writhing against him while ginger-colored light strained through the window, the frame of the bed creaking beneath us. Will grunting my name over and over and over until we were both finished.

AFTERWARD, WE RETREATED to the calm oasis of his library. I've never felt more at home in anyone's house in Cedartown than I have at Will's. Finally, someone in town with the same elevated appreciation for fine art, books, and decorating.

A painting hung over his desk—a portrait of a stunning-looking female, her form hidden behind a coral-colored flower—and as I sipped the rest of the wine we'd abandoned earlier, I studied her features. Almond-shaped eyes, the same turquoise as Will's, and dark brown hair flowing beneath her bare shoulders.

"That was my mom," Will explained. Though I already knew the story from Jen. "A self-portrait. She was"—he paused as if searching for the right words—"quite a woman."

"Was? Has she passed?" I asked, even though I knew the answer.

"Sadly, yes, I lost her years ago." His eyes twinkled in the late-afternoon sunlight, and it almost looked as though he had tears brimming.

Before I could be sure, he leapt up and padded to the kitchen to fetch the remainder of the wine.

I realized I knew so much about Will through Jen, and in the moments he was gone, my throat grew hot as I thought of her. She was liable to be even more devastated than Gerald if she knew what was developing between me and Will.

"What exactly is going on with you and Jen?" I asked him once he refilled my glass and settled back into his armchair.

His mouth hung open as if in shock that I was questioning him about her, but he quickly regained his composure, the features of his face pinching together in consternation.

"You know, if I'm honest, I was interested in Jen at first. I mean, she's your friend; you know how wonderful she is. But I think now what I was wanting with her was more of a friendship." He stretched his long form back into the chair, cradled his chin in his hand. "I thought I wanted it to be something more, but being with you has changed that. It's changed everything, actually."

His eyes roved over my face, penetrating, searching, and I felt my stomach drop at his admission. It all made sense—his continuing to push Jen off when things would get too heated, keeping her at arm's length.

Unlike me. This had been only my second tryst with Will and we'd already gone all the way. My insides felt uneasy, sad for Jen. I knew how much hope she had pinned on things working out with him, but I couldn't help what was happening between us. Something that felt so natural, so second nature, shouldn't be prevented. Especially if he really was just seeking a friendship with her.

He crossed the room then and took my hand, pulling me back over to his armchair so that I was sitting in his warm lap. Sweeping my hair over one shoulder, he pressed his lips to my ear. "You're who I want, Cynthia. Let's not worry about Jen. I'll find the right way to break it off with her."

I leaned my head against his neck, let my body go slack against his. We sat like this for a long time, no words passing between us, no unnecessary chatter cluttering up this perfect moment, the bond between us crystalizing with our silence.

BEING WITH YOU has changed that. It's changed everything, actually. Will's words echo in my head now; I can't stop replaying them, replaying us together. And I feel strangely calm about it all, because I know that being with him is the right thing. I can't even be bothered to think of the logistics—the biggest being Gerald, and Jen, of course. No, for now, it's as if an orb of sunlight is encasing me, protecting me, protecting us from having to share our secret, our connection, with anyone else in the world.

29.

Jen

MY STOMACH IS a roiling pool of unease. I'm pacing from room to room, chiding myself for going over to Will's just now.

Which is silly; I should feel every right to pop over, but now I'm feeling like it was a mistake. Because it was.

I hadn't heard a peep from him since Sunday, since he was here with me and Kasey, and it was starting to bother me. For some reason, I thought he would've come over again by now, and I couldn't quell my buzzing nerves.

At six o'clock, I dropped Kasey off at Mom and Dad's for the night, hoping I might get to be with Will. When we pulled up to their steep gravel-lined drive, Dad was parked in front of his barrel-sized barbecue pit, smoke foaming out of the top as a blackened brisket sizzled on the grate.

"Wanna stay for dinner, honey?" He flashed me an eager smile.

I briefly considered it. Other than the occasional pizza night in town, I haven't made all that much effort to truly hang out with them since we've been back and I need to do better. But the thought of waiting another hour or two until Dad deemed the meat ready, while thoughts of Will danced through my brain, made my skin crawl. Plus, they know a little about him, and I'm not ready to be peppered with questions, even though they'd be well-meaning.

"How 'bout next time? I'm actually gonna try and clean the house tonight." I hugged his sweaty body and then climbed the steps to their wraparound porch so I could say hi/bye to Mom as well. I felt bad turning him down—I really did—and vowed to have them over for a long Sunday brunch soon.

A S   S O O N   A S   I got back home, I plugged my curling iron in and waited for it to warm. I washed my face at the sink, lathering it with the remnants of my favorite pricey cleanser, which I'm too poor to replace, and began applying a light coat of makeup. A sweep of navy eyeliner, a dusting of rose-pink blush, a swipe of berry-tinted lip gloss. I wrapped a few locks of hair around the rod of the curling iron (the way my stylist in Austin had instructed) and spritzed my neck with perfume.

I decided to drive to Will's so my hair wouldn't sag in the humidity, stashing the top-shelf bottle of bourbon I'd splurged on at the liquor store earlier in the day in the passenger seat.

As my Honda climbed the hill, I saw his gleaming truck in the drive, parked in the shade of the tall pine that looms over his yard. My hands grew slick on the steering wheel; I was both nervous and excited, thinking about the possibility that this might finally be the night when we'd go all the way. A rush of heat poured over me as I imagined his fingers unbuttoning my blouse, lifting the hem of my skirt as he'd done on Sunday, and finally, removing my panties.

I pulled up to the curb and shifted into park. My hands were jittery, so I sucked in a few deep breaths to steady myself and clasped the bottle of bourbon before stepping out of the car. Heat radiated through the thin soles of my sandals as I headed up his walkway and the evening air hovered over me like a bog.

The lamps in the library weren't turned on, but the house was lit from within, most likely from the back rooms: Will's bedroom, the hallway, the kitchen and dining area. I knocked on the door. As I waited for him to answer, I shifted on my feet, the bottle dangling from my hands. I had decided I was going to be direct with him, tell him I was ready for sex and frustrated with waiting.

A few seconds passed. I stepped closer to the door, aiming my ear at it. I could make out the sound of Will's voice, low and muted, and also the sound of classical piano music. Perfect. He was probably on the phone, maybe fixing dinner at the same time. I pictured him in his kitchen, dicing juicy tomatoes, refreshing a glass of wine. I waited a moment longer before knocking again. I rapped my knuckle harder against the wood this time in case my first attempt had been muffled by his conversation and the music.

A beat later, I heard his footsteps padding along the paved floor. My breath grew short and staccato. He opened the door about a foot, keeping most of his body hidden behind it. His hair was slick and messy, his long-sleeved white cotton shirt rumpled and cuffed at the forearm.

"Jen!" he said, his voice bright and cheery. He flashed a smile and raked his eyes over me. But didn't budge from behind the door.

"I . . . I just thought I'd stop by. I picked this up earlier today, was hoping maybe you'd like to split it?" I stammered.

"Oh," he said, looking down at the glass bottle in my hands. "That looks . . . inviting. But the thing is, I'm tied up at the moment." He tilted his head as if in apology, eyes crinkling into a smile.

"I—um . . . Well, no worries! Another time!" My tongue grew heavy in my mouth and my words came out clumsily, awkwardly.

I should've turned to leave then, but I stood there, firm and planted, feeling stung by his dismissal. *I'm tied up at the moment.* What exactly was he tied up with? I felt like he should explain further. But he only lifted his eyebrows at me as if to see if I had anything further to say.

My feet felt like deadweights and my head spun. Why wasn't he coming out from behind the door? Why wasn't he leaning down to kiss me? My cheeks grew hot with embarrassment and confusion, and I finally came to my senses, regained my composure.

"Well! Till next time, then!" I chirped, clasping the throat of the bottle. There was no way I was leaving it with him.

"Till next time." He flashed another smile, then gave me a nod.

I turned to leave, my insides feeling hollow as I walked back to my car, wondering whether he was alone in there. I didn't exhale until I heard his front door creak shut behind me.

I'M TIRED OF pacing. I kick off my sandals, shrug out of my clothes, and slip into my pajamas. I go to the kitchen and crack the seal on the bourbon. It's so expensive, it has a bloody cork in it, and I wrench it out with a pop. The air immediately smells of oak and I pour myself a tumbler full, not bothering to put a drop of water in it the way Will taught me.

I'm mad at him. But more than that, I'm mad at myself. I knew it was strange that he hadn't come by after our dinner on the patio on Sunday, and now I really suspect that something is off. I should've waited him out, should've waited for him to make the next move. I've been so careful about protecting myself, about trying to hold on to a sense of power. But I just gave it all away by going up there when my instincts were telling me not to.

He obviously wasn't just on the phone. If that were the case, I'm certain he would've asked me in. No—the music in the background, the way he didn't give me any details, the way he shielded himself behind the door, that look on his face—there was something else going on. And I can't shake the gut-churning feeling that there was another woman in his house.

30.

Kittie

MY FEET ARE sore, so I'm stretched out on the sofa in the living room, kneading them, a glass of wine on the coffee table.

Hank has already turned in for the night. We're both bushed. He took off from work early today so we could sneak away to the Honda dealership to buy Chloe her Pilot as an early birthday surprise, like he had suggested. She told us earlier this summer that she wanted a pearl-white one to match Shelley's, which I scoffed at.

"Don't you want something that's distinctly yours?" I asked, scrolling through the selections on her laptop. "How about this nice cherry color? Or even this sapphire?" I tapped my fingernail on the screen.

But Chloe just shook her head. "Pearl. It's not just 'cuz of Shelley, Mom. I mean, she has a black interior and I *definitely* want the gray leather. Shelley's is fabric," she said, pronouncing the word "fabric" as if it were a thing of disgust.

I have to admit I felt a ping of glee at the thought of Chloe one-upping that nasty-acting Shelley.

"Okay. White with gray leather seats it is."

HER BIRTHDAY ISN'T until August thirteenth, still three weeks away, but Hank is right: it's time to get her driving lessons and she may as well practice on the car she'll actually be driving.

Even though we knew exactly what we were after and were paying cash, the whole process still took three hours, most of it spent traipsing around the lot, looking inside the dozen or so pearl-colored Pilots, each with its own bells and whistles. Because I wanted to look cute, I'd worn a pair of peep-toe heeled sandals and instantly regretted the decision after picking my way back and forth across the acre-long lot.

"Honey," I whispered in Hank's ear, "this is taking for-ev-er. Wrap it up. Wine Night tonight."

At last, we were seated in the showroom, signing papers and buying warranties.

We managed to sneak the Pilot into the garage (which Chloe never enters) before she arrived home from cheerleading practice. We want to present it to her this Friday, two weeks before her big birthday weekend.

CYNTHIA SKIPPED OUT tonight, citing the migraine she's been nursing since Saturday, when she declined coming over while the men were off at poker night. She thinks she might've accidentally ingested some gluten—Lord knows how; she's so OCD careful—but whatever.

So I was stuck all night with Jen. Jen, who downed an entire bottle of sparkling rosé all by herself, while cramming pineapple chunks in her mouth. I'd made a nice-sized fruit-and-cheese platter and Jen damn near devoured the whole thing as she stood over me, swilling wine and holding court about Will, her nerves ablaze.

"I mean, can you believe he just dismissed me like that? Do you think he was with someone else when I stopped by?" She paced the length of the patio in her sad faded yoga pants, literally wringing her hands as she spoke. "Am I overreacting? I mean, maybe it was work related? Was I stupid for going over there?"

Before I could respond to any of her missives, she'd launch into a whole new line of neurotic thinking. "Maybe I *shouldn't* have popped by. But that's what we've been doing this whole time. He's popped by my place, too! I think it's probably fine. I'm probably overreacting. I'm just being paranoid."

I wanted to grab her by her bony shoulders and shake her. Scream at her, make clear that he wasn't this knight in fucking armor that she believed him to be. But again, how could *I* be the one to tell her that yes, he'd already fucked around on her—with me?

I just listened, nose buried in my wineglass, nodding slowly at all the important parts. I felt awful for her, so in addition to wanting to throttle her, I also wanted to tuck her in for the night and tell her a bedtime story, press a cool rag to her forehead, make all her worries go away.

But something also began to gnaw at me while Jen was flailing on my patio—the thought that Will had indeed been with someone else on Saturday night. It sickened me, made my gut ache with jealousy.

"Could you just dig around? Ask Margaret Anne or any of the Leaguers if they've seen him around and about? Surely he's not with slutty Brandi, but could ya just see?"

Oh, there will be digging going on, all right.

31.

Cynthia Nichols's Diary

OH, DEAR DIARY, I have my own drawer! A lingerie drawer. At Will's house.

We've been together every day since last week, sneaking in a rendezvous whenever I can steal away. Saturday evening was poker night for the husbands—a perfect time to go unnoticed, even if I had to lie to Kittie about having a migraine. And Tyson didn't care. Quite the opposite. When I announced to him after our casual dinner of tuna melts that I would be heading over to a friend's house and asked if he minded, he practically sneered at me.

"God, Mom," he said, shaking his head. "Already told you earlier today I'm going over to Carter's. If I spend the night, I'll text you."

Clearly I'm a giant idiot. He bent his head back down toward his dinner plate, his sandy brown curls nearly covering his eyes. I wondered (and not for the first time) if perhaps Carter was more than just a friend. If I was not the only one getting action around here.

I also ditched Wine Night last night (but told Gerald that's where I was headed), and I'm glad I did. Kittie rang me earlier this morning to tell me how gut-wrenching it was, listening to Jen go on about Will. About how she'd dropped by his place Saturday night and he hadn't invited her in. About how she thinks he might be seeing someone else.

He is, of course; he's seeing me, and what an asshole I am, carrying on with him. And an even bigger asshole because I know I'm not going to stop.

We were lounging in Will's bed, post-sex, when we heard a knock at the front door. I had a hunch it was Jen. Even though I was tucked away in the back corner of his house, spread out on top of his fluffy white down comforter—the thread count so high, it feels like melted butter against your skin—I could hear her voice, brittle and thin, carrying through the walls.

I felt bad, of course, but also relieved that he turned her away without so much as a peck on the cheek. Relieved that he's telling me the truth about her: he wants to be with me and me alone. Not that I don't trust him. But it was good to see it with my own eyes.

It was that same evening, a few hours earlier, that he presented me with the white box lashed with a red ribbon.

"I got you something, something I think you'll like. And something I want to see you in."

He's already possessive over me, and tender, asking me if I've kissed Gerald, or had sex with Gerald (I have not, not since Will first crossed the threshold to my backyard a week ago). And I can imagine why he's like this, after getting his heart smashed to bits. I can't imagine, though, who would want to do that to him; I want to know more about her, but I don't dare ask him. Why would I? Why would I spoil our magical time together?

I untied the ribbon, opened the box. Inside, wrapped in crisp white tissue paper was a crimson-red cupless bra with a matching thong. I gasped when I saw them. They were racier than anything I've ever worn.

"Try them on for me," Will said.

I went to the bathroom and changed into them. My heartbeat banged in my throat as I took in my reflection, and before I chickened out, I stepped into the hallway, then into the library.

Will was sitting in his armchair, fully clothed. Chin resting in his hand, a lazy finger tracing his lips.

"Come here," he ordered.

I floated across the room and he pulled me into his lap, his eyes blazing, needling every inch of my body.

"I would've gotten you a ring, something delicate and gold, but I know you couldn't wear that out in public. But these things, you can. No one will see them. But you will think of me." His accent in my ear made my stomach twirl. "You can keep them here, too, though, if you like, so your husband doesn't find out."

Before I left his house that evening, though, I stashed the bra and panties in my bag. I wanted to carry a piece of Will home with me, and Gerald, of course, would never discover my unmentionables in my own lingerie drawer.

On Sunday afternoon, when Gerald was snoring in front of the television and Tyson was at Carter's house, I snuck away again to Will's.

He greeted me with a glass of chilled sparkling wine and another white box to open. This time, it was a sheer cream-colored negligee, the silk hem of which hit the tops of my thighs.

"You look even more exquisite in this than I imagined." He twisted a lock of my hair around his finger.

"Where are you even picking up these things?"

"Internet fairy."

We spent that afternoon in bed, as usual, and then in his library, discussing books, art, travel. Standing on my tiptoes, I ran my index finger along the spines of his design books, which are kept on a high shelf. I slid one down—*Medieval Architecture in European Cities: Castles and Fortresses*—then leafed through it, getting lost in its pages. Sitting in his library then, I strangely felt how I used to feel as a young girl, upstairs in the sanctuary of my own room, dragging charcoals across a sketch pad or working through math problems in a state of meditative bliss with time falling away—my most beloved years of childhood before my mother, Virginia, yanked me out of my reverie and onto the debutante track. I had, of course, briefly recaptured that rapturous feeling in college in painting class, but it was fleeting after Kittie's dismissal of my piece.

I gazed across the room at Will. I already knew I'd be skipping Wine Night, so I proposed that we also see each other Monday.

He didn't flinch. "I'll make dinner."

And he did. When I stepped through the front door, my stomach grumbled at the aroma of the elaborate feast he'd prepared: a lemon-prawn salad dotted with feta cheese, simple yet scrumptious spaghetti made with charred cherry tomatoes and rosemary (his mother's recipe), followed by a cheesecake made with Greek yogurt and drizzled with honey.

As we ate, Will kept his eyes trained on me, attending to my every need: refilling my wine, serving me second helpings, refreshing my water glass. And I imagined Kittie and Jen several blocks over, holding court without me.

I was glad to be with Will instead.

He sees me for who I truly am, understands me in a way that Kittie never will. I'll always be small-town Cynthia to her, stuck in our roles of homemakers and wives. And as for Jen, she's been my friend since childhood, but we've never been particularly close; our friendship is always hinged on Kittie's presence, a sort of isosceles triangle with Kittie being the base that holds us all together.

For instance, Jen and I never, or rarely, text or talk on the phone. And we never would hang out without Kittie around. I was excited when I heard she was moving back, genuinely eager to see if, in our adulthood, our relationship could develop and we could connect in a deeper way. Jen had lived this seemingly thrilling life in Austin (except for the divorce part) and I was ready to be exposed to her, to mine her for something more stimulating than the mind-numbing gossip of Junior Leaguers.

But as soon as she hit town, the three of us instantly reverted to our primal childhood mold, in which Kittie is front and center, directing the show. Though she comes off as the most self-possessed of the three of us, she is the least grounded, least secure, and she requires that Jen and I constantly prop her up, give her our undivided attention. Any connection that Jen and I have outside of Kittie's realm always gets muted.

And understandably, Jen hasn't been too keen to talk about her life in Austin with us. She wants to move on, rebuild. I know she thought Will was going to be a part of that, and I do truly feel horrible, but as it turns out, the cheesy old adage is true: you can't decide whom you fall in love with.

And I am in love with Will, as he is with me. Monday night after our dinner, he pulled me into the bedroom. I undressed and opened the top drawer to his dresser, pulling out the cream-colored negligee. He was on me in a flash, devouring every section of my body with his mouth, and before I could stop myself, the words bubbled out.

"I love you."

He froze for a moment; his body tensed, and fearing I'd made a huge mistake, I braced myself for the rejection that was soon to follow. But instead, he placed his hands squarely on my shoulders and cupped my chin in his hands. His eyes were deep pools of jade in the weak evening light, and it almost looked like tears were forming in them.

He leaned in close enough so that his lips tickled my ear.

"I. Love. You, Cynthia."

He lifted me on the bed then and took me, both of us feverishly moving against each other as if we were in a struggle.

AFTERWARD, WE DIDN'T speak of what we'd said to each other. We just lay side by side, legs fitted together like chain links, our chests rising and falling with calm breaths.

That's the nice thing about Will and me: we don't have to talk every second we're together. It's as if we already know each other even though we've just met.

One piece of worry pricks at the front of my mind, though. Jen wants Kittie to go digging around. To try and find out if Will is sleeping with anyone and, if so, whom. I would prefer for us to exist in peace, to have our time together protected, unbothered.

Because when Kittie wants to find something out, she will.

32.

Jen

SWEAT DRIPS ON my yoga mat and my hands slip forward, arrowing out from me as I try to get into downward dog. I'll need to stop soon. I've been out here on the back patio doing this flow for the past half hour, but now I'm drenched, making it harder to stay in poses. The yoga, though, has helped lift my anxiety about Will.

It's midday. Venting last night to Kittie at Wine Night also helped. She reassured me that I was most likely overthinking it. I'm letting my past experience with Felix color everything, and now it's threatening to undo my promising relationship with Will.

I know I need to cool it. He's told me, time and again, that he wants—and needs—to take things slowly. I should have more faith in myself and believe that he's into me, even if we're not having sex yet, and even if we don't see each other every day.

I've had enough counseling and read enough self-help books to understand this tendency of mine to "get lost in the other," as my old therapist, Annie, used to say. The first book she recommended to me was one I turned to this morning: Melody Beattie's *Codependent No More.*

I was still in bed, feeling sluggish and slightly depressed, when I raked it off my nightstand and fingered the dog-eared pages until I came across a passage I'd underlined and circled (and even drawn a star next to in the margins).

"Codependents are reactionaries. They overreact. They underreact. . . . They react to the problems, pains, lives, and behaviors of others."

Bingo. Just what I needed to read at that exact moment. I was guilty of reacting to Will's standoffish mood Saturday night, of taking it personally, when it probably had nothing to do with me at all.

My plan now is to take a breather and fill the well. I'm going to hit the "pause" button on thinking about Will (or at least thinking about him constantly) for the next week or two. Do things for myself that I've been putting off, like finally looking into exactly what it would take to become a yoga instructor. I need it not only for the money. I need it for my sanity.

I'll finally make a dinner date with Mom and Dad, maybe have them over to our place for brunch, do something nice for them for a change. I'll take Kasey on a movie date, a matinee; we can stroll downtown afterward and duck into the ice-cream parlor for strawberry-chocolate milkshakes.

And yes, in the meantime, I'll also be keeping my ears pricked to see if Kittie hears anything about Will. I can't help myself.

33.

Kittie

IT'S AFTERNOON. HANK is still at work and Chloe's gone out for a walk. She's going over to Megan's house, which is in the next subdivision over, and she practically skipped down the driveway just now as she headed out.

She's been in such a better mood since yesterday, when Hank and I presented her with the new car.

Hank's like a big kid; he didn't want to wait until our Friday-night family dinner, so as soon as he got home from work, he opened the garage and backed the car into the drive, fastening the cartoonish giant yellow bow that the dealership had given us on the hood.

"Go inside and get her," he said, his face crinkling into a grin. "I'll be off to the side so I can snap the pic!"

Chloe was in her room with the door closed. I could hear her through the walls, talking in a low voice on her phone. I strained to listen but couldn't make out what she was saying.

I knocked.

"Yes?" She sounded tense, irritated.

"Honey, can I come in?"

"Sure," she shouted in my direction.

I opened the door. Chloe was sitting cross-legged in the middle of her bed, her hair cinched up on the top of her head with a scrunchie, her cell phone planted to the side of her face.

"Gotta run. Call ya later."

She looked up at me with annoyance in her eyes. I wanted to turn from her room and snatch the car away from her, drive it back to the dealership, but I swallowed my ire and smiled.

"Can you help me bring in some grocery boxes? Dad's not home yet and I don't want someone snatching them from the drive."

She followed me outside, her flip-flops slapping the floor behind me. I led her out the back door and through the side gate to the driveway.

"Surprise!" yelled Hank, though it wasn't really a surprise at all; she had picked it out but had no idea we were giving it to her this early.

Chloe's face flushed and her eyes grew wide as a squeal escaped her lips. "Oh, my God! Oh, my God!"

Hank angled his iPhone toward her with his chubby hands, snapping a vertical and horizontal picture of Chloe before she bum-rushed him with a hug. Hank motioned for me to come over and Chloe grabbed my waist, pulling me into them, knotting the three of us into a group hug.

"You guys are the bessst!" Tears misted in her eyes, causing her black eyeliner to smudge.

"Well, climb in!" Hank said.

The three of us piled in, with Chloe in the driver's seat. She ran her fingers along the gray leather interior, tracing the seams along the dash.

"This is sick!!" she squealed, flashing us both a huge smile, giving us a thumbs-up.

IF I HAD known that bribing her with a new car was all it would take to get her to treat me with a modicum of respect, I'd have done it at the beginning of the summer. After she called and texted all of her friends to gush about the car, she actually hung out with us for the rest of the night. Hank grilled chicken on the barbecue. As we all ate together, she actually filled us in on her life, told us how cheerleading practice was going (pretty well; she was close to perfecting the pike), and admitted that she was nervous about her upcoming junior year (transitioning from a cheerleader for junior varsity football to varsity).

I tried not to interject at all, just listened and nodded and swilled more wine. I realized how on my guard I always am around Chloe, tiptoeing around her volatile moods. After one of our particularly nasty fights earlier in the summer, Hank had told me later that night in our bedroom that I needed to learn how to not "poke the bear." So that's what I did last night. I didn't poke the bear; I let Chloe bask in the glow of her shiny new Pilot and kept my trap shut for fear I'd say something to set her off.

And I'm glad her sunny mood has held over. Because right now my nerves are shot. I can't stop thinking about Will and what he might be up to. Now with Chloe gone, I'm in the bathroom primping before going to his place. I've squeezed myself into a pair of designer Daisy Dukes that are acid-washed with the hems frayed. Cost me a fortune at Mark's, the boutique downtown, but the saleslady literally hooted when I tried them on last week.

"You have *got* to have those," she said as I studied my ass in the dressing room mirror.

They were flattering, I had to admit, so I took them home with a faded graphic T that also hung nicely on my frame.

I'm wearing that T now, and as I study myself in the reflection, I almost feel as though I'm in high school again; I look so retro. Except for my crow's-feet, which clearly time-stamp me. I dot a little concealer over them, which helps some, but the crevices are still there. Oh, well. I'm still feeling sassy in my new getup, and before I leave, I apply a lipstick aptly named Dagger Red and refresh my perfume.

As I walk over to Will's, the air outside feels like warm lake water against my skin, making my mood even sultrier. I feel badly about Jen—I honestly do; he's obviously over her—but the scorching thought of Will and me repeating what we did the other day live-wires through me so that I'm nearly skipping down the street like Chloe.

I can't help it and I can't stop myself from walking on toward his house. Remembering the way he rode me from behind, the way he couldn't resist me, the way he panted in my ear, is like an addiction.

But what if he turns me away like he did with Jen? What if he thinks I'm ridiculous for coming back over? Presumptuous for thinking he'd want to see me again? That I'm nothing more than a quick good fuck. He doesn't even really like me, and I can't pretend that he does. Even though we had that searing afternoon together, there was still the way it ended, with him taunting me about Jen. *I can't imagine you're going to tell Jen, are you?* As if he'd just ensnared me in some trap. And then his final words to me: *See you around, Kittie.*

He certainly hasn't made an effort to seek me out since then. What if he really *is* seeing someone else? What if I get to his house and discover that she's there?

But I know how it felt to be with him—so hot, so urgent—and there's also the thrilling prospect that there's no one else at all, that because we've hooked up, he simply doesn't need Jen anymore; he's cast her off.

I round the final corner and my feet stutter on the pavement when I see him outside on the lawn, bent over a baby shrub. My heart beats against my rib cage and I lift my hair off my neck, fan myself for a moment before walking farther.

When I reach his walkway, he turns as if he can sense me. I wave and walk up the flagstone path, aware that his eyes are sizing me up, taking me in. Will stays crouched on the ground, his hands dirty with clumps of soil, the front of his white T stained with earth. A trowel lies next to a yellow-and-purple lantana flower—the petals so vibrant, they look like confetti—and the water hose dribbles out a slow stream, soaking the bed.

He looks up at me, a broad hand shielding his face. The sun is overhead, beating down on both of us, and his expression is practically a scowl, his eyes scrunched up in defense against the sun.

"Hello, Kittie," he says, still squatting on the ground, not rising to meet me.

"Hey there," I say, twisting a strand of hair around my finger.

Will swipes sweat from his hairline and looks up at me expectantly as if I need to explain my presence. My insides curdle. He's clearly not rushing to invite me in for seconds, but I'm not going to give up so easily.

"I just didn't want to be a stranger, ya know?" I say, planting my feet a little farther apart.

His eyes skim up my legs, causing my pulse to race. He dusts the soil off his hands, cocks his head to one side. A half grin plays on his lips and I can hear my heartbeat drumming in my ears.

"Oh, you mean—" He snorts and shakes his head, dropping his gaze.

Shame ripples over me and I want to evaporate; he's obviously not interested in going another round with me. But seeing the smirk on his face turns my shame into rage. Motherfucker.

"Fuck off, Will."

But he just keeps on sneering.

"And what about Jen?" My voice is raw, full of hurt I don't want him to hear.

"What about her?" He squints at me.

"You're a bastard. At least I don't have feelings for you, but Jen—"

"Let's just say I've moved on." He lifts his hands skyward as if in apology. "It happens."

My fingernails are digging into my palms. I want to smack that smirk off his face with the back of my hand, kick him in the balls, but instead of giving him any more satisfaction, I turn, put my shoulders back, and walk away.

I can feel his eyes on my ass, and I can't help it; I look back to check. Sure enough, he's gaping after me with a look of desire on his face that I know will haunt me.

What a bastard.

I feel sick. The heat coupled with my horror at what just happened causes sweat to sting my armpits and make my shirt stick to my chest. Of course he wasn't interested in being with me again; I'm such a fool. There I was, believing for a second that I still have it—that I could hook a man like Will, *really* hook him—but let's face it: I'm not the catch I used to be. He's a god, fucker that he is.

I look down at my thighs as I walk home. Sure, my quads are toned, thanks to hours on the Peloton, but they could be even more defined, less flabby. I'm an idiot for letting myself fantasize that we could have something ongoing, something more than the onetime, heat-of-the-moment episode we had. I still look good enough for *that*, just not for anything else.

As for Jen, she's in for a world of heartache. I won't tell her, of course, the evil thing he said—obviously she can never know I went over there—but I'm sure as fuck going to find out who he's moved on to.

34.

Cynthia Nichols's Diary

WE'RE GOING AWAY together, Will and I. He asked me earlier this afternoon, after we untangled ourselves from each other in bed and retreated to his library, glasses of wine in hand.

He stood before me, leaning against the bookcase. He tugged down a coffee-table book about architecture in his mother's native country of Georgia. Holding it up, he flipped through glossy pages of photographs of crumbling churches and fortresses.

"I want to take you to Tbilisi," Will said, the word on his tongue sounding like "Belize-y." It's the capital of Georgia, he explained. "It's truly the Old World, and I want to show you the sky, how it's the color of salmon before sunset; how the village people sell roasted corn on the side of the road; how the vodka tastes so smooth, it's like drinking silk."

As he spoke about this ancient land, his accent seemed to grow thicker.

I nodded. It sounded intoxicating to me.

Setting the book on a side table, he took a pull of his wine. "And I think we should go this summer."

"But it *is* summer," I said.

"Exactly." He winked at me.

He strode over to the empty armchair, sank down onto the gold-colored cushion. The sight of him sitting there—long legs stretched out, his eyes shimmering green—tugged at me, and I went and sat in his lap.

"So this is a yes?"

As he combed the hair off my neck with his fingers, I felt my stomach drop at the thought of traveling somewhere with him.

"Yes."

He told me that he's sick of sneaking around and that he wants me to himself.

He wants to take me to Georgia, Italy, Denmark. He wants us to be able to stroll the streets together, fingers laced; to eat at sidewalk cafés and lie side by side on sunbaked beaches (topless!) without the fear of getting found out.

I know it's crazy—really crazy!—but I couldn't say no. Will is the man of and from my dreams, from my vision, literally. The man whose hand is on my wrist leading me through cobblestoned alleyways. The man, I feel, whom I've been waiting for all my life.

WE ARE GOING soon, two weeks from now. On Saturday the tenth. We agreed that we'd tell no one, that I'd leave Gerald and Tyson a note. My stomach lurched as I thought about abandoning them so abruptly like that, but Will is right: if we tell anybody ahead of time, we'll be talked out of it; we'll never go through with it.

"When we will return?" I asked.

He stroked his jawline, looked pensive for a moment.

"Why do you have to plan it? For once in your life, can you not have everything planned out?" His serious look spread into a smile, taunting me.

"Okay. But are we talking days or weeks?"

"Weeks. And we'll see what happens. I will arrange it all and leave it open-ended."

As precipitous as this plan sounded to me, it also thrilled me.

For years I've begged Gerald to take me somewhere, anywhere. Sure, we went to Mexico for our honeymoon like everybody else from Cedartown, but other than weekend trips to Dallas or New Orleans, or a ski trip to Aspen, we've barely left the city limits.

I once went to the local travel agency and collected brochures for cruises. Gerald promised to book us one, but never followed through; he was always too busy with work, he said. But the truth of the matter is this: Gerald is a homebody and prefers the predictable routine of staying in his own domain versus all the unknowns and perils of travel.

So there was no way I was going to pass this up. This is my chance, and I'm going to take it.

"Your husband, your friends, and the neighbors will be shocked at first," Will continued, "but this way, everyone's anger will have a chance to dissipate by the time we return. It's better for all—letting people process our relationship on their own terms."

He roped his arm around my waist, pulling me in closer to his chest. "Because you and I," he said, lips on my ear, "we're only getting started."

35.

Kittie

I'M OBSESSED WITH Will. I can't help it, can't stop my mind from replaying the shame-inducing scene from the day before yesterday at his house.

I had to fake it through the start of dinner last night with Hank—Friday night was our date night—and my cheeks were literally sore from trying to keep a smile plastered on my face.

He picked up on it, though, even if he tried to make light of things. "I'm guessing it's your time of month, huh, sweetie?" He clapped me on the back, almost causing me to choke on my wine.

We were having dinner out on the back patio, chicken piccata with linguine, which I'd prepared in a savage way right before Hank was due home from work, pounding the hell out of the poor breast with a metal mallet, pretending in my mind the meat was Will's face.

"Shut it," I said to Hank. "Why do men have to blame everything on women's periods?"

"You tell me, sister," he said, breaking into a self-satisfied laugh.

I have to hand it to him: he's always had a damn good sense of humor. And after he emptied the rest of the first bottle of wine into my glass, I started to feel a little bit lighter, a little less ashamed.

But when I woke up this morning, there was a hard pit in my stomach, and I haven't been able to stop thinking about Will's rebuke of me.

I can't believe I put myself out there like that, gave that bastard the chance to reject me. And I can't stop wondering about who he's seeing now—if that's indeed what he meant when he said he's moved on.

That's why I'm driving over to his place now, to scope things out.

Harsh noonday light bleeds through the windshield, cooking the tops of my thighs. My hair is pulled into a ponytail; I didn't even have the oomph to shower this morning, and as I pull the visor down, check myself in the mirror, I see how feral I look: eyes wild and blood-shot due to my wine-soaked, restless night of sleep, stray hairs escaping the hair tie, wrinkles spackling my face.

I turn down his street, slowing the car to round the bend. In the distance, I spot his truck in the drive but don't see him in his front yard again, thank goodness. To be on the safe side, I tug down my shades. He doesn't own this fucking street anyway. I could be heading to Jen's (though it's the long way around Azalea Circle) or somebody else's house, and furthermore, *we* owned this block, and the woods around it, before Will came in and invaded everything.

I ease my foot off the gas pedal even more, so that I'm inching past, nearly idling. Will's car sits solo in the drive, and the lights in the library are switched off. I peer through the picture window into the library and try and see beyond into the hallway that leads to his bedroom. Nothing, no other lights appear to be on and the inside of his house is motionless.

What the hell does he do all day? Maybe he's in the backyard tending to a fucking rose garden? Or maybe he's at his new lover's house, whoever she may be. I put a call in to Margaret Anne this morning, League treasurer and gossip patrol, asking for her to put her feelers out. Told her it was Jen who was really asking.

"You think it's Brandi?" she asked, her voice rising in pitch at the end of her question.

"Probably. I don't know, don't really care, actually, but Jen does."

"I'm on it."

I PULL AWAY from Will's and coast down the hill toward the back of the circle, where the forest grows even thicker. On the outer ring of the circle at the base of the hill, there are no home lots, only a thick stand of trees—a tract of land that the home builders left undeveloped. Eden Place's nature preserve. It's here where cars can enter the woods by hopping a curb and following the red-dirt drive that winds through the rest of the forest, which rims the neighborhood and runs behind Will's house.

As I turn the corner, I spy Chloe sitting on the curb in front of the woods, a thin, jagged stream of white smoke rising over her. Cigarette smoke. Her head is turned away from my direction, her blond curls cascading down and forming a curtain around her. I see another pair of legs next to hers, and as the car approaches, Chloe drops the cigarette, stubs it out with her combat boot. She flicks her head in my direction, eyes going wide when she clocks my car. Sitting next to her is Kasey, and my heart melts at the sight of them together, knees practically touching. Tears flood my eyes and I feel almost wistful. I would love it if Chloe would date Kasey. He can be edgy and petulant with Jen, but he's such a good kid—always has been—and he's so much better than the rich little pricks running around town.

I panic and slow the car at first, but then wave and smile and accelerate away from them. I don't want her to think I'm keeping tabs on her, which is exactly what she'll assume.

I round the corner and slow the car so I can turn into Jen's drive. So I can have an alibi for Chloe for being in that part of the neighborhood. Jen is cross-legged in her front flower bed, planting what look to be strawberries, and she's just out of sight from where Kasey and Chloe were.

"Girl," I say to her as I climb from the car, "did you know about Kasey and Chloe?"

Even in her gardening clothes—a faded T and slouchy pants—and with her hair frizzy from the heat, she looks radiant. A natural beauty who doesn't need the aid of makeup like I do. Fuck Will for stringing her along and then casting her aside.

"I did not! What do ya mean?" She grins from ear to ear, stripping a dirt-soaked glove off her hand so she can mop the sweat from her brow.

"I saw them just now, sitting on the curb together by the woods." I nod in that direction.

I decide to not bring up the smoking thing. What the hell do I really care about her smoking anyways? It was in those very woods that my first boyfriend, Jason, taught Jen, Cynthia, and me how to smoke. He was playing Pearl Jam on his jam box and he passed out sticks of Merit Menthol 100s to each of us. Cynthia, predictably, went white as a ghost after she inhaled and then immediately proceeded to vomit.

"Ah! I love it. I thought Kasey was just hiking in the woods."

"Wouldn't that be the best if they got together?" Again, tears prick my eyes. I'm a mess; I'm clearly losing it.

"Well, yes!" Jen's sky-blue eyes sparkle with excitement. "He is totally crushing on her."

I lunge in and hug Jen's neck, feeling sick inside for what lies ahead of her in terms of Will.

"Call me later!" I scurry back to the car and head home.

I'VE BEEN INSIDE for exactly half an hour, waiting for Chloe to reappear. I can't sit still; I've been pacing from room to room, my nerves on edge about Will, my guard already up, anticipating Chloe's arrival.

I'm in the laundry room, standing next to the open dryer—the hot air licking my legs as I fold Hank's boxers—when I hear the front door burst open.

The soles of Chloe's boots clack along the wood floors, and I can hear from their frantic sound that she's going from room to room, searching for me.

I ease out into the hallway, meet her narrowed gaze.

"Mother, were you spying on me?"

Her arms are crossed in front of her chest and her face is balled up into a scowl.

"Of course not." I was spying on Will. "I was heading over to Jen's; I needed to talk to her about something."

Her jaws work her chewing gum; she smells like a mix of mint and tobacco smoke. I don't say anything about the smoking, but I can't help myself. My nerves are shot, so I poke back at her.

"I thought you were headed to Megan's." I cross my own arms in front of my chest, ready for the standoff.

Chloe rolls her eyes and throws her hands up before dramatically slapping the sides of her thighs with them. "Does it matter? I wasn't doing anything wrong." Her voice is just this side of a yell.

"So," I say in a warmer tone, "are you and Kasey seeing each other?"

She chomps her gum faster now, blows a tiny series of bubbles that, when they burst, snap the air between us. "No! We're just . . . hanging out."

Red seeps up from her neck to her face and I can tell she's lying. But I don't push her; I'd be thrilled if they were together. I can't tell her that, though. Then she'd definitely *not* want to be with him.

"Okay, okay," I say, raising my palms toward her as if I'm calling a truce.

"As much as you'd like to, you can't control me, Mother," she hisses at me before stomping to her room and slamming the door.

No, but I can take your car keys back from you, bitch, I think to myself but don't dare say out loud.

36.

Jen

I'M NEARLY FINISHED tucking the last of the strawberry plants into the front bed that rims the house. It's part of my new self-care routine—keeping my hands busy and my mind off of Will. So far, so good.

Kittie just stopped by and gushed about seeing Chloe together with Kasey. I had no idea; I thought Kasey was on a walk alone in the woods—that's what he told me he was going to be doing—but I was delighted to hear he was with Chloe instead.

I didn't mention to Kittie that we'd caught Chloe smoking the other night as she walked past; I didn't bring up, either, that she'd had a nice exchange with Kasey. I don't want to rat her out or get in hot water with Kittie for not telling her sooner about any of it.

Maybe Will's advice to Kasey worked! I can't wait to tell him about this latest development next time I see him, and I feel a surge of giddiness imagining that moment.

That's what I'm practicing right now: affirmations. Instead of wringing my hands, assuming the worst, I'm speaking the most positive outcomes out loud. "The next time I see him, when I talk to Will again, when we kiss again," and so forth. And this is also working. I've also added in a few about my future: "I will be able to provide abundance for me and Kasey; I will be able to be self-sufficient soon." I feel lighter; I'm breathing more deeply; I'm even sleeping better at night.

It feels good to take this breather. I know that we were moving too fast and hot and that I was veering into the dangerous territory that Annie had warned me about: losing myself to the other. I don't want to repeat the mistakes I made with Felix; I don't want to get so swept away with Will that I lose my grounding, forget about myself. I want to come to our relationship whole, and I want it to be a healthy one. And, hopefully, a lasting one.

37.

Cynthia Nichols's Diary

IT'S LATE. I'M out by the pool, catching a breath of fresh air. Gerald and Tyson are both inside—Gerald in his easy chair, remote in hand, watching the Golf Channel, and Tyson is in his room, plugged into his Xbox.

I couldn't stand to stay in the house any longer, so I brewed myself a cup of chamomile and came out here to sit under the glittering stars and listen to the crickets chirp.

I can't believe I've agreed to skip town with Will. I mean, there's no way I can resist him; there's no way I'm *not* going—I want to more than anything in the world.

It's just been sinking in on a deeper level these past few days. I'm not merely heading to Vegas with Kittie and the girls for a weekend.

This is me drawing a line in the sand, leaving my marriage and abandoning my son.

We'll be gone for a few weeks. Which means Tyson will likely start his senior year without his mother around. The thought of it makes me panic, makes me sick to my stomach, so I'm trying to plan ways in which to soften that blow. I'll stock the freezer in the garage with his favorite frozen pizzas; I'll leave him a bundle of prepaid Visa cards that he can use for meals out with Carter. I'll make sure we go clothes shopping together before I leave, and most importantly, I'll spend as much time with him as he'll allow.

As for Gerald, I've been moving around him like a buoy in the water these past few days: whenever he gets close, the motion makes me bob away. And I don't mean for sex—he hasn't even tried for that. I just mean for the small acts of intimacy that we share, like him putting his arm around me on the sofa or leaning in for a hug. I can't help it, but I've all but been flinching whenever he brushes past me.

I'm Will's now, and nothing else feels natural. These next twelve days before I leave Gerald, though, I'll do better. Not to lead him on, but to show him some kindness.

He's going to be devastated, of course, and also shocked. He thinks his quiet, meek wife is the calmest, most contented person in the world. He won't understand, and the thought of his confusion is what pangs me the most. Most devastating to Gerald, though, will be his embarrassment in front of our friends and neighbors. They are all going to roast me, and Will is right: it's best if we're far away when all that goes down.

I haven't even been able to stomach thinking about Jen. She's going to be crushed and humiliated, liable to hate me forever, but again, I can't help it that Will and I are in love.

I have no idea whose side Kittie will take, but she needs me so much in her life as a crutch that I know she'll eventually accept me back into the fold.

Not that I need or want that exactly. I mean, I still intend to be close to her, but I've always followed Kittie's lead with *everything* and I'm sick of it. I've always adopted her interests as my own—partying, hobnobbing with the others, hitting events with her just so she can be on display. I've always been her wing woman.

And it's time I stepped out of her shadow. And also out of the shadow of my marriage to discover who *I* want to be. I'm almost forty, not eighty, and I can have a second chance at life. That's what Will is giving me.

Will and I haven't talked in specifics about what our life will be like when we return, only that we'll be together. I imagine taking up residence in his house. That could actually work well, because I could still be near Tyson. Tyson would actually love Will's house, I think, and I can picture him coming to stay with us in the guest room every other weekend, practicing his flute, dining alfresco with us on the back patio. And if my suspicions are correct about Tyson and Carter, I can imagine Will being a safe harbor for him: somebody who would understand and be open-minded about his sexuality versus the other men in the neighborhood, including Gerald, who would likely shame him.

Tyson, though, will likely be humiliated about me, too, at first. And angry. His mother will be branded as the local whore, but I sincerely hope that one day he'll respect me for this decision. That he will be inspired he has a mother who was strong enough to stay true to herself, to follow her own path, despite what society thinks.

I've also already preemptively wound things down with Dr. Whitaker. I phoned her office this morning to say that I wish to pause my sessions for the time being. But I know I'm never stepping foot back in her office again. I'm so happy now. The truth is that there was never anything wrong with me to begin with. I just needed Will.

38.

Kittie

I'M IN THE drive-through at Starbucks. The coffee I made at home didn't cut it; I still have this throbbing hangover, so I'm headed to the gym next to try and sweat it out.

Even though I canceled Wine Night last night, I still managed to drink a whole bottle of sauvignon blanc by myself. My nerves were shot; I needed it. I haven't heard a thing about Will from any of my sources, and it's driving me crazy. So yesterday afternoon, I texted Cynthia and Jen to let them know it was off. That I wasn't feeling up for it.

I couldn't handle listening to Jen prattle on all night about Will; I just didn't have it in me. And thankfully, Hank took Chloe out for driving lessons and left me alone for a few hours.

"She's mostly going to be driving at night with her friends," he said, "so I'd better get her used to it."

Chloe was all aglow around Hank, but still giving me the cold shoulder because she thinks I spied on her when I saw her together with Kasey. Her stinging words haven't left my brain since she hurled them at me: *As much as you'd like to, you can't control me, Mother.*

When I set the table for us for lunch earlier, she picked up her plate of chicken salad and stomped out of the room to eat alone, slamming the door to her room behind her.

As a peace offering, I asked her the other day if she wanted me to throw a birthday party here by the pool.

"I can hire a DJ and order pizzas, and I promise Dad and I will stay inside. You can invite whoever you like," I said, referring to Kasey but not daring to speak his name out loud again.

Her feet were propped up on the breakfast table and she was shaping her long fingernails with a file, not even bothering to look up at me when she answered.

"Mmmm, no, thanks."

"Okaaaay," I said, trying to keep the bite out of my voice. "What *do* you want to do, then?"

She continued sawing her claws. "Shelley's gonna have a sleepover that weekend, on Saturday night."

Great. My stomach knotted itself into a fist. Shelley's mom is not exactly the type to keep tabs on the girls. She's like an older version of Shelley—wild haired and irreverent. But I couldn't tell Chloe no.

I sucked in a breath. "Sounds good."

So much for a party. Sweet sixteen my ass.

39.

Cynthia Nichols's Diary

I'M DISCOVERING SOMETHING new about Will almost every day. This afternoon, for instance, I learned that he's a perfectionist.

I'd snuck up to his house around two o'clock. We're leaving town in just a little over a week, and even though he's told me that he needs time to tie up loose ends with work before we go and that we might be seeing less of each other until then, I can't keep my hands off of him.

So after Tyson hopped in his car and drove over to Carter's, where he is practically living these days, I grabbed a bottle of wine, threw on a sundress, and drove over to Will's for a quickie.

He was just as hungry for me as I was for him. I barely made it through the front door before his hands were on my thighs, snaking up to my hips. After a few minutes of making out in the entryway, we tumbled into the kitchen so he could uncork the bottle.

I went to use the bathroom while he poured, and when I was finished, I stepped into the hallway. He was there waiting for me, pressing me against the wall, lips tracing my neck.

"Let's have a sip first, shall we?" he asked, unlatching himself
from me.

Instead of going into the library, I sank to the floor to admire his
ruby-colored Persian rug. The top of it felt like velvet and the intricate
pattern was different from all the other ones I'd seen before.

"This is absolutely luxurious, Will. I love Persians."

"I'm delighted you like it. It's actually Tibetan. Family heirloom.
It was my mother's. And her mother's before that."

I stretched my body along the length of it as if I were going into
cat pose in yoga. But with the intention of showing off my body in
front of Will and also because I wanted to feel its buttery-soft texture
against my skin. Running my fingers along a prism-shaped design, I
made the fibers stand up the same way that horsehair does when you
comb it in the opposite direction of its natural course. My hand hit
upon a pit underneath the rug, followed by a jagged lump.

I crawled to the edge of the rug and was starting to roll it back to
inspect further when Will raised his voice.

"Don't do that! Leave it alone!"

I immediately dropped my hand, feeling chided as his tone lashed
over me. It was so unlike him to snap like that. Before I could turn
and face him, he was behind me, arms roping around my stomach,
hot breath in my ear.

"I'm so sorry; I'm just embarrassed. Didn't mean to react like that.
I like things to be"—he paused, nibbling on my ear—"perfect. Like
you. And I want everything to be perfect *for* you."

My body went slack against his and I smiled at the realization that
we'd had our first spat. If you could even call it that.

"The pavers are chipped under there and I haven't done a thing
about it. It's one of the things I want to attend to before we leave."

He undid his pants, then peeled my panties off—a white lace thong he'd recently bought for me—and slid his hands down to my wrists, pinning me in place, lifting up my dress and taking me right there on the rug.

I STAYED FOR another hour or so after that. We sipped our wine in his bedroom as Will trotted out gift after gift for me. Ever since he'd invited me to go to Europe with him, he's been buying me outfits for the trip so that I don't have to pack a stitch, raise any suspicion before we take off. He even bought me luggage—a supple tan leather set from Saks—which is resting at the base of his closet, ready to be packed with my new things.

Before I left, he clasped his hands to my cheeks. "Sorry about earlier. Just feeling a lot of pressure to get things wrapped up. But soon we'll be gone, together, dipping our toes in the warm Adriatic Sea."

40.

Kittie

IT'S SIX O'CLOCK and I'm out back, churning in a figure-eight pattern on the patio. Cynthia and Jen are due here any minute for Wine Night. I have a few bottles of Pinot Grigio—the expensive shit—resting on a bed of ice.

I'm clutching a tall, slender shot glass filled with sipping tequila, blue agave—also the expensive shit—because wine's not gonna cut it for me tonight.

Margaret Anne called me an hour ago; I'm still shaking from what she told me.

"So . . . get this. Allie spotted Will today." Margaret Anne's voice buzzed with excitement, which set me on edge. "With Brandi."

I felt like someone had taken a two-by-four and knocked the wind out of me. Margaret Anne, our close friend, is treasurer of the Junior League and also treasurer of all local gossip. I knew this wasn't some mistake.

"Where?" My own voice rose in pitch and I had to remind myself to play it cool, to not blow my cover.

"Allie was leaving the spa, just after noon, and when she was getting into her car, she saw them drive past in Brandi's convertible. The top was down and Will was in the passenger seat. His arm angled toward Brandi as if his hand was resting on her thigh."

I know Brandi's car—a convertible red Mercedes with tacky personalized plates that read "BRANDIREALS" for real estate. So that's who he's moved on to. Fucking tramp. I knew she'd get her mitts on him eventually. The thought of them together made my stomach ache.

Tears flooded my eyes and I saw red; I wanted to tear over to Will's house just then, rip off his head, but decided I'm not going to give him any more satisfaction.

I guess he's fucking his way through town now. And I'm going to have to find a nice way to break it to Jen.

I slam the remaining finger of tequila in my glass and wait for the doorbell to chime.

41.

I'M IN MY little Accord, driving over to Kittie's house for Wine Night. Despite the mugginess, I lower my window and let the cabin suck in the boggy night air.

I missed this the most about East Texas when I moved to Austin. The climate down there is drier, more arid, downright Saharan even, but the air up here is heavy and humid and can envelop you wholly so that you feel as though you're floating in a warm, briny sea.

I suck in a deep breath, exhale. The tan leather interior of the Accord is webbed with little rivers of cracks and the AC whines through the grates, as if it's on the brink of sputtering out. I tap the small, feathery dream catcher hanging from my rearview and send up a small wish that with my new, hopeful stream of income, I'll be able to replace this car soon with another, newer one.

This morning, I finally dragged myself over to Yoga Blossom, the only yoga studio in town. I sat in on a hot yoga class and was actually impressed with the instructor (who is also the owner). It was all about the stretches and the poses, and none of this dropping of unwanted essential oil on your third-eye chakra as class winds down.

After the room emptied out, I lingered while she tidied up, toweling off the floor and stacking foam support blocks into a wide-rimmed basket.

"You're a new face; welcome," she said. "But clearly, not new to vinyasa."

"Thank you. I'm Jen."

I already knew her name—Susan—from both the brochure and from her introduction in the beginning of class. I liked her immediately. I pegged her as being in her early fifties. She exuded a calm confidence I'd like to someday attain.

Susan offered me a hot cup of green tea and we sat in the light-filled foyer and chatted. I found myself opening up to her, telling her all about Felix, the divorce, Kasey, and my desire to forge a new career path as a yoga instructor.

"I'd like for you to sit in on some more classes first, if you're open to it. Get a real feel for my practice, but I think there is a place for you here. Believe me, I've had a hard time recruiting dedicated instructors in this town."

We talked specifics—how much it would cost for me to get certified, when I could potentially start training (next week if all goes well)—and I was so giddy when I left, I practically skipped down the sidewalk back to my car.

It's not Rockefeller money, but the prospect of having my own income—especially after all these years of being dependent on Felix—has filled me with glee and I can't wait to share the news with Kittie and Cynthia.

I even got all gussied up for Kittie's tonight—I shaved my legs, spritzed on perfume, and applied makeup, though it's just me and the girls.

I'm also giddy because when I see Will again ("I will see Will soon, I will see Will soon," my mantra of the day on repeat in my brain), I'll have something positive about myself to share with him.

The call-and-response song of crickets fills the car as I slow to make the final turn onto Kittie's cove. Cynthia, in a pair of tiny shorts with a flowing blouse, is drifting up the sidewalk. I call out to her.

"Hey, woman!"

She spins around and flashes me a grin, waits for me on the side of the curb.

I park and walk over to her. She looks more radiant than I've ever seen her, teeth practically glowing against her dark-red-colored lips. Her long legs tanned and toned, her glossy chestnut-brown hair as smooth as glass, cascading in a sheet over one shoulder. But more than her appearance, it's the way she's carrying herself with a seemingly newfound verve and confidence.

"Look at *you*! You look positively gorgeous!" I gush.

"Well, thank you! And you, too!"

I'm about to say more but she starts walking at a fast clip, as if she can't get to Kittie's front door fast enough. Guess she's ready for a glass of wine.

She presses the doorbell and Kittie swings it open, pulling us each into a hug. Kittie clutches onto me for longer than what seems normal, and I swear I hear her voice crack when she tells us she has news to share. I'm certain it's going to be another long rendition of her latest blowout with Chloe, so when we settle around the glass-topped table and Kittie fills our wineglasses, I take the opportunity to spill my news first.

Kittie's eyes are bloodshot, as though she's been either crying or drinking too much—probably some of both—and when she hears about my prospects of becoming a yoga instructor in training, tears wobble in her eyes.

"Sorry, honey. I'm just hormonal tonight. And your news, well, it makes me *so* damn happy."

She leans across the table and snaps me into another long, awkward hug. Sister needs to get her period, I think to myself, but I'm touched that she's so happy for me.

"Congratulations!" Cynthia says, raising her glass to mine. "That's so fabulous! I can't wait to take one of your classes!"

Kittie tilts her shot glass toward ours and we toast. The tart, chilled wine makes my mouth pucker.

"I might even have to drag my ass to the yoga studio," Kittie says.

"So, what's your big news, lady?" Cynthia asks Kittie, arching her doll-perfect eyebrows.

A warm gust of wind sweeps over the yard, causing almond-shaped leaves from the enormous oak to pirouette into the pool.

Kittie grabs the tequila, dumps another shot into her glass. She stands and paces in front of us for a second before taking a sip, then exhales so fully, it seems as though she's in labor.

"So get this." Her piercing green eyes skitter back and forth between me and Cynthia. "Margaret Anne called about an hour before you guys got here."

The mention of Margaret Anne's name makes my stomach drop. I know Kittie is about to deliver a doozy about Will, about whom he might be seeing.

Kittie tucks a golden lock of hair behind her diamond-studded earlobe and drains the rest of her glass.

"Aaaand?" I ask, my voice splintering.

Cynthia swirls the wine around in her glass, uncrosses and crosses her legs as if she's as antsy as I am to hear the answer.

"So . . . she says that Allie saw Will together with Brandi."

"What do you mean, together?" Cynthia's voice rises as she asks this; she's clearly as outraged on my behalf as I am.

"Well, she was out earlier today, leaving the spa, and she saw them drive past in Brandi's vomitous convertible."

"And what else? Is that it? Is that all?" I ask.

Kittie lowers her gaze before delivering the rest. "Allie was pretty sure that Will's arm was on Brandi's side of the car. As if"—she pauses, shaking her head like she's swallowed something bitter—"his hand was on her knee. Like, they looked *together*."

Bile rises in the back of my own throat and my vision swims. My hands are shaky, so I set my glass down, clutch at my stomach. Kittie comes around the table, slings an arm over my shoulder.

"I'm so sorry, honey. I truly am. And I did *not* want to deliver this wretched news on top of your good news. But I had to tell you. What a giant fucking asshole he is."

I let her hot arm rest on me for a second before peeling it off and inching away. I need space, I need to process this—the horrible, unwelcome image of Will with Brandi. Jesus fucking Christ. Is *that* why he hasn't gone all the way with me? Because he's been banging her instead? I feel queasy, like my stomach is going to empty its contents.

As if she can sense this, Kittie scurries inside and returns with a tumbler filled with ice water. I take a small sip and try to breathe. And then I can't help it; tears form in my eyes and I'm sobbing, my spine hitting the back of the patio chair with each wave.

What a goddamn fool I've been, thinking that someone like Will would ever really be into me. That what we had was real. Images of *us* together fill my mind—our first kiss in his sunlit hallway, which I had initiated; me pulling his pants down in my garden, placing my mouth on him. Will consistently stopping short of consummating with me: *I'm not ready just yet. I just want to take this slow.*

And then the last time I saw him, he all but guarded his doorway, saying, *I'm tied up at the moment.* Probably because Brandi was inside with him.

"God, I'm such an idiot. I can't believe I thought he was actually holding out for me. What is wrong with me?"

"No, *he's* the idiot," Kittie says. "And a master manipulator. Any of us would have thought the same."

I see him standing on my doorstep, his broad hand clutching the bouquet he had handpicked for me. I feel his hands moving up my skirt, probing. He's standing shoulder to shoulder with Kasey, talking shop about the Land Cruiser. It all really *did* feel so real, like the beginning of something solid.

My mind bolts from anger and sadness to denial.

"Could there be some mistake? Maybe it wasn't him? Or maybe there's some perfectly good explanation as to why they were together? I mean, I *know* Will, and she's not his fucking type at all."

"Honey," Kittie says, "Brandi is every man's type."

I hear a squeak escape from Cynthia and turn to look at her. Her olive-toned skin has now turned a shade paler, and she looks as nauseated as I am. She parts her crimson lips to speak, then closes them tight. Studies the backs of her delicate hands, then folds them in her lap.

"Fucking slut." The words escape Cynthia's normally prim mouth with a hiss. "Sorry, Jen. I'm just *so* fucking sick for you."

"He's a bastard, Jen," Kittie says. "Plain and simple. So *fuck* him. And forget him. Easier said than done, I know."

I know Kittie's trying to make me feel better, but her slamming Will isn't helping. I'm still stubbornly clinging to the hope that this is all some big mistake. That Allie didn't see what she thought she saw, or that even if they were together, there's a good reason, other than him screwing her.

"Please, Kittie. I know this is salacious, and he probably is banging Brandi, but I'd like to hold off on any judgment until I can talk to Will myself."

Even as the words leave my lips, though, I can hear how lame they sound, how lame *I* sound. But I'm feeling oddly protective of Will all of a sudden, protective of a lingering idea of "us."

Kittie snorts, tosses back another shot of tequila.

I glance over at Cynthia, who's rubbing minute circles on her temples, her eyes shut. After a few seconds, she stands.

"I can feel another migraine coming on, damn it." She squints at me and her chocolate-brown eyes look glassy, almost as if she's on the verge of tears.

"Oh, for fuck's sake, really?" Kittie barks.

"Yes. I hate to leave you like this, Jen. I really do, but when these come on, all I can do is go to my room and lie down with the lights off. I guess I need to go to the neurologist or something."

"Whatever, Granny. We'll finish up here." Kittie lifts a dripping bottle of Pinot Grigio from the wine trough and uncorks it, filling my glass so full that it almost capsizes.

I crane my neck down to it and take a sip from it without lifting it off the table so it won't spill, like a dog lapping water from a bowl.

Fuck it, I'm getting bombed tonight. Kasey's at Mom and Dad's, and if I have to, I'll crash in Kittie's guest room. I need to process everything, but I also need to be numb right now, and Kittie's the perfect person to do that with.

"No worries, Cynthia. You know I understand. Hope you feel better," I offer.

Cynthia slips out the side gate, vanishing back toward her home.

"What a goddamn pussy she is," Kittie slurs. "Shot?"

"Please."

The tequila sears the back of my throat, but I welcome the sting, the pain.

"I honestly can't believe he'd stoop *so* low," Kittie says, starting back up again about Will. "I mean, what the fuck? Brandi? She's so low-rent. I'm really sorry."

"I still want to talk to him first, Kittie," I say sternly.

"Be my guest. But he's *such* a grade A prick."

I study Kittie's face. Her cheeks are flushed, likely from the booze, and her breath reeks of tequila. Annoyance bubbles up in my chest and I find that I want to strangle her for bad-mouthing Will. I mean, I want to strangle him, too, but *I* want to be the one to put him down.

And listening to her now tells me that she's probably always been put off by him; that she might have been rooting for me, for us, but that she's never really cared for Will.

"Let's assume that nothing is going on with them," I say, putting my hands up to preemptively silence her. "What do you have against Will? What do you mean, he's such a grade A prick?"

Kittie stares at me like I've just slapped her. She sucks in a breath and gazes into the dark sky behind me. She twists the top off the tequila, which is in a white porcelain bottle—some pricey brand—and splashes us each another shot.

"Drink," she orders.

Lifting the shot glass to my lips, I take another scorching sip. Globe lights are strung between the branches of the chubby oaks, casting a soft orange glow across Kittie's lushly landscaped backyard, and the alcohol is starting to work its magic: the lights look fuzzy and there's a soft halo around each one.

"I think he's a goddamn snob," she says, her voice thick with tequila and her words all stretched out. "Issss what I mean." She tosses her hands up in the air before slapping them down on her thighs.

I drain the rest of my shot, pull my wineglass to me, and start sipping that as well before it loses its chill.

"Okaaay," I say, my own drawl becoming more pronounced with the liquor. "What do you mean?"

"Oh, I don't know. How about his poetry lessons or whatever the hell he was doing with you? I mean, reciting poetry? What a pretentious douche."

And then it hits me: Kittie is *jealous* of what I have with Will. Or what I *had* with Will.

"But of course, *you* liked it; you would," she continues.

"The fuck is that supposed to mean?"

Kittie rolls her eyes, flips her hair over her shoulder. "Oh, nothing."

"No, let's hear it."

A long, exasperated sigh streams from her lungs.

"Ever since you left Cedartown and moved down to Austin, you've thought you were better than me and Cynthia. More cultured."

"I—"

"Shut it; don't deny it. I don't really care. It's true. You *are* more worldly and broad-minded than us. All's I was saying is that you and Will could've been a perfect match in that regard. But Brandi—" She shakes her head again in clear distaste. "Look, we all feel sorry for you about Felix. But it's obvious Will isn't a replacement; he's just another asshole, *just* like fucking Felix. He's no different."

My head is swirling. Kittie has just called me out on thinking I'm better than her and Cynthia. I don't, do I? I mean, maybe I do, but damn, has it been blatant? In many ways, I'd kill to have what she has: a huge gorgeous home, a husband who worships her, and zero money problems. But now I want to throttle her for throwing Felix in my face.

And also, the image of her standing on Will's front lawn, hip cocked to one side, flirting, floods back. She's pissed that I could hook him but she couldn't. And clearly pissed that maybe Brandi has hooked him as well.

"You're just jealous." The words float out of my mouth before I can stop them.

"Excuse me?" She crosses her arms in front of her chest, skewers me with her gaze.

"You're so transparent. I can't believe it's taken me this long to figure out. You're jealous that Will came on to me and not you."

Kittie narrows her eyes at me and her whole face darkens. And just when I think she's going to deny it and tell me that I'm wrong, the corner of her mouth lifts into a small grin.

It takes a second for it to hit me, for the truth to slap me in the face, and when it does, it's as if red-hot lava is filling every pore of my body. I'm so furious and so disgusted with Kittie that I want to turn her glass-top table over and shatter it.

"You have *got* to be fucking kidding me."

Kittie still wears the smirk; I want to slap it off her face.

"Yeah, I fucked him. Come on, it didn't seem like you guys were ever gonna get past second base. And also, obviously, I did you a favor. Like I said: grade A prick."

I feel like I did when I was eight years old in the surf of the Gulf of Mexico with my parents. My boogie board slipped out from underneath me, got sucked away by the tide, and then came crashing back into my chest. I feel like Kittie has just knocked the breath out of me.

I'm shocked she would do this to me. But also not shocked. Of course she would. It's no different from that shit she pulled in high school with my crush Craig. It's always been about her and her fucking ego above everyone else.

"Why?" My voice sounds feral and ragged when it comes out of me. "Why would you do this to me? Especially when you know all I've been through with Felix."

Kittie flinches back an inch as if I've just swung a punch, and I realize that I'm practically shouting. "You threw yourself at him, didn't you? You weren't over there that day at his house on my behalf; you were there for yourself. You *always* had to have every man. You are such an enormously selfish bitch!"

My words ring out over the lawn and I'm positive the neighbors can hear, but I don't care. In fact, I hope they do. I only wish Chloe and Hank were home to hear all about it as well.

"Jen, shhhh, calm the fuck down." Kittie tries to stand but her feet falter and she has to lean against the chair to catch herself.

She's drunker than I thought, not that that excuses anything.

"How many times?"

"What?" Kittie's bloodshot eyes are filled with genuine confusion.

"How many times did you fuck Will?" I pitch my voice even louder.

She drops her gaze, twists her hands in her lap. "Just once, swear." She looks up at me almost sheepishly.

"Then he was through with you, right? He'd gotten all he needed or wanted from you."

A small ashamed nod from Kittie. Even though I'm seething mad, I almost feel a twinge of guilt with my newfound cruelty toward her. I can picture it: Kittie flinging herself at Will with no remorse or concern for my feelings. And all the while pretending she was helping me.

I'm such a fool. For trusting Will. For trusting Kittie. I twist the knife in deeper.

"That's why you're acting like a jilted lover, right? Your eyes are puffy from crying about him earlier when Margaret Anne called. First, you were jealous of me—of what I had with Will, which is *way* more than you could ever dream of having with him—and now you're jealous of Brandi. Hell, you're even jealous of your own daughter."

I'm standing over her now, shaking with rage, my stomach beginning to turn sick from all the adrenaline zipping through me. Kittie wilts in her chair, eyes trained on her lap. That last blow I dealt about Chloe has flattened her.

"You disgust me," I say as I turn from her and walk toward the gate. "Don't ever call me again. Lose my number."

42.

Cynthia Nichols's Diary

IT'S LATE, NEARLY eleven o'clock. But Gerald didn't suspect anything when I came home—I often stay late at Kittie's on Wine Night, sometimes even until midnight.

He was sprawled in his easy chair in the den, dozing off to the Golf Channel, when I stepped through the front door. I passed by him, pecking him on the cheek before announcing I was going to take a shower to wash the sticky evening heat off of me.

It wasn't the sweat from sitting out by Kittie's pool; it was Will's sweat from our first make-up sex. I guess this was our second spat; well, actually, it was more than that.

I couldn't escape Kittie's yard fast enough when she told me what Allie had seen. I did my best to hold it together in front of Jen and Kittie, but when I thought of Will riding in Brandi's car with his hand on her knee, it was as if the patio tilted and spun. My insides clenched into a hard lump and I wanted to be sick.

I had walked over to Kittie's, so my car was at home, parked in the garage, and I couldn't risk sneaking into the house for the keys and driving to Will's, so I walked the mile and a half to his house, and by the time I arrived on his doorstep, I was panting and doused in perspiration.

I banged on the door as hard as I could, releasing my rage with each blow of my fist, until Will opened it, alarm registering in his eyes.

He was immaculately dressed as always in a button-down with slacks. His hair was slicked to one side, as if he'd just showered, and his mouth hung open at the sight of me.

"Is everything okay?" He drew me into him, shutting the door behind us.

I stood there, shaking against his chest, while a small cry snuck out of my mouth.

"Honey," he said, his voice warm and sensuous in my ear, "what's wrong?"

I pulled away from him, then stared down at my feet.

"What in the hell were you doing with that tramp?" I practically yelled the question at him, causing him to take a step back.

"Whatever are you talking about?" His eyes searched mine, and I wanted to strike my hand across his face for playing dumb.

"Don't fucking lie to me, Will."

"I would never lie to you, but I don't know what you're talking about." His own voice was rising in frustration and his face was a mask of confusion.

"Brandi. Brandi Stephens. The local-town-whore Realtor."

He exhaled sharply, blowing his bangs toward the ceiling. A small grin crept across his face and he reached out and placed his hands on my arms. I flinched them off.

"Now, *that* I can explain. But I'm sad you found out."

My vision started to go hazy again. So it *was* true about him and Brandi?

"What are you saying right now? That's it's true?"

"I'm saying that I wanted it to be a surprise. I met with Brandi about the house. But I wanted to surprise you."

"Will, I don't understand—"

"I made arrangements with Brandi to put the house on the market in the event we decide to stay over there. And it was easier to set up the paperwork in person. Not that we *will* stay; I just wanted to cover all bases and eventualities. But don't worry. I also had Brandi sign a nondisclosure agreement so she can't blab about it."

He sighed. "Honestly, it's one of the reasons I've been under so much stress lately. And I wanted to wait to tell you once we got to Europe."

The hard lump in my stomach softened and a warm pinprick stabbed my chest. The man of my dreams stood before me and I couldn't believe I'd doubted him. But then the vision of his arm slung over on Brandi's side of the car came roaring back. And Kittie's voice. *They looked together.*

"My friend said she saw you in Brandi's convertible. And that it looked like your hand was on her knee."

Will scoffed, rubbed his chin, and shook his head.

"Do you honestly believe that? I don't know who your friend is, but based on the rest of the women I've observed in this town, is it possible she could be embellishing things? Trying to stir stuff up?"

Yes, Kittie, Margaret Anne, *and* Allie could indeed be trying to stir the gossip pot.

Will closed the gap between us, leveled his sea-green gaze onto mine. "You know you're the only one for me, Cynthia. Please, we are this close," he said, pinching his fingers together, "to being away together, to me having you all to myself."

He grazed my cheek with the back of his hand, put his lips on mine. After a few seconds, I relented and allowed him to kiss me. His hands fumbled through my hair, trailing down my shoulders to the buttons on my shirt, which he undid in a fury.

Next my shorts, then my lingerie, which he flung in a wad across the hallway. He undid his own pants and slid his hands to my ass, lifting me and carrying me to his bedroom.

We passed through the library, and as we did, I noticed his desk was more disheveled than usual, with piles of papers on every surface. My eye caught sight of a listing agreement on the corner of his desk, presumably between him and Brandi.

When we got to his bedroom, I glimpsed both sets of our luggage at the foot of his bed, unzipped, as if he had been in the midst of packing when I had interrupted him by banging on the door. A blush-pink pair of linen slacks peeked out of the top of mine, like the tip of a cat's tongue, and in that instant, I chose to believe him and to believe in us.

I know in my heart of hearts that even though Brandi might attract most men, her kind would never appeal to Will. And the evidence of Will's devotion was all around me—him readying everything for us, down to buying me clothes, selecting my outfits, and packing for me; him setting things up legally with the house on the crazy off chance that we *don't* come back, at least not right away.

He took me right there on the edge of his bed, his eyes dancing over me with sweet anguish, the magical words leaving his mouth between each thrust: I. Love. You. I. Love. You.

Over and over again until we were both panting and murmuring each other's names.

"Just four more days," he said to me as I lay next to him, our fingers intertwined. "Give me these last few days to get everything sorted. I want—no, I *need*—to make sure everything is perfect."

I had learned recently that perfection was indeed important to Will, and I felt bad for the pressure he was under when all I had to do was slip away from my life without lifting a finger.

"I'll leave you alone, I promise." I felt myself grin at him as I dragged my finger along his bare chest.

"It'll be like the old superstition about the bride and groom not seeing each other before the wedding." He grinned back at me. "We just have to make it till Saturday morning. See you at six a.m. sharp?" He cocked an eyebrow. "Can we make it that long?"

"Of course we can. I'll see you then," I purred.

I covered his mouth with mine and we made out for another teasing half hour before I had him drive me home in his truck, letting me out half a block away from my house as if I were a teenager again sneaking around.

43.

Kittie

I FUCKED UP big-time last night with Jen. I took it too far. I can't believe I told her I slept with Will.

The tequila is partly to blame, for sure, but also, once I started, I found I couldn't stop. I wanted someone else to feel as wretched as I did about Brandi, and then I simply got carried away.

I totally blew it. I know I'll never forget the pained look of shock and hurt on her face when the truth hit her.

After she stormed out, I stayed up with the tequila, wading through nearly half the bottle until I couldn't feel anymore.

I'm a loser, just like she accused me of being. Everything she said punctured my gut, because it is true, all of it: my jealousy of her and Will, my jealousy of Chloe, my grasping at what I once was. I'm a fool.

I've lost Jen, and now I might lose Hank, too.

I've called her a dozen times today, sent her a pile of texts, but everything is going unanswered, ignored. I'm worried I'll never talk to her again, of course, but selfishly, I'm also worried that she'll tell Cynthia or Hank.

44.

IT'S MORNING, JUST past nine. I'm out on the back patio, forcing my way through a yoga flow so I can be prepared for Saturday, the day I return to the studio. I want to shine for Susan: more than ever, I need this gig. I need something to buoy me after Monday night's blow.

I drove home drunk from Kittie's that night, not caring about anything other than getting the hell out of there, getting the fuck away from her.

I never want to see her tanned face again, never want to hear her coarse laugh. I meant every hurtful thing I said to her—especially the part about her being an enormously selfish bitch—and even though I'm not exactly surprised she fucked Will, I'm still shocked she would do that to me.

I can't believe that after everything I've been through, and her having a ringside seat to my life bottoming out, she would pull this shit. We are so over.

What makes me even more ill than Kittie betraying me, though, is the undeniable fact that Will did, too. That what I thought we had was a sham all along.

He fucked Kittie, and he probably fucked Brandi as well, and I can't help but fixate on the fact that he *always* stopped short of having sex with me. Why *not* me? Are they really that much more appealing than I am? Really that much more irresistible? Or was I too needy for him? God, I'm a giant moron. I can't believe I was delusional enough to believe that he wanted something special with me, and that's why he was holding out.

I spent most of yesterday morning in bed, cotton mouthed from my hangover and feeling sorry for myself. I didn't budge until Kasey appeared in my doorway at ten, having been dropped off by my mom, who thankfully didn't come inside.

"Umm, you okay, Mom?" His brow was knitted together in concern.

I never sleep in like that. But there was no way I was prepared to tell him that Will and I were through. Thinking of that eventual conversation fills me with dread. "Hey, guess what, kiddo. Your dad cheated on me and now Will has, too, except Will and I weren't even a real couple."

"I'm fine, just tossed and turned last night," I lied. My stomach curdled with shame as I stared up at his worried, oblivious face.

After I showered yesterday and fed Kasey a gourmet lunch of frozen burritos and salad, I debated on going over to Will's and pounding down his door. Demanding an explanation, an apology. But I honestly couldn't muster the energy to follow through. What would I say to him? "Hey, I'm just stopping by because you fucked my best friend and probably Brandi, so why not me? Was I not good enough? How dare you, Will?"

No, I never want to see him again, either. I cannot believe he lives around the corner.

I feel stuck, trapped, moored in this neighborhood with two people I despise. Maybe after I get my certification, just maybe, Kasey and I can eventually return to Austin. God knows there's a plethora of yoga studios down there. Surely I won't have to stay in Eden Place for the rest of my life.

I told Kittie to lose my number, but she has decidedly *not* lost it. My cell's been dinging and chiming with calls and texts from her nonstop since Monday, a ticker tape of her bullshit.

> Jen, you have to let me back in. Let me explain. I'm
> so sorry.
>
> Please just pick up the phone. I feel terrible. I know
> I'm the worst person in the world and you never
> want to have anything to do with me but I'm
> begging for your forgiveness.
>
> Jen, please. Please call.

She can fuck right off.

I did, however, text Cynthia. I really want to talk to someone about this. Surely she doesn't know about Kittie and Will; she seemed downright horrified last night about Brandi, dashed for me. She's a true friend, at least. She's got my back. I hammered out a quick Call me, I need to talk message and am waiting for her reply.

45.

Cynthia Nichols's Diary

I CAN'T BELIEVE we're leaving tomorrow. That in less than twenty-four hours, Will and I will be sitting elbow to elbow, together in first class, floating over the Atlantic. Europe! I'm finally going to go to Europe.

I also can't believe I'm saying goodbye. To Tyson, to Gerald. Of course, we'll return in a couple of weeks. I mean, I'm touched that Will has planned for all contingencies, including one in which we remain overseas, but I couldn't bear to be away from Tyson at this stage in his life, with him entering his final year of high school. I won't tell Will this, of course, but no way I'll stay over there long term.

I nearly blew it this morning when he was headed out the front door with his flute case for band camp. I leaned in to hug him and then held on for far too long, even though I'll see him one last time tonight when he gets home from Carter's.

He pulled away from me, his face screwed into a puzzled expression. "Um, later, Mom," he said before skipping down the steps outside toward his gray Nissan, his sandy brown locks flopping as he moved. My heart cinched at the sight of him, always awkward-looking in his too-loose pants and glasses, a nerd since the day he was born.

How would he take the news of my leaving? Would it crush him? Or would he be relieved, actually, to have me out of his hair for a few weeks? I decided I had to believe in the latter version in order to follow through with it.

And Gerald. I honestly haven't allowed myself to fully imagine the blow Gerald will feel when he finds my note. The slump of his shoulders, the battered look of defeat on his lined face. I can't. I wouldn't be able to breathe or really go through with it if I focused on that for more than a second.

So today I kept myself busy, flitting about town on last-minute errands: to pick up more frozen pizzas for the garage freezer for Tyson, frozen steaks for Gerald, cash from the ATM. I've tucked my passport into my bag. And last, I sat down to write this difficult note.

My dear Gerald,

Please know, above all else, that this had nothing to do with you. You are one of the most wonderful men I have ever met and I will always be grateful you were my husband.

But here it is: I've fallen in love with someone else. Will Harding, the new person in town. This was nothing I chose; it just happened. You must believe me.

And this hasn't been going on for very long, I promise. But because I know Will is the person I'm supposed to be with, we've left town together for a few weeks. We're going to Europe, and I will call Tyson as soon as we land. I can imagine neither one of you will want to hear from me, but I'm hoping, over time, you'll both understand.

Cynthia

I know it's not perfect, but after tearing off sheet after sheet of stationery and composing several different versions, this is the one I settled on.

The note is tucked beneath my blanket on the chaise longue in my study for now, but when Gerald and Tyson are asleep for the night, I'll leave it on the kitchen table before I slip out at dawn to head to Will's.

I'm not telling Kittie or Jen, of course; they'll just have to find out when Gerald breaks the news to them. Jen texted me after Wine Night, asking me to call her, but I haven't and I'm not going to. I feel badly about it—my part in crushing her—but I don't want to listen to her dither on about Brandi, whom I've tried to force far from my mind.

So far, I've held true to my promise to Will: I've left him alone these past three days, as excruciating as it's been. Anytime I get the urge to pound the pavement to his doorstep, I check myself and envision us nestled together under downy hotel sheets, a sea breeze gusting through the open window, bathing us in warmth. Without a care in the world.

46.

Jen

IT'S CLOUDY THIS morning but already piping hot, the cotton-ball layer of clouds acting as a steam press against the heat.

I've been up since six, practicing yoga flows on the patio, trying to focus on my appointment with Susan this morning at Yoga Blossom. This is the first day since I found out about Kittie and Will that I haven't woken up and stayed in bed too long, a feeling of depression, sticky as glue, pinning me in place.

I feel a flicker of excitement about chatting with Susan again, about getting on with my own damn life. The only interruption has been another assault of texts from Kittie, all of which I swipe to clear and ignore.

I've just showered and am sitting on the patio, letting my hair air-dry, the clean herbal smell of my shampoo competing with the charcoal scent of an impending rainstorm, when my cell dings again.

Sigh. Another text. I reach for the phone, and before I can swipe to clear it, I see Cynthia's name in the text.

She never returned my text; I just assumed that Kittie had gotten to her first. That would be a typical Kittie move, trying to shore up sympathy from Cynthia, twisting the version of events around so that somehow she'd be the victim.

Jen. Call me. This is not about me. It's about Cynthia.

Clasping the phone, I step inside the kitchen to refill my coffee. Hmmm, Kittie's just trying to bait me at this point. I can hear her voice, low and concerned. "Cynthia's migraine has gotten worse. She's at the doctor's office this morning. Just thought you should know."

I clear the text, drop my cell into my bag. I'm not about to let Kittie fuck this day up, too. I top off my coffee and settle behind my laptop until it's time to leave for the studio.

I'm halfway through an op-ed in the *New York Times* about the joys of solo parenting (as if—give me a break) when I hear knocking on my front door, a frantic, staccato sound.

My first thought is of Will, and goose bumps dot my arms. Could it be? I creep toward the door, peer through the side window.

It's Kittie. My shoulders slump and I feel a fire-poker prick in my chest. I'm *so* not opening the door. She knocks again, this time so loudly, I flinch.

"Jen," she practically shouts, "I know you're on the other side of the door. I can see your shadow."

I step to the right, trying to make my shadow disappear.

"I can't apologize any more than I already have. But that's not why I'm here. I told you, it's about Cynthia."

"And what about her?" I shout back through the door, gearing up to tell Kittie to get lost.

"She's"—her voice warbles—"gone."

I hold my breath for a second, hear my heartbeat dong in my chest. Gone? As in she's dead? I wrench open the door. Kittie stands before me, looking diminutive for a change, her blond hair flattened by a canvas visor, her forearms wrapped around her stomach.

"Is she—?" I ask.

Kittie's cat-green eyes meet mine. Her mascara is matted in the creases of her crow's-feet as if she's been crying. She pushes past me into the house.

"No, she's not dead. Sorry. I didn't mean to scare you."

She's moving through the kitchen now, opening up the cabinets to drag out two tumblers. "Got anything to drink?"

The nerve. I can't believe she's asking me to serve her anything. As if she clocks my thoughts, she adds, "Believe me, you need a drink to hear this."

I fix her with a glare as I pluck open the fridge, clasp a bottle of white from the door. I place it on the counter and slide it toward her. I'm not pouring for her.

She fills two glasses but I shake my head as she tries to hand me mine.

"I have coffee. So out with it; I have somewhere to be."

She peers around the room, motions for us to move over to the dining table. Without waiting for me, she parks herself in a chair, digs her elbows on the surface of the wooden table.

I stay in the kitchen with the small of my back leaning against the counter.

"Gerald called me half an hour ago," she starts, eyes skimming over the surface of the wine, which she gently swirls in the glass. "Cynthia has skipped town." She stops her swirling, aims her eyes at mine. "With Will."

My lips part to speak, then seal together again. The room seems to spin in an almost-cartoonish fashion, and suddenly I feel too hot. I fan my face with my palm, train my gaze out the back window, and focus on the jewel-red hummingbird feeder to try and steady myself, stop the slow rotation of the room.

With a calm clarity, it all clicks into place: Cynthia not returning my text; Cynthia's overblown reaction to the news that Will had been spotted with Brandi; Will standing guard at his door that final time I went to see him. It hadn't been Brandi in there with him after all; it had been Cynthia. Maybe he's banging Brandi, too, but holy shit, he's skipped town with Cynthia?

"Jen." Kittie's voice cuts through the molded Jell-O of my thoughts like a butter knife.

Our eyes meet. Begrudgingly, I move to the chair next to hers and collapse into it. Kittie hops up, retrieves the filled wineglass from the kitchen, and places it in front of me.

I sip. Fuck it. There's no way I'm going to Yoga Blossom now. I'll have to go another day. Kittie's eyes bore into me. She looks sad and defeated, and it hits me that this news is most likely just as much a blow to her as it is to me. An ego blow to her, though, not the heartbreak I have endured, but a punch nonetheless. If I thought my heart had been wounded at Wine Night, it's completely punctured now. What a goddamn fool I have been.

Cynthia? I never saw that coming. It's always the quiet ones, isn't it?

"Where did they go?" The words tumble from my lips robotically.

"Gerald doesn't know exactly. She left him a fucking *note*, if you can believe that. He showed it to me. It was all: 'I never planned this but we're in love and we're going to Europe for a few weeks.'" Kittie flicks her eyes toward the ceiling, rolling them.

Europe. Of course. I'd long been nursing fantasies of Will taking me there to see his childhood home in Denmark, to the land of his mother's family in Georgia. My daydreams were even specific enough to include him crouched down on one knee, a band of platinum in his palm, asking for my hand in marriage.

"Jen," Kittie says, glancing up at me, "I'm sorry." Her eyes mist with tears and she reaches for my hand, but I yank it away.

"I'm sorry for what I did, for my part in this shit show, but I'm also sorry about Cynthia. I. Had. No. Idea." She says that last sentence in a low voice, emphasizing each word.

I can't tell if she's truly remorseful for how she betrayed me or if she's just sorry that Will found someone he favored over her. Someone so enticing, he left the country with her.

I decide I don't give a hoot about Kittie's feelings right now; I'm still trying to wrap my mind around this new reality. On the one hand, I'm ill with jealousy and rage—spiky anger against both Will and Cynthia—and I feel more rejected than I've ever thought possible. Even worse than when I found out Felix was fucking someone else. But on the other hand, there's a tiny glimmer of relief: clearly, Will is a psychopath who gets off on fucking with people, so his rejection of me is actually nothing personal.

"Told you he was a motherfucker. And Cynthia, she's left Gerald. For good. I can't believe it." Kittie interrupts my thoughts again, sighing into the rim of her wineglass. "He's a wreck, of course." She gives me a look as if she's sizing up my reaction, gauging whether I'll feel sympathy for Gerald, whether I'm interested in continuing this conversation with her at all.

I absolutely do feel sympathy, having been through a similar heartbreak. And I can picture mild-mannered Gerald, a single hair never out of place, falling apart over this news, which most likely came as a complete shock to him.

"I wanted to see if you'd actually go back over to their house with me." Her eyes are glassy with tears, which she brushes away with her hand. "Jen, it was a bad scene. He's a mess. And Tyson was locked in his bedroom with the music blaring. Wouldn't answer the door. I panicked and left, said I'd come get you and that we'd be back over." She scrunches up her face in defense, like she's waiting for me to yell at her for being so presumptuous, but I just nod and agree.

The need to comfort Gerald and, hopefully, Tyson outweighs my rage at both Kittie and Cynthia at the moment. And also, my need to find out more, any small detail, so I can pick up the pieces of this shattered mess, make some sense of it all.

"Let's go," I say in my chilliest voice, trying to make it clear that I'm still not happy with her, that I'm doing this for Gerald.

I FOLLOW KITTIE in the Accord. No way we're riding over there together. She pulls into the Nicholses' drive, and I slide in behind her. As we pick our way across the slate pavers that lead to the side door, it hits me that I haven't been to Cynthia's house since the day Will and I walked by it together. A key turns in my stomach and I remember the strange reaction she gave Will then and wonder if things with them had already started to develop.

I push the thought away when we step inside and spot Gerald in their dining nook, shoulders stooped over the kitchen table, gazing out the back window toward their shimmering lap pool. My eyes sweep over the view: the pool, the meticulously landscaped terraced gardens, the sleek patio furniture. Cynthia left all of this and left the sweet man who's been by her side since college. But I too well understand why: Will is irresistible. Bastard.

Gerald hears us approach, and as he turns, the feet of his chair let out a sharp bark against the high-sheen wood floors. He stands and shakes my hand, a gesture that seems too formal for this occasion, so I pull him into a hug.

"I'm so sorry. I don't even know what to say."

My voice is shaky, which seems to break something inside of him.

His chest heaves against mine and he holds me for a beat before pulling away, blotting his eyes with his freshly starched shirt.

"Gerald, have you eaten anything? Let me fix you some toast," Kittie says in a too-loud voice as if he's deaf.

She's never been able to handle strong emotions, only her own; she busies herself in their sunny kitchen, pulling bread from the plastic bag and placing it in the toaster oven.

"How's Tyson?" I ask.

Gerald lifts his palms up in a shrug.

"Want me to check on him?"

He nods.

I creep down the hall. Loud synthesizer music bleeds from under Tyson's closed door. I tap on the door first with my fingernails, then with my fist. It's not like I'm exactly close to Tyson, but I have known him since he was born, and I know he needs comforting now, like Kasey did when he learned his dad and I were separating.

I hear him lower the volume of his music, followed by the heavy sounds of his footfalls on the wooden floor. He opens the door. His face is mottled and it's clear he's been crying. But he eyes me with suspicion.

"Tyson, I—" I falter. "I just wanted to let you know I'm here, right down the street, if you ever need anyone to talk to."

He raises his chin to me as if appraising my sanity, shakes his head, and closes the door. He probably knows that I was seeing Will and, like everyone else, just feels sorry for me.

A sour feeling washes over me; I want to flee this house just as Kittie did earlier. I'll give Gerald another hug and tell him to call me, but then I'll take my leave. I turn and head back down the hall when I hear Kittie's voice clattering off the walls. She and Gerald are headed toward me.

"She must have packed *something*?" Kittie says, flinging her hands in the air.

They whoosh past me and I trail them into the master bedroom. I'm stunned when I step into the room and take in the bright fuchsia wall color—it's in such stark contrast to the muted tones of the rest of Cynthia's house, I wonder for a second if we've fallen into another dimension. But everything else in the room is pure Cynthia: the sleek headboard, the tidy matching end tables with lamps, the framed artwork on the walls. Opulent and also cold.

The sounds of clothes hangers scrape along the rod as Kittie paws through their closet.

"I don't understand. She didn't take *anything*?" Kittie's shrill tone sets my teeth on edge.

She jets across the room to the chocolate-brown mahogany chest of drawers and opens each of them, digging through their contents as if searching for clues.

"I'm just so sorry," I say again to Gerald, who stares blankly at the floor, eyes trained on his moccasin-style house slippers.

Kittie slams dressers behind us, huffing and puffing.

"Listen, I'm gonna give you some space, but call me anytime," I say lamely to Gerald. "I mean it. If you want help with Tyson, or just anything, please let me know."

I turn and walk out of the loud-colored room without even bothering to say goodbye to Kittie.

47.

Kittie

IT'S EVENING, SIX o'clock. I've been nursing wine since five. This day. This day makes me want to empty bottle after bottle down my throat. Hank is around the corner at Gerald's. All the men have gathered for an impromptu poker night in the hopes of taking his mind off of everything or, at least, getting him so drunk, he'll tip into the bed, sleep through the night.

And Chloe is at Shelley's for her birthday-party weekend. I've been a jumble of nerves all week about it—I have no idea what the girls are getting up to—but I bit my lip yesterday afternoon when I said goodbye to her, only saying cheery things as I clutched her neck. Her freshly washed hair was luscious against my cheek, carrying the scent of her new grapefruit-and-ginger shampoo, and she looked dazzling—her green eyes expertly rimmed in coal-black liner with specks of gold glitter on the lids. Sixteen. Whew. My throat swelled with emotion as I gave her a final glance before she broke away from me and galloped down the lawn toward Shelley's SUV.

I ' V E   L A I D   O U T a table of appetizers—crab cakes, purple-red grapes, and cheeses; Jen is due to arrive any minute now. I can't believe I convinced her to come hang out with me, but with the diary in my possession, she couldn't say no.

I'm still stunned that I found it. And that dopey Gerald hadn't yet combed through Cynthia's things. I don't know what came over me, but standing in their kitchen this morning, pouring Gerald coffee, I was seized by the need to rake through Cynthia's closet, see what seductive outfits she had chosen for her extended vacation with Will.

Will. I cannot wrap my head around the fact that they are together. It's impossible. Except that it's not. I've read her diary in its entirety. And now I have to share it with Jen.

I feel so betrayed by Cynthia, even though I know it's an irrational anger: she never even knew I slept with him, had a thing for him. But still . . . how could she do this to Jen? To Gerald and Tyson? But of course, I already know the answer: Will is undeniable, unavoidable. I would've done the same if he had asked me, no question in my mind.

My head is on a swivel from this news. Gerald called me, sobbing in my ear this morning before I'd even properly woken up, my eye mask still pasted on my face when I heard my cell chime.

"She's gone," he simply said.

I swiveled out of bed, crept from the room, leaving Hank snoring under the duvet.

"What are you talking about?"

And that's when he told me about the note, about Will. I felt like my chest had split into two, like someone had just snuck up behind me with a hacksaw and sliced me open. Not only was Cynthia *with* Will; she was leaving the country with him, abandoning her family for him.

They are clearly together. *She's* the one who hooked him. Mother-fucker that he is. Girlfriend had it bad for Will—I had to read some of the diary entries twice just to believe them. I'm certain that it won't end all in roses for her, either. But still . . . Europe together?

I tried to picture them, tried to imagine how long this had been going on under my nose, tried to wrap my head around the whole thing. In a way, it makes perfect sense. She is ferociously attractive, even if her beauty is a quiet one: understated, classic. I can see her feeding right into Will's hands, lapping up those lines he tossed her way. "You're beautiful, Cynthia. I've never seen anything so beautiful in my life."

Out of the three of us, she's actually the perfect puppet for Will, and as mad at her as I am for stealing him from both me and Jen, I'm also worried about her because she's so doe-eyed and almost childlike, he can shatter her forever with a single act.

I found the diary in the top drawer of her dresser, nestled under a pile of neatly folded panties. As soon as my hand landed on it, I in-stinctively knew what it was: it's *so* on brand for Cynthia to need to keep a secret journal. I glanced around the room, and while Jen and Gerald were talking, I slipped it into my waistband.

As soon as I got back to the house, I went to my bedroom to hide from Chloe and read. It cored me, reading about their escapades; making me feel foolish for thinking I could have ever held his interest beyond that one afternoon. The moment I shut it, I dialed Jen.

"Just come over tonight. We can flip through it together. Trust me, you don't want to read it alone."

A sigh hissed out of her, and she acquiesced.

I clasp the icy bottle of Pinot Grigio, tip the rest in my glass. I'm halfway through a glug when I hear the side gate being unlatched. One look at Jen's face, which is puffy and mottled, tells me she's been crying most of the day. But even with her swollen eyes, she looks striking—her blond hair tousled and beachy, her tan shoulders lithe and toned, yoga triceps. She's wearing a crisp free-form jumpsuit that looks new, and caramel-colored freckles dot her perfectly shaped nose.

She deserves better than Will. Than Felix. Hell, than me.

I hope I can make her forgive me. I need her now more than ever, especially with Cynthia gone.

"Hey!" I say. "You look gorgeous!"

Her mouth is a flat line. She flips her hair over her shoulder, then scans the table laden with appetizers.

"Red or white? Or both?"

She narrows her eyes at me. "Oh," she scoffs, "I'm not staying. I just came for the diary."

"Don't you want to have a bite?" She normally eats the world when she comes over.

A small terse shake of her head.

Sinking into a patio chair, she holds her palm out. "Let's have it," she says as if she's about to swallow acrid-tasting medicine.

I hand over the diary and settle into the chair across from her. My chest tightens as she opens the little black notebook; I'm bracing myself for what she's about to read.

She scans the first few pages quickly, eyes roving over Cynthia's words, until she gets to the good stuff.

She lets out a gasp and her hand flutters up to her mouth. When she looks away from the journal for a moment, fresh tears pool in her eyes.

"Honey, I know. I'm sorry—"

She shakes her head as if to shush me. I'm sure she's wondering who *I* am to give her any consolation, so I close my mouth, fill an empty glass to the top with red, and nudge it toward her.

Without acknowledging me, she sips and continues reading. Gasping. Pausing. Drinking. Crying. Reading.

The sun has faded behind the tree line, backlighting the clouds in amber and lavender. This sunset is too majestic for what's going on here; I wish the night would hurry up and take over, fade the sky to black to more properly match Jen's mood.

She's openly weeping now, but when I move to smooth back her tear-soaked locks, she bats my hand away, grabs the bottle of red, and dumps a healthy pour into her glass.

She closes the diary, flicks it away from her. Crosses her arms across her stomach, peers into the distance. "I can't read any more right now. I'll take it home and read the rest later."

I take a sip of wine, consider my words. "I told you that he was a prick."

She nods. She's tipsy; I can feel her coming around. I grab an appetizer plate, load it with crab cakes, and push it toward her, not wanting to lose any momentum.

Mindlessly, she retrieves one and shoves it in her mouth.

"I'm in absolute fucking shock," she says as she chokes down the crab cake. "How could I be so stupid? So blind?"

I shrug. First Felix, now Will. She sure can pick 'em.

"It's not *your* fault Will's a snake. Look what he's done with Cynthia. She's trashed her whole life because of him."

"Well, at least she had a life to trash!"

She downs the rest of her wine, waves the glass at me to refill it.

"Oh, honey—"

"I could strangle her for going behind my back with him. And I still can't believe you; *you* fucked him, too."

I flinch, pass her the wine.

"Why. Not. Me?"

"What?"

"What is wrong with *me*? Why didn't he want to have sex with *me*?" She strikes her chest with her fist each time she says the word "me."

"I told you. It's not about *you*. He's a motherfucker. Clearly, he got off on toying with each of us."

Jen seems to consider this, then shovels another crab cake in her mouth. She nods as if what I've just said is the Gospel.

"You're right, you're right," she says, her words blurring together. "I'm so fucking pissed! He's playing her, too, right?"

"Of course. I'm sure it's going to end in disaster," I offer. And I actually mean it.

"I can't believe I let him string me on like that. Motherfucker."

I can tell she's drunk, so I seize my moment.

"Does this make you less mad at me?"

A smirk creeps across her face. "I guess. Yes."

My shoulders relax and I exhale. Thank God.

From the edge of my table, my cell dings. It's nearly dark now and the pale blue light from the phone flickers like lightning. I grab it and swipe the screen.

It's a text from Chloe.

Having SUCH a blast! xo

She's attached a selfie along with the text, a silly picture of her, Shelley, Megan, and a few other girls crammed into the frame, all making clownish faces. It's still light out in the picture, so I know it's a few hours old. No telling what she's up to now, but nice work trying to throw me off track by sending a stale pic.

"Who is it?" Jen asks, her voice hazy with wine.

"Chloe. It's her sixteenth-birthday party this weekend. And I'm terrified. A sleepover at that snotty friend of hers."

Jen's sky-blue eyes crinkle into a smile. "Sorry."

"Hey, do you know if Kasey was going to stop by there?"

"I don't think so; he's at Mom and Dad's for the night, and was at home with me all last night."

"Okay, good. Maybe it's just girls, then. Whew. Have you had the condom talk with him yet?"

Jen places her wineglass on the table, nearly chokes on her sip. "I was going to leave that to Felix."

Shame burns my skin. "Oh, of course. Sorry, honey. I—"

"Don't be. It's just one of those things I thought Will would be good for. I really, really thought there was something between us."

She's not an idiot for thinking that. Will is just a gigantic mind fucker.

"I'm so sorry."

Jen lets out a ragged breath. "So. What was it like?"

I swallow more wine. "What?" I ask, even though I know exactly what she's asking.

"The sex with Will?"

"Awful."

"Come on. Tell me."

"Girl, you seriously don't even want to know."

Her posture deflates and she drops her hands into her lap, stares down. "I figured."

I want to walk around the table and hug her, but I don't want to push my luck. I'm glad we've broken through this far. Nothing better than a common enemy to mend fences with someone. And now we really have two: Will *and* Cynthia.

48.

Jen

THE ROOM WOBBLES around me; I drank way too much wine at Kittie's, but, I mean, how could I not have? I'm plastered against the sofa, Cynthia's diary in hand, determined to read the rest, even if I don't want to.

I'm a wreck, and I'm grateful Kasey's not home to see me like this.

The entry, so far, that cores me the most is this one, where Will said the following to Cynthia:

You know, if I'm honest, I was interested in Jen at first. I mean, she's your friend; you know how wonderful she is. But I think now what I was wanting with her was more of a friendship. I thought I wanted it to be something more, but being with you has changed that. It's changed everything, actually.

That motherfucker. And also Cynthia. I hate her for what she's done to me. Will's words are torturous—he was clearly into me before *she* came along; I could've had a chance with him. Reading about them together makes me ill, makes my insides quake. Him telling her, too, about the portrait of his mother, about his background—I thought all of that was special stuff he shared with me and me alone. *You're different from the others here.* He actually said that to me.

Fucking liar. Fucking bastard.

49.

I DON'T THINK I have much time left, but then, I have no concept of time anymore. At first, I tried to keep track by tracing the moon's arc in the sky, but now it's blotted out by the feathery treetops, which hiss against the wind.

I've lost so much blood that my body—which has been motionless for what must be hours—feels featherweight, as if I'm going to just evaporate into the swampy night. I can't feel anything else, really, but my cheekbone still throbs with pain. I wince when I remember the strike of his hand, followed later by the strike of the shovel blade, which opened up a gorge along my cheekbone and cracked my heart into two.

I don't even know if they'll find me. I'm just behind his yard, where he left me, but in addition to the night sounds of the woods— the sawing of the cicadas, the groan of bullfrogs—I hear the clink of the shovel against the red-clay soil.

He's digging me a grave; that's all I can think, and if I don't bleed out, he'll likely bludgeon me to death to finish me off. A gunshot would be too loud.

I can't bear to think of Tyson anymore, let alone Gerald, and the pain that I've caused them. Running away to Europe with Will was cruel enough, but now I'll just be a tragic footnote, the fool who threw everything away for a sociopath. The town whore.

I wasn't even going to leave the house tonight. I was going to stay in, try and curl up with a book while Gerald dozed on his side of the bed and Tyson was sealed up in his room. But the buzzing in my chest wouldn't stop—the anticipation of leaving the country with Will— and I couldn't quit pacing in the living room, cutting quick, tight circles on the hardwood.

I couldn't quiet my mind, couldn't stand to be inside any longer, so I threw on a thin hoodie and burst out of the front door—on foot, toward his house—into the balmy night.

I followed the buttery glow of streetlamps until I reached Will's. All the lights inside the front room were switched off, so I crept along the edge of the lawn to the rear of his house, where his bedroom is. I was going to rap on the window, wake him, invite myself in for a quickie.

That's when I heard them.

Branches snapping, her rough cackle, a snort of his laugh, followed by the throb of blood coursing in my temples.

Kittie.

My head spun and I wanted to be sick.

A crescent moon hung overhead and cast enough light that I could see a little ways in front of me as I stepped toward the murky forest.

I could just make them out as they were entering the woods through a slender corridor of vines behind the house. Her shiny hair glinting in the moonlight, his hand on the small of her back.

Kittie.

Or everything that appeared to be Kittie except the tight curls, which I glimpsed as I crept closer. No, not Kittie.

I shouted her name before I could stop myself.

"Chloe!" My throat burned as if someone had struck a match against the back of it.

Then I heard my name rolling out of Will's mouth, his voice lip-balm smooth as ever, trying to calm me down, trying to placate me.

She turned and saw me just then, and I'll never forget the look of hurt on her face when she registered that he and I were most likely an item.

Anger seared through me as it all clicked into place: Will had in-deed been seeing someone behind my back, but that someone wasn't Brandi—most likely anyways. It was Chloe.

Chloe. A child.

How the fuck could he have done this to me and how the fuck could he have done it to *her*? My own anger and confusion were re-placed by rage and the urge to protect her, so I charged toward them, slicing my bare leg against the thorns of a wild blackberry bush.

"It's okay," I heard Will say to Chloe as he mumbled something else. "I'll take care of her."

Her eyes clouded with uncertainty as she looked from him to me, but before I could reach them, she followed Will's command and van-ished into the woods.

"Chloe!" I screamed again, but she was gone.

I was on Will in seconds, slapping his face as hard as I could. His mouth hung open and he palmed the cheek I had struck with a look of astonished admiration in his eyes.

"Cynthia, I can explain—"

But I knew that whatever was coming next would be bullshit, so I raised my hand again to hit him, and that's when he grabbed me, wrenching me off the ground by both wrists.

He pulled me into his chest, lips grazing my ear. "If you will just *calm down* a sec," he said, loosening his grip, "and let me explain."

My wrists singed from his rough hold, I bit my tongue, fear already oozing over me. Part of me wanted to believe whatever lie he was concocting; part of me wanted what I had seen *not* to be true so I could wind the clock back to the part of our story where Will was my one true love and we were leaving together in mere hours. I couldn't unsee what I had seen: the way she had laughed, the way he cupped her back, the way they stood so close together, so intimate that I knew they were *together*.

"We just met, on the street just now," he said, his words floating past me. "She was wanting to get away from her friends, and I was just showing her—"

I twisted away from him.

"What are you thinking? That she and I—" His eyes skittered over me in mock concern. "Cynthia, please. I love *you*. We are leaving together in . . . what, less than seven hours? Do you really want to mess all that up?"

He slipped his hand on my spine, tried to guide me toward his backyard.

"Just calm down and come on in for a sec; let's have a drink."

I wavered for a moment. Could I have misheard what he'd said to Chloe? Was I blowing this all up? My head spun. I wanted to pummel him with my fists, make it all go away. But then I heard his words to Chloe again in my head—*I'll take care of her*—and it's as if a pounding surf knocked me down.

"No," I growled.

He tugged at my shirt, pulling me closer to the yard. I stumbled a few feet forward but then froze, refusing to budge another inch.

Will exhaled, unlatched the gate, and slipped inside. "Well, if you won't come in, then I'll bring a drink out to you."

I should have known then that he was up to something; it was taking him far too long to fetch that glass of wine. And I should have left—I don't know what compelled me to stay other than the fact that I wasn't finished with him; I needed to give him a bigger lashing.

He stepped out of the gate, smiling at me with his eyes. He looked me over, slipped a hand around my waist.

"You look ravishing tonight."

I wanted to freeze this final moment with him because I knew it was all over between us. He tried to place the wineglass in my hand but I shook my head, peeled his hand off me.

"Cynthia—"

"Get the fuck away from me," I said, my voice shaky and low.

He exhaled, placed the glass on the ground. Closing the gap between us, Will laced his hand around the back of my neck and tried to draw me into a kiss.

My fists were white-knuckled balls of rock; with them, I pounded his chest over and over again as a wall of tears cascaded out of me.

"We are through! How could you fucking do this to me? I was willing to give up everything for you!" My voice echoed, loud and sharp, throughout the forest.

Will peered around the woods as if checking to make sure the neighbors hadn't been disturbed.

He tried to pull me in closer again to his chest. This time, his grip was tighter.

"No! Get the fuck off me, you son of a bitch!"

That's when the first blow came, fast and hard across my face. The backs of his knuckles connecting with my cheekbone, sending a shock of pain up to my temple.

"You motherfucker," I gasped, holding my cheek. "You're going to regret that."

His prism-green eyes shone in the dark, glassy and glinting. "You're wrong about me, Cynthia, about me and Chloe—"

"Oh, no, I'm not. You're a fucking pedophile. A monster. And soon everyone in town is going to know the truth about you."

Will turned away from me then and walked through the gate. I thought he was just going to leave me there, steamed and enraged, and coast back inside his house.

My breath was ragged in my ears and my heart was pounding like a jackhammer. I couldn't believe he'd hit me.

Fucking bastard. But before I could ponder that fact any longer, he reappeared with the shovel, swinging it at my head.

Pain. White-hot blinding agony across my jaw, down my neck. Warm blood trickling from my ear, which felt like a hot potato, and blood sputtering from my cheek, which was split open. Unsteady on my feet, the forest spinning around me, I tried to regain my balance.

Then he shoved me to the ground. Swaying over me, inspecting the damage. Blood. So much blood that my body was slipping into shock. Skin clammy but limbs cold all at the same time. My vision foggy, the druggy sensation of utter fatigue.

He must have been satisfied with my condition because he turned away, retrieved the shovel, and dragged it back to his yard. I lay there motionless, unable to budge. He deposited the shovel and slammed the gate shut, the latch clanging behind him.

I could hear his footfalls next to my head; I braced for a kick to the temple. But he spared me, and my eyes followed his ankles as he made his way into the forest, toward her. Chloe.

Present

HE CAME BACK for me again. At first, my body was flooded with pure relief because he untied my wrists from the tree, freeing my arms to flop at my sides. But then he was over me, a dark look on his face. I flinched before he struck me across the cheek.

WHEN HE FIRST asked me to go away him, I couldn't believe it. I mean, to Dallas for a whole weekend? More than not believing he would even ask me, I can't believe I had the guts to agree to it.

But then Shelley came up with the perfect idea: she already had the weekend sleepover planned at her house for my birthday, and they would all cover for me.

Then, when he asked me a few days ago to bring my passport, it all started to feel a little freaky. I have one, of course, because my parents took me to Mexico when I was twelve. We'd spent a miserable rainy week crammed in a villa in Cancún during hurricane season, Mom day-drinking margaritas and picking on me and Dad.

Will wouldn't tell me where we were headed, only that it was a special surprise and that we'd be driving to Dallas, to the airport, and that I'd be back home on time Sunday so that no one would suspect a thing.

Butterflies had swarmed my stomach all week thinking about it; I worried that I'd get caught somehow but was also excited. I figured he was probably taking me to Mexico, to a beach somewhere because he said to be sure to pack my swimsuit. I couldn't help thinking about how jealous Shelley would be, how crazy it would make her once she saw the pics of us together, sprawled on the white sand.

But I kept Will a secret from her: I never told her who he was, never told any of them, and now, of course, I wish I had. But after she'd stolen Keith from me last summer, going down on him hours after he and I made out, I decided to keep any guy I was interested in away from her.

Kasey.

And Will.

It wasn't hard. Will and I never texted, for one thing. He doesn't have a cell, and he would never let me take his picture. So all I would tell Shelley and everyone else is that he lived in town but was out of school and older. On his own.

I had first seen Will at the pool party Mom threw for him and Aunt Jen. I couldn't take my eyes off of him, actually. I know he's just a little younger than my parents, so ewww, but he looks so much younger—late twenties to me—and I've never seen a guy this hot before. Only in the movies, not in Cedartown.

We never spoke but he caught me staring at him at one point and a small smile crept across his face. He lifted his chin toward me before looking away, and it felt like my whole body was on fire.

As if she had picked up on the whole thing, Shelley burst out into laughter and splashed us all in order to turn the attention back to her, like she's always doing.

"Who's the fucking hottie?" she shout-whispered at me. "I wanna go talk to him."

"No!" I dug my fingernails into the tops of her sculpted tanned thighs. "That's my mom's friend's new boyfriend, freak."

"Well, he's fucking delish if you ask me."

"I *didn't* ask you."

"Whatever. Chill out."

I made us all leave the party then to go for a walk. Plus, I was tired of watching my mom throwing herself at him; it was pretty pathetic.

THE FIRST TIME I actually got to talk to him was just a few days after that, while I was walking to meet Kasey for a smoke. I'd taken the back way around Kasey's circle so we could meet at the vacant lots in front of the woods.

I had no idea Will lived in the old Ellingsworth mansion, and when I saw him standing in the front yard, body coated with sweat from planting a tropical, my feet stuttered in place.

Upon seeing me, Will froze in place as well, just staring at me, drinking me in with his crystal-green eyes. My heart pounded in my chest and he finally broke the spell by raising a gloved hand, waving at me.

I waved back, turning my gaze to the ground so he wouldn't see the big grin spreading across it. And then I decided fuck it. I was going to walk over there and talk to him.

I was wearing my denim cutoffs and combat boots and a short red T-shirt that showed my abs (I was trying to look hot for Kasey), and as I moved toward his yard, his eyes were trained on my stomach.

I felt powerful then, holding his complete attention like that, knowing that he thought I was sexy. By the time I stepped onto his lawn, I felt like I had the upper hand.

He tugged his gloves off, extended his hand to me.

"Nice to see you again."

I wasn't sure if he had remembered me, which made me feel even more powerful.

"Chloe," I said, taking his hand.

"And I'm Will."

We held on to each other's hands longer than normal and chills tingled up my arm.

Will was wearing a white button-down with charcoal-gray shorts, and even doing yard work, he looked like a model posing with a shovel. His high cheekbones, his cotton-candy lips. His accent. My insides melted.

"It's so hot out here, and I'm so rude for not offering you a drink," he said after we had dropped our grasps on each other.

I just stared at him, deciding between playing it cool and seeing how far things would go. I opted for the former.

"Oh, thanks, but I don't have time," I said.

He lifted his eyebrows at me as if in question.

"I'm meeting someone, actually," I said, jutting my hip out and fixing him with a flirty smile.

His whole demeanor shifted then, his liquid green eyes turning frosty. He slipped his gloves back on, jabbed the soil with the blade.

"And I need to get this plant in the ground before it wilts."

THAT SHOVEL. I heard him digging with it while he still had me outside—the blade striking the soil like a woodpecker chiseling at bark—and I know what he was doing: getting ready to bury her.

I know what he did to Cynthia. I know he killed her. I didn't see it, of course, but I heard her shouting at him and then she went all quiet. At first, I thought she had just left, gone home, but then after he turned on me, I'm positive she's dead.

I'm in his cellar now, wrists tied—again—behind my back to a chair, my ankles lashed to the wooden legs of it as well.

When he untied me from the tree, he bent down and scooped me up. I couldn't fight him then—my body was limp from being bound, my face still bloodied from him striking it, my jawbone throbbing from where he kicked it—and he was clutching me so tight, I couldn't have budged if I had wanted to.

I didn't even know the creepy fuck *had* a cellar, though I've been in his house many times. He had the entrance to it covered up by a long rug in his hallway. The rug was rolled up and moved to the side, and the cellar door was open when he brought me in.

When his foot hit the first step down, that's when I decided to fight. I pulled my knee into my chest and then kicked at his arm, but it was pointless; he just gripped me tighter and hurried me down the stairs, squeezing me so hard, I was afraid my bones might snap.

He's upstairs now. I can hear him pacing back and forth above me. I squeeze my eyes shut to stop the flow of fresh hot tears.

50.

I'M POURING THE last of the coffee into my mug—it's inky thick now but I'm going to down it anyway—when Kasey appears at the back door, his hairline drenched with sweat.

I top the coffee with a splash of almond milk, which barely lightens the sludgelike color, but I need every ounce of caffeine I can get this morning; I'm finally going to meet Susan at the yoga studio and I need to be on my game.

"How was your hike?" I ask Kasey as he opens the fridge and retrieves a bottle of orange-flavored Gatorade.

"It was fine. Good. I saw Will. Well, I thought I did." He shrugs and breaks the seal on the lid with a hard twist.

His words make me freeze, but he must be mistaken.

"Oh?" I ask, aiming for casual, as I've never mentioned my and Will's demise to him; nor have I mentioned Will's dashing off to Europe with Cynthia just yet.

"Yeah, it was weird, Mom." Kasey downs half the sports drink, his Adam's apple bobbing with each gulp.

"What do you mean?"

"Well, I was hiking on the trail behind his house, you know? And, uh, I haven't seen him in a while. He hasn't been here recently, and so I wandered up to his house."

My stomach ties itself into a knot. But I just nod for him to continue.

"I walked around to the front and rang the doorbell. But no one answered. And so I kind of looked through his windows, too." Kasey's blue eyes skitter across the countertop. "But I couldn't see him. So I headed back toward the woods and that's when I saw something move out of the corner of my eye. I stopped and looked and I swear it was the top of his head just over the fence line, moving through the backyard."

My stomach clenches even tighter.

"And?" I ask, my voice rising in pitch.

"Well, I called out to him. And this is the strange part. Whatever I saw turned into a blur and I swear I heard his back door open and close. Like he was purposely ignoring me, trying to get away from me."

What in the actual hell? Surely he's mistaken.

Red streaks lash across Kasey's neck. I can tell the whole encounter has embarrassed and baffled him. It's time to come clean about Will and me at some point. But first, I need to press Kasey a little bit more.

"Honey, do you really think it was him? I mean, maybe it was his lawn man?"

"I dunno, Mom. Will is very tall; I swear it was him. I mean, I *know* what he looks like." His words jab at me.

None of this is making any sense. "I'm just saying that if it was him, there's no way he'd ignore you, ya know?"

He nods. "Yeah, I guess. But, Mom, why hasn't he been by here lately?"

Ugh. I don't want to get into this right now. I need to keep my head screwed on tight for the yoga studio, and also, I'm itching to call Kittie to tell her what Kasey just told me. So I lie.

"I'm just taking it slow with him, Kasey. After your father—"

"Hey, Mom, it's cool," he says with faux alarm in his eyes, his palms raised as if I'm aiming a gun at him. "I don't need all the details. I was just asking."

He's obviously satisfied by my answer and equally disgusted at my attempt to dump my feelings on him because he stashes the Gatorade back in the fridge and retreats down the hall to his room.

I slam the rest of my now-cold coffee before calling Kittie.

She answers on the second ring. "Hey, woman." Her voice is leaden, like she stayed up drinking even longer after I left last night.

In a lowered voice with my face aimed toward the window so Kasey can't hear, I tell her everything he just told me.

There's a pause before she responds. "Jen, are we even really sure they left town?"

Of course I've been wondering the same but I can't imagine why Cynthia would go through all that trouble—leaving Gerald a note, imploding her family—to not follow through with going.

"What if they're just shacking up at Will's, under all our noses, like naughty children or something? I can see him getting off on some shit like that."

Before I can reply, Kittie's voice crackles again across the line: "I'm going over there. I'll report back."

She hangs up, leaving me clutching my cell, my head spinning.

Present

WILL STILL PACES on the floor above me, a panther prowling in his lair. I can't believe that I'm tied up in his cellar, that he's put me in a gag. Fucking monster.

It's basically one long narrow room with limestone walls. Like a cave. No windows. Dark wooden bookshelves line one wall, just like in his library. The room is lit by wall sconces, giving it an even more dungeonlike feel.

It's creepy as hell down here. Especially with her watching me from all different angles. It's like a mini shrine to her. There're a dozen framed pictures lining the shelves, her dark eyes glimmering at the camera. She's so attractive, I can see how even Will couldn't hold her attention.

"Oh, wow, that's your mom," I said to Will as he was lashing my ankles to the legs of the chair.

By that point, I had changed my strategy with him: I was trying to engage him, calm him down, bring him back to me. To manipulate him into falling back in love with me. Or lust. Anything to save my ass.

He scoffed. "No, that's not my mother."

"Well, it looks just like the woman in the painting upstairs, so I just thought—"

"Well, you're wrong." He fastened the cloth around my left shin, tying the knot as tight as he possibly could. I winced at the pain jolting up my leg. Still down on one knee, he looked up at me then, an almost wistful look in his eyes. "You remind me of her, actually."

Good, I thought, maybe my line of questioning was getting me somewhere after all. I parted my lips, looked directly in his eyes.

"Oh, yeah?" I asked, trying to tinge my voice with a flirty tone. "How so? And who is she?"

He scoffed again, dropped his gaze to the ground. "Her name was Sasha and she was my fiancée."

"She's very beautiful. What happened?"

Wrong question. He looked up at me and his face hardened. "She fucked my best friend. That's what happened."

His jaw clenched and unclenched.

"Oh, I'm sorry. I—"

"You're just fucking like her. She was young like you. Nineteen. And wild like you, too. I couldn't control her, either."

Control her. He definitely thought he could control me. And when he led me to the clearing in the woods to our spot—the spot we'd sometimes go to to be completely out of sight from anyone popping over here—that's when I learned just how desperate he was to control me.

It's okay, I'll take care of her. That's what Will said to me when Cynthia showed up out of nowhere, screaming his name. I knew then that something was off, that there had been something between them, but I still hadn't wanted to believe it, so I walked to the clearing and waited for him.

"Sorry about that," he had said a little while later when he joined me.

"Will, what was she doing here?" I looked up at him, scanning his handsome face for any clues.

He cupped my cheeks in both hands and pulled me into a long kiss.

"Let's just say . . . Cynthia has grown fond of me. And obviously, it's one-sided. And she's upset about it. But don't worry. She's gone back home now."

I felt queasy thinking of him with anyone else, so I pushed the thought of her out of my mind. My own mother was drooling over him and I was certain every single woman in town had tried to land him, so why not Mrs. Nichols, too? But even then, I'd known there was something more between them. She was too upset when she saw me with him, for one thing.

He kissed me again, this time lifting me into his arms. I wrapped my legs around his torso and we continued making out.

"God, you drive me crazy," he said. And I felt that familiar all-powerful feeling that came with turning him on. "Happy birthday, Chloe."

I've never gone all the way with him; we usually make out for long stretches, but one time I peeled my top off and we touched each other. That's as far as we've taken it. It's not like I'm a virgin or anything; I shed my virginity last summer in a field with my then boyfriend, Alec. And I've been with a couple boys since, but Will never pushed it, and I'm not sure how far I would've gone with him anyways.

I'd kind of been crushing on Kasey lately—he's the one I really want to date but he's not considered cool or popular—and I'm not even sure how to classify what Will and I were doing. We weren't boyfriend and girlfriend; we were just hanging. I know he's too old for me and that I shouldn't have been seeing him, but he's so hot and so different from everyone around here that I couldn't stop myself. And he made me feel really special. I loved the danger of it—it was like a high. I knew how much it would piss my mom off and how insanely jealous Shelley would be, so I became addicted to seeing him in secret.

After the first time we talked when he was out in his yard, I walked by again the next day and there he was, outside again, covered in sweat, digging holes for plants.

That time, I took him up on his invitation to come inside and have a drink.

We sat across from each other in the library, underneath the gaze of that ginormous painting that I thought was his mother but who I now know is not his mother at all, but rather his murdered fiancée, Sasha.

We sipped tall glasses of icy handmade lemonade, spiked with vodka, and Will asked me all sorts of questions about myself. What grade I was in (sophomore heading into junior year—he was shocked by this; he had me pegged for a senior), what subject I liked most (art, of course), and what my other interests were.

I squirmed under his attention and tried to sound as sophisticated as possible, tossing out places I wanted to travel to—the Met in New York City, the Louvre in Paris—while trying not to constantly blush as he stared at me with his crystal-green eyes.

We were latched onto each other before an hour had even elapsed that afternoon, me in his lap, his fingers tracing my lips, him kissing me. He was the greatest kisser I'd ever been with and I've kissed a lot of boys so far.

"You are the most beautiful thing I've ever seen, Chloe," he said as he twisted a lock of my hair with his index finger. "You're different from the other women in this town. I can already tell."

My insides melted and I wished that Shelley had been on the other side of the window, looking in on us. Watching as he chose me over her and all the others.

His hand crept up my thigh until he reached the hem of my cutoffs. I didn't want him to stop; I wanted his fingers to go all the way to my zipper but he just fiddled with the frayed threads of denim, teasing me.

He told me that he didn't have a cell, so like some character from eighteenth-century fiction, I agreed to meet him on Thursday afternoons at two at his place. There was only one time when he wasn't home or didn't come to the door, and I had either walked home, sad and frustrated, or texted Kasey to meet me at the bottom of the hill for a smoke.

I've been into Kasey ever since he moved back. He became like Insta handsome since the last time I'd seen him a few years back. Also, more intense, which is not surprising, seeing what he went through with his parents' divorce. And he's so nice to me. But I almost died the day Shelley and Megan and I were walking by Kasey's house, smoking, and caught Will out front working on Kasey's car.

He flicked a glance at me and then dropped his gaze, so I followed suit. I didn't want anyone catching on to the fact that we were an item.

And when Shelley started pestering me about the mysterious guy I was dating, I gave her only those basic details: he was older, he had his own place, and he said I was the most beautiful thing he'd ever seen. That I was different from the others. And would only refer to him by his first initial, W. Drove her crazy but there was no way I was telling her about Will until I knew where things were going with us. Or, at least, until I sent her a pic of us together on the beach.

THE BEACH. IF only it had been so simple, and if only I had had the wherewithal *not* to react so strongly when Will told me what his real plans were.

"Happy birthday, Chloe."

"Thank you, Will," I said, mocking his serious-sounding tone.

A grin spread across his lips. He was still holding me in the clearing, my legs still wrapped around his waist.

"So, where ya takin' us?" I asked.

He set me down, never breaking eye contact with me, a hint of dare playing in his gaze. He swept my hair to the side, leaned in, kissing me on the cheek.

He was still twirling a strand of my hair, gently tugging at it, which gave me goose bumps, when he answered. His eyes glistened in the dark and my whole body danced with electricity in anticipation.

"Darling girl, I'm taking you to Paris."

My stomach dropped, but not in a good way. Paris? How in the hell was I supposed to pull that off? And more importantly, I didn't *want* to go to Paris with him. Dallas or the beach in Mexico was one thing, and that felt risky enough, but going halfway across the world with him? And then the way he was staring at me, expectantly, the grin across his face growing even wider. I suddenly felt repulsed. I'd thought what we had was something super casual and fun but now he was getting all romantic on me. Like, was he planning on proposing to me there?

He kept staring at me, waiting for me to squeal in delight or something—I don't know—but all he was met with was my baffled expression and the snort that had unfortunately escaped my nose. I felt like I needed to set him straight.

"Paris? For real? You're joking, right?" I instinctively took a step back from him.

He looked stunned for a moment, as if he were unsure how to respond. "Yes, Paris. And no, I'm serious. We leave in an hour. I've chartered a small jet to fly us to Dallas, where we'll catch the red-eye. First class. We land at four thirty p.m., Paris time, enough time to shower before dinner and our night out. But don't worry; we'll be home late afternoon or Sunday night. I know it's extravagant and a bit of a whirlwind, but you're worth it."

"I'm sorry, but I'm not really comfortable doing that, you know? I thought we were going somewhere close—"

"But you said you've always wanted to go to Paris, so I thought it would be the perfect birthday surprise. I've managed to get us dinner reservations at this incredible place and we'll hit the clubs later. And the hotel is right on the Seine River." A short pause as he searched my eyes. "You'll have your own room, Chloe. Don't worry."

"Yeah, I'm sorry. That's supersweet but I'm not up for all that." I didn't mean to but it's a bad habit of mine and I'm pretty sure I scrunched up my nose just then. Wrong move.

I was suddenly aware of being alone in the dark forest with him, with nothing but the trees and the chirping of crickets surrounding us.

The first hit came hard and fast and shocked me so much, I wasn't sure if Will had really just struck me or if I was imagining it. But my cheek flamed with heat and my eyes watered.

I shot him a withering look and then turned to leave. My heart was jackhammering in my chest but I took the path toward his house, my legs scraping against the vines, but then he was on me. His hand clamped on me, spinning me around.

"You ungrateful little bitch," he spat out. "I was going to whisk you away from this little Podunk town, and maybe if you loved it, we could stay. I was going to show you the world." Then he struck me again.

This time, it was enough to knock me off my feet, sending me down in the dirt. I didn't even have time to register more fear because he was over me, striking my face again with the back of his hand while I kicked at him.

AFTER HE FINISHED tying me to the chair, he started heading for the narrow staircase leading up out of the cellar.

"Wait! What happened to Sasha, Will?" I asked his back, my voice coming out more panicked than I had intended.

He stopped but didn't turn around as he answered me.

"No one ever found her, and no one will find you, either."

My body went rigid with fear but I managed to yell out, "But wasn't anybody looking for her? Her family?"

He turned around then. "Her family?" A smirk twisted across his lips. "What a joke. She was a runaway teen when I met her, from a broken excuse of a family in Eastern Europe. She was just starting to model but I *made* her. Her family stopped looking for her years before I came around."

"What about your best friend?" I couldn't believe I was even bringing that up but fear had pushed me beyond reason.

He stared at the floor. "He never even knew I found out. I— Well, I took care of her right after. And I told him some sob story over beers at the bar, about how she had left me. Why would he think otherwise? She fucked *him*." His eyes were manic and his hands shook as he said this last part before turning to walk away, leaving me tied up.

"Well, my mother will be looking for me," I wailed to his back. "When I don't text her back, she'll know something's up and she'll find me."

He barked out a laugh. "I've read through all your texts and I've already been answering her. I know what to say to her, know how to handle her, until I figure out what to do with you."

I screamed out as loud as I could, the rock walls absorbing my screech like a pillow, and that's when he crossed the room again, using another strip of cloth to tie a gag around my mouth. The corners of my mouth are cracked and burning, and I keep yanking my legs and wrists away from the frame of the chair, trying to loosen the cloth ties, but with each pull, I'm only making the knot tighter. And everything worse.

51.

Kittie

I PARKED AT the bottom of the hill, halfway between Will's and Jen's, in front of the vacant lots. I wanted to be undetected and to enter through the woods, so now I'm walking the trail I walked a million times in high school, but not once since then.

It's nearly eleven o'clock, and it's so hot out already, it's as if the forest floor is steaming. Orange pine needles coat the trail, brittle and crunchy underneath my feet. I walk up the hill in the direction of Will's and realize just how thick these woods are. I can barely see the fence line that marks the property line of homes on Azalea Circle. The woods are desolate, too, devoid of any other walkers, and the back of my neck tingles with fear when I realize I'm all alone out here.

I pick up the pace, even though it will make me sweat. I shouldn't care about such things but if Will is indeed home, I can't help it: I still want to look good. I threw on a button-down yellow blouse and a pair of khaki shorts and, yes, applied a fresh coat of lipstick.

The path narrows and I have to sidestep to keep my legs from getting clawed by wild blackberry vines. I'm getting closer to Will's. I can see the arched pitch of his roof peeking between the column of pines; I turn down an even narrower path full of brambles that leads to his place.

I'm at the back gate now, peering through the slats. I creak it open and step into his lushly carpeted yard of jade-green grass. In the far corner, near the back of the fence, there is what looks to be like a garden in progress. There's a recently made mound of dirt, which I recognize as a watermelon bed. When we first married, Hank and I actually grew a crop of watermelons out on our land, my only foray into yard work. Snap peas line a trellis running the length of the fence and clusters of tomatoes dangle from their vines like garnets.

Next to a tidy garden shed rests a shovel, newly caked with red clay, the earth next to it slashed open, awaiting more plants. A pair of gardening gloves rests limply on the shovel's handle like a dead snake—gardening left in haste.

I peer through Will's bedroom window. The bed is made as neatly as if a hotel cleaning lady had made it, and the room is dark, empty of Will. I scan the other windows and then step through the gate to circle the house, to check the rest of the rooms. I feel slightly ridiculous spying like this and hope to God I'm not spotted by a neighbor. I rush to the front hedge and look into the library through the big picture window but it's as lifeless as the rest of the house.

Kasey is wrong. Of course he is. He just wants Will to still be here, poor guy.

I round the corner and walk the length of the fence line toward the trail. I'm digging in my pocket for my cell so I can text Jen to let her know that Kasey has thrown up a false alarm, when I hear the click of a door opening, followed by the clap of it shutting. Coming from Will's yard. I spin around and look through the slats on the wooden fence and see him striding toward the corner of the yard where the garden lies.

My breath catches in my throat; I feel almost dizzy with adrenaline. What the hell? He's in a rust-colored T-shirt, his midriff soaked with sweat, and a pair of low-slung cargo shorts, which hang from his hips. He tugs on the gardening gloves, turns over more earth with the blade of the shovel.

Before I can even think, I find myself moving toward the gate, wrenching it open. It clanks behind me, a jarring sound that echoes through his yard.

Will looks up at me, surprise registering on his face, followed by a tight smile.

"Kittie," he says, giving me a quick nod while still stabbing the ground.

"Where is she?" My voice comes out like a howl, raw and primal and full of every ounce of rage I feel toward Will.

He stops his shoveling, spears the blade in the ground.

"Honestly, I was hoping you could tell me."

This stops me short, knocks the breath out of me. I'm completely bewildered. If he's here but Cynthia's not, where the hell *is* she?

I pitch my voice a notch louder. "What are you talking about?"

His eyes dart across to the neighbor's as if he thinks I'm being too loud.

"We had a falling-out, right before we were supposed to leave. She bailed."

He trains those eyes on me, which now appear filled with pain.

This has caught me off guard. I don't know what to say.

"A falling-out about what?" My voice is still edgy and loud.

His hairline is soaked with sweat, and as he swipes it with the back of his gloved hand, his shirt creeps up, exposing a sliver of flesh, that taut torso.

"Want to come inside and talk about it? Have a drink?"

I can't believe I'm even considering being social with him but my stomach is also buzzing with this news, with the thought that they aren't together anymore. And of course, I need to hear the full story.

I lock my eyes onto his and pause before I answer. "Sure."

Trailing behind him into the house, I'm caught in the jet stream of his intoxicating scent, the same scent I couldn't get out of my mind for days.

The back door opens into the hallway, and as we pass by his bedroom, he motions for me to sit on the love seat nestled against the wall. I do and he stands at the door, his arm slung on the doorframe, his shirt creeping up again.

"Well?"

"We had a fight about Brandi, that Realtor. I had arranged for her to list this place, in case Cynthia and I stayed abroad, and I did it in secret. My mistake. I was only trying to surprise her, but she got the idea that I had something going on with Brandi."

"Well, did you?" I arch an eyebrow at him.

He palms the back of his neck, a small grin tugging at his lips.

"Actually, no. I was besotted with Cynthia, but again, she wouldn't listen to reason. I'm coming to learn that all you women are crazy."

"Fuck off."

"I shall. Now, about those drinks . . . I'll be right back."

He's left me alone in this room, which is warm and coated with morning light. I can't help but remember what we did in here, what we *could* do again. I'd be lying if I said I didn't want to. I won't, obviously, and I hate myself for still being attracted to him after all the havoc he has wreaked, but damn it if I'm not.

I'm staying only to find out more about what went down with him and Cynthia. She's probably out at her lake house, weeping on the dock, trying to piece together how she's going to slide back into her life here.

Will returns with two very full glasses of red wine, and as he passes me one, his fingers graze mine. He sits on the edge of the bed across from me and I'm hyperaware of how inappropriate our proximity is.

I sip. "I would say I'm sorry, but I'm not."

He barks out a laugh, raises his glass to mine. "Don't blame you. I know I've been a scoundrel."

He's trying to sound light but his face looks solemn, lost. I'll be damned; Cynthia broke his heart. Good for her. He was only going to ruin her somehow anyway, not that he hasn't already destroyed her life. I find myself softening to him just a little.

"You're a bastard all right." I sip some more, the wine warming my already-overheated body.

"I can't help what happened. I fell so hard for her. I really did."

As he says this, though, he locks those crystalline eyes onto mine, fixing me with an intense stare. I squirm on the velvet-upholstered love seat, not wanting to care about his attention, but unable to stop myself. Because there's an irrational part of me that felt betrayed by Cynthia, too, and that same part now feels vindicated. The fact that she can't have Will, either, balances everything out.

"Life can be so crazy, you know?" he says, keeping his eyes level with mine.

Yes, yes, I do know.

He sets his wine down on the nightstand, the bottom of the glass thudding against the wooden surface. I melt into the love seat, unsure of what to do with my body. He leans in closer and reaches a hand around the back of my neck. I shiver at his hand on my skin but remain frozen. I think he's going to kiss me, but instead, he takes his hands and trails his fingers down the front of my blouse.

He stops at the top button, fiddling with it before undoing it, and then undoing the next two.

I don't stop him. The top of my blouse slouches against my shoulders, leaving only my bra covering my breasts, which Will drinks in with his eyes. He's staring at me just like he did that afternoon we were together—the same pained look of desire on his face—and I want to kiss him, rip off my bra, and re-create every sordid detail of what we did together that afternoon. No one would know.

But something is not sitting right. In Cynthia's diary, she talked about their fight over Brandi, but she also talked about how they resolved it. And how she had chosen to trust him.

Will doesn't know that she kept a diary, let alone that I've read it.

"This is embarrassing," I say, dropping my eyes to the floor. "But I need to use the bathroom." I place a hand on his knee, brush my lips against his cheek. "But I'll be right back."

I leave my shirt as it is, flung open and dangling from my frame, as I head down the hall in order to keep up the act.

Once inside the bathroom, I snap on the lights, hammer out a text to Jen.

> Something's not right. I'm at Will's. He's here, but
> Cynthia's not. Gonna hang around for a sec longer
> and talk to him. See what I can find out. Will let you
> know ASAP.

I make a show of flushing the toilet and twisting on the faucet to pretend I'm washing my hands when my cell chimes with an incoming call. Ugh, it's Jen I'm sure, and I'm instantly annoyed at her for not being able to wait for even just a few minutes so I can dig some more, get to the bottom of things.

But when I look at the screen, it's not Jen's contact that flashes up; it's Shelley's, Chloe's friend.

My heart pounds in my throat. Why is *she* calling me instead of Chloe? Maybe Chloe's cell battery is dead.

"What's up? Is everything all right?" I try to keep my voice steady, but there's a dagger to it.

"I was calling to see— I was—" She's fumbling. She sounds nervous, fearful, and her crackle voice sets my nerves on edge.

"For Christ sakes, spit it out, Shelley!"

"I was calling to see if you know where Chloe is."

Blood roars in my ears. "What the hell are you talking about? She's supposed to be with *you* at *your* house!"

"Well, she was, of course, but"—she pauses as if considering what version of the truth to tell me—"she left really late Friday night. And she was supposed to be back this morning. Like, we were covering for her, but she never came back. And I just thought, well, hoped maybe she was home with you. She's not answering her cell."

My stomach is filling up with acid and my pulse pounds jittery in my temples. Maybe she *is* back home by now, only her stupid mother is over at Will's.

"Shelley, where did she go?"

Another pause. Shelley sighs. And when she speaks again, her voice sounds small and meek. "She went to see this guy she's been hanging out with."

"Kasey?" I ask with hope brightening my voice.

"No, not him. There's a new guy. She won't tell us much about him. Only that he's older. I think he must be from Pine Tree."

Pine Tree is the neighboring town; their high school football team is the rivalry to Cedartown's.

I picture Chloe in the woods of our neighborhood, in a boy's sports car. Just like I was in high school so many times. Maybe I even unwittingly got close to her as I was hiking up to Will's.

It hits me that she quite possibly lost her virginity on her sixteenth birthday. As hollow as this thought makes me feel, I'm also relieved to think that she's probably at the boy's house if his parents are away, or even in the woods in a tent with him. We used to do that some-times, too. And now she's hanging out with him, endlessly torturing her friends as they sit at Shelley's and squirm and text her.

"I'll call you right back," I say, and end the call before Shelley has a chance to respond.

I follow Chloe on the app 360, so I'll check that first. My finger-nails click across the screen until I find the icon.

Next to Chloe's picture, the text reads: Notifications from this user have been disabled.

I feel the blood drain from my face. What the fuck? Chloe has never turned this app off before; it's one of our agreements. I don't usually check in on her, but when we first bought her the cell when she was thirteen, we immediately installed it, just in case. Now the one time I actually need it, it's not on.

I close out, go to my Favorites list, and tap on Chloe's name. It rings and rings before rolling over to voice mail. I hang up before leaving a message and punch out a frantic text instead:

Where are you?

Then another one:

Shelley just called. Said you haven't been at her
house since Friday night. Chloe, call me RIGHT NOW.
I'm worried SICK.

I stare at the screen. It says only DELIVERED underneath my texts, not "read." Well, at least her phone isn't switched off. But she'd better call or text me back immediately.

I swipe to Recents, tap on Shelley's number. She answers on the first ring.

"What's his name? Do you have a picture of him? Anything?" I realize I'm near shouting at Shelley.

"We don't *know* his name. She just started seeing him, and like I said, she's been super secretive about it. I think . . . I"—her voice is brittle—"I think she thought I would steal him from her."

"You don't even know his name?"

"No, she only ever referred to him by his first initial, W."

Great. That doesn't help me one bit.

"Shelley, is there anything else you can tell me about him?"

She lets out a ragged exhale. "The only other thing she told us was that W used to tell her she was different from all the other girls in town, that she was the most beautiful thing he'd ever seen. That she was exquisite. He really laid it on thick, but Chloe lapped it up and repeated it all the time. Sounds like a player to me, to be honest."

I chafe at Shelley's obvious jealousy, but then my blood goes cold. *You are different from all the others; you're the most beautiful thing I've ever seen; you are exquisite.*

I've heard those same words before, read them in Cynthia's diary. Those are Will's words, no mistaking it. And the W is for Will. What in the actual fuck? My daughter has been seeing Will? Impossible. Yet somehow it's hardly surprising that he'd prey on her. But if it was Will she was with, she's not here now, so where the fuck is she?

My head is coursing with rivers of thoughts when I hear a sound just outside the bathroom door.

I jam the phone back in my pocket, twist the knob.

He's standing right across from me, eyes as blank as stone. I'm not sure how long he's been out there and what all he's heard.

I decide my best play is to pretend as though nothing out of the ordinary just took place, that I didn't just get a call alerting me that my daughter is missing and that it's him who she's been messing around with.

I close the space between us, stand on my tiptoes to kiss him, my chest brushing across his as I do. He kisses me back, hot and urgently, then trails a hand up my back. I have no game plan here, only to find out where Chloe is, but before I can even plot my next move, Will grabs my hair, yanks my head back.

In his other hand, a paring knife, which he raises to my neck, pressing the cold blade against it.

He slightly releases the pressure of the knife and knees me in the ass while still wrenching my head back. His hard frame pushes into mine as he guides me down the hallway, back toward his bedroom.

Motherfucker.

My only thought is of Chloe now, seeing Chloe alive again—oh, please let her be alive!—and escaping Will. He releases the knife and shoves me so hard, I fall against his bed. Before he steps closer, I spin my body around, kick him as hard as I can in the groin.

He winces in pain, but then his hand connects with the side of my head, a blow that causes my vision to swim. He lifts me onto the bed, pinning one arm across my chest while still wielding the knife in his other hand. For the moment, I don't budge.

"Where *is* she?" I seethe.

Will lets out a sharp laugh. "Who? Cynthia? Or Chloe?"

"You fucking bastard!" I yell, kneeing his crotch as hard as I can.

At this, he edges the blade of the knife against my throat, the pressure of it causing me to choke.

"Don't move an inch, bitch."

With the knife still at my neck, he uses his free hand to jerk open the drawer on his nightstand, then pulls out the same white strips of cloth he tied me up with before.

But this time, he's tying me up for a very different reason.

"Now you *have* indeed been a very bad girl, Kittie. What kind of friend even thinks of sleeping with her best friend's love, not once but twice?" He ties my wrists to the bedposts so tight, I gasp.

"Fuck you."

"You just couldn't wait to get back in my bed, so now here we are. What should I do with you?"

He rakes the blade down my neck, resting it between my breasts. I can't tell if he wants to fuck me or kill me. The sick bastard.

"Don't act like you were coming over here to be a good friend, all concerned about Cynthia. You were snooping and you shouldn't have been."

His eyes dance over my body and I'm filled with dread, with repulsion. But I'm not worried about me, and I'm not even thinking of Cynthia anymore. I'm only fixated on Chloe. What has he done to her?

"But I must say, my thing with Cynthia," he says, emphasizing the word "thing," "proved to be a good cover for my relationship with your daughter."

His breath is wine soaked as he pants over me; bile surges up the back of my throat. I want to scream. I want to wrest myself free and choke Will with my bare hands, but I'm screwed. This time figuratively and not literally fucked in his bed.

52.

Jen

> Something's not right. I'm at Will's. He's here, but
> Cynthia's not. Gonna hang around for a sec longer
> and talk to him. See what I can find out. Will let you
> know ASAP.

Kittie's text rolls around in my head, over and over, while I walk through the woods to Will's.

I waited a little while after she sent it before bolting from the house. Something about it didn't land right with me. I mean, I was stricken with shock to hear that Will was indeed there, that Kasey was right after all. And equally shocked to learn that Cynthia was not.

As bitter as I am about the way things went with Will and me, I'd be lying if there isn't a real part of me that isn't crackling with utter glee that Cynthia's relationship with him has obviously met its demise as well. I'm still so hurt by her betrayal, and I'm glad she'll soon reap the consequences of blowing her family apart, without the prize of having Will.

No matter what went wrong with them—and I'm assuming something has, but I could be getting ahead of myself—it makes me feel less rejected somehow, less like a pariah, a castoff. Will truly is incapable of having a mature, adult relationship, so what happened with us truly has nothing to do with me.

I waited a second before texting Kittie back, but after sitting fully dressed in my yoga gear, hopped up on coffee, rocking back and forth on the edge of the sofa, my teeth sawing at my fingernails for a full ten minutes, I snapped.

And after another fifteen minutes without a reply from Kittie, there was no way I could stay contained in the house any longer.

Also, the pit forming in my stomach told me that she might be doing more at Will's than merely inquiring about Cynthia.

Bastard that he is, I know the pull he has, the spell he can cast. And I know—especially now—how dangerously addicted Kittie is to male attention.

And of course, an immature part of me can't help but wonder: if he is free of Cynthia now, *could* there be something salvaged between us? I feel weak and dumb for even allowing myself to entertain such a notion, especially after he slept with both of my best friends. The logical part of me—the part of me that's had years of therapy—knows he's damaged goods, but damn it, I fell hard for him; I can't help it.

I crest the hill that leads up to his place, my legs damp with sweat from being encased in these yoga pants. The forest this morning is saunalike, matching the inferno state of my thoughts.

But I'm grateful for said yoga pants when I have to wade through brambles of blackberry bushes, a thick tangle of them knotted at the trail's entrance to Will's backyard.

I'm not going around front and ringing the doorbell like I have in the past; I'm not signing myself up for the humiliation that will ensue if they don't answer. No, I'm going around back, so I can pound on the back door as loud as I wish until they answer, without the prying eyes of the neighborhood.

The gate is flung open and I step through it, survey the yard. It looks like Will did indeed catch the gardening bug from me; there're the makings of a basic garden in the far corner. A wide patch of earth is turned over, hungry for more plants, and I'm sick with the thought that this is something he might have enjoyed doing with Cynthia when it's something I had envisioned us sharing together.

I take the winding footpath to the back of the house, which is paved with flat limestone rock. From this distance, the windows look blank, the rooms empty and dark. Creeping closer to the house, I see something in Will's bedroom that makes me stop in my tracks, makes my breath catch in my throat.

It's Kittie, flat on her back, her wrists tied to the bedpost. And Will, on all fours, over her. Piping hot fury rips through my core; this is so much worse than I could've imagined. What the hell?

Fuck them both.

I want to turn around and flee from the yard before they see me. But I'm so lightning mad that I can't help myself; I charge toward the back door and tear it open. I've jerked it with such force the tiny panes of diamond-shaped glass flutter with the blow and I'm disappointed when they don't all shatter.

I storm down the hall toward Will's bedroom, my anger growing in decibels with each step.

When I reach the open doorway, they both twist toward me in surprise, their bodies shiny with sweat. Kittie's blouse is splayed open, her ample bosom cinched up in a front-clasp black lace bra. Other than that, they're fully clothed. Looks like I've interrupted them when things were just starting to heat up. My temples pound with white-hot hate and it's all I can do not to cross the room and slap both of them.

Then Kittie screams something that causes everything to go off-kilter: "Jen, be careful! He's got a knife!"

53.

JEN'S WILLOWY FRAME fills the bedroom doorway. She looks, understandably, both baffled and furious. I can't believe she showed; thank freaking God I texted her. I'm still seized with fear. For us both.

"Jen, be careful! He's got a knife!" I shout.

She looks from me to Will, scrutinizing our faces for clues. I know what this must look like to her, so, ignoring what Will might do to me next, I continue.

"He's deranged! Get out of here, please, and save us both!" My words come out as a frantic wail. "He's done something to Chloe and probably to Cynthia, too!"

Will slides off the bed, tugs the waistband of his shorts up, combs a hand through his hair.

"Jen," he says, his voice smooth like polished silver, "obviously we weren't expecting you, and this is awkward. But I must say, it's good to see you."

He moves toward her.

She flinches, steps back from him.

"Don't fucking listen to him! Run!" I scream. "Call the cops! I'm begging you! If not for me, then Chloe!"

Will barks out a laugh. "Nice try, Kittie."

"Kittie, what's going on?" Jen's voice is high and reedy, her face contorted with confusion.

Another sharp bark of a laugh from Will.

"I'm sorry, Jen, but what does it look like's going on?" He inches closer to her. "Your friend," he says, making rabbit ears for the word "friend," "showed up here a little while ago. She was allegedly checking on Cynthia but has been trying to seduce me ever since."

Jen narrows her eyes at me, surveying my nearly naked chest.

Panic crawls over me; how do I convince her this is not what it seems?

"Jen, no! That's not at all what happened!" My voice burns the back of my throat. "I know it looks like—"

"She's lying," Will says, stepping even closer to Jen. "She's trying to cover her ass. For trying, once again, to have sex with me. My only fault here is that I was tempted."

Jen's eyes are trained on Will's now, drinking in his words as if she believes his version of events.

"I told her all about Cynthia leaving me this morning, and in my weakness . . ." Will shakes his head. "Well, here we are. Kittie started to undress, asked me to tie her to the bed. Just like last time."

Jen looks ashen over his mention of our foray together.

"Were you really tied up last time?" Jen asks me.

"Yes, but it was his idea. And this time, he forced me into bed! Tied me up at knifepoint! You have to believe me; you know what a lying piece of shit he is!" I kick and buck and yank at my wrists to prove I'm being held against my will.

Will starts to turn toward me but stops himself. I'm sure he wants to hit me but has to restrain himself in front of Jen.

"Jen, listen to me!" I plead. "Shelley called—Chloe's friend—and she said that Chloe hasn't been there all weekend and that she's seeing someone that suspiciously sounds like Will."

Another guffaw from Will, his shoulders rising and falling.

"Your friend here is really something. Pathetic, really. She's reaching. I don't even know her daughter." He lifts a hand to touch Jen's cheek, but she bats it away.

"Will, where *is* Cynthia? And what exactly happened?"

"As I told *her*," he says, motioning with his hand in my direction, "she bailed on me this morning. Accused me of sleeping with Brandi, that Realtor. I couldn't convince her otherwise. So she left me. Every woman in this town is insane, I'm coming to learn, except for you. I messed up with you big-time, and I'm so sorry. But it really is so good to see you."

Jen looks as though she's going to melt right there on the spot. My head races; I'm not quite sure how to convince her I'm telling the truth.

"Jen, please! Get out of here! Call nine-one-one!"

"And tell them what? That you need to be arrested for being a tramp?" Will says.

"Did she ever tell you the whole truth?" he asks Jen. I have no idea what he's going to say next but my stomach buckles.

"The whole truth about what?" Jen asks, then peers around Will's shoulder and shoots me a withering look. "Kittie, what is he talking about?"

"That she came back over here after we slept together. It wasn't just the one time."

His words slap, and slap me hard.

"Jen, wait—"

"But I turned her down. I was still so into you, and I realized I'd made a massive mistake in sleeping with her the first time. But yeah, she came back, throwing herself at me again."

Jen swallows hard, as if she's just choked down a multivitamin.

"Jen, he's lying. You have to believe me!" I scream.

But Jen's face is streaked with red, her eyes flaming with fury.

"Paleez, Kittie. Save it. I should've known this was what you were really up to. You've been doing this *shit* to me since we were in high school!" The words "high school" come out as a bitter hiss; Jen's yoga-gear-clad body is shaking with rage.

"No!" My eyes fill with tears. I feel like I'm drowning. "Jen, please just untie me—"

"Untie you?" Her voice cuts through the room like freshly sharpened scissors. "Not a chance. It's what you obviously like, remember?" She shakes her head. Then in a low voice: "You fucking whore."

"Why don't we go into the library, talk alone. Just you and me?" Will says to Jen.

She pauses, then nods.

Turns on her heel and steps out of the room.

"Jen, please! He's going to kill us," I shout after her, but she keeps retreating away from me.

54.

HE TRAILS ME into the library. We enter the room—the room where so much did and also did *not* happen between us.

It is just as it was the times I was in here, only more unpacked, completely tidied as if Will were genuinely planning to leave the country for a while. The surface of his desk, which used to be a blizzard of papers, is now sparse, save for a neat stack of documents pinned down by a letter opener. An ornate letter opener enameled with a family crest on it, most likely Will's.

Above the desk hangs the portrait of his mother, her dark eyes brimming with sexuality. I remember how sorry I felt for him when he told me she had passed and how close he had been to her. It was one of the thousand things that endeared me to him—the fact that a grown man would so prominently display such an intimate painting of his mom, with pride.

I feel the heat of his body behind me as we pause at the desk.

I turn and face him.

His lips are parted, and a lock of sweat-soaked hair hangs over his forehead. Those emerald eyes sear into me and I drop my gaze to the floor.

"So, do you mean what you said?" I ask.

"About what?" Will's voice is low and husky.

"That it's good to see me. That you know you messed up."

He closes the space between us, lifts my hair off my shoulder, sweeping it to one side. "Even when I was with Cynthia, I couldn't stop thinking about you. Like I said, every other woman in this town is unhinged. But you, you're the real deal. I know that now, and I'm just sorry I gambled with you. With us."

His fingers feel like fire against my skin and I loop my arm around his waist, tug him into me. He leans down, as if he's going to kiss me, but I shift my head so that his lips land on my cheek instead. A moan erupts out of me.

Then I inch away from him.

"I need a drink."

"Fair enough. Let me get you—"

"No." I level my gaze with his. "I'll get it. I know where everything is, remember?" I say, winking at him. "Are you joining me? Bourbon?"

He hesitates, then answers. "Absolutely. Neat with a drop of water."

Before I go, I lace my hands around the back of his neck, kiss him long and slow. His hands rove over my back until he reaches my hips and presses against me. I break away, flash him a sheepish grin.

I exit through the archway that leads to the foyer. A pair of matching leather bags rests next to the front door—they must be his and Cynthia's carry-ons. I snake through the house until I reach the kitchen.

Like the library, the kitchen is spotless, not a dirty dish nor a used kitchen towel in sight. Even the espresso maker is unplugged from the wall, its cord wrapped around its body like a long string of black licorice. He was indeed clearly planning on being gone for a while, possibly forever.

As I'm frantically rifling the cabinets, I hear Will's footfalls approaching. My heart is a punching bag in my chest and my hands start to shake.

I bank myself against the wall, just next to the doorway that leads back into the entry hall.

"I wanted to see if you needed some assistance—"

His shadow bleeds onto the floor and I lift the cast-iron skillet I just grabbed and swing.

It connects with the side of his head, near the corner of his eye, the sound it makes like a hammer striking wood. My forearm vibrates from the force of my blow, and a geyser of blood spurts from the wound before Will covers it with his hand and staggers to the ground.

A low sound rumbles out of him, but other than his hand assessing the gash of flesh, his body is motionless, curled into the fetal position. The blood seeps around his head in an expanding circle and I involuntarily drop the skillet. It clangs against the tile floor. Leaping over Will, I head through the kitchen into the dining room, my legs pumping as fast as they can until I reach the hallway that connects to the back of the house. Rounding the corner, I hear Kittie sobbing.

I race toward her, and when she sees me, a nervous laugh rattles her whole frame.

"Was that sound what I think it was? Did you—"

I quickly nod, shushing her. "He's out."

I can't imagine the state of shock she's in. My fingers work as fast as they can, untying the tight knots on the strips until I free her wrists.

"I thought you didn't believe me. I was *so* scared you were siding with him. You really had me convinced!"

"Well, I had to fool him, didn't I?"

"I'm so glad you did. Now let's call the cops."

"We will, but first, we have more to put him through. Also, if they show up and start questioning him, I'm scared he'll just deny it all and then we'll never find Cynthia or Chloe."

I practically choke on Chloe's name. "Don't worry; we *will* find her."

"What gave him away? I mean, why *did* you believe me? I know I wouldn't have."

"Because of what he said. That he didn't even know your daughter. You never once mentioned Chloe was your daughter."

Kittie massages her wrists, which are streaked with purple marks.

"C'mon, we need to move him."

Kittie buttons her top, smooths the front of her shirt down. I gather up the strips of cloth and shove them in my back pocket.

In the kitchen, Will still lies on the floor, face upturned in a puddle of blood. He's still alive, though; his eyes open and shut at the sight of us.

"You take one leg and I'll take the other," I order Kittie.

Together, we drag him to the library, his skull knocking against the milk-white pavers.

"What are we doing?" Kittie asks.

"Tying his ass up."

We pull him toward the desk, binding his legs together with one strip and, with the other one, tying his legs to the feet of the desk.

I double-, then triple-knot it. Bastard's not going anywhere.

From the floor, he squints up at us, a piercing look of distaste on his face.

"You're not going to get away with this," he says.

"Oh, goodie, you're conscious. Now tell us where the fuck they are."

He's lying flat on his back, underneath the gaze of his mother, which I find very appropriate.

"I told you already: Cynthia took off on me and I don't know a thing about Chloe."

"Jen, let's stop fucking around. I need to find my daughter. Get your cell and call nine-one-one," Kittie says, her voice shaky and scared.

"He knows exactly what he's done to them. Fucking piece of shit. Where the fuck are they, Will?"

He shuts his eyes, lets out a soft whistle. "I. Don't. Know."

"Well, then you can bleed to death here. Kittie, come with me."

She looks at me as if I've lost my mind, but I yank her by her shoulder, pull her along with me into the back hallway. Kneeling, I start to roll up the exquisite rug like a yoga mat.

"What the hell are you doing?" Kittie asks.

When I pieced together the fact that Will was lying to me in his bedroom, something else came to the forefront of my mind, something that's been gnawing at me ever since I read about it in Cynthia's diary.

Her entry about their spat—the one about the pavers being messed up in the hall, the one about Will being a perfectionist. I, of course, read the diary more than once—how could I not?—and this entry always bugged me because it was so random. Like Will was actively trying to hide something from her and she was too dim to realize it. I myself had stubbed my toe on a ridge underneath the rug and now I was eager to find out if there was more to the story.

"You're wasting our time; we should be calling the police—"

But Kittie stops speaking when I finish rolling up the rug, exposing a brass handle bolted to the floor.

"What the fuck?" she says.

"I'll explain later, but let's open it."

She kneels and clasps the handle, pulling it open. It's an entryway to a room below. Beneath us, a flight of stairs descends into the cellar.

55.

Kittie

STEPPING DOWN INTO the cellar, the first thing I notice is the smell: chalky and cavelike.

How Jen knew this was down here is beyond me. I shuttle down the steep steps into the darkened room, lit only by flickering wall sconces, and am bombarded by a guttural sound. A female voice moaning; a muffled scream.

When my eyes adjust to the dark, I see her. Chloe! Gagged and bound to a chair. Adrenaline snakes through every nerve fiber of my being. I can't hear her voice anymore over my own because I'm shouting her name over and over again.

Jen stops trailing me, no doubt giving me space with Chloe. I reach my daughter and gasp as hot tears flood my eyes. Her hair is a mess, a tangle of leaves and dirt. Her gorgeous face is a kaleidoscope of gashes and bruises. Her left eye is swollen, a lump the size of a buckeye protruding just underneath it. Dried blood is matted on her skin and hair, and her legs are so clawed up, it looks like she's been trapped in a sleeping bag with feral cats.

My baby. My Chloe. I dissolve into gut-racking sobs and fall to my knees in front of her, smoothing her hair down and holding my face to her chest.

I release the gag from her mouth, which sends her into a coughing fit. I scan the room for water, but of course, there is none.

When she speaks, her voice comes out strained and raspy. "He killed her, Mom! He killed Cynthia!"

Trembling as I work at the knots on her legs and arms, I stifle the urge to keep weeping because I don't want to traumatize her any more than she already has been.

I have no idea what she's been through. Did he rape her? Make her watch as he killed Cynthia? Tears leak from my eyes as I finish freeing her bruised limbs. I take her in my arms and hold her as delicately as possible.

"I've got you now, baby. You're safe from that motherfucker!"

"Mom, I think he buried her out back—"

I think of the shovel outside and the freshly turned earth, and shudder. Poor Cynthia. Queasiness splashes over my stomach but I push those thoughts away; I have to focus on Chloe.

"Ssshhh, we'll talk about that later. Let's get you out of here first."

Her body is so cold, I want to rub my hands against her skin, but I'm afraid I'll hurt her even more.

I turn to find Jen, who's standing in front of a wall of shelves, her arms crossed in front of her chest.

"What in the hell—?" she says, almost as if to herself.

"He killed her, too!" Chloe screams in that same raspy tone. "His fiancée. Sasha. She cheated on him with his best friend and he killed her. And yes, that's the woman in the painting upstairs—"

The sound of stairs creaking makes us all freeze. Will's long legs. His feet poking each step as he ambles down. He's moving slowly, clasping the side rails, as if they were a walker. Blood paints half of his face and his right eye is swollen shut.

"Jen," I shout as soon as I spot the knife in his hand.

She scrambles to join us, the three of us now facing him.

When Will hits the floor, he pauses, sucks in some deep breaths. He clutches his stomach, then balances himself, leaning against the stairwell.

In his right hand, he wields the knife, shiny and glinting in the dim light.

The same knife he held to my throat. He must've cut himself out of the ties with it. I'm kicking myself for not checking him, but he seemed like he was done for.

"Fucking creep!" Chloe yells at Will. I hug her to my side.

He scoffs. Shakes his head. Twirls the knife in his hand.

"You know what, Chloe? If you had only stuck to our plan, none of this would've had to happen. Now all three of you have to die."

"Jen," I whisper to her, "get your cell and call the cops."

Jen slides her hand down her backside, twists around, and searches for it.

"Damn it," she mutters.

"Looking for this?" In his other hand, Will shakes Jen's cell above his head.

"Motherfucker," Jen seethes under her breath next to me.

"Yeah, that kiss you gave me in the library, did you really think I fell for that? That I was running my hands along your ass because I wanted to?"

Another snort from Will.

"Fuck you, Will," Jen says.

"Oh, I'm sorry that you were the only one who never had the pleasure," Will says.

My throat grows dry and my face burns.

"Chloe, did your mother ever tell you that we slept together? This was before"—he waves the knife around in the air as if to punctuate his meaning—"you know, you and I—"

"You fucking monster!" I yell. I can't believe he preyed on Chloe, slept with her.

"He's lying, Chloe." Jen's voice comes out solid and strong, and I want to hug her for covering for me.

"Oh, no, I'm not. Chloe, your mother is a whore, just like you."

"Bastard!" My throat burns as the word leaves my mouth.

"But it doesn't matter," Will continues, stabbing the air with the knife at each of us. "I'll be long gone by the time they find you three. Once I lock the latch, there's no way to escape and you'll all burn down along with the house."

He turns toward the stairs. I want to run over to him, bum-rush him, but I know that even with his head wound, he could take me out. Same for Jen. And Chloe is in no condition to fight.

He's mounting the first step when I hear Jen's voice, full of taunting, float through the air.

"Why'd you do it, Will? Why'd you kill Sasha?"

His form goes rigid on the stairs but he keeps his back to us.

"Let's recite some poetry, shall we?" Jen continues. "This is one of Will's favorites! Mine, too. Here goes. 'That's my last Duchess painted on the wall, looking as if she were alive.'"

I've never heard this poem, of course; I don't really know any poetry, but this makes Will twist his body around, descend the last step.

"She's not alive, though, is she, Will? And that's not your mother in the portrait upstairs. That's her, Sasha. And this"—Jen fans her arms out like a model posing in front of a showroom car—"is some kind of sick shrine to her."

Darkness clouds Will's face and the muscle in his forearm flexes and unflexes as he squeezes the knife.

"Shut up, Jen," Will says.

"I'm not finished with the poem. Let's continue; this is fun!" Jen's eyes sparkle and she clasps her hands in front of her.

"'And seemed as they would ask me, if they durst, how such a glance came there; so, not the first are you to turn and ask thus. Sir, 'twas not her husband's presence only, called that spot of joy into the Duchess' cheek.'"

She pauses, seemingly for effect.

"Who called up that spot of joy in Sasha's cheek, Will? Who was it that was so dashing that he could take her attention off the great Will Harding?"

I'm seriously impressed with Jen, but she's also making me nervous. Will takes a few steps toward us.

"Maybe stop now," I whisper to Jen.

"I'm not finished," she announces loudly. "I haven't gotten to my favorite lines of all!"

The knife continues to twist in Will's hand. His gaze is narrowed, shooting bullets at Jen.

"'She had a heart—how shall I say?—too soon made glad, too easily impressed; she liked whate'er she looked on, and her looks went everywhere.'"

Chloe cackles, "Oh, my God!"

"Who was it, Will? Sasha was stunning and it's clear you were in love with her, so . . . do tell us. Who swept her off her feet? Who did Sasha screw behind your back?"

"Shut the fuck up now," Will says through clenched teeth.

But Jen continues. "'She thanked men—good! but thanked somehow—I know not how—as if she ranked my gift of a nine-hundred-years-old name with anybody's gift.'

"And thus concludes my poetry lesson. But you still haven't told us, Will, who Sasha let bang her. Oh, Chloe told us it was your best friend, but we want to hear it from you! He must really be something, something so fetching that gorgeous Sasha just couldn't resist."

Will charges the length of the room, staggering a bit, but he reaches us in a blur and I grab Chloe and pull us to the ground while he lunges at Jen with the knife.

I close my eyes, bracing, then hear the wretched sound of metal slicing through flesh. Followed by a howl.

But it's Will's voice that's howling and I look up to see Jen sliding something from his leg. A letter opener now coated with blood.

"Where in the world—?" I ask.

"Grabbed it from his desk," she says, cutting me off. "Now run!" she screams.

I sling Chloe's arm around me, wrap my hand around her waist, and hurry her to the stairs. Jen follows behind us closely.

Chloe limps—both her ankles are shredded from being bound— and I practically drag her until we hit the bottom of the staircase. We stop and heave in huge breaths of air before continuing farther.

I glance behind us at Will. He's still crouched on the floor, trying to use the bottom of his shirt to bandage his thigh.

"Go!" Jen orders.

Chloe grabs the rails and groans. "It's hard to step up, Mom!"

"Baby, you have to!"

I place my hands under her bum, shove her up the first step. It works but this is going to be a long process.

Step up. Groan. Pause for breath.

"I'm getting dizzy." I can hear the tears in Chloe's voice.

Jen's breath is hot and panting on my back.

"Keep moving!" she orders.

Finally, we make it to the top. Chloe collapses on top of the white pavers; her chest rises and falls as she struggles for breath. I study her legs. Zigzags of scratches slash over her skin, the blood congealed within the cracks. My chest constricts with sadness. That fucking freak.

Jen creaks the cellar door shut. There is no lock in sight to bolt it closed, so we dash to the back door.

Which is double bolted. My hands shake as I undo the locks, both of them, the doorknob slimy in my hand from my sweaty palms. I step out into the yard and climb down the few steps, turning around and reaching out for Chloe. Jen is behind her and she tucks her hands under Chloe's armpits, lowers her down to me.

We stand face-to-face for a moment, tears washing both of our eyes, my hands instinctively smoothing down her rat's nest of hair.

Jen steps around us, tugs me by the wrist.

"Let's get the fuck out of here."

We move toward the back gate, my breath a jagged ocean in my ears.

The sun has slipped behind a slate-colored storm cloud, almost making it feel like nighttime. We pause at the watermelon patch, which I now realize is most likely Cynthia's grave. I look over at the shovel, glazed with red clay, and feel newly sick to my stomach.

"That's her, isn't it?" Chloe asks, and then wretches on the ground.

Jen's eyes fog with tears but she whisks them away with the back of her hand. "Fucking Will," she says.

We take another moment with Cynthia, as if out of respect, and then another shadow darkens the ground around us. I think it's a cloud but then I smell him, ripe and fragrant all at once.

Will.

I turn around; he's two feet away. This time with a butcher knife.

Jen rushes to the back gate and rattles it, but it's been dead-bolted; it makes a jangling sound like a horse trapped at the starting gate.

"Shit shit shit!" she yells.

Will hobbles toward me and Chloe.

I plaster my hands in front of her body as if that's going to protect her from him.

His arms are long, and the one holding the knife snakes toward Chloe until the tip of the blade is resting just under her chest, where her heart is.

"You fucking little tease," he jeers, making Chloe jump. "You move an inch and you're a goner."

Her green eyes shine with tears.

My insides squirm; I feel helpless, panicked.

"Will, let her go, please," I plead, trying to locate some human core in him I know doesn't exist.

"Stay out of this, slut."

At this, Chloe's leg explodes in the sky, her foot launching and connecting with Will's arm. The knife falls into the squashy grass without a sound.

"You little bitch!"

In a flash, Will is on Chloe, tackling her to the ground.

"Wanna know why I turned you down?" Chloe asks as Will pants above her. "Because you were too needy. It grossed me out."

A crack of Will's knuckles across Chloe's cheek.

"Fucking bastard!" Jen yells, but I'm already on him, clawing at his spine, punching the back of his head.

He pushes himself off of Chloe and flings me to the ground. Hard. The back of my head lands on a rock, the nauseating pain making me draw my knees into my chest.

Jen rushes over to us, but Will's arm slithers through the yard and clasps the knife.

He slashes it at Jen's legs, slicing open her yoga pants and sending blood spewing out.

"Fuck!" She falls to the ground, clutches her calf.

Will climbs back on top of Chloe, pinning her down.

"You know you were in love with me," he grunts.

I inch myself up, crawl toward where Cynthia now rests.

Clasping the handle of the shovel, I spin around.

As if he can sense me, Will climbs off of Chloe, rises to standing.

He hobbles toward me.

"Mom!" Chloe's shriek explodes through the yard.

I raise the shovel, squint my eyes, and swing it as hard as I can, like a baseball bat.

My arms go all rubbery as the spade strikes Will's neck, causing him to fall to the ground like a downed tree.

"Good one, Mom!"

I cast the shovel aside, stand over this pathological pile of shit. His neck is a monsoon of blood; he's not going anywhere this time.

As if to make sure, Jen walks over and places her foot on the base of his chin, before giving it one hard kick that cracks through the air like a branch snapping.

Chloe joins in, stomping Will's face with the sole of her black leather combat boot.

A final groan oozes out of Will before his body goes slack, before those cat-green eyes seal shut forever.

56.

I'M SITTING BY the pool with Mom and Dad. It's early evening, just six o'clock, but it's already dark out because of daylight savings.

A chill hangs in the air, so I wrap my black cardigan tighter around me. It's knee-length and I'm glad, because the cold air stings my skin through my fishnets.

I'm dressed to go out with Shelley and Megan, who'll be here in an hour to pick me up. But first, sigh, dinner by the pool with the parents. I'm at one end of the table and they're at the other, Dad rubbing Mom's back, their chairs scooted so closely together, it appears as though she needs his help feeding her. The sight of it makes me ill.

There's been a lot of that going on these past few months. Dad massaging Mom's back, Dad rubbing the top of Mom's forearms. Dad always now spring-loaded to be at her beck and call.

And mine, too. I can hardly leave the room now without one of them asking if I'm okay, where I'm going, if I need anything. It's driving me a little insane, but you know I'm milking it. Whenever I so much as frown, Dad slides his Platinum American Express card from his wallet, tells me to order whatever I want off the Internet. And we've spent more than a few weekends in Dallas at the Galleria, me in a fevered state of ecstasy as I grab whatever I want off the racks without Mom's nagging or disapproval, as Dad sits in the food court, sipping foamy beers and watching the Cowboys game on TV.

Shelley and Megan are so jealous of my new outsized wardrobe. And also a little jealous, I think, of all the attention I've gotten since the whole thing happened.

I could also swear that—even though she won't admit it because it would make her look like a shit bag—Shelley is jealous of my thing with Will, even if it did end in spectacular disaster.

AFTER I FINISHED stomping his face with my combat boot, Aunt Jen knelt and dug her cell out of Will's back pocket. The screen was smashed—a glass spiderweb—but she was able to power it on and dial 911.

Her sandy blond hair was frizzed around her face; her expression looked haunted and wild as she spoke.

"My emergency? My friend and I just killed a man in self-defense. Will Harding. We are at his house. Eight-oh-two Azalea Circle."

She ended the call, tucked her phone into her back pocket. They stood on either side of me as I slung my arms around their shoulders. We wove our way back inside Will's house so we could exit out the front door.

While we waited on the front lawn for the police to arrive, Mom held me in a tight clasp.

In that moment, I felt like I never wanted her to let go of me. I couldn't believe that she had rescued me, couldn't believe that I hadn't actually died in that forest; I was overcome with guilt for all the nasty things I'd ever said to her.

"I'm so sorry, I'm so sorry," I said as a gush of tears poured down my cheeks.

She just held and rocked me, ssshhing me while smoothing down my hair. I knew I was going to be in deep shit later for sneaking around with Will, *really* deep shit, so I was happy for us to stay like this for as long as possible: as victims and survivors of something terrible.

I felt bad for Aunt Jen, too, who stood next to us, hugging herself, running her hands up and down her arms as if to warm herself.

I knew from Mom—and from the pool party Mom had thrown for Jen and Will—that Jen had been in love with him, had fancied herself his girlfriend at one point. Kasey also had talked about Will to me, and I felt ill thinking about how hard he would take the news about what I had done.

So far, he's barely spoken to me since. But I have hopes that he'll forgive me soon, that maybe we'll even hook up eventually.

I found out the truth about Miss Cynthia as soon as the police arrived. Mom and Aunt Jen told them all about her diary and the note she had left for Gerald and Tyson.

What a fucking psycho Will was. Leading Miss Cynthia on, fucking around with her even while he was trying to drag me to Paris. Mom later told me that Will had said to her that his fling with Cynthia had been a good cover for my relationship with him.

Even after the one female cop had endlessly questioned me about Will—did we have sex ever, did he rape me?—Mom kept grilling me once we got home that night, her green eyes bloodshot from crying.

I swore to her that we only ever kissed—there was no way I was admitting everything else we had done—and I'm positive she didn't buy it.

I was basically locked in the house for the first month. The police along with my school counselor (ick, why does everyone in this hideous town have to get involved?) suggested I go to therapy, so for weeks afterward, my life was basically: hang out with Mom all day while Dad was at work, have Mom drive me to therapy twice a week, eat dinner with Mom and Dad. Repeat. I felt like I was going to throw up constantly or lose my mind. But one upside of therapy—even though I think the woman is a dipshit—I got a nice little script for Valium. You know, for my anxiety and all.

Not that I haven't had my share of nightmares about Will. I have. Recurring ones. In all of them we are standing in the clearing of the forest. Even though the moon wasn't full that night, it is in my dreams, glowing so vividly, it almost seems like daytime. Will's snaking his fingers through my hair and we're making out. But when I pull away from him and open my eyes, it's Will's body, but he's got a wolf's head. With teeth bared, gums bloodred.

Ever since I got the Valium, though, the nightmares have stopped. I don't take it every night; I don't really like feeling that out of it. I just pop it whenever I'm bored. I've slipped a healthy amount to Shelley because Mom counts them, wants me to be on them as prescribed.

Dad and Mom also decided that I wasn't ready to get my driver's license just yet. They are making me wait until next spring. I mean . . . They promise it's not to punish me, only to keep me safe, blah, blah, blah, but I know Mom's behind it. Dad would cave in an instant if she would let him, and I hate her for doing this.

I feel like for sure she's punishing me, even though outwardly she's been nothing but all doting mother and gooey ever since we stood shoulder to shoulder on Will's front lawn. She would be viewed as *such* an asshole if she were mean to me. But still, I can't shake the suspicion that keeping me from driving that brand-new Pilot is some kind of payback. I sometimes wonder if she's jealous of me.

Of what I had with Will.

And what she could never have had with him.

Not only did I see the pathetic way she acted in front of him at the pool party, all head cocked and high-pitched flirty voice, slutted up in her most flattering dress. I also learned something she doesn't know I know.

Something that could ruin her.

A few nights after the rescue at Will's, Aunt Jen came over. Dad was down at Gerald's with the other men having drinks and trying to help Gerald sort out the arrangements for Miss Cynthia's funeral.

I told Mom that I had just popped a Valium and was going to bed. She bought it, of course. Instead, I lifted my bedroom window a crack so that I could hear everything she and Aunt Jen were talking about out by the pool.

They must have split three bottles of wine between them, because by the end of the night, they were both slurring so much, I had to choke back a laugh. What I heard was this:

"I haven't thanked you yet for covering for me," Mom said, sniffling.

"What do you mean?" Aunt Jen asked.

"You know . . . with what Will said," Mom said, pitching her voice a little lower. "In front of Chloe."

Aunt Jen was quiet for a second.

"Of course. She doesn't need to know, and I wasn't letting that bastard get any more satisfaction."

So Will had been telling the truth. Mom had spread her legs for him. Jeez. Believe me, I had wondered if that was true.

And what Aunt Jen didn't explicitly say was that she hadn't done it for Mom's benefit; she was doing it for mine. I wanted to raise the window and high-five her.

"Does this mean that you'll, ya know"—Mom was bumbling around, which filled me with glee—"never tell anyone else? Like Hank? I mean, I know I don't deserve it, but if the police ask more questions, et cetera. I just want to know where I stand."

The sound of wine glugging out of the bottle, splashing into a glass. I walked over to the window, peered out to see Aunt Jen emptying it into her glass.

She leaned back in her chair, twirled the stem around in her hand. I could see only the backs of their heads, but I could make out Mom's bright pink manicure clicking atop the glass table as Aunt Jen tortured her with silence.

"Deal. I like Hank, and I wouldn't want to hurt him. But just tell me one thing. You asked Will to tie you up?"

Mom poured the rest of her wine down her throat before answering. "No, honey, I didn't. It's just something he did when we . . . um, you know—"

My stomach hardened into a rock.

"Oh, for fuck's sake," Jen said.

"Sorry. I wish you'd never had to hear that detail."

Jen's shoulders slumped as if she were a balloon losing air. "It doesn't matter; none of it matters. And when you went over there looking for Cynthia, did you throw yourself at him like he said?"

Mom exhaled a gust of breath. "God, no. All of that was lies."

They sat in silence for a while after that, the only sound from the yard the gurgling of the pool filter.

I'm certain that Aunt Jen didn't believe Mom. I don't believe her, either. Because she's lying.

NOW DAD PATS his stomach before sliding the plate of pork chops toward my end of the table.

"Have another one before your friends get here, C. You're skinny as a rail."

I spear one with my fork, lift it from the platter. As I saw into it, Dad winks at me before turning back to Mom and continuing to massage her back.

Gag. Retch. Hurl.

It makes me sick to think she got away with what she did with Will, makes me sick to think of what she did behind Dad's back. It also makes me sick that Dad thinks she so perfect while I'm the one being punished, my brand-new car wasting away in the garage.

But I'm biding my time, waiting for the perfect moment to unleash. To let her in on the fact that I know her dirty little secret. And what it's going to cost her.

Acknowledgments

Writing and publishing a novel is very much a team effort, and I'm lucky to work with one of the most supportive and brilliant teams out there. My gratitude is due to many.

To Victoria Sanders, tireless champion and incredible friend, you keep making my dreams come true, and your unwavering faith in me means the world. I will never stop thanking you.

To Benee Knauer, thank you for pushing me to jump right in and get this one underway (well before the pandemic set in! Like, did you know?). Seriously, thanks for being such a lifeline and story wizard and incredible editor. I could not do it without you.

Massive thanks as well to the rest of the amazing team at VSA— to Bernadette Baker-Baughman, Diane Dickensheid, and Christine Kelder. I cannot thank you enough for your steadfastness and diligence on my behalf, which makes me breathe so much easier.

One of the bright spots of the pandemic has been meeting my dear friend Josh Sabarra. Josh, I simply can't thank you enough for being such a stellar friend and dreamy publicity guru. I owe you big-time.

Enormous thanks are due to my wonderful and brilliant editor, Danielle Perez. I am insanely lucky to be working with you! Thanks so much for all your extraordinary, incisive edits, which always make my novels so much better. I couldn't ask for a more supportive partner, and I'm thrilled for all the books that are yet to come!

To the entire team at Berkley, thank you for being such an incredibly warm and wondrously creative publishing home. Huge hat tip to Loren Jaggers and Jessica Brock, publicists extraordinaire, and huge high five to marketing firecrackers Bridget O'Toole and Natalie Sellars. Ginormous thanks as well to Ivan Held, Craig Burke, Jeanne-Marie Hudson, Claire Zion, Christine Ball, and Candice Coote. I'm so fortunate to get to work with all of you!

Huge thanks are also due to my amazing film/TV agent, Hilary Zaitz Michael at WME.

My writing career would not exist without the support of my family, and I must first thank my best friend, my mom, Liz Hinkle, who continues to inspire every novel I write. I will never understand how I got so lucky as to call you Mom. I love you.

To my fabulous sisters, Beth and Susie, who are *always* there for me, and to my b/f/f/e/a/e/a, Amy Thompson, first reader and first responder. I love y'all, and what the hell would I do without you guys?

To my sweet father, Charles, how can I ever thank you enough for everything you've done for me and C and J? I can't, so I'll just say I love you.

Big thanks to Paul and my darling nephews, Xavier and Logan, and also thanks to Joni, Courtney, Buddy, Theresa, Marc, Kip, and Mac. Thanks also to my husband's family, Jake and Stephanie, Amanda and Matt, Pam and Kevin, and especially Martha and Larry Lutringer.

Thanks to my extended family: Delena and Rex; Slade and Keegan; Jessica, Noah, and Trevor; and T-Pa and Feeney. Huge thanks to Slade for all the late-night pep talks.

A giant thanks to my East Coast family, starting with Dorthaan Kirk. *Bright moments*, Nana! Special thanks also to April, Yolie, Iris, and all the Grands. Big thanks to my Houston family, Charlotte, Shan, Kia, Bailey, and Akyla. And I'm forever indebted to Rahsaan Roland Kirk, my forever muse.

Massive thanks to my wonderful friends Kim and Chris and Elliot, Shannon and Drew Crawford, Sarah King, Lauren, Lori, Jackie, David and Clara Ward (seriously, David, thank you for the Jell-O and all the pre-orders!), Bo and Laura Elder, David Hess, Mark and Dan, Betty Neals, Lew Aldridge, Sara Zaske, Cody Daigle-Orians, Alex Giannini, Bob and Shirley, Carole Geffen, Dave and Joyce Dormady, Ron Shelton and Lolita Davidovich, Kellie Davis, George and Fran Ramsey, Henry and Patricia Tippie, Terri Whetstone, Adam and Colette Dorn, Stanley Smith and Mee-Mee Wong, Guy and Jeska Forsyth, and Sumai and Hannibal Lokumbe.

To Carmen Costello, I can't believe you're no longer with us, but I'm not going to say I miss you, because we are *always together.*

Many thanks as well to Tanda Tashjian and the Zhang family: Li, Bob, Don, and Sharon. Also much gratitude to Kayla, Kristen, Marissa, Erica, Lynne, and Kelsey. And unending thanks to Laura LeBlanc—you're the best.

To the warm and supportive crime fiction community, especially Riley Sager, Jen Dornan-Fish, Laurie Elizabeth Flynn, Samantha Bailey, Eliza Jane Brazier, Samantha Downing, P. J. Vernon, Jesse Sutanto, Amy Gentry, Sharon Doering, Chandler Baker, Sarah Pearse, Vanessa Lillie, Zoje Stage, Amina Akhtar, Andi Bartz, Jeneva Rose, Megan Collins, Kellye Garrett, and Robyn Harding.

Huge thanks and all my love to El Poquito and Cathy Fast Horse. I'm ready for that in-person campfire whenever y'all are!

The writing community in Austin is pure gold, and giant thanks are due to my writing friends here, starting with my work wife, Marit Weisenberg, as well as Amanda Eyre Ward, Owen Egerton, my dear friend Suzy Spencer, Stacey Swann, Kathy Blackwell, Mary Helen Specht, Hillery Hugg, Beth Sample, Alyssa Harad, Maya Perez, Stacy Muszynski, Carolyn Cohagan, Nick and Jordan Wade, Michael and Stephanie Noll, Meghan Paulk, Michelle Cullen, Becka Oliver and the Writers' League of Texas, and the LLL.

Huge gratitude to Katie Gutierrez (for everything!) as well as the incredible Stacia Campbell, Roxanne Pilat, Elia Esparza, and the entire Cabin 20. Massive thanks to Luis Alberto Urrea, who saved my writing life years ago by inviting me into the Cabin. Also big thanks to Kassandra Montag and Clare Empson.

Thanks as well to the fabulous Arielle Eckstut and David Henry Sterry (a.k.a. The Book Doctors).

And enormous thanks to all the wonderful booksellers, bookstagrammers—especially Abby with Crime by the Book—and librarians who truly keep books alive, with a special shout-out to Sally, John, and McKenna at Murder by the Book, Barbara Peters and the Poisoned Pen, Scott Montgomery at BookPeople, as well as Pamela Klinger-Horn, Maxwell Gregory, Mary O'Malley, and also the good folks at Book Soup.

My biggest thanks of all go to my amazing husband, Chuck, for being the most supportive partner, story collaborator, and best dad ever. I love you.

And, finally, to my magical son, Johnny, who teaches me every day that miracles exist; I am so lucky I get to be your mom.

My
Summer
Darlings

MAY COBB

READERS GUIDE

Questions for Discussion

1. Early in the novel, we learn that Kittie is mourning the passing of her once-striking looks. Even though she is still stunning, in her mind her beauty has faded, and we find out that she's actually jealous of her teenage daughter's figure and good looks. Could you relate at all to her feelings? What did this make you think about Kittie?

2. When the novel opens, Jen—recently divorced and for all purposes a single mom—has moved back to her hometown and into her parents' rental house. Unlike the well-to-do Kittie and Cynthia, Jen is in financial straits. Did her plight make you feel more sympathetic toward her than the other women?

3. Each of the main characters—Jen, Kittie, and Cynthia—eventually falls for and becomes obsessed with Will. In Kittie's and Cynthia's cases, they even go behind one another's backs.

Were you rooting for any of the three women, and why? Which of the women did you relate to the most?

4. Each of the women falls for Will pretty hard and fast. Could you see this playing out in real life?

5. What role did the insular East Texas setting play in the novel for you?

6. How did you feel about Cynthia making the drastic decision to leave with Will?

7. One of the themes of the novel is the increasingly toxic relationship between teens and their parents. This is especially shown with Kittie and Chloe's relationship. Did you find yourself understanding both Kittie's and Chloe's strained feelings about the other? Was there a teen you related to the most?

8. Were you shocked to discover what Will was actually up to?

9. Were you surprised when you discovered who the victim was (or victims were)?

Don't miss May Cobb's next suspenseful read . . .

A Likeable Woman

Kira's back in her affluent hometown for the first time in years and determined to unravel the secrets of her mother's death—hidden in the unpublished memoir she left behind—even if it kills her. . . .

Prologue

IT'S NIGHT. NEARLY eleven and pitch black on the street.

Elsewhere in the neighborhood, streetlights cast golden pools of light across the pavement, but not down here on the edge of the circle, near the entrance to the woods.

I can barely see my shaking hand in front of my face, but it's so cold out my breath clouds white in front of me. And other than the wind, which rattles through the tops of the pines, it's quiet.

And dark. So dark.

Good. She can't see me.

But I can see her. Through the chain link, which is strangled by vines that should have been weeded a long time ago. She probably thinks it looks so cool.

Through the silver net of fencing, I see the white, wooden shed. The light is on inside; she's sitting at the table. My blood boils at the sight of her. Her hair draped around her, her face made up like a whore's.

She thinks she can get away with anything. Well, she's about to learn that I'm putting an end to all that tonight.

Kira

MIDMORNING SUNLIGHT WINKS through the glass slat windows, but I'm still lying in bed, the black paper invitation shouting at me from across the room. It's sitting upright, resting atop a stack of junk mail on my wooden café table where it's been since Friday evening after I retrieved it from the mailbox.

20 years and still going strong!

We'd be delighted if you'd join us,
Chad & Genevieve Greer
as we retie the knot with a
Vow Renewal Ceremony

Saturday, October 15th at 6 p.m.
The Walters's Farm
7328 Pleasant Green Road
Longview, Texas
Please RSVP by September 15th

The envelope it came in—black on the outside, bloodred on the inside—is gashed open, the tiny RSVP card peeking out like the tip of a cat's tongue.

I can't pull it out yet and mark "Attending" or "Not attending" because I can't decide.

Of course Genevieve wants to throw herself a bash. She's always been attention-seeking, and from the group text I've been ignoring since Friday night, it's clear that it's not just the ceremony itself but a weekend full of eye-rolling events she has planned for us.

Friday night at the bowling alley, kids welcome. Saturday morning ladies' brunch at The Farm (No doubt some farm-to-table BS.) followed by crafts of some sort (WTF, are we five years old?), ending with a spa day complete with mani-pedis and a wine tasting.

The guys, of course, get to do the fun stuff on Saturday—canoeing, archery, and duck hunting. Chased with a private uncorking of a local distillery's batch of bourbon made exclusively for the occasion.

I'm certain the entire event will be just a giant Band-Aid on what has, from all accounts, been a very nasty marriage. But it's not just the spectacle that's making the pit of dread in my stomach expand. It's the prospect of having to go home again. A place I fled over twenty years ago, after I lost her. Mom.

I've returned only the one time, for my father's funeral.

All eyes were on me the entire day, to see if I would shatter. I'm the fragile one, the potentially unstable one. *Just like her mother*, they shout-whispered. And also, I'm the only one who believes my mother was murdered, that she didn't die by her own hand.

I've put acres of auburn desert land between me and East Texas, moving as far west as I could without plunging into the Pacific. But every so often—especially for events like these—East Texas tugs at me, threatening to yank me back into its pine-soaked atmosphere and engulf me. Just reading the invitation has landed me in bed for virtu-ally the entire weekend.

Especially because of the venue: The Farm. The last place anyone saw her alive.

She wandered into the woods. She'd been having one of her spells, they said. Sadie. Always quick to tears. Hysterical. They glanced up from the bonfire and saw the shock of her platinum hair, her russet-colored fox-fur coat, before she slipped into the forest.

Now I'm up, pacing the thinly-carpeted length of my six-hundred square foot apartment in the Hollywood Hills. I make a pass by the invitation, wanting to snatch it and shred it into tiny pieces, but instead, I continue on into the galley kitchen where I open the fridge and drag out a paper carton of pad thai. I eat it cold from the container, leaning against the counter.

WHEN I OPENED the mail on Friday evening after work and my cell starting exploding with the group texts from my childhood friends—Genevieve being more frenemy than friend—I ordered four servings of pad thai and three bowls of coconut and mushroom soup, knowing I'd be moored at home for days.

I sat parked at my tiny café table, staring at the invitation, swirling the steaming noodles around on a plate, forcing myself to eat small forkfuls.

And I texted Jack. Jack Sherman, my childhood best friend and former crush. We were each other's first kiss, four years old and zipped up inside his Incredible Hulk sleeping bag. An odd kiss where our teeth knocked together. We only ever text now to wish each other happy birthday—his on October tenth, mine August third—and I took this as an excuse to check in. Pathetic, really, since he's been blissfully married for a decade now and has a real life, unlike me. He's a neurosurgeon, at Johns Hopkins and has a three-year old son.

Me: Ummm . . . you guys going?

Jack: Ummm . . . hi! And hell no ☺.

A sinking feeling spread over me. Even though I didn't want to return home, the chance of seeing Jack again after all this time cast butterflies across my chest.

A few seconds later, the three dots starting leaping again, letting me know he was writing more.

Jack: Why? Are you?

Me: Don't know yet. Probably not.

Jack: Well, Melanie's going. I told her she could have a girls's weekend, drop Aiden off at my parents—so they could look after him while she gets her drink on. But she's pissed. Wants me there with her. It all sounds so ghastly to me. I just . . . I'm not really like those guys anymore, you know? And I can't imagine you wanting to go, either.

This was the most we had texted in years, and my pulse jangled in my neck, my face flush from this new contact with him. I could hear his voice across the line, as if he were speaking in my ear. That rich oaky-voice, which was never bent with the twang of the region but always sounded sonorous and kind. And yes, sexy.

Also, Jack was the one who came to my side the night they found her. When I was shaking, when I wouldn't let anyone else near me, he asked my father if he could see me. I remember him standing in the doorway to my bedroom, his fifteen-year-old bulk filling the space. A silhouette of strength leaning against the frame. I was in bed, buried under my floral-printed bedspread, eyes bloated from wailing.

He'd been at an out-of-town football game that night, a few hours away. He was a second-string running back, usually sitting on the bench—sports were never his forte; he only played football because the rest of his friends were doing the same—and he told me he'd come as soon as he'd gotten off the bus and heard the news.

He crossed the room, slid into bed, and roped his strong arms around me.

"You're not alone, you're not alone," he whispered in his soothing voice, over and over again as more hot tears gushed out of me. Somehow, he knew those were the very words I needed to hear then, because my mom and I had been simpatico. Best friends. Tethered by our artistic souls, misunderstood by Katie, my older and more sensible sister, and my cold-faced father, Richard. We had existed in a kind of bubble, and Katie had been part of it at first, but then she grew out of it, drifted away from us.

I'd spend bottomless hours in Mom's art shed as a little girl, our knees touching as she guided wax over cotton sheets for her batiks while I moved globs of paint around on poster paper. I can still hear her voice in my head, sometimes singsong, sometimes frantic, sharing things with me she probably shouldn't have been. Always followed by a "don't mention that to your father, Kira."

She named me Kira after Olivia Newton-John's character in *Xanadu*, one of her favorite films. She'd seen it at the drive-in years before I was born and loved the music, the mythology, the story of nine muses who cross back and forth between time. When it finally came out on VHS, she made me watch it over and over with her.

After I couldn't stomach anymore pad thai, I peeled the plastic lid off the soup as I considered how to respond to Jack. I knew what he meant by *And I can't imagine you wanting to go, either.* He was referring to Mom, but I didn't want to get into that with him, to prick at that old wound again, so I dodged the subject.

Me: I need time to figure it out. But I was thinking about it.

Jack: Well, I'll only go if you go, so let me know.

I sent back a simple thumbs-up emoji and placed my cell facedown, cradling my chin in my hands.

I WOKE EARLY this morning, before the birds started their chirping and when the sky was still a deep indigo, and dragged my laptop into the bed. I emailed in sick to work. I sat there, cross-legged in bed, my laptop baking my thighs, looking at flights before slamming it shut without booking anything.

I shouldn't go. I shouldn't put myself through all that, but as pitiful as it sounds, I want to see Jack. I want to see myself reflected in his face, the strong girl I was once was, his neighborhood friend who he admired. *I'll only go if you go.* Sounds like he wants to see me, too. And now, I have to decide if it's worth it. My vision blurs around the edges when I think about facing the others—Genevieve, Katie, not to mention Jack's wife, Melanie—and also returning to The Farm.

I refold the carton of pad thai, shove it back in the fridge. Drag myself the few steps back to bed, where I wilt under the covers and feel myself sinking back down into sleep.

Photo by Steven Noreyko

MAY COBB earned her MA in literature from San Francisco State University, and her essays and interviews have appeared in the *Washington Post*, the Rumpus, *Edible Austin*, and *Austin Monthly*. Her previous novel is *The Hunting Wives*. A Texas native, she lives in Austin, Texas, with her family.

CONNECT ONLINE

MayCobb.com
🐦 MayKCobb
📷 May_Cobb

Ready to find
your next great read?

Let us help.

Visit prh.com/nextread